Unclean

The Sanctwood Series, Book One
Keller Hayden

Contents

Trigger Warning

This book contains themes and scenes that may be difficult for some readers. These themes include parental loss, religious extremism, persecution based on identity, imprisonment, suicidal ideation, and physical and emotional trauma. Please read with care.

For anyone who's ever felt like they don't belong—you do.

Everywhere.

Exactly as you are.

Chapter One

Ria

Ria Halrowe knelt on the forest floor. Her hands dug into the earth as her tears fell, soaking the moss-covered ground beneath her. She could hardly breathe.

One week.

That's all she had before her son turned eighteen, and she would lose him to the world he was always meant for–one far away from the suffocating watch of The Order.

And she'd be left here, in this Gods damn forest, alone. Wrestling with the idea that maybe that's what *she* had always been meant for.

Ria had been dreading this day for years—the day she had to tell Kalen the truth about who he was and what he was up against. What and who they'd been hiding from.

His aging had always been inevitable, and no matter how she ached for more of it, time was a thief—and it was here to collect.

The Awakening was coming.

Every hybrid's rite of passage into adulthood. The night he would come into his full power, and he had no idea.

She had been keeping the secret long enough.

Her nightmares had gotten worse, too.

Blood.

Screaming.

Gone.

She couldn't let the same thing happen to Kalen, but the thought of letting him go was suffocating.

"I can't do it," Ria whispered into the darkness. "You were supposed to be here." She dug her fingernails into the loose soil, grabbing two fistfuls in a silent rage. "You were supposed to help me through this."

The leaves stilled, as if the forest was listening to her too. Making space for her grief, the way it always had.

Trembling, she pressed her dirt-streaked hands to her temples and closed her eyes. A memory, a fleeting moment of what could have been, flashed before her.

Her soulmate. *Alive*, kissing her rounded stomach. The point of his fae ears, her witch heritage, a love forbidden by The Order. And the miracle growing inside of her.

Her beloved Kalen.

She shuffled her legs out from under her and leaned back against her favorite tree. The giant oak was just a short walk from their home. Sometimes she was glad the trees couldn't talk. Because this one had heard too much.

She came here on the days her mind felt foggy. When she needed to scream about the life she'd never have because of her choices. And tonight, to cry about all she lost.

Even through the pain, she wouldn't have changed a thing. She often wondered if that made her selfish. Her choices had been the reason *he* was dead. The reason she was losing Kalen, too.

But wasn't it also the reason that she experienced love like this? The love of a mother. Deep and unending. Unconditional and infinite. The reason saying goodbye would be so hard.

Taking a deep breath, she grounded herself; smelled the scent of rain long past, felt the cool breeze tickling her cheek, heard the distant caw of a crow, and felt her heart breaking.

She hadn't been with him on the day he was taken by The Order. She never got to say goodbye.

The memories keep him alive, she thought as she reached her hand back to her temples, trying to remember what it felt like to be wrapped in his embrace. Trying to find a semblance of peace within the sorrow that covered her.

It was a gift of her witch magic—memorywalking. It gave her the ability to relive moments of her own and those around her. But today, it felt a bit harder to stay tethered to the flashbacks of her past.

Today, the gift felt like a curse.

She couldn't smell him like she used to, the scent of ash and cedar—she wished she had been able to bottle it. To hang it like an herb and dry it in her kitchen to smell when she walked into her home. To keep it near her forever.

She couldn't feel him either. Where she used to feel the strong pull of his hands, she could only feel a phantom touch. The fingers of a ghost. Of love lost forever.

Gods, she missed him.

And she was furious he wasn't here.

But at the edge of her anger was fear. The two emotions held hands as if they were partners to her brokenness. It was impacting her magic in a way she hadn't felt since The Order killed him like he was no one. Like he meant nothing. Because of his disobedience. For his *uncleanliness*.

For falling in love with her.

She heard the soft, familiar crunch of a leaf and opened her eyes. You could barely hear her, unless you knew she was coming. Eugenia arrived, just as she promised. And Genie always kept her promises.

"Ria?"

"I'm here," Ria called through her tears, sorrow dripping from each word.

The two had been best friends for as long as she could remember. They met in the village of Evermere as young witches trying to fit in until they quickly realized all they needed was each other. They were soulmates of a sort–Ria and Eugenia. Genie and Ri. Her confidant. Her sister. Two witches who had an indescribable tie to one another. She didn't trust anyone the way she trusted Genie. Not even herself.

"Oh, honey," Eugenia crouched low and swept Ria into her arms before falling back into the tree where Ria once leaned. They sat silently as Ria's sobs shook them both. Eugenia held her close, steady and strong, just like the tree they were resting on.

"I know it's time," Ria wept, "I'm just not ready to let him go." Her breath hitched as she tried to calm herself down. "How do I let him go?"

Her best friend was here. She was safe. But it didn't change the truth; she didn't know how she would live without Kalen. She didn't know how to face her impending loneliness.

It wasn't supposed to be this way.

"You don't have to be ready, Ri. You just have to be brave," Eugenia said softly. "And you've always been the bravest person I know."

Ria raised Kalen alone. Well, mostly alone. Eugenia was the only person who knew Ria had fled Evermere after the murder of her soulmate.

She was pregnant and grieving, and Genie was there for all of it. It was uncommon for a witch to give birth to a male. But Kalen was special, and Eugenia never cared how he got here. Just that he did it safely. That she managed to escape The Order before they captured her, too.

And especially before they found out about Kalen. The child of a witch and a fae. A miracle.

A threat to their beliefs.

The unclean incarnate.

Eugenia taught Kalen everything she knew. About salves, herbs, and creating the right potency to heal brutal wounds. She taught him how to forage, to sort out poisonberries from sweetberries, the perfect way to cook healing mushroom stew, and how to become one with the land.

"You take, but you give, too." Eugenia always told Kalen. Kalen understood what his Genie was saying. He'd always understood people fundamentally.

But even more than he knew people, he appreciated the earth.

He carried a reverence for the wild. The forest was his home; the magic hummed through the roots the same way it hummed through his veins.

She would watch him touch a tree and close his eyes, like the two were talking without saying anything at all. He would always end each small interaction by patting the bark with a clever grin like he knew something she didn't.

She was willing to bet that was true.

Kalen's small ritual made foraging adventures last exponentially longer–but she would not be the one to sever his bond with the world around him. It was part of what made him who he was.

Ria taught him what she knew, too. Memorywalking and rootweaving. But only for restoration, for peacemaking—never for harm. She made a promise to herself she'd never be like them–like The Order, not after what they'd done to destroy her life.

She vowed to raise Kalen that way, too.

Kalen didn't know who his father was. He brought it up once or twice, but Ria couldn't talk about it–and he never pushed.

He understood how some pain was just too great to put words to. He would hug her waist, tell her he loved her, and then run out the front door and into the woods.

She wasn't ready to tell him about his father's murder at the hands of the Head Cleanser. She didn't want him to blame himself the way she'd blamed herself all this time.

The guilt was heavy, but she chose to carry it alone–she had to.

Until now.

"I know it's hard," Eugenia said, "But Kalen can do this." She was talking as if she were running through a list, "He'll make it through, and we will see him again." She placed a kiss on top of her best friend's head. Her hands brushed through Ria's hair. Eugenia could heal more than physical wounds, especially for Ria.

"Do you think they'll accept him at Wyrdbrook?" Ria's voice had grown steadier in her grief. "What if they call him names?"

"Then they call him names," Eugenia breathed. "There are things now that are out of our control." She pulled Ria closer. "What I do know is there is no one like Kalen Halrowe. The people at Wyrdbrook will see it too."

Eugenia squeezed her friend's hand three times. A reminder of the words they lived by.

Kind. Brave. Gentle.

"You know he can't stay here, Ria."

"Will you please come with me to tell him?" Ria asked quietly. "I'm scared I won't go through with it."

"I would go to the ends of the earth for you," Genie replied as she shifted her body to cup Ria's face. She wiped a tear with her thumb before it fell. "But you have to do this part on your own."

"Send a flower to bloom by my doorstep in two days' time and I'll meet you here to say goodbye to him," Eugenia said, standing up and pulling Ria to her feet.

She exhaled. "Okay. Two days' time. I'll see you then. I love you, Genie. Thank you."

"Anything for you, Ria. Always."

The two witches gave each other a farewell hug, and Eugenia slipped into the night, disappearing into the trees, as if she had never been there at all.

Ria slid her hands down her skirt, brushing off the dirt and moss from where she once sat. With one more deep breath, she pulled her shoulders back and began the walk to her cottage.

It was time to tell Kalen the truth—about the Awakening, about his Father, about The Order. About everything.

Kind. Brave. Gentle. I can do this, she whispered under her breath. She willed one foot in front of the other until she reached the front door of her cottage. She'd never be ready, but she didn't have much of a choice.

Chapter Two

Kalen

His mother had been gone for over an hour now.

Probably foraging for dinner and lost track of time, he thought, as he swept their small cottage floor for the third time.

It wasn't unusual for them both to spend hours in the woods each day. It was a part of her, as much as it was a part of him, maybe even more.

Probably not more.

The Sanctwood Forest was right on the edge of the local village, Evermere. It was vast and unexplored, wild and untamed. It was perfect for him and his mother. For the small, secluded life they've always lived.

Most of the citizens of the town stayed within the city limits, never venturing into the forest. They spent their time living well beyond their means, too fancy for the Sanctwood.

Their loss.

He'd never met anyone from Evermere, not really. Once, a decade ago, he'd met another child–Tessan Duscaire, Eugenia's niece. But beyond that, it was just him, his mother, and, as always, his Genie.

Every once in a while he'd doze off high in a tree and wake only when he heard the sound of hooves growing nearer.

He loved getting a peek at the riders, usually men, dressed in all white garb and adorned with fine golden jewelry. He had no idea who they were, but each time they were in the Sanctwood, they seemed to be looking for someone.

They never stayed long. But their presence unnerved him all the same.

Kalen had thought about jumping down a few times to ask what they needed, but he heeded his mother's vague warnings about staying hidden. About how there weren't many people in their world whom they could trust. But really, there weren't many people in their world at all.

How could there be, hidden deep in this forest?

He enjoyed the freedom he had in the Sanctwood, though. Living in isolation never really felt like a prison to him. Not when the forest danced with the breeze, or a woodland jumping mouse hopped by to say hello. His life was gentle, slow, and full of love.

It was everything he needed.

And it was all he knew.

But he did wonder, every once in a while, what lay beyond. *Who* lay beyond. It made him feel guilty, but it also made his heart race.

The daydreams about what his life would be like with friends. Would they like the forest as much as he did? Would they stay up all night talking about their favorite birds? Did other teenagers even like birds?

When he was feeling especially curious, he sometimes wondered what it would be like to fall in love. The way it would feel to hold someone's hand. To share secrets, to pass love notes. It would never happen to him.

Because the list of people he knew was short:

Ria Halrowe

Eugenia Duscaire

He'd asked his Mom why they lived in the forest a few times, and she always mentioned she'd tell him when he was ready. He never knew what that meant, and usually, that didn't bother him, but today, it did.

He'd be eighteen in a week, and his best friend was his mother.

And while she was the best, it would be nice to know someone else, too.

Because no matter how much he loved his life in the Sanctwood Forest, this was the one thing he and his mother didn't talk about. Maybe the only thing they couldn't.

Why don't we live where everyone else does?

Seventeen years of isolation from Evermere, and he had no idea how they ended up here in the first place. He'd only visited the village once, and he was too young to remember much of anything except for where Eugenia lived.

Kalen may not know much, but he knew things like this didn't happen by accident. People didn't leave all they ever knew for a life in the middle of a forest. They were hiding. He just didn't know from what.

The caw of their crow, Wen, snapped him out of his daze. He paused and listened, counting the birds' calls.

Four. She's close.

Nothing ever happened in the Sanctwood, but his mother insisted he memorize her song anyway:

One caw for yes,
Two for no.
Three for run,
Four — I'm almost home.

She'd been singing the rhyme to him since he was a young boy. Sometimes he'd race around barefoot in their cottage, flapping his arms, and cawing repeatedly; his silly way to make sure she knew he understood what she was telling him.

She'd chase him, laughing, through their small sanctuary, the one Earth Mother helped her build. The one she used her magic to create. Their game always ended the same way, in a tight hug.

"You're the light of my world, little crow," she'd whisper softly.

And Kalen never had to wonder, even for a moment, if he was loved. He still didn't.

What a gift.

But he'd been changing lately. It was slow, but with intention. Like it was out of his control but demanded his attention. It was unlike anything he'd ever felt.

And he could talk to trees.

That part made him feel kind of crazy.

He knew his mother had seen it, too. She spent more time crying, more time away from their home. She'd been avoiding him, and they didn't do that. They never had, and it made no sense for it to start now.

So tonight, he was going to ask for answers. Tonight, he would finally learn the truth.

Because the Sanctwood had always felt like a safe place for them both. But lately, it felt like even the trees were holding their breath.

He needed to know what they had run from.

And why it felt like it was finally catching up.

Chapter Three

Ria

R ia held out her hand as Wen swept down to take the small worm she'd dug up for him.

When Kalen was a toddler, he hated that she fed the crow worms. He'd beg her to feed him berries instead, even if it meant he had less for dinner.

Kalen had always been that way: gentle and aware. He was a boy who understood the suffering of all things.

Even the worms.

It broke her heart, and healed it, too.

They were in an easy rhythm, Ria and Wen. He kept them safe, she kept him fed. She patted the black bird on the head, "Have a safe flight. I'll see you tomorrow," and off the crow went. Quickly and quietly, the darkness of his feathers faded into the night sky.

She knew she'd see him again and again, no matter the weather, and that stability kept her grounded a bit more than she'd like to admit. But after spending the last seventeen years in isolation from almost everyone, talking to a bird seemed like a reasonable thing to do.

Wen showed up several years after they arrived in the Sanctwood, and she quickly realized how important his presence could be for Kalen's safety.

She still remembered the day Kalen named the bird.

"I'll name you Wen," he giggled. *"Like the wen in the sky."*

Of course he meant wind, but the name stuck around. And so did the crow.

She trained the bird daily as Kalen grew, rewarding him for learning to differentiate his calls, and teaching him to do four in a row when she was getting close to home.

She would do anything it took to keep Kalen safe from The Order, including feeding this crow every day for the last thirteen years.

The Gods damn Order. She despised them. They ripped everything they could from her without hesitation, without pause. Her love. Their life together. The opportunity for Kalen to know his father. And they didn't care.

She was dreading having to tell Kalen everything. She should have been preparing for this over the last several years. Maybe she'd figure out how to avoid it?

No. Get it together, Ria. It's time.

She spent most of her walk home sorting through a mental checklist of what she'd tell Kalen when she arrived. Her footsteps grew as heavy as her heart the closer she got to their cottage, forcing her to slow down.

To appreciate these last few moments before everything changed again. Before the last part of her heart was ripped from her.

Her brown leather boots felt too tight, and her flowing green tunic was constricting her chest, making it hard to breathe. The path she'd walked a thousand times now felt foreign beneath her feet, as though it had closed in on her, mirroring the tightness in her chest.

I should have told him this sooner; he deserved to know.

What was the path of least resistance? She wasn't sure it existed.

"Kalen, your father was fae, and because I'm a witch, he was murdered for loving me."

"Kalen, The Order doesn't know you exist, and they would chase you to the end of the earth if they found out."

She didn't know if there was a *right* way to do this.

But she felt certain she could do better than that.

This part of being a mother typically came easily to Ria–the conversation. But tonight felt different, because tonight would be the hardest conversation she'd ever had with Kalen. With anyone, really.

And maybe ever would.

How would she explain to her son that he could be hated for simply existing? That people who have never met him want to get rid of him just because of who he is? Something he had no control over.

The idea of anyone hating him, this boy who was so good, made her stomach churn.

He deserves more than this.

She rounded the last tree, the one that blocked their home from the view of unsuspecting visitors of the forest. Her eyes quickly locked on the wispy brown hair of her sweet Kalen. Sitting at the kitchen table, picking at his fingers, and lost in deep thought. A perfect view of her boy.

Though she had told him more times than she could count to stop picking at his fingers.

Gods, he looks so much like his father.

He hadn't noticed her yet. His face was softly glowing in the candlelight. She had seen that look a thousand times. Tonight, though, she took a mental picture.

She couldn't believe how much he'd grown this year. The once young boy, now on the cusp of becoming more. Becoming whole.

Whatever that meant.

Where his face was once soft and round, the edges were now sharp and pronounced. His dark brown hair had grown as wild as the wind that carried her feet here. Where he once met her hip for a hug, he now towered over her, as tall as the Yew tree they planted together when Kalen was seven. But what remained the same were his eyes. Her favorite.

Because, for some reason, they looked almost exactly like Eugenia's. Brown, with a golden inner rim. It made sense to Ria that he was a reflection of the two other people she had loved most. But it made tonight's conversation feel a little bit harder.

If she believed in the God of The Order, she'd curse him for his cruelty.

Instead, she wiped her eyes, lightly smacked her cheeks, and put a smile on her face as she opened the door of the small oasis that had kept them both safe for the last seventeen years. She was out of time.

And there was no place left to hide from the truth.

Chapter Four
Kalen

The door creaked faintly as his mother stepped inside.

She'd been crying, though the smile she had written on her face was a weak attempt to hide it from him.

Even if it had been convincing, Kalen could somehow *smell* her sadness–it was one of the things that had been changing lately; his sense of smell. Things just smelled...different. Everything was more. More intense, more fragrant, more pungent. It gave him a headache to experience another's emotions so vividly, but in some ways, he was grateful for this...gift? He wasn't sure what to call it. He just knew it was different. That *he* was changing.

"I'm glad you're back," he said meekly as she shut the door behind her. "I was getting worried until I heard Wen's cranky ass caw."

He had only briefly lifted his gaze to confirm if the scent was correct–and it was, she had clearly been crying tonight. Her swollen eyes and red nose were an easy tell, but he didn't want to ask her about it. He'd give her the space to do that when she was ready. He went back to picking at the beds of his fingernails.

She chuckled in response, deep and honest. "I won't tell him you said that."

A soft smile bloomed on his face. If he could choose one thing about his mother he loved the most, this may be it. The ease with which they existed together.

He had barely finished the thought when he felt the shift in the room–the air tightening, making it harder to breathe somehow. There was something that was going to happen tonight. And Gods help him, but he felt like he could smell *that* too.

"I picked your rosehips, by the way. I put them over by the plantain to dry." He was trying to ease the tension, buying a bit more time for them both to sort out how they were going to do this. Whatever *this* was.

It wasn't working.

The silence took on a life of its own, growing deeper and wider. One of them would have to make the first move.

And it would have to be his mother.

"Hey, Kale, can we talk for a minute?" Ria walked over to him and planted a kiss on the top of his head. "It's important."

She'd read his mind.

His mother pulled her seat away from the kitchen table, the wooden legs dragged along the freshly swept floors. She was moving in slow motion, and he felt the thump of his heart as she sat down.

There was no running from it now; they'd always agreed kitchen table talks were reserved for serious conversations. And she didn't ask him to move to the common room.

He finally looked up at his mother's face. It was worn, lined with exhaustion. The heavy bags under her tired eyes, her typically bright blue irises rimmed in red.

This level of sadness was unfamiliar to him. What had been on her mind the last couple of weeks had begun to take its toll.

He didn't respond; he didn't need to. She sat in front of him, the words stuck in her throat. Until finally she exhaled and began to speak to Kalen.

"Your father loved you more than you could imagine," his mother started. "You need to know that he gave up everything to keep you safe."

This is about my father? Why now?

Kalen knew his father was dead, but that had always been the beginning and the end of the conversation.

He didn't know how he died, just that it happened before he was born, and it had been tragic.

He always knew when his mother was thinking about him. She'd lift her head up and to the right. She'd shut her eyes tight, face to the sun, and then look back at Kalen with fondness.

"Can I show you?" his mother asked gently.

His mother was a skilled memorywalker—she'd taught him how to do it, too. To use the gift he inherited from her. But when she taught him, they never explored old parts of her memory. They'd use it to relocate a patch of berries, or to remember how to get home if they went too deep in the Sanctwood.

But never like this.

He nodded in response. Consent was a moral and ethical necessity when you could enter someone's mind.

What's about to happen?

His mother reached out and touched Kalen's temple. He froze just a bit, bracing for impact.

But the landing was soft, as he became an observer caught in his mother's memory. They stood in a village, bustling crowds surrounding him.

And his breath caught when he realized why.

Kalen froze mid-step.

He stared in disbelief. The man running through the market might as well have been his reflection. He was older, broader, and real.

My father.

This man, this stranger who shared his face, just ran straight into a young woman.

Mom?

"I'm so sorry," his father said coolly as he stooped low to help pick up the cloudberries his mother was carrying. "I'll pay for them, I promise. How much did you expect to make today?"

"You really don't have to do that." Kalen watched as she picked up the berries herself. "The forest provides. I'll just pick more tomorrow." She wiped her hands on her apron before she looked up. "I do appreciate the offer."

He watched intently as her eyes grew wide, seeing his father for the first time, a pink blush settling on her cheeks.

She looked away quickly.

His father did not.

He was studying her face as she continued to salvage as many berries as she could. The erratic movements of her hands gave it away—she was so nervous.

And his father was taken. He looked at her with such curiosity and wonder. As if there was a question begging to be asked between the two of them.

Would one of them make a move?

Kalen was living proof they would. He knew how this story ended. And now he got to be there when it started.

Through labored breaths, Kalen watched the unfamiliar man. His father's hair was shoulder-length and wavy, just like his. Kalen reached up and put his hand through his own as he was noticing, taking inventory of all the ways they would have been the same. All of the small features they would have shared.

His skin was tanned, and he looked powerful. Strong. Kalen could have sworn his bicep was as large as his head. This time, Kalen reached up and felt his own arms, small and lean.

I guess I didn't inherit those genetics.

He heard his father speak again and quickly dropped his hand from his bicep. He wouldn't miss any of this, especially to compare the size of their arms.

"Well, can I make it up to you another way, then? What about dinner?" he asked confidently.

There it is.

"I don't even know your name. Why would I spend an evening with you?" she replied curiously, her eyebrows furrowed.

Kalen huffed out a small laugh. He'd never seen this side of her before.

"I will tell you my name over dinner. Please?" He clasped his hands together as if he were begging. "Meet me inside the Sanctwood Forest tonight, right by the giant oak tree. You can't miss it." He flashed a grin and then stood up. "I'll see you there."

Before she could answer, he took off. Kalen reached out to try and stop him, to try and grab his shirt before he got away.

He wanted more time. To see his mannerisms, to learn his face, to see the parts of him reflected back into his father. But he was gone. Again.

He'd always be gone again.

Because this was nothing but a memory.

His mother dropped her hand from his temple, and he was back in their small kitchen. His arm was still raised, an attempt to grab the ghost of the man he'd never know.

His mother continued slowly.

"Your father was self-assured and stubborn; unshakable and convicted." She sniffled, then let out a small laugh. "He was so charismatic and full of joy. He was the greatest person I had ever known until I came to know you." She reached out and grabbed his still-outstretched arm and rested it on the table in front of them, holding onto his hand.

"He wanted to meet you so bad, little crow," his mother's face grew dark as she continued. "But he was a member of The Order–a group of fae, witches, and humans who worship the High God, Athero." She scowled, shaking her head. "Like many members of The Order, he was raised to believe Athero provided blessings for those who remained loyal to his ancient teachings."

"What kind of blessings?" Kalen responded curiously.

"Power, mostly," his mother sighed. "You'll learn in time that people will do anything for power."

"Athero is said to exist before time itself. An all-powerful, all-knowing God who believed in the segregation of His creation. Athero pictured a world in which purity was the goal, magic bred magic, and order was maintained. Evermere was his first creation, his first attempt at building the world he wished existed."

"He raised the mountains with nothing more than a thought; grew the trees with a single blink, created the sea with a snap of his fingers," his mother snapped her own. "And when that was done, he whispered to the wind to create the mighty winged fae. He sent rain to the soil to bloom the witches of the earth. And when the dust had settled, he turned it into humans–the only group that didn't hold magic, the ultimate test of his Creation."

"Athero assumed there would be no way fae or witch would be interested in humankind. They held no power and no status–and the two magic bearers had no need for something that wouldn't strengthen their own bloodlines."

Athero? The Order? Purity?

Kalen's head was spinning.

He'd been living here all this time and had only heard about The Order in passing, and even *that* was by accident.

Eugenia had taught him how to sneak around the forest without being heard by anyone or anything. It came in handy one day as he heard his mother and Eugenia speaking in hushed tones.

"Things have changed, Ria," Eugenia spoke quietly. *"The Order is everywhere."*

Kalen had always felt like Eugenia knew that he was listening. That she knew the lessons she provided him would be used for something other than foraging or hunting.

He learned that day that The Order had grown in popularity over the last 10 years, and most of the village of Evermere now believed in the teachings of Athero. That purity was power—and power was everything.

It was clear his mother was a staunch non-believer. He was finally understanding, just a bit more, how dangerous *that* could be in Evermere.

And his father...a member of The Order?

How could she have looked past that?

She continued, "But Athero couldn't have planned for the power that went beyond bloodlines or beliefs. Power that went beyond magic." She paused. "What is forged between two people when they fall in love."

I guess that's how.

She shook her head, trying to rid herself of a memory. Kalen had seen her do it a thousand times before.

"The Order's sacred vow is *Purity Above All*—of bloodlines, of magic, of faith," she pushed on. "These teachings, these beliefs..." She scoffed. "They ensure the members of The Order adhere to their covenant at all costs. And any Orderly who is found to be in violation of the covenant is publicly, brutally punished."

"Why would he believe in something like that?" Kalen asked curiously. "Why does it matter if people are different?"

The question made him feel naive. Was there something he was missing? He'd lived life mostly alone, and he couldn't imagine separating himself from people by choice.

"Sometimes people inherit the beliefs that are passed down to them," she shrugged. "Your father's parents were both Orderlys. He didn't know how to question anything about what he'd been taught." Her face was stained with sadness. "Until us."

This was a grief so deep and wide. If his mother had been treading water before, her head was almost underwater now. And he didn't know how to help.

She reached out to him again–a simple movement to acknowledge she was done talking, that there was more to show, instead.

He nodded again. If it meant he'd see his father, he'd nod and nod until they both fell unconscious.

He felt the buzz of her magic pulsing through him again, but this time, he was in a more familiar environment. The sharp smell of pine needles, the soft mossy floor of the earth. He was near his home in the Sanctwood, right beside the giant oak.

He was standing next to his mother now as she was hiding behind a nearby bush. He could hear her heart pounding in her chest as she watched his father set up a small meal for the two of them, the giant oak serving as an awning from the setting sun.

His *parents*.

Was this the beginning of their love story? What could have gone so wrong that his father was *murdered* by The Order? Despite the unanswered questions, he found himself grateful to witness this small moment between the two people responsible for his existence.

He'd wondered what his father was like for so long—if Kalen was anything like him at all. And now he was sitting right in front of him.

Sort of.

He would have never asked his mother for this–to relive all of these moments. He couldn't imagine how painful it was for her to have been blessed with this magic. To be able to revisit the past and know her life would never be the same again. That she'd never see him again except in her mind.

He had the ability to memorywalk, too, but he had never been through anything like this. Nothing to break him. He'd really never been through anything at all.

His mother began to move toward his father now, and he slowly followed. He knew he couldn't be seen; that this was just a memory, but he felt like an intruder. He treaded slowly and kept his feet light, just as Eugenia had taught him.

"You came," his father said with a smirk. His voice was calm, but he was looking at her with unspoken adoration. Like he had never seen someone so beautiful.

He had looked at her like that in the market, too. Kalen had noticed, but his mother had not.

"Well, you promised me dinner, and considering I wasn't able to pay for my own due to *someone's* clumsiness," she laughed softly, "it seemed to be in my best interest to show up."

His father looked up at her and smiled, bright and enamored, and then patted the mossy ground next to him—an invitation to officially join the small meal he had prepared.

His mother sat down happily.

"I think that makes me the luckiest man in the Sanctwood Forest," his father said as he popped an olive into his mouth.

"You're probably the *only* man in the Sanctwood Forest," she shot back playfully.

"Semantics," his father winked with a chuckle.

Kalen sat down across from them—his mother and his father...and listened for what felt like hours, as his parents introduced themselves to each other.

And fell in love.

Chapter Five

Ria

R ia hadn't revisited this memory in a very long time. She tried not to, even on the days when she missed him most. Because this pain was almost worse.

He'd been gone for 18 years now. Sometimes it felt like yesterday, and sometimes it felt so long ago she'd wondered if their love had even happened at all. But then her heart would ache in the morning, and it was a reminder that it had.

It was hard to see him like this–so full of happiness, replaying the quiet moments they shared together on what was certainly a date, even if they never said it out loud.

Alive.

Letting Kalen in on these moments was never the plan. She thought she would just share the truth about who he was, not give him a front row seat to their love story. But he deserved to know his father in some small way, and this was all she could give him.

It was all she had.

He deserved so much more.

She wondered what he was thinking as he saw his father for the first time. Was it just as hard for him as it was for her?

Regardless of the pain, tethering to this memory was easier than she'd expected. She would never forget how the forest smelled that day, how he smelled, either.

Everything was in bloom, and the breeze carried the scent of honeysuckle and lavender to cover them both as they sat nestled under the shade of the giant oak. The sun was setting, but the Sanctwood felt alive. Like the trees knew a union was forming that had the power to change everything.

"Ria Halrowe," she heard herself say, putting her hand out to shake his.

"Ria Halrowe," he repeated her name back like he was singing a song, trying to taste the syllables. Like he knew he'd be saying it forever.

"I'm Westin Vale," he grinned. "You can call me West, all of my friends do." He took her hand and shook it, never breaking his stare from her own.

"We'll stick with Westin, then," she chirped back, smirking.

Their conversation was enchanting. They spent as much time laughing as they did talking. He was every single thing she had no idea she'd ever find.

She remembered the way her heart fluttered when he flashed his smile, how her face flushed when their hands accidentally brushed as they both reached for a berry.

She knew the moment she met him that there was nothing that would have stopped her from falling in love with him.

And on most days, she was thankful.

But on some days, she wished she could stop time before what came next.

They were finally getting to the end of this date, and Kalen was about to see the moment that changed everything for her.

For all of them.

She found herself holding her breath on the other side of the tether. If only the Ria of then knew.

Would anything have changed?

West looked over at her, his hair hanging like vines in front of his face. "Can I walk you home?"

"You cannot, Westin Vale. The forest looks after me; I don't need you to do the same," she nudged him, "but thank you for the offer."

"Fair enough." He put his hands up in an easy surrender. "Can I at least see you again?"

"I'd really like that," she replied without a second thought.

She took one last bite of the bread he had bought from the market; the spread of fig jam and goat cheese lay out in front of them, almost empty. Ria was smitten by the man in front of her and stuffed by the food he brought. Everything about the night was so full. Her stomach, her heart. She couldn't have imagined her evening would have turned out like this.

It had been the best night of her life.

Until right...now.

West began packing up his things, his long hair clinging to the sweat on his forehead, blocking his view. He was so effortlessly beautiful. She couldn't stop herself from reaching up and tucking the piece of hair behind his ear.

His *pointed* ear.

His Gods damn pointed ears.

Westin Vale was fae.

She remembered the way her heart had stopped. The butterflies in her stomach had suddenly caught on fire, turning to dust. She should have left right then. Told him she'd never see him again, but she couldn't move.

And if she had moved, she would have never had Kalen.

She realized in that moment she was in more trouble than she originally thought, and for an entirely different reason.

She was falling in love with a fae. She was a witch.

The Order declared it forbidden. But she was never one to follow their rules.

And it came with a cost.

A life lost.

A love lost.

A hidden son.

It was time to get back to her real life; it was time to tell Kalen the truth.

Chapter Six

Kalen

Kalen's head rushed. Like the information was too much for his brain to hold, to process. The corners of his vision started to blacken. His father was fae...his mother, a witch; that made him...

What does it make me?

"I don't understand." He looked at his mom with betrayal. He didn't want to be angry, not after everything she'd shown him tonight.

She looked away.

He reached across the table and grabbed her hand, a peace offering.

The hand of the woman who had given up everything she knew in Evermere for *him*. He realized she could have chosen a different path; that hiding him in the forest for all of these years was a sacrifice she had made to keep him safe. His anger simmered.

Maybe there was more he didn't know.

"Why didn't you tell me before now?" Kalen whispered.

"Because my love for your father killed him, and I can't bear the same outcome for you," his mother choked out.

"The Order found out about us somehow," she said. "Your father, being an Orderly, defying their covenant so blatantly, it was unforgivable to them. I didn't get to say goodbye."

The silence settled between them for just a beat.

"But they don't know about you." She looked at him now. "And I plan to keep it that way."

"I've always known you were special, Kalen. From the very second I laid eyes on you. Our magic hummed together, and I knew you were going to be powerful in a way people wouldn't understand. You made me whole again in ways you can't begin to imagine."

"But your father told me to prepare you for what was to come, if we both survived. That on your eighteenth birthday, you'd likely have to endure the Awakening–a painful transformation all hybrids are bound to."

The Awakening?

A hybrid?

"How did he know about it? Was he a hybrid, too?" He asked, head still spinning.

"No. He was fae. The Order teaches all of its followers about the Awakening so they know how to...track hybrids."

Kalen was going to be sick. No wonder they'd stuffed him in the corner of the forest. They were almost impossible to find here. And if people were trained to *track* him?

He stood up from the kitchen table and began to pace.

"So, I'm some kind of hybrid?" Kalen turned on his heels, rubbing his face in disbelief. "Are there others like me?"

It was all making sense. The heightened sense of smell, the ache he felt everywhere as he lay down each night for bed.

He was changing.

His body was preparing for this...Awakening? And it had been for a while.

What could he even expect from something called *the Awakening*?

Would it hurt?

How long did it last?

Would he become more powerful?

He had too many questions, and he knew his mother didn't have the answers. For now, he just needed to know if he'd have to face this alone. If there were other people who had done this, too.

"I don't know," she said, with regret on her face. "I've heard The Order drove most of them away." She stood up with him, urging him to stop pacing. To listen.

She lowered her voice now. "But up in the Peaks, there is a small, hidden village for people like you." She grabbed his hands. "It's called Wyrdbrook. Eugenia has a connection there and sent a post through Wen about a year ago asking them to prepare for your arrival."

Wyrdbrook.

Something inside him hummed at the name.

"They're expecting you in three days," his mother finished.

Three days? I can't leave in three days.

He released his mother's hands and made his way back to the kitchen table. The room was spinning as he sat down, throwing his hands on his face, he tried to process all he'd learned.

He had wanted answers. He had planned to ask for them. But nothing could have prepared him for this.

A hybrid hidden from an oppressive force, fleeing his home. And what's worse is she'd had it planned for a year?

He trusted his mother and Eugenia. They'd never led him astray before, and he knew they wouldn't now. But this felt bigger than what he was expecting.

It's not that they *didn't* go to Evermere. It's that they *couldn't.* That *he* couldn't.

That it wasn't safe.

"Now you know, my love." She walked back to the table, sitting across from him. "Why I had to run, why we have had to stay hidden all of these years." She sniffed. "Your father died for us. And it gave me time to escape before they really found out who I was. Before they found out about you."

A sacrifice Kalen couldn't bear to swallow.

He died for...me?

"I know he wouldn't have changed a thing." She rested her hands on the table. "But I wish he were here to meet you. To see who you've become. To help you discover who you're about to be. You have no idea how much I wish it didn't have to be this way," she finished.

"Me too. But it is." Kalen didn't know how to accept what he'd learned. There was no bringing back his father, there was no changing his bloodline.

He was exactly who he was, and there wasn't a thing he could do to change it. But if given the option, would he?

Knowing he was a hybrid didn't change anything he knew about who he was fundamentally.

Right?

Kind. Brave. Gentle.

It was just one part of him.

One giant, uknown part of him.

"When do I leave?" Tears began to sting his eyes. He couldn't imagine a life different from this one. Who would spend time with his mother? Would she be alone? How long would he have to be there? Could he ever come back home?

"You'll leave the day after tomorrow. It takes about a day to get to the Peak, so you'll have time to settle in before the Awakening." His mother leaned across the table, clutching his hands, a new resolve shining in her bright blue eyes.

"This is an adventure for you, Kale. That's all this is. It doesn't change one single thing about what's in here." She softly poked his heart. "Or up here." She flicked his forehead, and he let out a laugh.

It doesn't change a single thing about me. He kept his mother's words close to his heart.

She tousled his hair and then brought a hand down to his chin, forcing him to look at her as she continued.

"You can *do* anything. You can *be* anything. Labels are created by those who need control, and The Order fears what they don't understand." His heart warmed at the words. "But hear me when I say this, you're just you, Kalen Halrowe. You were born of love, so you are love personified. You are going to be okay. I promise." Her lips tugged upward in a soft smile.

He smiled back and put on a brave face, standing once again to wrap her in a tight hug.

I'm going to miss this.

Exhaustion began to weigh heavily on him. He needed to get to his room. He needed to be alone.

"It's been a hard night. You should get some rest," his mother said, understanding what he needed before he had to say it.

That was the gift of being loved by Ria Halrowe.

"Thanks for all of this," he replied genuinely. "I know it was hard on you, too." He let go of his mother and walked toward his room.

She nodded in response.

"I love you, Kalen," his mother chirped after him as he headed to his bedroom.

"I love you, too," he called to her, choking back the tears that were threatening to fall.

Kalen shut his door and collapsed onto his bed. Face down on his pillow, he thought briefly about how it would feel to scream. To get out these big feelings while they were so fresh. To make space in his brain to surrender to his exhaustion.

Instead, he continued to carry the weight of a feeling he'd never known, and let the tears he held back begin to fall.

Kalen silently wept until his eyes ran dry and sleep finally claimed him.

And for just a moment, he was able to forget about the day that had changed his life forever.

The forest felt different today, like it knew he was leaving.

He'd spent yesterday packing his life into the leather bag his mom had carefully made for him. One bag for 17 years. How could that even be possible?

This morning, though, was dedicated to foraging for the provisions he'd need to make the trip to Wyrdbrook.

What kind of a name is Wyrdbrook?

He carefully plucked berries from a thorny bush, his calloused fingers making it quick and painless. He was especially grateful for how thoughtless it was, considering his head was stuffed too full.

Kalen had replayed his conversation with his mother more times than he cared to admit.

A hybrid. He was a hybrid.

He was trying not to let the truth of who he was change him before the Awakening inevitably did–whatever that meant.

But how could he not?

He'd been lied to. Almost everything he knew about himself was a lie, and he needed to mourn who he thought he was...*what* he thought he was. And while he knew it was never his mother's intention to hurt him, her impact remained the same. He didn't want to leave home, and he had no choice.

This was the last day of the only life he'd ever known.

The sun began to creep higher, the strong light casting shadows of the leaves on the forest floor around him. It was getting close to his departure, and he needed to get back to say his goodbyes.

He closed up his sack, stuffed to the brim with his favorite berries, and whispered a word of gratitude to this place that provided for him for so long.

His home.

He was leaving his home.

I hope to be back soon.

He inhaled deeply, remembering all of the ways the Sanctwood raised him. The way the forest taught him to thrive and showed him the gifts that bloomed right under his feet. He'd miss this so much.

A twig snapped in the distance, breaking the calm that had washed over him. Kalen's senses shifted into high alert.

Someone was here. Was it The Order? Had his luck finally run out on the day he planned to leave?

No one came to this part of the forest. He'd never seen anyone here for as long as they'd lived in the depths of the Sanctwood.

Whoever this was had been tracking him specifically; he was being followed, and he'd missed it. All of Eugenia's lessons about moving stealthily through the forest had been wasted because he'd missed it. How would he ever do anything on his own?

Shit, shit, shit.

He quickly shuffled up the nearest tree, watching as a hooded figure scanned the forest. They were small enough Kalen felt confident he could fight them off and get back home. His heart slowed.

If he got his timing *just* right, he should be able to jump down and—

"Kalen?" a familiar voice whispered. "Where did you go..."

What the hell?

Kalen hopped out of the tree with a lightness, landing with an unfamiliar grace.

Maybe I really am part fae.

Could he even say that before the Awakening? He still didn't know how being a hybrid worked.

He raised his fists playfully. "Remove your hood, stranger, and no one has to die today," his voice boomed as he tried to hide his bubbling laugh.

Eugenia turned around and cackled loudly and freely before throwing her hand over her mouth. It was clear she was trying to be quiet, but why?

"You're an idiot," she said with adoration. "I'm glad I caught you before you got home."

Weird.

"I need to talk to you, and we don't have much time," she spoke quickly.

"When you get to Wyrdbrook, I need you to find Liam. It shouldn't be hard; everyone up there knows him. He's going to make sure you are settled in and your questions are answered. Do you understand?"

"Liam. Yeah, I got it," Kalen responded casually. "But why are you here, Genie? I thought you were meeting us at the house to say goodbye?"

"Because I needed some time away from that nosy mother of yours," she joked.

But then her face lowered, and she grew serious. The sudden shift in her mood was enough to tilt the solid ground they were both standing on.

"Listen, you're going to find out some things over the next few days that aren't going to make much sense to you. About yourself, the Awakening. And about me. And I know..." her voice trailed off, Kalen could smell the now familiar scent of sadness dripping off of her. "And I know...I know it may change the way you feel about me." Kalen watched, confused, as her eyes welled with tears.

"But when you love someone the way I love you and your mother, you're willing to do whatever it takes. Do you understand? That was the promise I made to your father. That was the promise I swore to keep. Whatever it takes, as long as you're both okay." She inhaled before continuing.

Why did these two women, who have always been so forthcoming, suddenly have so many secrets? What could she have promised his father that made her this upset?

"But Genie–"

She cut him off quickly.

"I need to get to the cottage to tell you goodbye officially. Give me a head start?" Her voice was light, but her eyes were pleading with him.

Please don't ask me any questions. Please don't make me lie to you.

It wasn't fair. But nothing about today was fair.

"I'll see you there," he responded, nodding toward home. And he watched as his Genie took the first step on the long trail headed toward the cottage, skipping her usual shortcut.

His mother wouldn't suspect a thing, and he knew that was the point. For all of the quirks about Eugenia, none of them surpassed her cleverness.

Kalen knew he needed to make one last stop, and now that he had to give Genie some space to go ahead, he didn't feel so bad about being a few minutes late.

It didn't take him long to come upon the giant oak tree. The one from his mother's memories.

He'd passed this tree thousands of times. Had climbed its branches and sought shelter from the blistering sun under its long leaf-covered limbs. But he hadn't known his father once sat under it, too. That it was the place where his parents talked about their lives, their faith, where they discovered who they were—a witch and a fae, and chose each other anyway.

It changed the way he approached it. Tenderly, respecting its history. Wondering if the roots felt the way his parents fell in love. He'd ask them to tell him their story if he weren't so pressed for time.

He sat down under the tree, his legs stretched out and crossed at the ankle. Remembering the easy way his father existed, he leaned back on his elbows.

"Feels kind of cruel to be sitting where you once were and knowing I'll never be able to say this to your face," Kalen said into the nothingness.

The wind stilled, and the caw of a crow in the distance was all he could hear.

He didn't know what came after death, if his father could hear him, but he continued anyway.

"Thank you...for what you did. I know it was really for her, for Mom, but you gave me the best life I could have imagined by letting her go."

His throat began to close up, but he didn't stop his tears as they slid down his cheek. He didn't wipe them away, either. He wanted to sit with this sadness–this longing for the man he'd never met, and all he missed out on because of it.

"I don't know how it's possible to miss someone you've never met. But I do miss you," Kalen sniffed. "I know she does, too. I hear her crying sometimes at night. She doesn't know I can. But I guess thanks to you, I can hear better than she thinks." He let out a breathy laugh.

His hand casually went up to the tip of one of his rounded ears. Would they be pointed by the end of the Awakening? He laughed a bit more at his cluelessness before continuing to talk to the sky or the earth. He still didn't know how this worked.

"I'm traveling to Wyrdbrook today. Alone. And I don't know if you have any influence wherever you are, but if you could try and help me make some friends there, I'd appreciate it."

Kalen heard Wen caw again from a distance.

His mother had planned his whole trip, down to the minute. She had warned before he left that morning that if he didn't stick to the schedule, she was going to send Wen after him. The crow's call was her loving nudge to get him moving.

It was time to head to Wyrdbrook.

"I have to go now, I guess," he said as he looked to the sky, watching the birds overhead. He was jealous of them–of their freedom to move from place to place. They could go wherever the day took them, never having to worry about whether or not they belonged there.

How could they carry on as if they didn't know this was his last day around for a while? Maybe forever. He knew the forest had been here long before him, but how could all of it still exist and thrive without him around? How could this place not miss him the way he would miss it?

He took one last look at the Sanctwood Forest.

"Take care of my mom," he whispered to the breeze and the earth, to the trees, and to the ghost of his father.

To anything that would listen.

Kalen stood up, patted the giant oak, and ran toward the only home he'd ever known.

Hurrying off to say goodbye to the two women who raised him.

Both carrying secrets of their own.

Chapter Seven

Ria

Ria thought the day West died would be the hardest of her life. This one was worse.

Her mother had told her that she'd never understand love until she had a child. She'd always say that loving Ria felt like her heart was physically walking around outside of her body. Unprotected, vulnerable, with no real way to guarantee that other people would keep it safe. Ria always thought that was an exaggeration—until she saw Kalen for the first time. Until the first time he held her finger or cried for her in the middle of the night. Until right now. Because she could feel herself breaking. Like someone was sinking their claws into her heart and ripping it apart from the inside.

You need to be strong for him.

"I'm here! I'm here!" She looked up to see Kalen running down the path toward her and Eugenia.

Her boy.

Sprinting toward her heartbreak.

Yes, she thought, *this day is definitely worse.*

Eugenia reached out and gave her hand a quick squeeze. Three times, like she always did. *Kind. Brave. Gentle.* A subtle reminder from her best friend. The only thing holding her together.

"Late to your own going-away party, Kale." She smiled. "I thought I raised you better than that."

Kalen threw a glance at Eugenia before looking back at his mother.

"You did!" he replied, still catching his breath from his run. "I hit the jackpot foraging and lost track of time."

What was that look about?

"I didn't think you'd be so excited to send me off," he joked back.

Her face scrunched, and her heart stung.

She knew it was a joke, but no matter how light she was trying to keep this goodbye, no matter how desperate she was to keep him safe, she was never going to be ready to let him go.

She handed him his bag reluctantly. She wished she could freeze time and stretch out this goodbye.

"Have everything you need?"

"I think so." She watched him intently, noticing his throat bob up and down. He was trying to be strong, too.

She turned to Eugenia. "Can you give us just a minute? I promise I'll get you before he leaves."

Eugenia nodded and headed inside, giving them both the space they needed for a proper goodbye.

"I know you're scared. It's okay to be. You know that, right?" she prodded him, ignoring her heartbreak to focus on her son.

"I know. I'm just going to miss this." He gestured to the forest and let his arm fall slack to his side. "And you."

"Me too, little crow." A lump formed in her own throat. "We've been sad a lot lately, huh?"

"Well, we've had a lot going on," he countered.

She closed the distance between them and embraced her son, wondering if she'd ever be able to do this again.

She broke away first and put her hands on his shoulders, steadying them both.

"What if no one likes me in Wyrdbrook?" He was days away from being eighteen, an adult, but right now, she just saw her little boy. He was five again, needing her as badly as he did when he'd fall and scratch his knee.

"Impossible," she responded, lightly grazing his cheek with her thumb.

"I need you to write to Genie while you're away, okay?" She noticed the confusion on his face instantly.

"I can't risk anyone intercepting a letter here. It's too dangerous."

He didn't respond as his tears began to fall silently.

This is the first time Ria had ever felt regret for falling in love with West.

She gained love, but at what cost?

That love gave her Kalen, and now it was ripping him away.

"Remember, this is just a new adventure." She forced herself to smile and pinched his cheek. He hit her hand away and let out an airy laugh.

They were going to be okay. She would see him again.

Gods, I hope I see him again.

"Genie!" she yelled, coaxing her best friend to come back outside.

It was time for them to say goodbye.

Kalen hugged Eugenia first. They mumbled a few words to each other and then pulled away. Eugenia looked at Ria with sorrow. She knew this was going to be the hardest part for her.

The look was Eugenia's promise: *I won't leave you.*

Finally, Kalen walked over to Ria and they hugged again—a tight and quick embrace, like ripping off a bandage.

"I love you, Mom," he said.

"I love you, too, Kale," she replied.

That was all there was left to say. They'd spent the last seventeen years filling all the little corners of their lives so neither of them ever had to wonder. Love was the beginning and the end; it was the thread that carried them both through.

So Ria watched as her son, her Kalen, her heart, walked toward his new life.

Knowing there wasn't any way hers would ever be the same again.

Chapter Eight
Kalen

K alen was exhausted. Beyond exhausted. The path was straightforward, but the time it took to arrive was dragging on. He knew he was getting close to Wyrdbrook, to his new *home*.

Home.

He rejected the thought; he'd already had a place he called home. And it wasn't Wyrdbrook.

He'd been traveling all day, but being alone in the forest felt like second nature to him. It's how he had spent his entire life. But he wasn't entirely alone on this trip.

He looked up to see Wen flying overhead, a thoughtful companion to guide his journey. Eugenia had suggested the crow come along, and Kalen found himself grateful for the last bit of his old life following him to his new one.

"Wen knows the way," she had whispered to him as they said goodbye.

He was dreading the moment Wen dropped him off and left. The isolation from everything he'd known before, the absence of everything familiar.

He'd be in a new place, to endure something he'd never even heard of until three days ago.

The Awakening.

He still wasn't sure what it meant for him. And that made him more nervous than he cared to admit.

He tried not to let his mind wander too much into the unknown. He knew there was no real use. He could think about it all he wanted, but he wouldn't get answers. Not until Wyrdbrook.

So he needed to stay the course, get there safely, find Liam, and then get his ass to sleep. He turned eighteen in just a few days, and beyond the exhaustion he was currently feeling, he could tell his body was growing tired.

He didn't have time for anything else. Not yet. He didn't know how to make new friends or meet new people. He'd never had to do it before.

And while he'd found himself wishing for those relationships just a week ago, today, he felt like his brain couldn't handle the idea of anything else new. It was too much. He'd just need to get through the Awakening. Then, he'd focus on friendship, or whatever else came next.

Wen let out a caw to grab his attention, and then dove, taking a sharp turn down a path Kalen wouldn't have noticed on his own. He followed the crow deeper into the forest until they hit an uphill slope.

I guess this is why they call it the Peaks.

Ducking under tree limbs and climbing over rogue rocks, he began the ascent. The brush up the mountain was thick and steep, hiding it from unknowing eyes and deterring anyone else who happened upon it. This was the final push to Wyrdbrook.

Kalen climbed for what felt like hours. Building a steady rhythm despite his bleeding hands and cramping thighs, his body was screaming at him to take a break, but it wasn't an option. He had to get there tonight. He could see where the Peaks plateaued. He could feel the magic of Wyrdbrook beginning to hum through him.

Was this excitement? Was this exhaustion? He didn't care as he muscled his way up.

He'd made it.

Finally, he'd made it.

And there was nothing there. Just trees, as far as he could see.

This has to be a joke.

Wen landed on a branch nearby, and Kalen snapped his head toward the bird.

"Please tell me we're not lost," he said plainly. "Please tell me we didn't come all of this way to a village that doesn't exist."

A twig snapped in the distance, interrupting their conversation. If he could even call talking to a bird a conversation. Wen took flight, continuing his work as Kalen's protector.

Three caws rang out from the distance.

Run?

Kalen moved quickly, trusting the crow despite the fact that he had gotten them lost. Sprinting in the opposite direction Wen flew, he hid behind a tree, deep enough to see where he once stood, while praying he was too deep to be seen himself.

It didn't take long before a group of men came through the clearing.

Is it? Why would they be up here?

Kalen felt his blood grow cold.

He couldn't see much of the men's faces through the dark of the night, but they did not attempt to hide their conversation. They didn't know he was here.

Thank Gods.

"It was right here just last week," one of them said with confusion in their voice.

"I knew I shouldn't have trusted you, Acer," another spat in his direction. "How dare you?"

Kalen could tell that was their leader, somehow. His voice brimmed with power.

"I'm sorry, sir. It was a white orb. I swear it. It was just here..."

"Enough. You have wasted my time. And my time is very valuable," the leader shot back.

Smack.

Kalen didn't have to see to know the man had just been hit.

The casual cruelty confirmed what he already knew: The Order was here.

"Let's get back to Evermere. There's nothing for us here," the powerful one declared. And the group turned around, coming back the way they came.

Kalen stood there for what felt like hours. Frozen in fear.

He finally got the courage to make his way back to where he had started.

Well, I guess something else is here.

Wen flapped back to Kalen now, perching on his shoulder.

"That was too close," he said to the bird, patting his head. "But where's Wyrdbrook? I don't get it."

Kalen noticed a light coming from deeper within the forest.

"Do I..." he stumbled over his words, "um, follow that thing?" He pointed in the direction of the light, frightened.

One caw for yes.

This must be right, then.

The crow looked at him smugly, almost as if to say, "I told you so."

Kalen walked slowly toward the light, admiring the way the faint glow illuminated his path–a beacon. Calling him in somehow. He hadn't been sure this was right, leaving the Sanctwood. His mother.

Until now.

The light of the white sphere felt like a familiar hug in this foreign place.

"Well, what the hell am I supposed to do now?" he called to Wen. "Touch it?"

The crow cawed once in response, a confirmation for him to move forward.

"Here goes nothing," he said, as he closed his eyes and outstretched his hand to make direct contact with the glowing sphere. He winced, waiting for whatever came next.

Nothing.

"You're kidding me, Wen," Kalen huffed as he opened his eyes to scold the crow.

Just in time to see a protective veil over the hidden village dissipate.

Oh my Gods.

Kalen had made it. He'd done it.

Wyrdbrook.

And it was more beautiful than he could have imagined.

But more than that, he felt it.

This was where he was meant to be. Something within this ancient village was welcoming him here.

Wyrdbrook had been waiting for him all along.

Kalen's eyes grew wide, scanning the village for the first time.

A beautiful, hidden oasis. Unseen by anyone except those who lived there, and people like Eugenia, who just knew everything.

The anxiety he had before arriving was slowly fading away, making room for wonder.

Wyrdbrook *felt* old.

Where the Sanctwood was sturdy, Wyrdbrook was fragile. Where the Sanctwood was mostly untouched, Wyrdbrook was worn and lived in. Where the Sanctwood was just him and his mother, Wyrdbrook was lined with *people*. Real people.

His anxiety was back.

Kalen couldn't tell the difference between fae and witch, human, or *hybrid*. Everyone was talking, laughing, and existing together without a single trace of fear about what lay beyond the enchanted forest. Without a single worry about The Order.

Kalen forced himself to begin walking through the village, admiring the cottages nestled on either side of the lit path ahead of him. Wondering if one of them would be for him.

Something of his own. Where he wouldn't have to hide.

He was so tired from his journey, but he found himself in perpetual awe of this place. The smell of pine and patchouli, the sky so wide open he could count the stars. It felt like something out of a dream.

Maybe this won't be too bad.

His priority hadn't changed, though–he had to find Liam. But how?

He heard the chatter of people all around him. People paired off, holding hands. People in small groups walking into cottages. Friendships. Relationships. Two things he's never really had, and never thought he would.

Kalen looked around, unsure of where to go, until he heard a boisterous laugh coming from a group to his right.

He'd start with them.

You can do this. Kind. Brave. Gentle. Kalen reasoned as he walked toward the group.

He wasn't ready to make friends quite yet, but he was eager to talk to someone other than his mother or Eugenia for the first time in years.

"Excuse me?" he said as he walked up to the mingling group. "I'm, um, sorry to interrupt, but do you all know Liam?" He tried to maintain eye contact, tried to show these people he was used to having conversations with folks he didn't know.

He wasn't sure it was very convincing.

You won't have to hide in Wyrdbrook. He remembered the promise his mother made him one night before he left.

He relaxed his shoulders and unclenched his jaw.

He belonged here.

"Hiya! You must be new," a cheerful fae responded. Kalen noticed the tip of one of her ears stood tall and sharp, while the other was dull and scarred.

"Everyone knows Liam," she continued. "He should be in the big building right over there," she said as she pointed beyond the edge of the path.

He didn't understand how he'd missed it before. Draped in vines, he could feel the magic of the building calling him inside. Maybe that's what he'd been feeling since he got here.

He pulled his eyes away and regained focus on the conversation in front of him.

"Thanks. I'm Kalen, by the way."

So much for not making friends.

"It's really nice to meet you, Kalen." The fae reached her hand out in greeting. "I'm Victoria, this handsome person is Shu," she pointed to her left, blushing, "and *this* sassy one," she lovingly put her arm around the person next to her, "is Tessan."

"Tessan?" Kalen asked in disbelief.

There's no way the one person he'd met in his childhood would somehow turn up at Wyrdbrook. But it had to be her. He remembered her ice-blue eyes. His mother's eyes were blue too, but not like Tessan's. He wasn't sure anyone's eyes were like Tessan's.

The last time he'd seen her, he was a buck-toothed boy who barely stood as tall as her shoulders. She was a mean witch with a quick wit who poked at him for his height.

She still stood tall, taller than the average witch, though now she hit right about at *his* own shoulders. Kalen straightened up a bit.

Her raven colored hair was slicked back tightly, every single piece had its place. The juxtaposition of her dark black hair and blue eyes made his breath hitch.

He couldn't believe she was here.

"I know, I know, it's kind of a weird name..." Victoria trailed on happily, but her words faded into nothingness as Kalen focused on Tessan.

Would she remember him?

Should he ask?

He was going to ask.

"Are you Tessan Duscaire?" He blurted out.

Victoria stopped talking abruptly. Kalen's cheeks reddened.

Oops.

Socializing like this was going to take some time to figure out.

"I'm so sorry I cut you off. This..." he gestured to the group in front of him, "is new to me."

Victoria gave him a knowing smile. "Don't sweat it, Kalen Halrowe."

Okay, so everyone knows my name?

It made him uncomfortable.

"Victoria, please," Tessan spoke with a playful edge. "You're going to scare the poor guy, and he just got here." Tessan stretched out her hand, offering him a handshake. "It's good to see you again, Kalen."

She smiled. Eugenia's niece in Wyrdbrook. A piece of home here after all.

Maybe making friends wasn't so bad.

"I can't believe Eugenia didn't tell me you'd be here," Kalen replied, confused.

Why did she keep so many secrets from him?

"Well, you know her. Her secrets are as deep and vast as her herbal cabinets," Tessan retorted.

So it's not just me, then.

His laugh quickly turned to a yawn. It was getting late, and his day of travel had finally caught up to him.

He needed to find Liam and get into one of these cottages. Catching up with Tessan would have to wait.

"I'd love to stay and talk, but I have to find Liam before I collapse. It was nice to meet you all," he nodded to Victoria and Shu.

"Maybe we can meet up again sometime?" he asked Tessan directly.

"I'll see you around, Kalen," Tessan responded with a smirk.

Kalen didn't know if that was a yes or no, but he was too tired to unpack it. He'd either see Tessan or he wouldn't. And as of now, she was just a stranger he'd met what felt like a lifetime ago.

Kalen waved to the group and headed toward the vine-covered building, trying not to think about Tessan and why on earth she was also in Wyrdbrook. And why Eugenia didn't tell him.

And what the hell was up with that orb?

Kalen's thoughts consumed him long enough that the walk to the building flew by. And it was even more beautiful up close. The moon shone brightly on the vine-covered walls, as if Earth Mother Herself was highlighting this place. Demanding that whoever passed pay attention to what lay in front of them.

Under the vines were hand-carved wooden walls, intricate details of lives and stories Kalen had never heard before–stories that had been lost to time, or left in a cobwebbed corner on purpose.

Kalen put his hand up to knock when the door opened.

"Oh, sorry, I was just knocking. I'm looking for—" Kalen started.

"I know exactly who you're looking for," the stranger cut him off. "Come on in, Kalen. We've been waiting for you."

Waiting for me?

Kalen followed the stranger inside, peering up at the ceiling, still admiring the beauty of this ancient space.

"Welcome to the Veilhold," the stranger said, as Kalen appreciated the mural on the wall. "It's beautiful, isn't it?"

What on earth is this place?

"I just told you, this is the Veilhold. It's the heart of Wyrdbrook. The place where our goodness grows. The place that keeps us safe." He murmured, "I don't know, I'm trying a few taglines. What do you think about them?"

Wait, did I say that out loud?

"Of course you didn't. You don't know who has magic around these parts, my friend." The stranger let out a deep laugh. "Gotta be careful with those thoughts." He tapped the side of his head.

"You can read minds?" Kalen gaped. "I didn't know magic like that existed."

"Almost. I can read energy. When you spend all day working with people and their needs, it's pretty easy to figure out what energy means."

"Are you Liam?" Kalen asked. "Eugenia told me to find you."

"Woah, now. I thought I was the one who could read minds." He threw his hands up in front of him in surrender. "Yes, I'm Liam. I'm the Overseer of Wyrdbrook. Eugenia is a dear friend to us here."

A dear friend? How long had she known about this place?

"Long enough to make sure you got here safe," he shrugged. "Follow me?"

Eugenia was right, he would be finding out a lot about her while he was here, he just didn't expect to find out so much on his first day.

The two walked in casual conversation until they reached a room off the main hall. He didn't care to ask Liam where they were going; he found himself trusting him implicitly.

He knew Liam didn't end up in this position by accident; whatever ancient magic existed here in Wyrdbrook trusted him, too.

"I'm sure you have a lot of questions," Liam said seriously. "We don't have time to get into much of it tonight. I have much to do, and I'd like to get you to your cottage as soon as possible. I'd also imagine those long legs are tired from your travels." He laughed again and turned his attention to the door in front of them.

Liam slid his fingers along the door, following a hidden pattern Kalen couldn't see. He heard a small click as it unlocked, revealing a room lined with narrow wooden shelves, each lined in rows of small white orbs of their own. He wasn't sure he'd ever get used to the magic this place held.

They slowly walked into the room, and Kalen could feel the energy buzzing from every corner.

Yeah, he definitely wouldn't get used to this.

"Take this orb," Liam said, handing a smaller version of what Kalen had touched to get into Wyrdbrook.

"Put it in the box by your door. It's spelled to only allow those you wish to enter into your space," he continued. "So choose wisely."

"Each resident has their own. Think of it as a special lock to keep your home sacred."

Kalen took the orb, and a small shock startled him. Whatever it was made of had just connected to magic of his own.

Liam handed Kalen a small map of the village, "And use this map should you need to find your way around our small village. But keep it safely within your belongings. Folks in Evermere don't know we're up here, and we'd like to keep it that way," Liam said seriously.

"Got it. The orb is the key; keep the map safe. Is there anything you need from me before I head to my cottage? I'm really looking forward to sitting down soon." Kalen lightheartedly joked.

He wondered if he should tell Liam about the men he saw earlier in the forest. The ones who had been looking for the white orb. The Order.

"Nothing at all. I'll get back to it. The work as the Overseer never stops. Can you believe I get to do this?" he sang out, gesturing to the room around him.

"It seems pretty incredible," Kalen responded genuinely.

He'd tell him about the men in the forest tomorrow.

Liam smirked. "Welcome to Wyrdbrook, Kalen. Come see me the night before your Awakening. There is much you need to learn before it starts."

Kalen knew it was time to leave, but hated saying goodbye to Liam.

He admired the way the Overseer balanced his wisdom and his humor, and Kalen found himself wanting to learn more about his life, about the stories he held.

Another time.

Liam walked him to the door of the Veilhold, "I'll see you around, little crow." Liam grinned and walked back inside, shutting the large wooden door behind him.

Little crow?

He knew Kalen would have questions, wouldn't he? How did he know his mother called him little crow? Was it a coincidence?

If he weren't so exhausted, he'd beg for answers, but his eyes were crossing.

So instead, he begged for the relief of a good night's sleep. He'd have time to learn from Liam.

Kalen pulled out the map and quickly found his new home. *His.* The first time he'd be living by himself. He already missed the smell of his Mother's stew, but he had to do this alone. Maybe it wouldn't be that bad?

Everyone he had met so far had been incredibly kind. And Tessan was here. Though he wasn't sure if that mattered yet.

He placed the orb down, just as he was told, and it flashed yellow before going white again.

That's probably a good sign.

He pushed the door open, grateful it swung easily as he entered the dusty and humid room. The home had been sitting empty for a while. He let out a small cough, waving the dust away from his face, while he searched for a lamp to light. He was excited to explore this place. It wasn't perfect, but it didn't have to be.

He struck a match and lit a lamp he found sitting by the door. He waited just a moment, letting the lamp catch fire, before picking it up to get a better view of his space.

The lamp was roaring now, serving him as a small source of heat and a large source of light. The cottage was cozy and cramped. A small couch sat in the common room, tiny holes like freckles marked the walls—a reminder of the people who were here before him and the lives they lived. The art they hung. He wondered what their stories were. Where they all went.

Kalen felt lucky to be the one here now.

On the counter sat a small bundle of dried herbs someone must have left behind. He picked them up and inhaled deeply, their once rich fragrance now faded with time.

His mother does that—keeps herbs on the counter. He missed her already somehow. He couldn't let his mind stay there for long, though. It was too soon; he just got here. How could he already be homesick?

Maybe he just needed to sleep.

Getting more familiar with the layout, Kalen finally reached for the door handle of his bedroom. His last stop before sleep. He yawned, setting down the lamp on the small desk by his door.

A draft of air caught his attention and blew out the fire in the lamp, leaving him in total darkness in an unfamiliar room.

Shit. Someone left the shutters open.

Kalen clumsily shuffled over to close them, careful not to break anything along the way as he navigated the darkness. He was fumbling through the room, following the cool, wet breeze to the open window. He yanked the shutters closed and slid the small lock into the latch so it wouldn't happen again.

Finally, sleep.

Kalen was trudging over to where he believed his bed was, a little quicker than he should be in his new environment.

He could not wait to lie down.

Faster than he could catch himself, Kalen's foot was tangled in a blanket, and he was falling, hard and fast, straight to the floor.

"Gods!" he yelped, grabbing his arm; he flipped over to his back, writhing in pain. His wrist had taken most of the impact in an attempt to save the rest of him.

"I just want to sleeeeeeep," Kalen moaned in frustration into the nothingness.

"Are you okay?" A concerned voice rang out from the darkness.

Kalen froze in fear.

He knew this voice from somewhere. Was it one of the men from the woods? How did he not realize someone was in his home? He talked himself down.

Don't panic. Act like nothing's wrong. Don't give anything away about who you are. You can do this. Make up a good story, be convincing.

"Oh, woah, I didn't realize someone was here!" Kalen kept his voice light and airy, an attempt to disarm the person in his room.

He didn't know if it was working.

"I think you're in the wrong place. Don't worry, this happens all the time," he continued, hoping his tone would keep this person from doing anything rash.

He needed to get out of here, fast.

Think, Kalen, think.

He stood up quickly, wincing as he grabbed his wrist and continued with his story, praying to anyone who was listening that the intruder would let him leave in peace.

"There must have been some kind of mix-up." Kalen's voice quivered with the lie. He cleared his throat. "I'll go talk to the Overseer and we'll get it sorted out."

Kalen hurried toward the door. Besides the immense danger he was in, he couldn't believe he was further from sleep now than he was when he walked in. He was in his bedroom, on the way to his bed. He could practically feel its warmth from here.

"Kalen, wait," the voice said softly.

He stopped. He *did* know that voice. But there was no way...

He listened intently, his heart thundering in his chest, as he heard the intruder stand up. He watched as one palm of the stranger in front of him created a tiny spark and flicked it toward Kalen's lamp. Kalen jumped when the flame made contact with the wick, bracing his head and expecting the worst. But nothing happened.

All was bright again.

He lowered his hands from his head.

He had to be dreaming.

This can't be right.

Because Kalen was looking into the face of his father.

His dead father.

Impossibly alive and standing right in front of him.

Kalen stared at him in shock, the man who shared his face. He wasn't supposed to meet him. He wasn't supposed to be here.

This can't be right. My father is dead.

Kalen's head was spinning as his throat tightened.

I can't breathe.

He was on a descent into panic, and he couldn't escape.

His Dad. Here.

This can't be right.

Does my mom know? Why has everyone I've ever loved been lying to me?

The edges of his vision were going dark, and there was no way Kalen could dig himself out.

Everything in his world had changed in four days. It was too much. It was too fast.

"Hey...breathe," the voice whispered. Trying to anchor him to reality. But it was too late.

His father's voice was the last thing he heard before the darkness took him.

Kalen's vision was blurry. He blinked away the fuzz that clouded his eyes, only to realize he was still in his room in Wyrdbrook. He had made it to his bed after all.

He thought he remembered what had happened right before he fainted, though he still didn't know if it was real or some version of magic that had come to taunt him.

His father, alive? Nothing made any sense anymore.

What day is it, even?

"You've been out like a lamp for the past two days," the hushed voice belonged to Liam. Of course it did, because Kalen knew he hadn't asked that question out loud.

And that means if he'd been unconscious for two days...

The Awakening is tomorrow.

He couldn't catch a break.

The Overseer walked over to him slowly, kindly, and put the back of his tattooed hand on Kalen's forehead. Checking for a temperature, checking to make sure he was okay. Kalen felt himself relax in his presence. He was safe with Liam here.

For now.

"How are you feeling? You had a nasty spill. Scared us all," Liam kept his voice low, and Kalen was grateful, considering the ringing in his head.

"I feel like I was hit by a damn tree," Kalen said in a haze. "Can we even say damn here? Or will some ancient God of Wyrdbrook strike me down?" Kalen softly laughed. He propped himself up on his forearms, trying to sit up to look at Liam but having trouble getting oriented in the still-spinning room.

Maybe the fall was worse than he thought.

"You can use your words however you want, as long as they're not meant to harm those around you," Liam answered. "Do you want to talk about what happened?"

Kalen assumed the Overseer could sense the unease building in his stomach.

"Is my Father alive?" Kalen choked out in disbelief. "I could have sworn he was here, but I was so tired..." he trailed off. He knew Liam would pick up on the rest of this thought.

Did I dream it?

No, he was standing there in front of him. Kalen heard his voice, and he saw him. He could have reached out to touch him. It was real.

Right?

"Do you really want to know the answer to the questions you have?" Liam responded, patting his hand. "You've been through a lot these last few days."

Kalen nodded in pain and let his heavy head rest back on his pillow. Staring up at the ceiling, thinking about the question he needed the answer to the most.

"Is he really here?"

"Yes." Liam's voice was steady, giving Kalen the courage to continue.

"Can I see him?"

"Of course. And if you're ready now, I'll leave you to it." Liam stood up from the chair he'd moved by Kalen's bedside.

He gave Kalen a hint of a smile. "Find me later, Kalen. Or send word that I should come back here if you're not feeling well. We still have a lot to discuss before tomorrow's ceremony."

"I will," Kalen started. "Thank you for taking care of me the last couple of days. Despite it all, I'm still happy to be here."

And he meant it. He didn't understand how this could be happening, but he knew this was the place he needed to grow through it.

"Don't thank me. Thank your father." Liam's expression was unreadable. He headed toward the door before turning around again.

"I am hesitant to tell you how to feel," he said. "But consider that we all have to make sacrifices for those we love. You'll understand one day, even if you don't understand now."

With nothing left to say, Liam left his cottage, and Kalen was alone with the silence.

He wondered when his father would be here.

Would he walk through the front door and greet him like they'd known each other forever? Would he apologize for being alive for the last seventeen years and abandoning him and his mother?

Would Kalen like him at all? Or was the idea of who he was built up in his head too...big?

He had never dreamt of preparing for this conversation. He'd never had to. His father was dead. Except he wasn't. Except, he never was.

Kalen glanced around his room, quietly passing the time before his father arrived, finally able to see it in the daylight for the first time. It was small but spacious. A closet in the corner, the same desk with the same lamp that lit his way around the house just a couple of days prior.

And that window. That damn window.

Open again.

Kalen wanted to get up to latch it, but couldn't find the strength or stability within him to move quite yet.

He decided to close his eyes until his father got here, doing his best to stay in the world that exists just between real life and dreaming. He could picture it here, the life he could have had if both of his parents had been around.

His father teaching him how to climb trees, kissing his mother when he got home from a day out in the Sanctwood, tucking him into bed at night, and telling him stories of other villages and people, of fae and witch and human. Of hybrids, like him.

Maybe they wouldn't have had to live in the Sanctwood at all? Maybe they'd have been vendors at the market in Evermere. And they'd have been neighbors with Eugenia.

Maybe he and Tessan would have grown up best friends or fallen in...

Wings ruffling in the windowsill brought him back from the world that would never exist.

"Well, look who it is," he glanced to see Wen perched in the window. "Did Mom send you here to check on me?"

He had to admit, it was good to see the crow. "I wondered where you flew off to when we got here."

The bird glided into his room and a couple of throaty caws left his beak.

"No, Mom didn't send you here. Whatever you say, Wenny." Kalen jeered.

"I guess you've just been hanging around and fattening up on whatever berries you can find in this new part of the forest, then. You're such an opportunist. Have I ever told you that?"

Kalen chuckled again, closing his eyes and continuing to chat to the crow.

"I'm going to tell you this because it's almost as crazy as the fact that I'm holding a conversation with you," Kalen said lazily. "I met my father last night, I think. He's supposed to be on his way here. Can you believe that? He's alive. The irony is that I think it would kill Mom if she knew."

Kalen let out a deep breath and settled further into his pillow.

"That's why I'm going to ask you not to tell her," a deep voice spoke from the middle of the room.

Kalen jolted up far too quickly for the pain he was still feeling. His father was here. He put his hand on his head to steady himself.

"Careful now," his father said, inching closer to him.

Kalen felt his body physically tense with his father's presence. His father noticed too, as sadness laced his eyes, and he stopped walking toward Kalen.

"When did you get in here? How did I not hear you?" Kalen spat out and immediately regretted it.

The first words he ever said to his father knowingly, and that's the best he could do?

"Spoken like a true teenager," his father laughed easily.

Kalen didn't think it was funny.

"I've been here, Kale," his father said seriously, picking up on the cue that it wasn't time for jokes.

"No. You don't get to call me that. My *mother* calls me that. People who *know* me call me that," Kalen snapped back.

He could feel the tears forming in his eyes. How dare he act like he was familiar? Kalen didn't know him. They shared blood, but that was it. And he was learning that wasn't enough for him. He was surprised by the anger rising in his body.

"Fair," his father responded tenderly. "Maybe we can just start from the beginning?"

Kalen couldn't move, as his father continued, assuming his silence was an invitation forward.

Kalen hated that he was right; that he somehow knew him in a small way already.

"I'm Westin Vale," he said, putting his hand on his chest. "I'm your father. And yes, I'm supposed to be dead. I think you know that part already," he finished smoothly. He clearly hadn't changed much in the last seventeen years.

He was still tall and broad, still charming and smooth. But he looked tired, like life had been unkind to him. His hair was shorter now, and a bit more gray, but his stature remained. Kalen scanned his father, seeing so much of himself reflected back to him.

Maybe too much of himself.

It made his stomach hurt.

He finally drew his eyes up to his father's ears, the mark that proved he was fae, the symbol that showed his mother the lineage he carried. The mark that had forbidden their love.

But where the points declaring him fae once stood sharply, jagged scars remained. Mutilated. Someone had cut off the tips.

Kalen's eyes widened in horror.

And his father noticed, swiftly dipping his head in shame, and began to wring his fingers. Was he ashamed?

His father quietly continued.

"Listen, I know you probably have a lot of questions. I think I could answer them if I just...show you?" He was asking for Kalen's consent before he undoubtedly learned something else that would send him off the deep end.

But Kalen didn't know what to say. He *did* have a lot of questions. There was no way whatever he wanted to *do* would answer any of them.

Oh, what the hell.

He tentatively shook his head yes anyway.

And in a flash, his father was gone. The room shivered with a familiar magic.

Kalen shivered with it.

He can shift? Kalen's mouth was open in amazement, and he really wished it wasn't.

He wished he didn't care about his father's magic at all. That he could just shake off this meeting like he was anyone else Kalen would be meeting over the next few days.

But he wasn't just anyone else. He was his father.

Here.

He wished he didn't want to know him so badly. He wanted to remain in his anger, *needed* to remain there. He was disappointed by the fact that the man he could have learned from, the man who could have raised him, chose to stay away from him, from his mother, for all this time.

It wasn't until he heard the ruffle of feathers that Kalen jumped out of his bed in disbelief.

Because where his father had once stood, a crow now perched.

But not just any crow. Kalen gulped as the realization sank in. Wen.

His father was Wen.

Kalen stormed out of his bedroom. He had to get out of here. He needed some space to process this, to run to the forest and clear his head. To sit among the giant pine trees and feel small again.

My father is Wen?

For the first time since arriving, he wished he were back in the Sanctwood.

If I had just stayed home, none of this would have ever happened.

He hurriedly grabbed the bag his mother had made for him. He needed to forage. That would make this feel better. He'd find some new place here where he could decompress while he sorted these feelings out.

Wasn't this always going to be his future? Here in Wyrdbrook? Navigating new feelings, people, and relationships alone because his mother was a witch and his father was fae, and that made him a hybrid. Unclean to The Order. A danger to their purity. A nobody.

Gods damn The Order.

His father had been near him all along? Near his mother? And *he* didn't even want them? It felt unforgivable.

Is this unforgivable?

He shook the thought from his head.

Kalen was almost out the door when he felt another shiver of magic and heard his father's hurried footsteps running toward him. Kalen turned to face him, his eyes pleading with Kalen to stop moving, to give him some time to catch up.

"Please, Kalen. Just let me explain," he gasped, sucking down the still air in the room. His magic clearly took quite a bit out of him, but Kalen wasn't familiar with shifting—with fae magic.

Maybe he would be if his dad had actually been around as a human and not a Gods damn bird.

He could feel the heat rise in his stomach again, his hands were shaking as he opened his mouth.

"What is there to explain? That you've rendezvoused as our family crow and didn't feel like it was worth your time to show your face?" Kalen said with exasperation. "You don't know me, so whatever. You don't owe me anything." He noticed the wince on his father's face but continued anyway.

"But my mother? She's been crying over you for years," Kalen felt his voice rising with his internal temperature. "She deserved more than this. *You* could have given her more." Kalen was yelling now. These feelings, this anger, were unfamiliar to him, and he didn't know how to come back down from it.

"I could have known you." He shook his head at his father, disgusted.

Readying himself for the final blow, he took a deep breath. He wanted to hurt his father the same way his father had hurt him.

"But now, I don't think I want to," he ended quietly. He knew his words would sting no matter how loudly he said them.

That was the point.

He didn't know if he believed the words he was saying. Could he really pass up the opportunity to know his father? Could he find it within himself to really listen to him? To hear him out?

He couldn't answer those questions right now. He wasn't ready.

Kalen started toward the door again before turning back around to look at his father. "Don't follow me." His voice was firm, but he hoped he heard his plea.

Please don't disappear again. Please be here when I get back.

Kalen stepped out of his home and into the sunshine. A stark difference to the storm brewing inside of him. He needed this—the quick connection to nature to bring him back to himself. He could feel it slowly working as he walked away from his home.

He hadn't had the chance to see Wyrdbrook like this yet, in the daytime. If he thought it was beautiful in the night, what he saw before him was blowing him away.

And just for a moment, he forgot he was angry at all.

The evergreen of the forest was a perfect background for this sacred place. Cottages scattered in rows around the village, all unique in their own way, built by the people who settled here and created this haven for people like him.

Kalen turned back to look at his own. He loved it.

His new home didn't look built, it looked grown somehow. The stone steps leading up to the doorway lay crooked as if whoever once lived there would hop to and from each one. Kalen could almost picture it.

If he weren't so damn mad, he would have smiled.

Vines similar to the ones he'd seen at the Veilhold tangled up the stone walls, weaving an intricate web that took Kalen's breath away. It felt intentional, like Earth Mother wanted folks to notice the little bits of beauty she left in the world. Kalen always tried to.

His mother had taught him that.

But what caught Kalen's attention most about his new home was the door. The weathered wood stood firm and strong, even though it had likely been here for hundreds of years, its burls and knots showing signs of the life it lived before it was repurposed for this.

He sent out a quick whisper of gratitude to the tree it once was, just in case it could somehow feel it. The trees always could.

Kalen recognized that staring at his home may be sending the wrong message to his father inside. Likely watching him take in this new village, assuming he was contemplating whether or not to come back inside and talk to him.

He wasn't.

He sent out that thought, too, just in case his Dad had magic that could pick up on energy like Liam did.

I am not ready to talk to you. And I may not ever be.

His hands balled into fists. The unfamiliar anger covered him again.

He turned on his heels quickly, heading toward the forest. He'd keep his head down, he'd get somewhere safe, and then he'd work this out.

Alone.

"Escaping already? I know it's not the Sanctwood, but surely it's not *that* bad."

Tessan.

Kalen stopped and peered at her. She was, unfortunately, an innocent bystander caught in his fury.

"You have no idea what the last few days have been like for me," he snapped.

He didn't mean to.

She didn't seem to care. Because Tessan Duscaire was unfazed. Her icy eyes stayed locked on his muddy brown ones, her face neutral. It almost felt like she was challenging him somehow. Like she was giving him evidence she could handle whatever mess he was planning to throw at her.

His thoughts were confirmed as she slowly began to walk toward him. Her long black hair was still perfectly in place, despite the whip of the wind around them.

Proving to him she wasn't scared of his pain, of the anger boiling inside of him, she smirked as she made her way closer.

"Well, lucky for you, I have time to learn." She looped her arm in his. "Walk with me?" she said softly. It was different from the first time they met. It was gentle, sincere.

Kalen could feel his heart steady, just a bit, as Tessan extended this olive branch. This friendship. Something that he'd never experienced before.

A nod that, whatever was happening to him, she could help him shoulder it. That she'd be here if he wanted her to be.

He didn't know why or how, but he believed her.

So she led them to the forest. As Kalen began to unwind, he told Tessan everything that had happened since he'd arrived at Wyrdbrook.

Kalen didn't know how long he and Tessan had been talking. He just kept going until all of his feelings didn't feel so big anymore. Until they took up less space in his brain and he steadied himself.

They didn't walk for long before Tessan showed him to a small stream to sit for a bit. Tessan knew the way there, as if she'd spent time here alone, too. His heart warmed at the idea of her sharing this place with him.

As if she knew his worries would be carried as far as the stream could take them. The trees were sparse, making way for the wide open sky in front of them, the sound of the birds serving as a soundtrack.

It was peaceful.

He needed that.

He'd told her everything–about Eugenia's meeting with him in the woods before he'd left, about his father being alive *and* his crow.

She was steady through it all. Unflinching. Occasionally, she made small noises to affirm she was still following along, but was careful to never interrupt.

Her presence made him warm in the way the sun did. Like it could sustain him–allow him to grow. But in the same way the sun demanded your respect, so did Tessan. Don't look too long, or it will hurt your eyes; don't get too close, or it will burn.

He'd take the risk for now.

"I feel like I've been doing most of the talking," Kalen said, embarrassed. "Sorry."

"I know. I was honestly wondering when you'd stop," Tessan replied blankly.

He looked in her direction, and his cheeks grew pink.

"I'm just kidding, Kalen." She gave him a light bump with her shoulder.

"I'm glad you told me. I'm sorry all of this has been so hard on you."

There was that sincerity again.

She's much nicer now than she was when we were five.

"I think I'd actually like to talk about something else," Kalen said as he looked into the distance. "Why are you here in Wyrdbrook? I thought this place was only for those who were *unclean* like me," he asked curiously.

"Unclean?" She looked at him with disgust. "Using that language only perpetuates and affirms The Order's purity bullshit," Tessan said firmly, popping a small berry into her mouth. She'd snagged a few from a nearby bush before she sat down.

"Wyrdbrook is for anyone seeking safety and community, not just for hybrids." She continued, "Sorry to disappoint, but we witches belong here, too." She gave him a sly grin.

"I'm not disappointed," he responded a little too quickly.

Be cool, Kalen.

"I'm just curious how you ended up here when it seemed like you had a full life in Evermere."

Nice save.

"Things aren't always as they seem, huh?" she started seriously. "I mean, you just told me your dad is also a bird, so I think you get it." Tessan chuckled.

He laughed with her, and a knowingness washed over him. This was all Tessan could give him right now–a vague version of a truth he hadn't earned.

He was willing to put in the time.

For now, though, he needed to get back to Wyrdbrook.

"I should go," he sighed.

He wished he didn't have to, but life was moving at a pace he wasn't used to lately. And if he slowed down, he wasn't sure what would happen. Maybe he'd break for good? Maybe his heavy feet would carry him right back to the Sanctwood.

Kalen stood up slowly, reaching down to offer his hand to Tessan.

She didn't take it.

Of course she didn't.

They started back toward the village, a knot twisted in his stomach as he got closer to his reality.

The Awakening was tomorrow, and he needed to talk to Liam. His father was in his cottage, and he needed to talk to him, too.

While the conversation with Tessan was a welcome reprieve, the relief was temporary. Talking about it made him feel better, but he had to go back to the village to truly face it all.

He still didn't have an answer to his question: was this truly unforgivable?

But first, he'd say goodbye to the witch at his side. The stranger who spent time talking him down.

"Thanks for today. It helped," he said truthfully. "I've never had a friend before."

"Who said you have a friend now?" Tessan winked as she jogged ahead of Kalen, disappearing into Wyrdbrook.

Kalen laughed. If she hadn't been so receptive to everything he'd just told her, he might have been embarrassed by her response. But he was coming to learn that the witch in Wyrdbrook could handle complexity. And that she might be a personified version of it herself.

Kalen looked around at the village before him, knowing he had two choices, both full of unknowns he'd have to face one way or another. For now, he'd head toward the Veilhold. He'd talk to Liam first.

His dad could wait a few more hours. He'd made Kalen wait seventeen years.

Chapter Nine
Kalen

Kalen's heart was steady from his conversation with Tessan as he approached the Veilhold. She gave him a hard time, but he wondered if they really would be friends one day.

He hoped so.

"Liam?" he called as he walked the halls of the empty building.

He didn't know what to expect from the Overseer about the Awakening. What else was he going to learn today to prepare him for tomorrow?

Can anyone actually be prepared for something called the Awakening?

He wasn't sure.

Liam was nowhere to be found. Kalen kept walking along the halls, paying more attention to the intricate wood carvings–the stories told on the walls of this sacred place honoring the memory of what once was. He realized they were a lesson to those looking: *Don't forget this. It could happen again. And how will you show up, if it does?*

Some of the carvings were so brutal they made his stomach churn. Fae and witch alike, on their knees with their hands shackled behind their backs, head nestled in the hole of a guillotine.

Depictions of the sharp, pointed ears of a fae being severed.

Kalen reached out and touched the carving in front of him; a deep ache panged his heart as the realization set in.

This is what happened to my father.

"You're right," Liam's voice answered from right behind him.

Kalen jumped.

Where did he even come from?

"I'll let your father tell you about what happens at a Severing on his own." He waved his hand, gesturing to Kalen to follow him. "But you have a big day coming up tomorrow, and much to learn. Come on, little crow." Liam swept down another long hall.

"Why do you call me little crow? Did you know my mother calls me that?" Kalen asked, hitting a slight jog to keep up with the Overseer. He was surprisingly fast for someone in such a long robe.

"I know you're mad at your father." Liam paused for a moment, giving Kalen the time to catch up. "However, you look just like him, whether you like it or not. And, sorry if this is too soon, *but* he can shift into a crow, so I feel like the rest of it is pretty self-explanatory." Liam chuckled as Kalen let out a huff.

"Oh, don't get your tunic in a twist. He's a very handsome crow, at least," Liam laughed again. Kalen rolled his eyes.

He grinned a little, too.

They kept up easy conversation until finally they reached a door with *The Overseer* carved on the front.

"After you." Liam motioned into his office, allowing Kalen to get the first look at his private space.

Filled with deep shades of brown and lush green, Liam's office felt divinely inspired. Thick vines of pothos draped through shelves of books, like the plant was keeping the ancient texts safe, or making sure they knew they weren't alone. Kind of like what the Overseer did, too.

The centerpiece of Liam's office, though, was the stained-glass window behind his large hand-carved desk. Kalen drew closer to the window in awe. He'd seen a lot of beautiful sights in Wyrdbrook, but none like this.

This was intentionally made for the space. Pieced together with so much care, Kalen was sure it would start moving soon if he looked too long. He stared in wonder anyway.

Whoever did this must have spent months on it.

"I did," Liam said, eyeing the stained glass. His eyes shone with pride over what he had created.

"What...what is it?" Kalen replied, forcing himself not to touch the colorful glass, to admire the piece for what it was, without putting his fingerprints all over it.

He couldn't believe the Overseer had the time or the space to create something so beautiful.

"What do you see?" Liam countered simply.

Kalen studied the glass art more. It almost looked like someone had picked up the village of Wyrdbrook and dropped it in the dead center of another one. Like the two villages had...combined?

"Is this," Kalen said, pointing to the unfamiliar village surrounding Wyrdbrook, "supposed to be Evermere? I've only ever been one time."

Liam nodded, confirming his belief.

"And this in the middle...is Wyrdbrook."

"That's exactly right," Liam said again.

"What does it mean?" Kalen wondered out loud.

"I hope that's our world one day," Liam said, walking forward, standing shoulder to shoulder with Kalen. "That we don't have to stay up here hidden in the Peaks forever." He turned to Kalen, "That eventually, the folks in Evermere and The Order see all of us as valuable members of society, and we can rejoin them. Peacefully."

"Yeah. That sounds nice." Kalen tried to imagine a world where he wouldn't have to hide. It was challenging.

Being alone was all he had ever known.

They stood there in silence, still peering at the colorful glass in front of them. Letting the moment breathe. Kalen wondered if a world like that could exist. He didn't know much about this ancient village that was now his home.

Why is the village hidden? Who helped build it? Kalen found himself with a lot of questions.

"Another time, my boy. I promise," Liam said assuredly.

"For now, let's get you geared up for the Awakening." He clapped his hands together, shifting the energy in the room immediately.

"How are you feeling? Are you ready?" he asked with glee.

"I have no idea what it is, so I don't know if I'm ready or not," Kalen responded truthfully.

Liam poked Kalen's forehead softly, "If this part of you is ready, the rest will be no problem at all."

He glided past Kalen and made his way to his bookshelf, carefully pondering his enormous collection until he pulled out a small leatherbound journal and made his way to the desk.

He signaled Kalen to sit in one of the guest chairs in front of him, and he swiftly sank into the warmth of the room. If he was going to learn about hard things, he was grateful to at least be sitting on a soft chair.

Liam cleared his throat as he began to read aloud.

"The Awakening is an ancient phenomenon that occurs on a young hybrid's coming-of-age day." Liam looked up, raising his eyebrows with a grin. "Shall the young hybrid reach this fated age, they will undergo a physical and mental transformation of power, strength, and magic."

Liam looked up again. "Cool, right?" Liam kept going before Kalen could respond.

"Each hybrid will begin the Awakening with the power blessed upon them by their mother; either witch or fae magic, or nullified if born of a human woman."

Wait, there are human hybrids?

"Yes," Liam confirmed. "The fortnight leading up to the Awakening, the young hybrid may start to notice new powers beginning to come forth. These are the powers blessed upon them by their father; either witch or fae, or nullified if born of a human man."

Well, that explains the scent and hearing thing...I wonder if I'll be able to shift by the end of this? Maybe I'll shift into a hawk and chase that crow's ass into oblivion.

"The Awakening must take place in a sacred space with only those whom the young hybrid trusts most. During the Awakening, the young hybrid's physical body will shut down, as the mind endures a grueling transformation to connect pathways to new magic."

I hate the word grueling...does it have to be grueling?

"Any tampering of the Awakening by another can result in dark magic, lost magic, or death of the young hybrid. It is advised to use extreme caution to determine the placement of those who attend a young hybrid's Awakening ceremony."

Holy shit.

"Please quiet your mind. I'm almost finished reading, and then we can actually talk about this," Liam said firmly.

Kalen would do his best.

"The Awakening can last from three days, up to a fortnight, with the shortest ceremony documented completing after one sunrise. The duration of this ceremony depends on the young hybrid's ability to accept the power laid before them," Liam continued.

"Upon their return to their physical body, the young hybrid may feel many changes. These changes can include physical differences, mental clarity, and new magical capabilities, though not all young hybrids experience all three. It is most crucial for the success of any newly awakened for a mentor in their untapped magic to show them the ways of their new power."

Liam slammed the book shut. Kalen jumped.

That's it? That's all I get?

"Well, it sounds fun, doesn't it?" Liam exclaimed playfully.

Kalen put his head in his hands. He dragged his fingers down the length of his face until his chin rested on his clasped hands.

"But what happens when I wake up? Will I even recognize myself?" Kalen ran his hand through his hair.

"I hope not," Liam responded with a grin.

"What is that supposed to mean?" Kalen moaned. What was so wrong with him now that he couldn't stay the same?

"I mean," Liam leaned in, closing the distance between the two of them, "staying the same means we never grow. And there's a lot of good left to bloom inside of that big heart of yours, Kalen Halrowe."

Kalen warmed. His mother had always instilled the Halrowe way to him–kind, brave, and gentle–but something was affirming about hearing he was good from someone he had just met. Someone who didn't really know him.

Liam continued, "I know you've had a hard week. I know these learnings can feel overwhelming. But any hesitation to fully engage in the Awakening can be dangerous." He looked away nervously.

How am I supposed to fully engage with something I still don't really understand?

"I know. I know," Liam answered Kalen's thoughts.

"Truthfully, I was worried about your father showing up now, the timing so close to such an important transformation for you." Liam's eyes met Kalen's again. "But you need him, Kalen. You need him to get through the Awakening, and especially for what comes after."

Kalen pondered his words.

"I just don't know how I can trust him," he answered softly.

He hated saying it out loud. The admission made it more real. He didn't want to feel this way toward his father; he wished he had just been able to hug the man he'd spent his whole life missing.

"I know." Liam stood up and walked around his desk, opting to sit next to Kalen for the remainder of their conversation.

"Your father showed up here about a year ago. I thought a crow had just flown in to deliver Tessan a message from Eugenia, but he shifted right in front of my eyes." Liam was looking off into the distance, recalling the memory.

"He got down on his knees, right here in my office." He pointed to a spot behind them. "And begged that I let his son live here. That Wyrdbrook would prepare for your arrival and ensure your safety. A young hybrid hidden in the Sanctwood Forest who'd be coming of age in about a year."

His son.

It's what Kalen had always dreamt of hearing from his father. From this faceless man who lived within his mind for the majority of his life, until his mother showed him her memories not even a week ago. Until he met his father face-to-face just last night.

How did his father manage to care so much about someone he didn't know? About him?

But he did know Kalen, in a way, didn't he? He'd been there for years as Wen. He knew the sound of his laugh, of his voice. He knew his favorite berries and what he liked to forage. Kalen was the one who didn't know *him* at all.

And maybe that's what was holding him up.

Liam continued, breaking Kalen from his thoughts.

"His desperation blew me away. And then I realized who he was. Westin Vale. The Orderly. Alive by some miracle. Begging us to make space for you."

"We didn't know there were any hybrids left around here." He grew serious. "After what The Order did to your father, people understood the danger of loving across bloodlines. Hybrids slowly started to disappear; either claimed by death, stolen by The Order, or they fled Evermere in search of a better life," Liam shuddered.

"I'm not sure anyone even knows you exist, outside of Wyrdbrook, your mother, and Eugenia. Ria did all she could to keep you safe."

Because she kept him hidden.

"But why didn't we just come here from the beginning? To Wyrdbrook? We could have been here all along, couldn't we? Together?"

As a family.

Kalen didn't understand.

They'd lost so much time together; how could they make it up now? What would his mother think?

"Your mother didn't know about Wyrdbrook, nor did Eugenia, until about 3 years ago. When Tessan arrived."

Tessan has been here for three years?

"It's not my story to tell," Liam leaned over and put his hand on Kalen's arm. "For now, you need to know that I'm glad you're here. Your father showing up at Wyrdbrook was a gift. For you to have a shot at a better life. And for us, because now we get to know you."

Liam stood up, keeping his eyes on Kalen. "You should go and talk to him. Keep this..." Liam put his hand over Kalen's heart. "Wide open, little crow. Let him surprise you."

Kalen stood up, too, and gave the Overseer a tight hug.

There was a lot he didn't know, and right now he was just piecing together things he believed could be true. But there was no good in assuming. Not when the truth bearer was within reach.

Kalen had made it to the door before he looked back at Liam. The Overseer had already settled back into his desk, quill in hand, flipping through the parchment in front of him. Focused on the next thing. Kalen wondered if he ever rested, or if he was always busy taking care of the people and things around him.

"Hey, Liam?"

Liam looked up; his green eyes were a perfect complement to the colors of his office. Earthy and knowing–full of wisdom, and a hint of sadness Kalen couldn't place.

"Would you mind being there? At...my Awakening? I understand if you're too busy." Kalen asked, his voice shaking. There was a declaration in his question.

I trust you.

Liam's lips lifted to a grin.

"I wouldn't miss it, Kalen," he responded, before shifting his attention back to his work.

So Kalen walked out of his office, down the halls of the Veilhold, and into the sunshine of Wyrdbrook.

It was time to talk to his father for real.

To figure out if he could trust him, too.

Chapter Ten
Kalen

Kalen stood at the front door of his new home, blankly staring at the worn wood, wondering if his father was still inside.

He didn't know if he was prepared for this conversation. He was unsure if he would be able to do what Liam asked–keep his heart open, let him talk.

Because he was mad for himself about everything he missed, but he was furious when he thought about his mother.

He wondered how soon he could get a letter to her. How soon he could let her know that his father, Westin Vale, was still alive. If he made it through the Awakening, it would be the first thing he did.

Kalen could almost hear his mother's voice now, encouraging him to step into his home. To stop avoiding the hard thing.

Kind. Brave. Gentle. You can do this, Kale.

Mustering all of the courage he had left, he stepped inside. His father owed him answers, and Kalen couldn't be scared of his past any longer.

He wouldn't be.

And there he was, sitting on the couch, head in hands, so deep in thought he didn't hear him come in.

Kalen cleared his throat–his father still didn't look up.

Damn it.

Kalen took a deep breath before starting, "I'm not trying to scare you, but I am ba–"

"Shit!" His father yelped, startled by Kalen's presence.

"I'm sorry! I cleared my throat first, and you didn't hear me!" Kalen hurled back.

"No, it's fine, it's fine," he exhaled. "I'm fine," his father reassured him.

He noticed his father seemed overwhelmed, too. Like the same thoughts had been in his head on a loop since Kalen left hours ago. It lowered Kalen's guard just a bit. In some small way, it made Kalen feel bad for him.

At least he knows how I feel.

"You came back," he followed up more clearly, settling into the easy nature Kalen remembered from his mother's memories. Kalen could hear the hope in his voice. *Maybe we can fix this.*

"Well, this is my home. So..." Kalen trailed off.

"Yes, of course. Still, I'm glad you're here," his father quietly said.

"Can we skip this part? I know you're sad. I'm sad too. But even more than that, I'm mad at you. And I'm not going to apologize for feeling this way," Kalen huffed out, bracing for his father's response to his attitude.

He didn't know him, but he was still responsible for giving him life. And Kalen was definitely ignoring the whole *respect your elders* thing. Or whatever that even meant in this scenario.

"I'd never ask you to," his father responded.

Wait, what?

"Great, because I'm not going to," Kalen spat out, feeling more confident now.

"Great," his father replied with a smile.

I wish he'd stop being so nice.

"Stop smiling at me," Kalen glared at him.

"Okay, sure. Sorry. No smiles. In fact, I won't even look at you," his father said, turning his back.

And Kalen watched as his shoulders began to shake.

Is he...is he...laughing?

"Are you laughing right now?" Kalen yelled. He couldn't believe it. The nerve of this *stranger* to come into his life unannounced and then laugh at him?

He could feel his internal temperature rise again, the heat behind his eyeballs convincing him they may actually be turning red.

"I'm sorry, Kalen! I just don't know how to do this with you," his father could barely speak through his laughter.

"You're so wound up...and so seventeen. It's just...I don't know, it's funny! I'm sorry. I'm going to stop laughing."

But he couldn't. His father let out a hearty, giant laugh. An infectious laugh. The kind of laugh that rolls through a room and drags you along with it. And it wasn't long before Kalen joined in against his will.

He hated that. But he couldn't help it, and he felt his guard lower a little more.

"Doesn't that feel better than being so damn mad at me?" his dad said with a lightness in his voice. Kalen noticed he was still treading lightly.

"It does. But I am still mad at you," Kalen agreed, his lips tilting to form a small smirk.

His father just nodded in return, "That's fair."

The air between them had tightened again, though the heaviness had slowly dissipated.

It was time for Kalen to get his answers.

"Who else knows about Wen?" he started quickly, getting straight to the point. He didn't have time to waste anymore. The Awakening started in the morning, and he needed to figure out if he could trust his father to be with him. To stay here afterward.

If that's what he even wanted in the first place.

"Eugenia."

What the hell. Of course she does.

"How long?"

"Thirteen years."

THIRTEEN YEARS?

Kalen's heart shattered. His Genie, his mother's best friend. Withholding the truth for so long...just watching as his mother suffered. Watching as he grew up without him. And knowing he was alive all this time.

"It's not what it seems," his father responded, sensing Kalen's pain.

Oh, this ought to be good.

"Prove it then," Kalen challenged with resolve. "Show me."

Memorywalking.

Kalen hadn't practiced in a very long time and had never tried to see someone else's memories, although he knew it was possible. His mother told him very clearly the boundaries of his magic from a young age.

"You can only memorywalk with permission, little crow." He recalled the sweetness in his mother's voice. *"Especially when reaching into someone else's mind for their own memories. Any alteration of the past could change who someone is. You have to treat your gift with the care it deserves."*

"Okay," his father answered with certainty.

"Okay?" Kalen looked back at him, puzzled.

That was easy.

"Why not?" he shrugged. "I've hidden the truth long enough, don't you think?" His father approached him now. "Should we sit for this?"

He sensed no fear in his father, so Kalen gestured to the seats at his kitchen table.

Kitchen table talks are reserved for serious conversations.

"Do you know how this works?" Kalen asked genuinely.

"Yes, Kalen," his father answered, almost annoyed. "I used to force your mother to replay the moment we met just so I could see her for the first time over and over again."

Gross.

Sweet.

Kalen rolled his eyes.

"Are you ready or not?" he responded.

"Have at it, boy. Good luck in there...scary place." His father winked, as Kalen lifted his hand to touch his temples.

And he was transported back thirteen years ago.

His eyes adjusted as he sat in pitch darkness and viewed the world as his father did.

Chapter Eleven
Kalen

*W*here are we?

He didn't know if his father could hear his thoughts while he was exploring his memories, but he figured he'd try just in case.

There was no response.

Shit.

This was different from what he'd experienced with his mother. With her, she was building the world around him– he was watching as a bystander, experiencing the sights and smells as an unassociated, but *kind of* associated, party.

This, though, felt like he was living it. He could smell the damp, rotting scent of his surroundings. He could feel his father's physical reaction to wherever they were. His heartbeat was slow; not because he was calm, but because his body was breaking down.

Physically, mentally, and emotionally, things were *off*. This was not the man who stood in front of him just a few seconds ago. Wherever he was, it was bad.

Really bad.

"Wake up, you lousy piece of shit," Kalen heard someone say as they banged on something solid metal. A jail cell? Had his father been captured?

What is going on?

The stranger lit a small torch, pointing it into where his father was sitting. Where *he* was sitting. Kalen was seeing everything through his father's eyes. He was reliving the moment from his point of view.

He didn't know it would be this intense.

"Hungry yet? You haven't eaten in days, have ya?" the voice grumbled.

"Fuck off, won't you?" His mouth was moving now, but it was his father's voice speaking.

Gods, memorywalking is weird.

"It's been over four years, Westie boy. Tell us the bitch's name, and maybe I'll convince The Order to get you into a better room. Maybe even a protection program?" The guard sneered.

"Let ya run free from this hell hole, huh? She's probably out fucking another fae by now anyway, yeah? Do you dream of her, West? Do you dream of her mouth on your fuckin—"

"I SAID FUCK OFF!" his father yelled furiously at the stranger. "I will die before I tell you one Gods damn thing about her."

"Shame, then," the stranger chuckled and backed away. "Someone so powerful, wasting away forever here." He leaned in closer to the cell.

"You coulda had it all, Westin." Kalen noticed his yellow teeth and could almost feel the evil radiating from his skin. "Instead, you're just an unclean bastard."

Kalen's father never took his eyes off the man.

"Ah, well." He hit the bars again. "Enjoy the darkness." The stranger spat at his father. He jumped as Kalen could feel the wetness land on his face—could smell the man's rancid breath. "Just a little something to remember me by."

The man chuckled as he walked back down the hallway.

He couldn't believe this was what his father endured.

"FUCK!" his father yelled. He was going mad. Kept in solitary for Gods only knows how long, Kalen couldn't blame him.

How did this even happen?

"I have to get out of here. I have to get out of here. I have to get out of here," his father was whispering to himself, holding his legs up to his chest in an effort to keep himself warm.

"Think, West, think."

His eyes quickly caught on the golden shackles binding his wrists.

What are those for? It's not like he can get out of here.

What he could see of his father's wrists were torn to shreds. Ribbons of red streaked where the cuffs lay connected over his skin.

He had been trying to get them off. But why?

"HEY! GAGE!" his father called out.

The arrogant man with the bad breath slowly came back, stomping down the concrete hall. Kalen could feel his father's heartbeat pick up a tick.

What was he up to?

"What do you want?" Gage had finally made his way back to the cell, standing about a foot away from his father, separated by the bars between them.

"I'll tell you. About her," his father said softly and dropped his head.

No. He can't do this. Don't do this.

"Speak up, you stupid fuck," Gage replied. "I can't hear you when you whisper."

"I said, I'll tell you about her," his father repeated in the same quiet tone.

"What don't you understand about I can't fucking hear you when you whisper?" Gage said angrily as he came closer to the cell.

Faster than Kalen could blink, his father jutted both hands through one of the gaps in the cell bars and looped the chain of his handcuffs around the back of Gage's neck. He pulled him tight against the cold metal of the cell, trapping his face between the silver cylinders.

Looking directly into the guard's eyes, his father started.

"I'm going to give you two options, you useless, pathetic man," his dad spoke calmly to the guard.

"You're either going to give me the key to take these Gods damn shackles off of my wrists. Or I'm going to kill you and take the key myself."

"You're going to burn in the underworld," Gage struggled to get the words out. His breath became labored, but Kalen's father didn't dare loosen the pressure of the chain against the man's neck, despite the weakness Kalen felt in his biceps.

"I'll see you there," he felt his father wink and spit back in the man's face before he quickly yanked back toward himself with all of the strength he had left.

Snap.

He unlooped his shackled hands from the man's head, and Gage's dead weight fell to the floor.

He'd killed him.

Holy shit, he killed him.

Quickly, his father shuffled the guard's body toward him, doing the best he could with two hands still cuffed together, and found what he was looking for.

A small skeleton key–his chance at freedom.

Kalen watched as his father used the key to free himself from the handcuffs. His hands were steady and sure, despite the loud thump of his heart.

His father quickly unlatched the cuffs, squeezing his hands and flexing his wrists to get the blood flowing in them again. Kalen wondered how long he'd had the shackles on. Had it really been over four years?

He immediately felt something new coursing through his father's body. Something strong, rushing forward to latch on to his being. Kalen knew that buzzing feeling.

Magic.

The magic had been suppressed by the golden cuffs, and he finally had it back, after all this time.

Kalen was speechless.

It didn't take long before his father had shifted into his beloved crow, Wen, and made a beeline toward the exit.

A graceful, unsuspecting, black bird, soaring through the sky. Toward liberation of some kind.

It was then that Kalen realized what he might have known his whole life, somehow.

That he would never be free, not really. That his life would always include running away from something, from someone.

And what kind of existence was that?

His father looked back as he escaped, staring down at a large stone building, his heart rate still high from what had just transpired inside.

Where are we?

Maybe he'd never know the answer to his questions. Maybe he was too scared to ask some of them, and to face the rest.

For now, Kalen was going to enjoy the breeze and watch as they headed toward what he could only assume was the village of Evermere.

His father was headed home.

He'd never experienced anything like this.

Flying.

Seeing the world from this high up. He was nauseous, but curious about what his future held. Would he inherit something like this from the Awakening?

I guess I'll find out soon enough.

His stomach did a backflip as his father dove lower into the village of Evermere.

Kalen marveled at the bustling streets.

So many things he'd experienced in the last few days had been new to him, but maybe none had felt as strange as knowing this town had been next to him his entire existence.

Unattainable.

Nothing more than an idea of what could have been, had his parents never met.

Other than the fact that he wouldn't exist without them meeting, did he really wish that for his mother and father? That they didn't meet—hadn't once loved each other?

Could they still love each other?

He had spent a lot of time wrapped up in what he lost because of their love–his freedom, a chance to know his father, a shot at a normal life.

He hadn't spent much time thinking about what they had lost, or *why* they had to lose it.

Because The Order said so? Because an institution declared their love unclean?

The more he thought about it, the less sense it made. He'd sort it out later, with the rest of the things he'd learned over the last week.

He slowly felt himself drifting away from the memory, noticing the edges of his vision were going black. He was untethering, and he needed to focus.

Because he needed to know more. This was his best, and maybe his only, shot at knowing the truth. He zeroed back in on his surroundings.

While the town was full of people, a quiet tension filled the streets. Strangers were talking, but keeping their distance. Were they trying to figure out where the other stood? In The Order, or not? Was this person worthy of their time, or not?

Maybe I didn't miss out on much after all.

His father had swept low enough now that Kalen could make out the tops of strangers' heads. Flying street to street, it was clear he was in search of something. Or someone.

Was he looking for me and my mom?

THWACK!

Kalen felt a sharp pain against his head; it felt so real that he had to remind himself he was just experiencing his father's memories. His vision went blurry as they were spiraling out of the sky. He hit the ground hard before the world went hazy. His father's eyes were slowly shutting now, drifting off into unconsciousness, but a voice was drawing closer to him.

He could feel his father trying to hang on to the light, but he was fighting a losing battle. He was at the mercy of whoever found him on the street. Kalen couldn't tell much, but he knew the knock to the head had severed his tie to Wen. He was just Westin. Westin, who had just escaped The Order. Prison.

Lying in the street.

"James! I know for a fact your mother told you not to shoot rocks at crows with that slingshot of yours!" the voice rang out. "You'd better hope the poor thing is okay when I find it, or I'll be knocking at her door later tonight!"

Eugenia.

On a mission to find the wounded animal.

A healer. Always in the right place at the right time. She'd found him.

He wanted to soak in the familiarity of her voice for a little longer.

"Oh, Gods," he heard her whisper before looping her arms under his.

Somehow, knowing he was safe, his father lost consciousness completely.

And Kalen couldn't see or hear a thing.

His father's eyes opened again, and the memory was back in view.

He was nestled on a couch, covered in a blanket. He'd been here before. Once. The dried herbs and tinctures were strung about, the smell of chamomile filling the room–a tea kettle boiling over the flame.

Eugenia's.

His father refocused on the witch in front of him, slowly moving his arm up to the top of his head before wincing. She was pacing, her nails in her mouth, deep in thought. Her worry was palpable. Kalen could smell it.

When she noticed the small movement, her eyes whipped to his own.

From worry to fury.

Uh oh.

"Oh, thank Gods you're alive so I can kill you myself," she spat in his direction.

"The absolute nerve of you to show up in Evermere. You're supposed to be dead, Westin. DEAD," she yelled, a finger pointed at his face.

"Eugenia, let me explain," his father said softly. Kalen could feel the pain pounding in his head getting worse from Eugenia's elevated tone.

"Does Ria know?" She began pacing again. "Actually, I'm sure she doesn't," she said flippantly, pausing and crossing her arms.

"You know what, West? I never trusted you. I told her from the beginning that if you lied to her about being fae, you'd lie to her about anything." She could hardly take a breath between the words.

Kalen felt his father's mood shift too, confusion was giving way to anger.

Oh no.

Laid before Kalen was a battle between two people who didn't like to lose. He didn't know much about his father yet, but considering he just broke out of prison and killed someone, he couldn't imagine he'd be one to back down from an argument.

And Eugenia, well, Eugenia never lost them.

Kalen settled in for the show.

"So that's how you treat me after all this time, Genie?" his father said smoothly. It disarmed Eugenia, just enough.

Kalen needed to take notes on the way his father navigated conversation–equal parts charisma and truth. It took a lot to rile him up outwardly. He held his cards close to his chest, always put his best foot forward.

At least, he did back then.

"Save the shit, West. How is this possible?" Eugenia asked curiously.

"The last time I saw you was right after the Severing." Her eyes dropped to the floor. "I thought you were dead. I told her you were dead."

"I know. They wanted everyone to think I was." His father sat up now, patting the cushion beside him, an invitation to handle this like adults.

"I was supposed to die that day..." he trailed off. "But something happened." He shook his head. "Like some sacred magic reached out to protect me." He looked at her. "I don't know, Genie."

Eugenia nodded, encouraging him to continue.

"They bloodied me up enough during the Severing that I was so close to letting go." He began crying. "But I kept hearing her voice in my brain, you know? *Just hang on for us, West.*" He exhaled. "Anyway, after they figured out I wasn't going to die, they drug me into the basement of the High Seminary and they've been torturing me there ever since."

Holy shit.

"I escaped today. By the skin of my teeth. I did it," his father continued, swiping a hand through his dark, wavy hair in disbelief. "Shifted into a crow and got to Evermere as fast as I could."

Eugenia's face was skeptical, but had softened quite a bit from the initial rampage.

"I just want to see her, Eugenia. And then I am going to leave. I swear it. Leave her alone to love whoever she wants. Let her live the life she deserves." His voice was shaking now. "She was the only thing that kept me alive."

"Of course she was. She's the best," Eugenia said, treading lightly. "But why didn't we know you could shift?"

"She did, but life was just *better* in this form when I was with her." He shrugged, a tear slipping free. "I told her one day I'd do it when she least expected it, just to freak her out." He chuckled weakly at the memory as more tears spilled down his cheeks.

"Obviously, I never got the chance to before those bastards got me," he continued.

Kalen instinctively reached up to wipe his father's tears, and instead, felt his own.

"It was a boy, you know?" Eugenia said softly.

"A boy," his father repeated back. "I hope he's nothing like me."

That might not be so bad.

The thought surprised Kalen. He'd barely spent any time with his father, but he'd seen the way he moved through the world in small glimpses. Felt the way he cared for Kalen by not begging him for his forgiveness.

And he was seeing now how deeply he loved his mother. Which maybe mattered to him most of all.

"Oh, he's better than all of us combined, and he's only four years old," Eugenia said, warmth covering her voice. "Whip smart, gentle as the breeze." Kalen understood why his mother trusted Eugenia so much. She had always loved him like he was hers.

"And looks exactly like you," she finished hesitantly.

Eugenia's words were enough to send his father to his knees. Sobbing on the hard wooden floor, slamming his fists against the ground. The pain was unrelenting now. His father's cries sounded like a plea to whatever God was watching over him, to please make it stop. To make it go away. To give him an opportunity to love his family right.

Is he this upset over...me?

Eugenia crouched beside him, the floor groaning lightly, as she put her arm around his shoulder and her head on his back.

The room was silent, save for his father's sobs. They sat there for a while, just like that. There was nothing to say.

A simple knowing was passed between them in the silence. The Order made the rules, and that meant they couldn't ever be a family. Not like they all wished.

"You know she can't know, right?" his father whispered.

Eugenia lifted her head.

"What do you mean she can't know?" Eugenia looked at him wide-eyed. "I can't do that to her, West. Surely you'd never ask me to."

"They'll kill her, Genie. You know that. And they'd kill the boy." He looked her squarely in the eyes. "The Order will chase me to the ends of the Earth, especially now that I've escaped." He pointed toward the door. "They're probably organizing a search party already. I can't put them in that kind of danger."

"This is insane, West." She lowered her voice. "You all can leave Evermere together. Go somewhere The Order can't reach you." She was frantic now, her panic was sharp.

"And then what? The Order's power is only becoming greater. There are more followers now than there were years ago." He shook his head no. "Trust me, Eugenia. I know them. You don't. They'll stop at nothing to find me, find *us*." He grabbed her hands. "They asked about Ria every single day. And they don't even know about the boy."

"You can't just leave now that you're back. No." Eugenia pulled her hands from his. "No. I'm not letting you do this to her."

"It's not *to* her, don't you get it?" his father cried out, exasperated, "It's *for* her. Everything is for her!"

He was yelling now, but it wasn't at Eugenia. It was at the cruelty of his life. At the powers that had kept him from his great love. The Order.

They found themselves in silence again. If Kalen knew Eugenia at all, she was trying to sort out another way to make this work. An alternative to this reality they'd been handed.

"Kalen," Eugenia said, breaking the silence between them.

Kalen swore his own heart stopped beating entirely.

"What?" his father asked.

But Kalen felt it. His father's magic pulsed within him at the sound of his name. Like some missing piece of him had finally been found and snapped back into place. Like he was whole again.

"His name...it's Kalen," Eugenia said quietly.

"Can I see them?" The question was soft and full of hope. His father was bracing for the answer, "Please, Genie."

Eugenia stared down at him, shaking her head in solemn disbelief.

"I'll take you to them," Eugenia said, reaching out to help him up. "But not like this. I have an idea."

Kalen was jolted back to the familiar scene of his cottage, the tether to the memory severed. His father had pulled his head back from Kalen's touch, leaving them both sitting in silence.

He was exhausted. Sad. Left with more questions than answers.

He looked up at his father, ready to ask more, but paused as he took in his face. Tears slowly dripped onto the kitchen table, and his head dipped low in pain.

His questions could wait a little longer.

Chapter Twelve
Kalen

A new understanding had passed between them.

His dad loved him and his mother so much that he stayed hidden in plain sight. To his own detriment, at his own expense.

All of this time.

"Eugenia told me she'd show me where you all lived in the Sanctwood as long as I showed up as a crow," his father continued. "I didn't plan to stay."

He let out a laugh, smiling through his pain.

"I saw your mother first. And she seemed so sad. But looked so beautiful–and she was so attentive to you." He chuckled again. "Because you were a little shit that day. Really testing her limits."

His laugh grew deeper as he wiped a tear from his eye.

"She must have told you to get down from a tree five times in a row before you listened to her once."

Kalen joined in on his laughter.

"I was surprisingly good at climbing trees around that age, though." He chimed in playfully.

"Oh no, I know, I was very impressed," his father responded with joy.

His laughter faded quickly, a longing straining his voice.

"I could have stayed in that tree forever, just watching you two. So in love, so safe."

His father let out a deep breath, and his bottom lip began to shake again.

"But I knew it was time for me to leave. To tell you both goodbye forever."

He closed his eyes now as he sank into the memory, lost in the moment as he continued.

"It would have been enough. If that was all I had with you two. It would have sustained me for the rest of my miserable life. But then you tugged her tunic and looked straight at me and said, 'Look ma, that crow is lookin' at me. Hi, crow!'

"In that moment, I knew if I had to sit on that same damn tree every day, I would. If it meant I didn't get to miss anything else. If it meant I could just see the two of you exist."

"So that's what I did. I showed up every day after. Every night when I was certain you were both asleep, I'd go forage and keep myself hidden and fed. And I wouldn't change a thing about any of it."

Guilt bubbled in Kalen's stomach. He and his mother were having homemade dinners while his father was in the woods struggling for years—just to stay close to them.

He wished he had known–but he understood now why he couldn't have.

"Well, except for those disgusting worms your mother insisted on giving me during the day–I would have changed that. I did much prefer the berries, by the way." His father winked.

"So I just became Wen. The crow that never left. I wanted more than anything to hear you call me Dad, for you to really know I was there, but I was just grateful when you'd take the time to talk to me at all."

Kalen's words were caught in his throat. He was processing the immense pain his father endured to escape from The Order, to gain his freedom, just to be put back into a different kind of prison, the body of a bird, watching his family move on without him. But they never really did. He was always the hole that existed in their family. Surely he knew how much his mother missed him. How much Kalen wished he had known him.

How many times had he looked at Wen and just given him a quick nod and carried on? How many times had he run past the crow without acknowledging him at all?

He couldn't fathom enduring that kind of heartache, and he found himself wishing his father hadn't either.

Kalen stood up from the kitchen table, his father's face twisted in confusion as he outstretched his arms. Inviting the man who had loved him from afar for so long into a hug.

His father moved quickly and crashed into Kalen. It knocked him off balance, but they held onto each other tightly anyway.

Silently crying on each other's shoulders. Father and son.

Together for the first time, and finally on the same page.

Kalen was the first to pull away.

It was getting late now, and the Awakening was in the morning; he wasn't sure what was going to happen, but he could feel his body begging him to prepare.

To rest.

"So why did you show up now?" Kalen broke their silence, wiping a tear from his face with the back of his hand.

"I was hesitant to. But when I came here the first time, I met Liam and told him about you. We talked about the Awakening," he continued. "He told me there would be no one here to help you through it like I could."

"I tried to convince him you wouldn't want to see me. That being here," he gestured to Kalen's home, "would mess this whole thing up."

"But he said something I'll never forget." He looked up at Kalen. "He said, 'Let people surprise you, Westin.'" His father changed his voice to sound like Liam's. "So here I am."

Kalen rolled his words over in his brain—remembering the way Liam had shared that same advice with him.

Let people surprise you.

His father was *here*. He had been with him all along, and now they had the chance to get to know each other. *Really* know each other.

Could that be enough for him?

There was nothing he could do to make up for the time they'd lost. Was that a reason not to see what the future could hold?

Forgiving him came easier in that moment than he expected it to. The anger of the day had fallen away from his heart, making way for whatever came next. If this was the only chance he'd ever have to know him, he couldn't let it slip away.

"I'm kind of glad you're here," Kalen confessed uncomfortably.

"I just told you I broke out of prison, killed a man, and lived as a crow for thirteen years to stay close to you, and you're *kind of* glad? Damn, kid. Tough crowd."

His father was playful in a way that didn't feel like he was trying too hard. It was warm and kind, and it never meant to hurt anyone.

He understood why his mother chose to be with him, despite his fae heritage. This was a man Kalen wanted to be like one day. That he'd aspire to be like.

"But for what it's worth, I'm kind of glad I did, too," his father finished.

"So what's next?" Kalen asked curiously, yawning. The exhaustion of the last few days was catching up to him. He stretched his arms over his head, a deep stretch settling in his upper back.

"Next is rest. You prepare your body and your mind for what's to come in the morning." His father looked at him with worry, and Kalen was doing the best he could not to take it on as his own.

It wasn't working.

"There's a lot we don't know, Kalen. But Liam will be here with you the entire time, okay?" His father gave his shoulders a reassuring squeeze.

"This is just stepping into your birthright. Alright?" He lowered his eyes to Kalen, forcing him to pay attention to what was next.

Kalen saw himself so clearly reflected in his father's eyes. His wavy brown hair, his dark brown eyes with the golden rims, his square jaw, and his strong nose. But where his father had stubble, Kalen was smooth-faced, and where his father's frame was broad and strong, Kalen stood long and lean.

His *father*.

"That's all this is. Just a fancy name for inheriting the power owed to you." His father's face had shifted from worry to confidence.

Kalen felt his own worry shift, too.

"You are Kalen Halrowe." He put his hands on either shoulder. "Son of Ria Halrowe. A powerful hybrid. The Order is scared of you because they fear what they do not know."

"But I know," his father said smoothly, refusing to break their eye contact, "I know you're going to change everything. That you being here, alive, now, is going to change everything."

"No pressure." His father winked.

I need to work on my winks.

"You and Mom really were perfect for each other." He rolled his eyes at his father and laughed. "She gave me a similar speech when I left the Sanctwood."

He took a deep breath.

It was hard for him to imagine he'd really change anything. One week ago, he was a nobody who grew up isolated in the woods, and now he's here. Stepping into the unknown.

He appreciated the belief his father had in him, but he didn't understand where it came from. It felt unearned. Kalen had done nothing. He'd *experienced* nothing.

"Okay, off you go." His father shooed Kalen to his bedroom.

"I'll be gone in the morning. I'm just going back to Sanctwood to check in on your mother before she thinks something happened to dear ole Wen," he cawed jokingly.

I still can't believe my dad is my bird.

"I'll be here when the Awakening is complete—if you'll still have me."

The unasked question lingered between them.

Am I welcome here? Do you want me here?

Kalen nodded and took off toward his bedroom. A pit was carving itself into his stomach.

This day had been more than he could have anticipated. From the anger that coursed through him as his father showed himself, to this moment now. The clarity Kalen had, the agony of what his father endured to be here for him in this moment.

He wanted his father here, with him, when the Awakening started. For everything.

He could hear Liam's voice in his head, replaying their earlier conversation.

"Any tampering of the Awakening by another can result in dark magic, lost magic, or death of the young hybrid. It is advised to use extreme caution to determine the placement of those who attend a young hybrid's Awakening ceremony."

I do trust him. I do want him around.

The thought stopped Kalen in his tracks. He slowly turned back, facing his father once again, choosing his next words carefully.

"Do you think you could be here when it starts?" Kalen looked down. "The Awakening? And maybe go check on Mom after? When I'm unconscious or whatever the hell will be happening to me?" Kalen spat out the ending too quickly. He held his breath and looked at his father, waiting for the response that could change everything.

But his father did nothing to hide the joy on his face. Where a smooth and confident fae once stood, Kalen just saw a happy dad, not trying to be anything else. No posturing, no extra effort. *Just* Westin Vale. *Just* his father.

Kalen felt confident he'd chosen the right words and made the right choice by asking him to be there.

"Of course I will. Thank you for asking me," his father said genuinely.

"Yeah, no problem," he responded, the newness of their relationship still settling between them. It will feel easier someday.

He was grateful for the possibility of someday.

"Goodnight, Kalen," his father said as he turned to leave his home. "I'll see you in the morning."

"Goodnight, Dad," he answered in return, the word slipping out of him before he could stop it.

Dad.

Shit, please don't make it a big deal.

His father stilled for just a moment before recognizing the fragility of the moment, and then smiled as he continued out the door.

Moments later, Kalen heard the beating of wings as his father flew away from his home, off to find a comfortable place to perch beneath the stars.

But not before he heard six rapid caws. Kalen didn't know what it meant, but he hoped it was his father's way of celebrating his reunion with his son. His Kalen.

His little crow.

Chapter Thirteen
Kalen

Kalen didn't sleep much that night.

He didn't think it'd matter, considering he was about to drift off into a magical unconsciousness.

It was his birthday. Eighteen. The day everything would change for him. He felt ready for whatever was next.

He hoped he was right.

Kalen lay there in his bed for just a little while longer. He was going to clear his head this morning, before he made his way to the Veilhold for the Awakening. He wanted a few more hours as *just* Kalen.

He needed to forget about what the day would bring, just for a moment. To enjoy his morning doing one of his favorite things–spending time in the forest.

He wrapped himself tightly in his blanket and imagined he was a kid again, spending his birthday with his mother. This is the first one she'd ever missed.

I hope she's doing okay today.

The sun began to creep through his window, and a soft orange hue covered the floorboards. A signal to him that it was time to get moving if he wanted to have a chance to enjoy any part of his day.

He quickly hopped out of bed, slipped on a shirt, grabbed his bag, and was out the door. He knew exactly where he wanted to go, and it wouldn't take long for him to get there.

He arrived quickly at the stream he'd visited with Tessan yesterday. He couldn't believe all that had happened since he'd arrived. All that had happened over the last week. And it all led up to this.

The Awakening.

He let the gentle sound of water moving slowly over the stones in the stream carry him away. He closed his eyes and listened to the birds in the distance—the same thing he used to do with his mother in the Sanctwood. He could picture her here now, their backs propped up against a tree, eyes shut, guessing which noises came from which birds.

He wished she were with him.

Crow. Too easy. Wood Thrush? Oh, that's definitely a woodpecker.

He could stay here all day.

Except he couldn't.

For now, he'd enjoy the peace and quiet of this moment, of being alone with the trees and the birds. With Earth Mother.

He didn't believe in Athero.

He believed in this.

In nature. In the clarity he got while existing among the flowers.

"I figured I'd find you here," a voice snapped him from his thoughts. He jumped at the sound piercing through the quiet. It felt unnatural for anyone to talk at all in a place like this.

"How?" Kalen asked in wonder as Tessan moved closer to him. Her eyes asked him if she could stay a while.

He smiled in return, an easy yes.

"It's your birthday," she tried to state plainly, but Kalen noticed there was a bit of joy in her inflection. "Happy birthday, by the way." She nudged him.

He wasn't sure how she knew it was his birthday. In the same way he didn't know how Victoria knew his name upon arrival.

It seemed it was just part of living in Wyrdbrook, the village was so small, and people just knew things. He wondered if he'd ever know things like birthdays or names of new arrivals.

Would there be any new arrivals while he was here?

He was warming up to the idea of being here for a while.

"And I know the Awakening is today." She gestured around her. "And this is kind of familiar for you, so I figured you'd come here to clear your head," she said easily. "Not so bad for a not-friend, right?" She smirked.

"Not bad at all," Kalen agreed.

Tessan surprised him. Granted, they'd only talked a few times. But that was a lot of one-on-one conversations for someone whose best friend growing up was his mother and his bird-dad.

Gods, my life is weird.

"Well, now that you've crashed my birthday party," Kalen poked at her. "Can you tell me something? It can be anything. No limits," he continued, wanting to learn more about her.

"Maybe that will help me take my mind off of what's going to happen today." He leaned back on his hands, his legs in front of him, trying to play it cool in front of her.

"What do you want to know?" she responded curiously.

"We'll start easy," Kalen replied. "What's your favorite color?"

"Oh, that is easy. It's lilac," she stated.

"Lilac," he repeated. "What's your favorite food?"

"Deer liver stew."

"That's disgusting, Tessan," he barked back, laughing. "Whose favorite food is Deer liver stew?!"

"Mine! It reminds me of my mom." She was giggling too.

"I've never tried it." Kalen picked a blade of grass in front of him.

"Well, don't expect me to make it for you." Tessan shrugged. "I can't cook at all."

He chuckled.

"What *can* you do?" he asked curiously.

She pushed him. "Don't be an ass. I can do a lot of things."

"I meant with your magic." He put his hands up innocently. "Don't all witches have magic?"

"Good save." She rolled her eyes and laughed. "Most of us have the ability to heal or harm. There are basic spell and potion books passed down throughout our bloodlines and kept alive through those who practice. I don't practice much, though." She diverted her eyes. "Some witches can do more than that, too. But it's pretty rare."

"Like my mom and her memorywalking?"

"Yeah. No one in my bloodline could do anything like that." She shrugged and laid down on the grass. "Okay, you get *one* more question."

One more?

There was so much left to learn about Tessan Duscaire.

"Why are you in Wyrdbrook?" Kalen leaned on his elbow, shifting his body toward her. His hand served as a small pillow for his face.

The question sucked the air out of her lungs. Kalen watched as she digested what he'd said. Like she was considering what her response would mean for the moment—for their friendship.

Would she answer? Did he go too far?

Shit.

"I came to Wyrdbrook three years ago because my dad was hitting me."

Oh, shit.

Kalen sat up quickly, and the smile fell from his face. Wiping the dirt off his hands, he turned to face Tessan fully. He didn't know what he expected her to share, but it definitely wasn't this.

"He is Genie's brother. Where she is everything healing, he is everything hurting," she started. "I'm not completely convinced that's not the reason she became such a skilled healer, honestly. To try and cancel out her brother's brutality." She spoke softly, running her hands through the blades of grass surrounding her, playing with them between her fingers. Trying to look everywhere but Kalen.

He wasn't going to push her until she was ready. He was used to letting the women in his life share things on their own time. He'd learned his own curiosity didn't matter as much as their feelings.

"But he could heal, too, in his own way. He'd beat the absolute shit out of me and then force me to take a healing or glamor tonic to cover up the bruises and speed up the healing process," she said stoically. "And then he'd do it again."

"It wasn't always like that, though. With me, at least," she sighed. "He showed violent tendencies toward my mother when I was young, but she always assured me she was okay. I wish I hadn't believed her." Her voice grew quiet.

"She'd come in my room and sit on the edge of my bed and rub my feet when she thought I was asleep," Tessan took a deep breath. "And she'd just cry and cry. I think she stayed in there because she knew he wouldn't follow her."

"But when she died," she paused, "he needed a new punching bag. So he turned to me."

Kalen had no words.

How could a parent do that to their own child? Forget their innocence? Steal it?

"Anyway, one day, Genie was over. We were talking in my room, and she saw one of the healing tonics on my dresser and asked about it. You can't get anything past her–but I tried anyway." She chuckled softly.

"I told her I was on my monthly cycle and just needed something for cramps."

Kalen involuntarily flinched when she mentioned her cycle.

He always tried to be a grown-up about things, to treat big moments with the respect they deserved. He grew up around women exclusively–he knew all about a monthly cycle. But every once in a while, the fact that he was a teenager bubbled to the surface. And it just did.

It was the wrong time.

He hoped she didn't notice the small movement. But Tessan's eyes met his for the first time since she started talking, and he knew she had.

Shit.

"Oh, grow up, Kalen," Tessan laughed.

"I am so sorry," Kalen spat out apologetically, frazzled by her callout. "I just really didn't expect that."

Way to go, Kale.

"It's okay." She leaned up and squeezed his leg with affection. He could tell she meant it.

Oh, thank Gods.

It made his stomach warm.

"Genie knew better than to believe me," she continued as if the moment had never happened.

"She knew him, you know? They grew up in the same house. He'd done such a good job hiding it all of those years, so she thought he'd really changed." She huffed. "But does a monster ever really stop being a monster? Or do they just figure out how to make everyone else believe they did?"

Kalen had found himself in hard conversation after hard conversation, recognizing everyone around him was carrying something too heavy for them to shoulder alone.

This was the gift of community. The ability to carry those burdens together. He had only ever really known isolation, but he'd always needed this.

A friend.

"I'm so sorry, Tessan." Kalen's throat was tight, thinking of all she'd been through. He didn't have anything else to say. What else was there?

"I know." She looked down again, breaking their eye contact. "Genie saved me, though. She told me to stay with her for a few days while she figured out a permanent solution away from him. Where he could never find me or hurt me again," she continued. "I don't know how she found this place, but she did. She met Liam, and a few days later, I was here in Wyrdbrook."

"Damn," Kalen responded in disbelief.

"Yeah. Damn," Tessan replied.

"So anyway, Happy Birthday!" she exclaimed.

And they both burst into laughter.

"Nothing like a good old-fashioned trauma dump to really celebrate the day," she continued, tears falling from her eyes.

She wiped them gleefully, her laughing turning softer now. Like it was a release for all of the emotion that had been stored in her body. Like she was letting little pieces of the past go with each tear that fell.

"Thank you for telling me, Tessan. Genuinely," Kalen responded.

"Yeah. Don't expect to learn anything else about me for at least a year," she clapped back playfully.

"Deal," Kalen agreed, appreciating the acknowledgement they'd keep doing this, whatever this was, for longer. That he had more to look forward to when he woke up in a couple of weeks.

"I know you said you didn't want to think about it, but are you doing okay? It really is a big day for you," she asked curiously.

"I think so. My dad and I are okay for now. Liam is going to be there. I don't know if you can ever fully prepare for a magic ceremony." He laughed. "But I do feel okay."

"It's going to be fine," she responded seriously, a calm reassurance in her voice.

"That's what everyone keeps saying," he said quietly in return.

Tessan stood up now, signaling to him that it was time for her to go.

He didn't have much alone time left, and while he hated the idea of her leaving already, he knew his mind had to be focused as he headed to the Veilhold.

"I'll come find you after. I expect you to be super ripped and way cooler than you are now. So, don't let me down," she teased.

"No promises," Kalen replied.

Tessan grinned in return.

"I'll see ya soon, friend," she said as she turned on her heel and walked back to Wyrdbrook.

Friend.

He could get used to that.

The sun had hit its peak now, and Kalen knew it was time for him to head to the Veilhold–the sacred place where he'd begin the Awakening.

He rose from the smooth rock that served as his chair for the last hour, his muscles aching from his stillness. The air had changed, too, the morning mist making way for the beaming sun.

Kalen turned his head toward the source of warmth, soaking in what it felt like to be here, in this moment. Knowing it was the last time he'd be in nature unchanged.

He knew the stream would continue to flow while he was unconscious. The birds would still sing, the trees would sway and creak with the wind, and the flowers would still bloom.

He guessed he'd be blooming in some way, too.

The trek back to Wyrdbrook was easy enough. The village was quiet, still waking up with the sun. He passed a few cottages on the way, windows cracked, welcoming in the cool breeze.

It was odd to think about how one of the biggest days of his life was just an ordinary day for someone else.

Loose dirt and gravel paved the path to the Veilhold, a sharp contrast to the ivy-covered building. Kalen felt like the place was calling to him louder today, beckoning him to begin.

He wondered if his story would one day be carved into the walls. If people would see his Awakening sketched into the wood and ask about the hybrid Kalen Halrowe.

He chuckled away the grandiose thought.

The door of the Veilhold was cracked open when he arrived, an invitation for him to enter when he was ready. He had no choice.

No turning back now.

He took a deep inhale, turned one more time to look at Wyrdbrook, and then stepped inside.

His own footsteps were the only thing he could hear as he entered the building. Where the Veilhold typically felt sacred and mysterious, today it felt different. Dangerous.

"Liam?" he called loudly.

"Dad?" he whispered, less confidently.

He was still getting used to that.

There was no response, just the echo of his voice as it bounced off the walls of the hallway.

Where are they?

Fear began to sweep over him with each step he took closer to the Overseer's office. He wasn't sure where Liam was, but he figured that was as good a place as any to begin the search.

"Please be okay, please be okay, please be okay," he softly chanted as he got closer to the large door.

Maybe Liam just didn't hear him come in? The door was open, after all.

Maybe he was early? They didn't talk about a time. Maybe his dad couldn't make it?

I hope Dad made it.

Slowly, Kalen pushed the office door open. The sun refracted through the stained-glass window, throwing a rainbow of colors across Liam's desk in the otherwise pitch-black room.

His heartbeat was running wild now.

Something isn't right.

Kalen closed his eyes and focused on his surroundings—channeling the limited fae hearing he had access to. He was trying to find something, *anything*, that he could latch on to.

There.

He heard someone in the office. Breathing. Deep and steady, trying to remain silent. It sent chills down his spine.

Why today? Why now?

He had no choice but to face this person, whoever was waiting for him.

He wouldn't be scared now. Not when there was so much at risk with the Awakening going wrong.

"Hello?" Kalen said firmly. "I know someone is here."

He heard the stranger shuffle toward Liam's desk. Kalen was careful to stay locked in on the sound, turning his body to follow the noise until the stranger got closer to the desk, the deep colors of the stained glass lit just enough that Kalen could vaguely make out the shape of the person now. He was huge.

Kalen braced for whatever came next.

Wait...is that...?

"Dad?"

"SURPRISE!" his father yelled, quickly flicking his wrist, using his traces of fire magic to light the candles placed around Liam's office.

For me?

Kalen's eyes took a moment to adjust to the sudden light, and when they did, he was at a loss for words.

He didn't know when they'd found the time, or how they'd done it–but someone had managed to decorate Liam's office.

A birthday party?

For him.

Small pieces of colorful leaves littered the floor, the contrast of the burnt oranges and bright reds against the dark wood were a symbol of celebration. And right in front of the bookshelf, on the large tea table, sat a birthday cake.

He continued looking around, noticing a large banner that simply read *Happy Birthday Kalen* draped across the bookshelves, stitched together in a patchwork of beautiful hand-dyed fabric. He'd seen his mother dye fabric in the past when she'd mend their garments.

He wished she were here to celebrate. To see all of this.

He couldn't believe it was for him.

"Happy Birthday!" a cheerful group of voices rang out from behind him now. Liam, Tessan, Victoria, and Shu were also here. Kalen felt like he might be the luckiest person in the world somehow.

He'd never forget this feeling. His first real party. That someone cared enough to make him feel seen and celebrated. To make him feel loved.

His father walked over now, clapping him on the shoulder. "What do you think?" His voice was thick with happiness.

"We wanted to give you a proper send-off before the big event."

"I can't believe this," Kalen responded simply, still awestruck.

"I know," he responded gently, matching Kalen's tone.

"It was Tessan's idea." His father nodded toward her, and her cheeks reddened.

"Yeah, well, Shu made the cake," she redirected.

"I don't know what you like, so I just went with chocolate. Hope that's okay," Shu responded happily.

"It's...perfect. Thank you so much." Kalen walked over to Shu before turning to the group. "Thank you all. I really didn't expect this."

"We were happy to celebrate you!" Victoria rang out. "Now, let's eat cake."

Kalen agreed. The idea of being unconscious on a stomach full of cake didn't seem so bad.

The small group continued their celebration—laughter and conversation filling the room. Kalen basked in the joy of the moment. He wondered how he'd lived so long without it. The thought felt like a betrayal to all his mother had done for him.

As if he could read his mind, Liam made his way over to Kalen.

"Walk with me, little crow."

Kalen set down his plate, waving at his father on the way out, and followed the Overseer out of the room. They walked far enough down the hall that the laughter that had once filled his ears was now a distant echo.

"It's finally here," Liam started the conversation. "How are you doing?"

"I'm good, I think. Right now, all I can think about is cake." He let out a small laugh.

"I'm glad," Liam responded flatly, his voice joyless.

"Is everything okay?" Kalen asked. There was no sense in waiting to find out. He was almost out of time.

"It has been a long time since we've had a documented Awakening, Kalen." Liam stopped walking now, shifting his focus to face him. "I just want you to come out the other side of this alright."

"Oh," Kalen responded softly. "Should I be worried?"

"There's no sense in worrying about the things we can't change," Liam responded. "I guess I should take my own advice." He grinned at Kalen.

He waved his hand, pushing the previous thought to the side. "Enough of that. I actually brought you here to give you this." He pulled a letter out of his pocket and handed it to Kalen. "It's from your mother. She made sure your *crow* got it here right on time. It just arrived this morning. It seems as though your father has had a very busy day already," he said. "They both love you very much."

"I know." It was all Kalen could say as he took the letter from Liam's hands.

"I'll leave you to it, then. Come back to us when you've finished up." Liam turned swiftly back toward his office, leaving Kalen alone in the hall.

He stood there for a moment, holding the letter in his hands. It hadn't been long since he heard her voice or gave her a hug, but after spending every single day with someone for almost eighteen years, even a couple of days apart felt like a lifetime.

He was lucky to have a mother who was so easy to miss.

He made his way to a small bench that sat lonely beneath a large banner in one of the corridors. He opened up the letter, took a deep breath, and began to read.

Happy Birthday, little crow.

I am hoping you are finding your way in Wyrdbrook. I can imagine you've made friends already and are enjoying what life could have been like for us all along had our circumstances been different.

I miss you, but I wouldn't change this. I need you to squeeze every ounce of experience you can from there. I need you to live. Maybe you'll even fall in love? Genie told me that niece of hers is there, too. I hope you're being kind to her.

I know you are.

The Sanctwood is too quiet without the sound of your feet following me around, but I'm doing just fine. Wen is still here to keep me company most mornings, and Eugenia insists on visiting every night for dinner. She never brings the food, though. You know how she is.

I know you're likely nervous about what's in store for you today, and if I could give you sage advice, I would. But the truth is, I don't know what's going to happen. I don't think anyone does.

I only know you are good. That you're meant for more than the life you've always lived.

And you're going to change the world somehow.

Call it a mother's intuition.

I hope to hug you soon. Until then, you're in my heart, always.

Kind. Brave. Gentle.

I love you,

Mom

Kalen held the letter to his chest before folding it back up and putting it in his pocket. He wished he had the time to write her back—to let her know he missed her, too. To tell her about his new friend Tessan, about the spot by the stream, his new home...about his dad.

That'll have to wait until I wake up.

The letter renewed him in a way. Like the last thing that had been weighing heavily on him had finally been shaken free. His mom was okay. He needed that.

He wondered if she had told him on purpose to ease his mind, and whether it was true or not, it worked just enough.

Kalen could feel a new energy forming inside him now. It was pulling him under, telling him that his body was ready for the Awakening. He'd need to get back to the party to tell his friends he'd see them again when he woke up–because he was going to wake up.

It was time.

He had almost made it back as Tessan was walking out of the door.

"Hey!" he yelled after her, hitting a small jog to catch up.

She turned to face him, and a grin spread across her face as he grew closer.

"Thanks for doing this. You've officially thrown me my first birthday party." He smiled back at her.

"Don't mention it," she replied. "No, seriously, don't. If you tell anyone it was me, I'll deny it," she joked.

"My lips are sealed," he shot back, acting like he was locking his lips with a key.

Their eyes met for a beat longer than usual. His stomach did a flip.

I can't do this, not right now.

"Well, I gotta get to it," he said abruptly. He could feel exhaustion creeping over him now, his eyelids feeling heavy, weighing him down.

"If you want to stop by while I'm unconscious or whatever, you can. Maybe read my body a book? I don't know if my brain will hear it, but it would be nice to have some company."

"I'll think about it," she responded with ease, but Kalen saw something small flicker across her face.

"Cool. See you when I wake up."

He turned and headed into the office, not giving her time to respond—a taste of her own medicine.

"Real smooth, buddy," his father said as Kalen walked in.

"Stop," Kalen moaned, embarrassed that his father had heard him. He needed to change the subject before he crawled out of his skin.

"I think it's time. I can feel something happening."

"Okay." His father nodded to Liam. "It's time."

Liam walked over to the bookshelf, carefully avoiding the proof of celebration that had been left behind. Kalen felt bad that he wouldn't be around to help him clean up.

Liam unclipped the banner first and then began touching a few books, purposefully, as if entering a secret code—the same thing he had done to the door when Kalen arrived the first day. He listened intently, a small click, a hiss of pressure being released, and then the bookshelves split straight down the middle, revealing a hidden room.

Woah.

All this time, it was right here.

The room was stale and cold, a wildly different environment from Liam's lived-in, warm office. There was nothing more than a bed in the middle and a table sitting off to the side.

Kalen's magic began to stir the closer he got to the room, and his already heavy eyelids began to feel like lead.

"What's this?" Kalen asked. Is this where he'd endure the Awakening?

"It is," Liam responded, sensing Kalen's curiosity. "It's the safest place in Wyrdbrook, and we can't take any risks."

"Will you all be able to visit me, though?" he responded with panic.

"Every day," Liam reassured.

"And don't worry, we'll make sure Tessan can too," his father jabbed at him.

Kalen's cheeks grew warm, despite the frigid temperature of the small space.

"What West is trying to say," Liam corrected, "is that if you've granted someone permission to visit you, they will have access." The Overseer glanced at his father with a warning in his eyes.

"You can do this, Kale." His father moved closer to him, masterfully dodging the look from Liam. "We'll be here the whole time."

"Do you promise?" Kalen responded vulnerably.

"I'm not going anywhere. Never again." His father hugged him now, a quick squeeze to solidify his words.

There was nothing left to say.

He couldn't stop what was coming; he just had to surrender.

So he lay down on the bed, shivering, ready for whatever came next, as Liam shut the door and Kalen was left in the darkness.

It wasn't long before his body gave in.

Here we go, Kalen thought, as he drifted into an unconsciousness he couldn't control.

Welcoming his new life.

Welcoming the Awakening.

Chapter Fourteen
Kalen

The air reeked of sun-baked fish.

Not cooked.

Fish that had been sitting in the sun for far too long.

It was disgusting.

How did I get here? Where am I?

The last thing Kalen remembered was lying down in the small room at the Veilhold.

He looked around, trying to anchor himself to anything familiar. There were bustling people everywhere, jam-packed in front of vendor tables, shouting their orders at artisans, trying to buy what they needed before the goods ran out.

Wait...is this the Evermere Market?

It had to be, he saw a small glimpse from his mother's memory a week ago. But what was *he* doing here?

He knew he wouldn't find out if he just stood there in shock.

Kalen walked from vendor to vendor, making conversation with the artisans, learning about the love they put into their goods.

He didn't have any money on him to barter, but he'd pretend he did anyway.

"How much for the loaf?" He leaned into his imagination, trying to channel the people around him.

This is fun.

"That's seven purits!" the baker yelled back.

He wasn't going to buy it, but it felt good to just exist in the Market today. To play the part as if he were just any other citizen of Evermere, not a forbidden hybrid. He'd never been here before, not like this. Out in the open, free. No fear of what could happen to him.

Well, maybe he had a little fear.

People were shoving now, trying to make their way to the front of the sourdough vendor. Kalen felt happy for the baker, knowing he'd make enough purits to take home to his family that night. He knew Evermere's classes were very distinct; the vendors could hardly afford to get by, while the rest of Evermere lived in luxury.

These people really should learn how to forage; it'd change their lives.

Kalen chuckled to himself lightly before making his way to the next vendor. He was looking at the scented beeswax now, inhaling a smell that reminded him of the Sanctwood, when a booming voice cut through the marketplace, ripping Kalen's attention from the booth.

"Citizens of Evermere, please report to The Hollow by order of Head Cleanser, Sir Hauke Elowen. I repeat, all citizens of Evermere, please report to The Hollow by order of the Head Cleanser."

What the hell?

The market was immediately abuzz in a different way. Where there was once a lightness to the people's banter, something much darker loomed.

They scattered from the booths quickly, hurrying off to a place he'd never heard of before.

The Hollow.

What's going on?

Whispers now replaced the shouting. People were pairing off together, clutching each other's arms, walking quickly, making their way out of the Market.

Kalen's curiosity bested him as he took off with the rest of the crowd. He casually joined the group, unsure of where they were going.

What even is a Cleanser? And who names their kid Hauke?

He weaved through the crowd, making his way to the front with little trouble, careful to apologize to each person he bumped into. He didn't know what was going on, but his mother taught him manners, regardless. The crowd slammed to a stop in front of a large building. Kalen looked up, taking in the new surroundings.

What is this place?

The building towered over him, making him feel small in a way he'd never felt before–like he didn't belong here after all. A chill slithered down his spine, goosebumps raising on his arms.

The structure in front of him was made of solid stone. Large depictions of winged fae, witches, and humans served as the pillars in the front. The landscape was lush and green, perfectly kept.

It made him miss the wild of Wyrdbrook, of the Sanctwood, where things could grow as they wished without disturbance. Everything here was in perfect...*order.*

Oh, shit.

From where he was standing, you could barely make out the writing etched front and center.

The High Seminary.

And below, in big, bold letters. A warning.

Purity Above All.

Shit, shit, shit.

He was standing in the stomping grounds of The Order. In plain sight.

Sweat started dripping from his brow, despite the cool breeze accompanied by the sun.

He wanted to run, to make a beeline for the Sanctwood, but his feet wouldn't let him. Maybe it was best to stay here, anyway. To let down his fear and experience the moment. He listened to that feeling, but remained on high alert anyway.

To his left was a small platform in front of a small arched room. The Hollow. The platform was made of solid white marble, completely spotless. So clean that you could eat right off of it. A small symbol of power to those who were paying attention.

Someone cleared their throat, and Kalen's attention turned to the archway. Inside was enough room for one massive chair, and it was occupied by a man.

I've seen him before...

"All kneel before the Honorable Hauke Elowen," a voice boomed.

Kalen followed the lead of the crowd, quickly dropping to his knee while looking up at the man in front of him, trying to rack his brain about where he'd seen him before.

The man from the woods.

This was the man from the woods.

But what was Hauke Elowen doing trying to find Wyrdbrook?

Hauke was seated in his solid white robe, a reflection of the marble floor that lay in front of him. He was the most regal person Kalen had ever seen.

His tanned skin was a perfect contrast to his long white hair and green eyes. He was adorned in jewels and gold, a message to those in Evermere–he was not only powerful, he was powerful and rich. And that was maybe the most threatening thing a person in his position could be.

"All rise," the voice called out moments later. Kalen's eyes remained fixed on the Head Cleanser, taking in his face, his features. His ears.

He wore two golden cuffs atop his ears—a solid curve rather than the pointed tips of a fae.

Is he human or a witch?

Kalen's thoughts were interrupted as The Cleanser stood.

The crowd went silent. So silent that Kalen was scared to breathe. He couldn't draw attention to himself, not like this. He'd have nowhere to go. The goal was to blend in as much as he could until he could get out of here.

"Good afternoon, citizens of Evermere," Hauke's voice rang out to the large crowd that was ordered here in his name.

"I am honored you took the time out of Market Day to come witness this most storied event."

The crowd remained silent. The anticipation of what was to come was buzzing around him.

"As you know, The Order takes the word of Athero as law. For He is the One True God."

People were nodding around Kalen now, agreeing with the words being spoken from The High Cleanser.

"It has come to our attention that one of our very own, *an Orderly*," Hauke sneered, "has broken the covenant of Athero, a crime in which we have not seen the likes of in all of my years in The Order."

Gasps rang out in the crowd as two armed guards dragged a man onto the stage. The Order had cuffed his hands and feet, and a heavy white bag had been slipped over his head. He was struggling to break free of the guards, but there was no use. He couldn't outrun his fate. The thought of that alone made Kalen sick.

I don't think I can do this.

Kalen wasn't built for whatever came next. He couldn't stomach watching this person be executed, or whatever the hell The Order planned to do to him. He just wanted to go home, back to Wyrdbrook.

Home.

He had to leave. So he would. He didn't care now who saw him; he'd run faster, he'd get to safety. He'd figure out a way back.

But weaving through the crowd was a bit harder now as folks were trying to push to the front to get a better look at the man.

How could they revel in someone's pain like this?

Kalen heard the crack of a heavy whip and flinched. The crowd was shouting now. But not in agony for the man they didn't know. They were already celebrating his punishment for the crime they thought he had committed.

He was already guilty to them; it didn't matter what he did. Or *if* he did it. All that mattered was that Hauke said he did.

I have to get out of here.

"Quiet now, please." The Cleanser's voice was still booming where Kalen stood.

"Let this be a lesson to you all, when you engage in Unclean acts, The Order must intervene for the betterment of Evermere. For all of you."

Unclean?

Kalen slowed to a walk. Maybe he could listen without having to watch.

He'd never had this kind of exposure to The Order before; maybe he'd learn something he could take back to Liam.

He heard the ripping of fabric now, and another crack of the whip.

The man screamed out in pain.

Crack. Crack.

The whip rang out rapidly twice more.

More screams. The crowd was drunk with glee at the stranger's suffering.

"Get him!" he heard the strangers around him yelling. "Hit him harder!"

"Purity Above All!"

The crowd was growing violent now, chanting The Order's sacred vow.

"Purity Above All! Purity Above All!"

People were shoving Kalen out of the way as he continued to make his way back toward Evermere. It wasn't until he heard the sound of the guards removing the heavy hood from the man that he considered turning around.

Every single person in this crowd, save for him, wanted to see this stranger's suffering.

The thought stopped him in his tracks.

Would turning around and remembering the man's face serve as a moment of resistance against this force that sought to harm him?

Maybe he'd be the last person the man saw before the moment grew more violent.

Maybe he'd recognize in Kalen's eyes that he'd hoped he would make it out okay somehow.

Hauke continued now, "Westin Vale is a traitor to the covenant, and therefore has been stripped of his title as an Orderly. As a result of his vile behavior, he will now undergo the Severing."

No.

Kalen grew dizzy at the mention of his father's name. He turned around now, sprinting again toward The Hollow.

He had to get back to the front. He had to save his dad.

The crowd was shouting in outrage. He couldn't stomach the names these strangers were throwing at his father. He didn't deserve this for loving his mother—for loving him.

But what came next almost sent Kalen to his knees.

"Upon the completion of the Severing, Westin Vale will be sentenced to death," The Cleanser boomed, a slight smile at the reaction he knew it would elicit from the crowd.

And he was right.

They erupted, forcing Kalen to throw his hands over his ears. Now, he elbowed the onlookers, trying to swim through this body of people.

"Let this be a lesson to you all." Hauke gestured to the crowd. "Long live The Order."

This isn't real. This can't be real.

"Guards, please prepare the traitor for his Severing." Hauke pulled a knife from his white robe. The sun reflected off his jewel-crested blade, causing a shimmer of blue and green light to hit the crowd.

They cheered in awe.

He had to hurry. He had to make it to his father. He couldn't lose him again—not like this. Not after everything.

The guards smashed his father's head against the cold ground; his left ear faced The Cleanser. They were preparing him for the Severing—a removal of the points of his ears.

His father's bloodline. The thing that marked him as fae. They were removing it before they killed him. Just to prove their power. A symbol that The Order did not care who you were, they did not care what that meant.

They are the ones in control. They own you.

Don't test them.

The rage propelled Kalen's feet faster through the crowd.

The edge of The Cleanser's blade moved closer now. Inch by excruciating inch, Kalen watched in agony as his father's eyes were closed, tears landing on the cold white marble below him.

This is a nightmare.

"No!' Kalen cried out. "Stop!"

But no one could hear him over the droning crowd. Or no one was paying attention to the lone voice standing against their cruelty.

Either way, he wasn't going to make it in time. He couldn't save him.

"Please! Stop!" he cried again.

He was frantic now.

But The Cleanser didn't stop moving toward his father.

"Hey!" Kalen yelled in exasperation, his final plea to grab the man's attention.

The Cleanser paused, locking eyes with him, his knife less than an inch away from his father's ear.

"I beg of you. Don't hurt him," Kalen huffed out, breathing deep, trying to catch his breath.

He'd done it, he'd stopped it.

He'd saved him.

But then Hauke Elowen smiled directly at Kalen.

"The Order does not make deals with the unclean."

And he watched in terror as Hauke Elowen swung his blade down to his father's ear.

Kalen screamed as the knife sliced through the air. Until the air left his lungs, and his vision went dark.

When he woke, the air reeked of sun-baked fish.

Not cooked.

Fish that had been sitting in the sun for far too long.

It was disgusting.

Oh my Gods.

Kalen jerked his head side to side, his pulse picking up.

The baker? The beeswax?

He'd been here before.

Not just here in the Evermere Market.

Here, in this moment. He was just here.

He was just...

The Awakening, Kalen realized. *This isn't real. This isn't happening.*

The Awakening is a loop.

Chapter Fifteen
Tessan

Tessan took a step out of her cottage door, the scent of Wyrdbrook welcoming her in. The crisp air crept over her cheeks, and the birds sang the greeting of a good morning.

I love this place.

It was mid-week, her day with Kalen. It was one of her favorites.

Though she didn't always like to admit that.

Seeing him, reading books together, and sharing updates on how her week was. He'd slowly become her best friend, somehow. The boy from the forest with no real social skills and a crow for a Dad.

She shook her head, laughing, as she walked toward the Veilhold.

She couldn't believe it either.

She did the same thing every single week. The routine had become second nature to her.

Lace up her boots, head out the door, swing a left, up the gravel path. Say hi to Victoria, leave berries for West, and ask Liam how he's doing.

And it was the same outcome every single week.

It had been two years.

Kalen was still in the Awakening.

Still asleep.

And it was torturing them all.

Liam assured her he was in there, whatever that meant, but she was losing hope.

Everyone was.

"Hey, Tess!" a playful voice shouted to her.

"Off to see Kalen?" Victoria followed up.

Something like that.

"Yep," Tessan responded plainly.

She was running out of things to say to her friend, to everyone. It was the same damn thing every single week.

"Today's the day! I can feel it!" Victoria chirped back.

"You say that every week, Vic," Tessan responded.

"Well, one of these days, I'll be right!" she laughed.

Tessan chuckled too. Anything to move past this moment–to get to Kalen quicker.

"Hey, do you mind dropping these berries off at Kalen's house? You can leave them by the door, and West will be by to get them," Tessan said quickly, changing the subject. "I'm running behind this morning, and it would really help."

"Oh, absolutely! I may have to sneak a few and convince Shu to make me a tart," Victoria remarked cheerfully before taking the berries and turning back into her cottage.

She checked two more things off her mental list–*say hi to Victoria, leave berries for West.*

She started toward the Veilhold. Toward Kalen. Or some version of Kalen she didn't understand yet.

Why won't he wake up?

Tessan didn't like thinking about the truth she couldn't outrun. She didn't know if he was going to wake up at all. No one did.

Liam kept the details of Kalen's Awakening quiet from everyone who wasn't intimately involved. The people in Wyrdbrook knew he'd been asleep much longer than anticipated, but Liam never let them worry.

Tessan could almost hear his voice now.

"Kalen's transformation is happening in the way that is best for him. We can't expect every outcome to be the same for everyone. That wouldn't be any fun, would it?" he'd chuckle. *"He'll come back to us when he's ready."*

Liam told her and West to keep what they saw quiet, too. Between the three of them, they were the only ones allowed within the small secret room in Liam's office. They were the only ones Kalen had permitted two years ago, before he started the Awakening.

She'd bet he would have made his list a little longer, had he known how long he'd be gone.

Regardless, she understood this bizarre twist of events was Kalen's story to tell, even if he wasn't *here*, not really, to tell it.

She really hoped he would be soon.

Tessan reached the Veilhold, her cottage was not far from the heartbeat of Wyrdbrook. The building was one of her favorite parts of the village, and she'd spent more time in it than ever these last two years.

She had memorized the wooden carvings in the walls now, the way the magic buzzed when new people entered the building, making space for more power.

Sometimes when she'd look out her window at night, she swore she'd see the vines that crept up the exterior faintly glowing. Pulsing in a rhythm.

It was beautiful.

And sometimes, she wondered if it had anything to do with the sleeping hybrid inside.

It was wishful thinking.

Muscle memory carried her down the long hall in the Veilhold to the Overseers' office. Before she knocked, she sent up a quick prayer to whoever was listening.

Please let him be okay.

"Come in!" Liam responded jovially.

Tessan stepped into his office, shutting the door behind her. With the bookshelves closed, no one would ever know Kalen was just on the other side. She guessed that was the point.

Liam and Tessan were alone in his office. After everything that had happened with her father, Tessan felt trepidation being alone with men. But never with Liam. She knew he was the reason she loved Wyrdbrook so much, the reason why she was even allowed to be here in the first place.

She owed him her life. Literally.

His office hadn't changed much in the last couple of years. He somehow had more books and taller stacks of paper on his desk, but the rest of it remained unchanged. The stained glass art was still the focal point as you entered his sacred space.

Still serving as a reminder of what the world could become.

He never asked Tessan why she kept showing up week after week. He just smiled and let her into the small room when she was ready to see Kalen. She knew he could sense her energy, the anxiety that coursed through her skin, but he never asked if she wanted to talk about it.

He knew her well enough to know she didn't.

What happens if I'm in there when he wakes up? What if he's different now? What if he doesn't recognize me?

Because the truth was, they had only spoken just a few times, spent only a few meaningful moments together on his first couple of days in the village, before all of this. What did she expect from him, two years later?

That he'd miss her, too?

She wasn't holding her breath.

But it didn't change the fact she'd felt connected to him somehow. Even when they met as children, she remembered wondering if she'd ever see him again.

Like he was someone she needed to make sure was always okay. Like he was someone who was going to protect her, too. But not in the patriarchal bullshit way; in the way a best friend would.

Because it wasn't a soulmate thing. She didn't think it was, at least.

But he was the first person in a long time who made her feel seen as more than the sum of her past. He had a gentleness about him she hadn't experienced before. She hoped it wouldn't change when–*if*–he woke up.

"Hi, Liam. How's he doing today?"

She called to him easily, trying to avoid giving away too much of how she was feeling to the Overseer.

She knew there was no point; his magic made no sense to her.

"No change, I fear." He didn't look up from the stack of papers in front of him, as if he didn't want to confront the truth, either.

"I did manage to source a few new books for you, though. A couple of them are really lovely. I think Kalen will enjoy them." The Overseer pointed to the stack of books on the tea table, still refusing to make eye contact with her.

Tessan didn't respond; instead, she walked over to the stack of books, thumbing through them until she found one he might like. She was always drawn to the covers that had flora or fauna.

She knew he'd like those best.

She grabbed a book while Liam stood up from his desk and walked toward the bookshelf to unlock it. Liam was the only person in Wyrdbrook who knew how to. She wondered if one day there would be another Overseer who could do the same thing.

Her thoughts were interrupted as the bookshelves began to swing open, just enough for her to sneak through before Liam quickly shut them behind her. The maneuver was always fast, and they'd gotten faster over the last two years. They couldn't risk anyone in Wyrdbrook knowing where Kalen's body was.

They were always prepared for what would happen if The Order showed up somehow. Liam made sure of it. He was a damn good Overseer. An even better person.

The familiar darkness of the room enveloped Tessan as she made her way toward Kalen.

Once Liam had realized Kalen wasn't going to wake up after two months, he made a small desk and chair for him, Tessan, and West to sit at while they visited. It was adorned with nothing more than a small lamp, a pack of matches, and the occasional book one of them left behind. Sometimes they'd all read Kalen the same one, hoping the continuity could break him out of whatever state he was in.

They all wanted him back.

Tessan felt around for the pack of matches on the desk and quickly struck one to light the lamp.

The room was so small that the flame felt as powerful as the sun. It quickly illuminated the space—uncovering everything she wasn't yet ready to accept. There he was, just as she had left him last week.

Kalen Halrowe.

Still fast asleep.

Tessan pulled the chair up to his bedside. The steady state of his breath was a reminder that somehow, someway, he was still in there. She rubbed her thumb across his cheek.

"Sorry I was late. I know you've been waiting on me."

She laughed at her own joke. She had no idea if he could hear her, but she'd talk to him anyway.

"Liam got us some new books, so that should keep us busy for the next few months, at least."

She grew somber now, lowering her voice.

"But I wouldn't mind if you woke up before then."

She gently moved Kalen's long brown hair out of his face, studying him, the way she always did.

He'd changed so much in the last two years, somehow. The long and lanky boy who arrived at Wyrdbrook wasn't the man she was looking at today. His face was sharper, his hair longer, and his muscles had somehow grown despite his completely sedentary state.

She didn't mind the changes, if she was being honest. But she wasn't ready to unpack what that meant to her just yet.

Instead, she cracked open the book and started, just as she had every week for the last one hundred and four weeks.

"Chapter One."

And she read to Kalen until the lamp dimmed and faded to black.

Until any hope she had felt for him to wake up that day had faded, too.

Chapter Sixteen
West

om,

I miss you.

I hope you know I think about you every day.

How are you? Is Eugenia still stopping by for dinner?

Things are going really well for me here.

I've learned so much from the Overseer about the history of hybrids. I think I'm starting to understand how I fit into the world. Thank you for giving me the gift of time, for being able to figure it out.

I've made some great friends, too. Tessan and I spend time every week together reading books and chatting about our lives. I never thought I'd say I have friends my own age.

I never would have if you hadn't sent me here. I owe you everything.

I'll be home soon.

Until then, I'll continue to write.

I love you,

Kalen

"'I've learned so much from the Overseer?'" West huffed. "Surely you can do better than this, Liam."

He slammed the letter on Liam's desk. "The letters are getting too repetitive. This is the same shit you've been saying for over a year. She's going to figure it out."

"Take a deep breath, please. Tessan is in the next room with your son, and it's important we keep our energy stable." Liam set his pen down on his desk, folding his hands in his lap. "I know it's hard, Westin. But this is the only way to keep Ria away from Wyrdbrook. And it's been working. The letters keep coming. What has changed for you today?" Liam looked at West with curiosity.

"I feel bad lying to her," he responded.

"I don't say this to harm you, but you've been lying to her for far longer than the last two years," Liam replied gently.

West flinched. The truth landed like a blow to his gut. But the Overseer was right; of course he was.

He sat down, slumping forward in the chair in front of Liam's desk. With his elbows resting on his thighs, he buried his head in his hands before throwing his head back and taking a deep breath.

"I just need him to wake up," West confessed with the sadness only a parent could carry.

He was devastated that Kalen was still asleep. He'd *just* gotten him back. They'd *just* broken through that wall.

He'd just called him Dad.

He barely had time to process it.

And then Kalen was gone.

The irony of the situation wasn't lost on him. A version of Kalen was there, but it wasn't one West could get to know. All he could do was watch as his son changed in front of his eyes.

It had been the sad truth of his existence. Witnessing Kalen grow from toddlerhood through boyhood into adulthood. Longing to be with him, with Ria.

To be a family.

And accepting the fact that they were both out of reach.

When West found out he'd have the opportunity to be with him, really know him, after the Awakening, it changed the course of his life.

It affirmed everything he did was right, despite how hard it was. He stayed away long enough to ensure his son stayed alive. And then he would have the honor of watching him grow up close.

They'd grow together.

Gods damn Awakening.

"He'll wake up when he's ready, West." Liam looked him in the eye now. "We can't speed this up."

"I know that." West stood up now, pacing in front of Liam's desk, racking his brain for the things he hadn't done yet. Trying to figure out how to snap his son out of his stupor.

Maybe he was being selfish, but he didn't care. He was losing time, and he'd come close enough to death to know that time wasn't an infinite resource.

He needed his son to wake up.

"When was the last time you made sure he was–" West began his sentence but abruptly stopped as he heard a chair clash to the ground from behind the bookshelf.

He ripped his gaze from Liam, turning his attention to the small room where his son had been sleeping for the last two years. Something wasn't right.

A sudden banging rang out against the wall, and books tumbled from their shelves to the floor. Tessan was pounding her fists against the wood, begging for someone's attention.

"Liam!" They could hear Tessan's muffled screams from inside the room.

The Overseer sprinted to the bookshelf, enchanting it quickly. He didn't understand what was happening, but he knew he couldn't let anything happen to Tessan. Kalen would be crushed, especially if he was the one responsible.

There was something about the way she looked at Kalen. The way Kalen looked at her. It reminded him of–

"Liam! Please help!" The doors on the bookshelves swung open now, interrupting West's thoughts.

Probably for the best.

Tessan's face was sheet white.

She took a deep breath before recognizing he was standing behind Liam.

"Oh, thank Gods you're here too." She nodded at West.

"Something's happening."

West stepped past Tessan now, careful not to knock her over in the cramped space. He was terrified to see Kalen's eyelids fluttering, but not yet opened, his fists clenching at his sides.

"Liam?" West called to him, worried. "What's going on?"

"I...I don't know," Liam answered truthfully.

"I thought you knew everything!" he shouted back.

"Energy, West," Liam spoke to him calmly as he approached his side, putting a knowing hand on West's shoulder. A gentle reminder—*I know this is hard for you. I wish I could help.*

"I called for you as soon as he started moving. He's never done anything like this before," Tessan chimed in, moving toward the two men. "I was just about to leave and head home for the night."

"I'm glad you were still here, Tessan. It seems Kalen is stable, though moving," Liam noted, reading the energy of the room. "Why don't you head home? West and I can take it from here."

West looked at the witch now. She wasn't looking at him, though; she was looking at Kalen. Her worry was obvious, and under different circumstances, it may have warmed his heart. West was grateful that Kalen was able to make an impact on anyone that quickly. But he wasn't surprised; he knew his son was special.

"Hey," he reached out to squeeze her hand, breaking her focus from Kalen. They'd grown close in the last couple of years, a shared sadness quietly exchanged between them. "I'll come get you if he wakes up."

That seemed to be enough for her, as she grabbed her things and exited the room, leaving Liam and West alone.

"Um, hey, West?" Tessan called out from Liam's office.

"Yeah?" he said, turning around to respond. But she wasn't alone. And somehow, they hadn't heard anyone else come into the office.

Eugenia stood behind her.

Oh no.

"I knew something was off about these Gods damn letters." Eugenia calmly walked toward West and Liam. The two of them had subconsciously joined shoulders, a wall to block her from seeing the sleeping hybrid that lay behind them.

In her hand was the letter from Liam's desk, the letter from "Kalen" to Ria.

West could have sworn he saw the smoke coming from her nose.

Fuck.

Chapter Seventeen
Kalen

K alen was losing his mind.

He guessed maybe that was the point.

He didn't know how long he'd been stuck in the Awakening, but he was exhausted.

He had no real connection to the world outside of his brain. He could occasionally hear the echo of a voice, but it sounded muffled, as if he were six feet underwater and the voice was begging him to swim to the surface.

But he couldn't. He was stuck.

Though he couldn't control his mind, he recognized the aches in his body as growing pains. He'd felt them years ago, when he hit a growth spurt in his middle teens, but they were nothing like this. He could feel his bones aching, crunching, as if they were making space for more of him. He could feel muscles forming where there was once just a bit of skin and bone.

It hurt.

But at least he'd come back bigger than he once was. He guessed that was the least he could do for Tessan, since she asked so nicely.

He couldn't even laugh at his own thoughts, not where he was. Wherever the hell that might be.

And he was beginning to have trouble discerning what was real and what was a product of this cruel magic testing his limits.

He had coined this place as the In-between. Once he realized the Awakening was a loop, he started to move more slowly, more thoughtfully. He didn't want to trigger the reset; he couldn't relive all of it again.

If he felt that he was going crazy now, he couldn't imagine what one more loop would do to his psyche.

He'd witnessed his father's Severing twelve times before he realized how to get past the first part of this violent loop.

He didn't remember how long ago that was.

It felt like yesterday, it felt like months ago.

He'd tried to stop the Severing himself, over and over and over again. He began running to the front of the crowd when they left Evermere Market, yelling at The Cleanser to put down his knife and change his decision earlier in the loop. He'd tried to tackle the guards. He tried to jump on the stage at The Hollow and get the crowd to rebel against The Order's cruelty. One time, he even tried to run back to his mother's home in the forest. That was the moment he knew he was coming undone.

Because each time, he failed.

Each time, he was put right back in Evermere to start all over again.

He'd realized on the twelfth loop that he had to do something else. The Awakening wasn't about the ways to save his Father, it was about how *he* was changing. About the magic he was born into, the magic that was his birthright.

He wished he could stop time anyway. That he could walk up to his dad, on the stage in The Hollow, and ask him more questions about the magic he was about to inherit.

He knew there was fire, and he knew he could already memorywalk, but what else? Was there anything else? If there were only two, maybe he could get out of here soon.

Maybe he could get back home.

It was then that he decided to change course. He'd have to observe, be a fly on the wall, and see what happened after the Severing.

He couldn't have anticipated that what came next would be torture.

He hoped he could be cleansed of these violent memories when he woke up.

Because the Severing, every single time, was brutal.

But what came next...Kalen tried to shake the thoughts from his mind.

The rickety wooden wheels of the guillotine slid smoothly across the white marble floor of The Hollow. Their soft squeaks sang the song of death as the guards rolled the heavy wooden contraption on the stage.

It was all you could hear over the silence of the crowd.

That, and his heartbeat. He swore he could hear it, too.

Kalen realized after the first loop that the slick white floor was a deliberate choice made by The Order. The bloodshed against the bright white served as a brutal reminder to all of the onlookers. What was even more chilling was the way it felt to see the white marble shine again when the loop reset and he was back where he started. As if it had never happened. As if it didn't matter at all. As if all of their lives were disposable. Replaceable. Nothing. Erased.

He had to get out of here.

Kalen watched in disgust as the guards left the sides of the guillotine and rushed to his father. Blood splattered on his face. Cartilage from his butchered ears hung on like a piece of string from an old tunic.

Kalen's stomach turned at the display of their brutality.

This isn't real, my dad is in Wyrdbrook. This isn't real, my dad is in Wyrdbrook.

But he'd never forget how it felt, even with the knowing that this was some alternate version of reality.

How vomit crept up his throat as they shoved his father's head into the small hole.

How his own tears fell as he watched his father close his eyes. Accepting what was to come.

Kalen couldn't say the same.

Something began to buzz inside of him. He reached for the magic, trying to taste it, to name it, to break from this haze he was in and remember who the hell he was, and what the hell he could do.

The magic felt like the Earth.

Like an evening in bloom after a soft rain. Like fresh-cut cedar or sticky sap from a maple.

Like Rootweaving.

His mother rarely used Rootweaving when he was growing up. She didn't have to rely on her abilities to manipulate nature because she became the forest's closest friend.

She didn't have to tell the berries where to grow, because she trusted they knew where to thrive.

She'd asked him to promise to do the same.

Promise me you'll only use your magic for restoration, for peace-making. Never for harm, little crow.

He hoped she'd understand why he couldn't today.

The magic was begging him to be let free. To unleash on the injustice in front of him. To become more than he was.

To save his father.

So, he let it.

With nothing more than a thought, the small pebbles on the ground began to shiver.

Holy shit.

The crowd gasped, unsure of what was happening around them, and the shivering grew more prevalent. The rocks sounded like an earthquake as the group of people began to move away from him.

Kalen hoped it sounded like a warning to Hauke. That going any further would result in a danger he'd never known.

Hauke's eyes lifted, but he wasn't looking at the pebbles. He was looking at Kalen. He could feel the man's eyes burning holes through him, begging him to look up at him. To face him.

Shit, not again.

He had to remain focused. He could do this; he could move past this part of the loop. He just needed to do something to distract them. To break his father out of the guillotine. Maybe he'd send the rocks flying at the guards? Surely that would do it. Then he and his father could escape, and he'd figure out what came next.

He couldn't live through this again.

Please. Please.

Hauke tisked in Kalen's direction, belittling him, "You're going to have to do better than that." An evil grin spread across his face. Kalen looked up at The Cleanser as he heard the slice of a rope, sending the sharpened blade toward his father's neck.

"NO!" Kalen screamed in agony, sprinting toward the white marble stage.

But it was too late.

Because before he knew it, he was back in the Evermere Market.

And it smelled like fish.

Chapter Eighteen
West

"Hi, Genie." West looked at the witch fondly.

She'd kept his secret safe all of these years, despite how much she disagreed, because she knew it would ultimately protect Ria.

Protect Kalen.

He didn't know how he'd ask her to do it again. He wasn't sure she would. He wasn't sure he'd blame her if she didn't.

It had been so long since she'd looked at him like this—as a man. He never showed himself to her again after the day in her home all those years ago. When he flew to the woods as Wen, she never saw him again as West.

Part of him hoped she'd forget it was him when she looked at the crow. He knew she never did.

She carried the pain of knowing for more than a decade. And the weight of that was what brought her here.

"Westin Vale, I swear to Gods," she snarled, stalking toward him, voice low.

He wasn't convinced he'd be able to talk himself out of this one.

"It's not what it seems," he stuttered. Pulling his body closer to Liam's, tightening the space between them. Trying to ensure Kalen stayed hidden.

"It's never what it seems when it comes to you." She was standing shoulder to shoulder with Tessan now.

"Hi, my love." She turned toward her niece, kissing her forehead. "You look good, Tess. But I'm afraid I'll have to deal with you later."

She nodded toward the door, silently prompting Tessan to leave.

West looked at the young witch, wide-eyed, pleading.

Please don't leave us here with her.

West was hopeful that if Tessan was in the room, maybe Eugenia would be a bit more even-tempered.

His stomach turned as Tessan grimaced at him, mouthing a quick confirmation.

Sorry.

She was going to do as her aunt asked. There was no real alternative she wished to be a part of.

He couldn't say he blamed her.

Eugenia followed Tessan out of Liam's office, giving her a quick hug before walking back in, slamming the door upon her entrance.

"I need answers. Now," she demanded harshly. She was not holding back the fury in her voice.

"Eugenia, it is a pleasure to see you again," Liam interjected. "Wyrdbrook has continued to thrive due to your generosity."

Liam was trying to buy them time. Trying to talk her down. He appreciated the effort, but if he knew anything about Eugenia Duscaire, it wouldn't be successful.

In so many ways, West couldn't have asked for a better person to have his family's back.

At the end of the day, they were more hers than they were his.

The thought caused his heart to crack back open, right along the slightly perforated lines where it had been healed by Kalen two years ago.

Was this whole thing a waste of his time? If Kalen knew Eugenia was here, would he even want *him* here?

"You, too, Liam. I appreciate your kindness, but I am not in the mood for niceties," she stated plainly, her steely eyes shifting between the two men in front of her.

"Where is Kalen?" She moved toward them with purpose, holding the letter over her head, a declaration of their lies over the last two years.

"And don't give me any more of this 'I have to keep him safe' bullshit, Westin," she taunted. "I'm done with it. Where is our boy?"

Our boy. At least she recognizes that much in her anger.

"I'll tell you everything." He tensed as Eugenia got closer to them. "But I need you to calm down." Eugenia's eyes flared.

He'd definitely said the wrong thing.

Shit.

"Calm down? HA!" Her voice went higher, fake laughter spilling out.

Shit, shit, shit.

"I'm going to lay this out plainly, so that your little bird brain understands exactly what I'm saying."

The air in Liam's office had stilled. Eugenia had sucked all of it out to make room for her anger.

"If Kalen Halrowe is harmed, I will take my ass back to Evermere. I will walk directly to the High Seminary, I will go straight to Hauke Elowen, and I will tell him where you are."

West gulped. He knew she wasn't bluffing.

"No, you know what. Change of plans. I'll bring you with me. How's that? Are you up for a trip to Evermere? The city really is beautiful this time of year."

This was the rage of a woman who loved fiercely, deeply, and fully.

This was the rage of a woman whose lies of preservation had led to this moment, who couldn't bear to look her best friend in the eyes and have to do it again.

"I hope I've made myself clear." She was now standing face to face with him, the top of her forehead hitting right at his chin. He could feel the heat radiating from her face.

This anger was pure.

"Crystal." He smiled at her–he couldn't help it.

He couldn't bring himself to be mad at Eugenia. To take her threats to heart. He was taking them seriously, yes, but he could never blame her for showing up here.

He knew it was always a *when* and not an *if* with Eugenia.

"I'm glad you understand. Now, where is Kalen?" It wasn't a question this time; it was a demand.

West looked at Liam, asking permission to break apart. To show her the sleeping boy behind them both.

His son. Trapped in some sort of purgatory.

How could he explain this to her? How could he convince her not to bring Ria here?

He couldn't imagine their reunion, if they'd ever have one. He needed to take things one step at a time, and he couldn't do *that* while Kalen was still asleep.

Liam lowered his head to West before looking at Eugenia.

"Eugenia, Kalen is still in the Awakening."

Eugenia, and all of her fury, froze in shock. Her breath grew lighter. The confusion in her eyes deepened.

"He's shown us he's still in there. That he's still alive," Liam shared softly before he looked at the floor, ashamed and preparing for what came next.

"But we don't know when–or if–he'll wake up."

The impact of the words sent a shock through his office.

If?

In the last two years, Liam had never muttered an "if." He'd been the slow and steady voice of reason. The one who kept them moving toward the hope that Kalen would wake up.

If.

It wasn't sure enough.

Westin couldn't handle an if.

"I need to see him," Eugenia muttered. West wondered if she had felt the weight of Liam's words, too.

Liam looked at West, with a new sorrow in his eyes–*I'm sorry I can't fix this.*

And in an unspoken agreement, they stepped apart from each other, making way for Eugenia to see the sleeping boy behind them.

"Genie?"

West turned around sharply at the sound of a voice he didn't recognize.

It can't be.

A voice that didn't sound like the one he'd heard two years ago. It was lower, it was deeper.

It is.

It was his.

Kalen was awake.

Finally.

Chapter Nineteen

Kalen

The air felt different now.

So did he.

He had lived a thousand different versions of his life while he was in the Awakening.

How could he be sure this wasn't just another one?

He made a slow attempt to gain his bearings. Steadily blinking away the haze from the corners of his vision, doing his best to remember where he was. To anchor himself to this reality.

He remembered this hidden room in Liam's office from...before.

Would that always be how he'd measure time now? Before the Awakening and now?

Before the suffering, and now.

Before all of his power, and now.

The still, small room somehow felt smaller than it did when he fell asleep.

Kalen began to wake his body up, his new magic a steady hum inside of him, a reminder that what he endured had a purpose.

But Gods, did his muscles feel stiff.

He heard a muffled conversation ahead of him and barely lifted his head to see who was there. It looked like the back of Liam and his father, but he was staring Eugenia in the face.

Wait, what's she doing here?

Eugenia hadn't been in a single version of his Awakening.

Does that mean...? Am I finally back home?

"Genie?"

Stunned silence filled every corner of the room. Kalen swore even the birds stopped chirping and the wind stopped blowing.

Like Earth Mother had been waiting for him to come home, too.

And then he saw him, turning around in a frenzy. His father.

Still alive.

His butchered ears had faded scars, and Kalen's stomach turned at the memory of what he'd seen. But the scars were faded. That meant...

He couldn't trust it yet. The idea that he had broken out of the loop.

If this were another version of the Awakening, he didn't know how to make it through. And he couldn't risk starting back at the beginning.

"Kalen?" His dad spoke tenderly, in disbelief. Tears began to well in his eyes as he ran closer to his bedside.

Kalen flinched at the movement. He couldn't believe this was truly happening to him, not yet. And he couldn't set himself up for more heartache. For more torture.

His father noticed Kalen's hesitancy and slowed to a stop.

"You okay, Kale?" The tears were falling down his face now, a mix of relief and pain.

He'd missed him.

"How do I know I'm really here with you all?" Kalen asked quietly, shifting to sit further up on the bed.

"What if this is just another version of the loop? I can't do that again. Please don't make me do it again."

He looked down now, shame filling his gut. He hated having to ask the question out loud. He felt exposed by the damage that had been dealt by the Awakening. He hoped they'd understand.

If they're even here.

"Hey..." Eugenia stepped forward now, slowly moving toward his bed, before stopping shoulder to shoulder with his father.

"Look at me, Kalen."

His eyes lifted toward the woman who'd seen him grow. Who'd walked with him through the forest and taught him all she knew. The healer from Evermere. His mother's best friend.

His Genie.

He took a deep breath, trying to ground himself in the moment. He just needed one sign that he was here. Anything that could help him to believe, fully, that he was back in Wyrdbrook.

"You're safe, little love," she said softly.

Kalen didn't move; his eyes remained locked on the witch.

Despite all he'd learned about her since arriving in Wyrdbrook, despite the years of lies shared between the people in the room around him, he still trusted her. Not like before, but enough for this moment.

So he nodded his head, just slightly. A signal that she could approach.

Close enough to softly push his hair out of his face, to run her hand along his cheek, wiping away a tear, before gently grabbing his chin.

It made him miss his mother.

"Not so little anymore, huh?" she grimaced, her eyes filling with tears, too.

How long have I been gone?

And then, in only the way Eugenia could have, she reached for his hand and squeezed three times. The unspoken pact they'd both made with his mother.

The reminder of who they were, in the moments they felt the least like themselves.

Kind. Brave. Gentle.

He was home.

Emotion quickly overwhelmed him as he reached for Eugenia's tunic and pulled her in for a hug. Where the room was once holding its breath, everything and everyone loosened.

Especially Kalen.

He was sobbing without shame. Openly, exposing the wounds of his soul. He didn't care. And he knew they didn't either.

They had no idea what he'd just been through. He swore he could still smell his father's blood, still see the images of his butchered ears, of his headless body hanging limp in the guillotine. Of the calluses on Hauke Elowen's hands as he threw him into a torture chamber.

He wasn't ready to relive everything. Not yet.

The truth was, he didn't know how to tell them that the boy who went into the Awakening was not the one in front of them now.

Maybe they already knew.

That in the darkness, a new knowing took root deep inside of him: The Order must be stopped.

And that because of what he went through, he may just have enough power to be the one to stop them.

But for now, he needed to stretch his legs.

Chapter Twenty
Kalen

Kalen slowly let go of Eugenia, her hair sticking to his tear-soaked cheek as they pulled away.

They both started to laugh at the sight of one another so exposed.

"It's good to see you, Genie," he said lovingly, glancing over her shoulder to the man who shared his face.

He was waiting patiently, the same way he had when he first met Kalen. He didn't push him; he was letting Kalen acknowledge him when he was ready. On his terms, on his time.

So he did.

Slowly swinging his legs off his bed, Kalen took a quick breath before attempting to stand up. His steps were strong and sure as he walked toward his father, though his brain was still having trouble processing the legitimacy of this moment.

He'd spent almost his entire life thinking the man in front of him was dead. And then he got just a few days with him before experiencing the horror of seeing him mutilated and murdered, over and over again. He knew it would take time to cleanse himself of the psychological damage of the Awakening, but it made one thing very clear to him.

He loved his dad, and he needed him to be okay.

Seeing him here, standing in front of him, confirmed it. He could forgive him for his lifetime of being an onlooker, for the lies, for being

Wen, because he got a front row seat to some version of what he endured to make sure he and his mother were safe.

Kalen embraced his father tightly, grabbing a fistful of his tunic and pulling him in close. His father returned the squeeze, hanging on as if Kalen was the thing that tethered him to the world. As if he was scared that if he let go, he'd lose him again.

Kalen felt the same way.

They broke apart after what felt like minutes of their silent reunion. His father squeezed his shoulder, just like he did before the Awakening, and looked Kalen square in the eyes.

"I really missed you," he said plainly, exposing his vulnerability and staring at Kalen with profound grief.

"I missed you, too, Dad." Kalen was confident in the word after what he'd endured. He'd earned the relationship, the title. What was once fragile felt forged. He'd waste no more time trying to determine whether this man was worthy of his love.

Kalen turned back to Eugenia now, a skeptical look on her face. She hadn't seen the reunion of the two upon Kalen's arrival at Wyrdbrook. Didn't know the walls they had to break through to get to this moment. Didn't know the pain he'd endured while he was sleeping. Kalen looked at her with a challenge in his eyes.

Don't forget your part in this, too.

She looked away, knowing him well enough to understand that it wasn't the time to start trouble.

"Kalen." The third voice in the room startled him out of his trance.

Liam.

Kalen's heart warmed at the sound of the Overseer's voice. He had almost everyone he cared for in the same room. He was just missing his mother and Tes–

"I think we have quite a bit to catch up on, little crow," Liam followed up lovingly. "No need to rush to it, but I'd love it if we could get this room closed up before someone else shows up here unannounced." He winked at Eugenia.

She scoffed in return.

Gods, it's good to be home.

"Oh, yeah," Kalen responded genuinely. "Would you all give me just a few minutes?"

The three of them exchanged worried glances. He knew what they were thinking before they said anything at all.

What could he possibly need alone time for? He just got back.

"I promise it won't take long," he tried to reassure the group. He was okay—he just needed to take a minute to say goodbye. To close the chapter of his life that changed him. He hoped they'd respect his request.

He had a feeling they would.

"We'll be in my office." Liam looked at Eugenia and his father, nodding toward the exit. He recognized they were both reluctant to take the first step.

"Don't take too long, okay?" Eugenia chirped as she walked past him, reaching to mess up his hair before pushing him away.

"I promise, I'll be right out." Kalen grinned at the easy interaction. "Shut the door behind you?"

"Just knock when you've finished up, and I'll let you out," Liam called back, and they headed out the door, carefully latching the bookshelves back into place.

Kalen lit the small lamp and gently set it on the desk. But not with the match, with a small flicker of a flame that came from his palm, just like his father.

He laughed in amazement.

The silence in the room caused a low ringing in his ears. He had so many unanswered questions, but right now he wanted to lie back down in the spot where he awoke anew.

The bed was quite uncomfortable now that he was back in it. The imprint of his body had formed deep into the mattress, squeezing him like a too-small glove.

He stared at the ceiling in deafening silence.

He knew he'd find out soon how long he was in the Awakening. He could tell by the way everyone was acting, by the way his body felt sinking into the bed, by the worried lines embedded deep in his father's face, that it had been a long time. Longer than two weeks.

But how long?

He wondered what the world was like for them on this side while he was away. Had much changed? Did they come to see him every week? He wouldn't blame them if they had stopped. If some of them never came at all. He imagined this room could feel a bit suffocating if you spent much time inside, especially if you were spending time with a practical stranger.

He'd tell them about what he endured when he was ready. About the magic pulsing through his veins that wasn't there before. About what he had to do to escape the loop.

But for just one more moment, he was going to close his eyes and reflect on the Awakening.

The darkness he endured had made way for the light inside of him to burn a bit brighter than it did before he got here.

Despite it all, he was thankful for that. For the way it changed him. For the way he grew.

But it was time to leave this place behind. Physically, at least. He'd be fine if he never had to open the bookshelves' doors again. Mentally, though, he knew he'd carry it with him forever.

Kalen stood up, blowing out the desk light, and knocked three quick times on the door, just as Liam said.

But when he opened it, it wasn't Liam standing in front of him.

"About Gods damn time you're back."

Tessan.

"Missed me, huh?" Kalen smiled at her, towering over her in a way he hadn't before.

"Yeah, right," the witch said, rolling her eyes, before walking into an embrace. It was uncharacteristic of Tessan, but Kalen didn't mind.

"I missed you, too," Kalen replied, wrapping his arms around her.

Yeah, it's good to be home.

"Okay, now who's hungry? I could go for anything but fish." He released Tessan, heading back toward his father, patting him on the shoulder. "Long story."

The group laughed and headed out of the Veilhold toward Kalen's home. He was looking forward to being back in his small cottage. Sleeping in his own bed for a change.

Although right now, he didn't feel like he'd need to sleep again for the next week.

The sun on his face felt like freedom. He was exactly where he was supposed to be.

But damn, he wished his mom were here.

The walk back to his home was full of cheers from the villagers. Strangers he'd never met, rushing to tell him they were glad he was okay. Victoria and Shu ran up to him cheerfully, too, almost tackling him to the ground in a hug.

"We're so glad you're back!" they sang in unison before running off holding hands toward Victoria's cottage.

That's new?

He looked at Tessan with confusion to confirm the relationship between the two. She smiled and shrugged in return.

The group talked and laughed all the way to his front door. He felt his senses tick up when he put his hand on the doorknob. He was still getting used to these new powers. What they all meant.

Right now, he was just happy to be back home.

He looked back at his father as he pushed open the door. "Did you decorate for me while I was gone?" he chuckled.

But his father wasn't looking at him.

He was staring straight ahead, his eyes wide, as if he'd seen a ghost.

Kalen turned to look into his house for the first time since he'd been gone.

But he wasn't drawn to the new tapestries hanging on the walls. Or the smell of dried herbs lying on the countertops.

Because he came face-to-face with his mother.

With the same wide-eyed look as his father, as if she'd also seen a ghost.

And for her, she had.

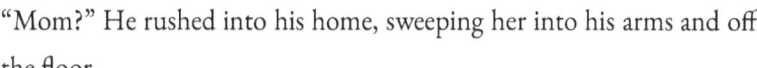

"Mom?" He rushed into his home, sweeping her into his arms and off the floor.

His person was here.

He'd been so grateful for his father, Liam, Tessan, and Eugenia.

But no one would ever be Ria Halrowe. His mother. Not for Kalen.

She felt stiff, resisting falling into the moment, still focused on his father in the doorway, too stunned to move.

Kalen sat his mother down now and looked back at his father. The top of his head was almost brushing the doorframe, his eyes a mix of sorrow, longing, and grief. Kalen understood he hadn't been prepared to see her again like this.

Maybe he never would have been.

But it was happening now, whether he was ready or not.

How is this going to go?

"Westin?" She squeezed Kalen's hand as she stepped past him. A quick acknowledgement that she was grateful to see him, but had to figure out if the man in front of her was once the man she loved, or a cruel version of a magic she wasn't familiar with.

Her bare feet slid with grace across the floor, making her way closer to his father. Like they were drawn to each other, like he was the moon pulling the ocean to the shore.

Kalen couldn't believe he was witnessing his parents together, in the same room, for the first time.

What a gift. What a day.

His mother was close enough now that she could have reached up to touch his father's face. Her skin was a shade of light green, nauseous and unbelieving.

The man she'd loved.

Alive.

Kalen had been there, but it had felt different. It felt like a betrayal when he found out about his father.

This was heartbreak on a different scale.

It was devastating and haunting. A reunion that should have never come to pass.

He watched, holding his breath, as his mother gently reached up and cupped his father's face. His father leaned into her hand and closed his eyes.

Kalen exhaled deeply, swearing something in his heart he hadn't known was broken had just snapped back together.

His parents. Here. Together.

Finally, a family.

SMACK.

Oh, shit.

The same hand that rested gently on his father's face just moments before reared back and landed with a disbelieving blow. It was enough to send an echo through the room. The softness of her hand, of the moment, followed up by the force of her swing, almost knocked Kalen off balance.

He'd felt that bit of his heart break wide open again.

"I never want to see you again," she whispered before stepping around him and walking out of Kalen's home.

"Ria!" Eugenia yelled after her, quickly dashing after her best friend.

"Wait, Genie," Kalen grabbed her arm gently. "Let me go after her. We'll be back."

I hope.

He locked eyes with his father now. The man hadn't moved from where he was planted, as if he'd grown roots himself. The bright red handprint shone brightly on his face, but he remained stoic, staring straight ahead to where Kalen's mother once stood. Silent tears fell from his eyes.

"Give her time, Dad," Kalen spoke softly. "She'll come around."

His father inhaled shakily before turning his head and looking to the ground. "It wasn't supposed to be like this."

They would never be able to go back to how it used to be. The secrets that had been forged in years of deceit were exposed in a matter of moments.

Nothing would be the same again. But Kalen had already known that when he woke up this morning.

"We'll figure this out, okay?" Kalen stepped in front of him, forcing his father to look at him. "Together."

Kalen waved at Liam, Eugenia, and Tessan before running out the door, yelling for his mother. Wyrdbrook wasn't *that* big, but it was big enough for him to lose her quickly.

He ran toward the forest. Until the voices faded, and all that was left was the steady caw of an unfamiliar crow.

The irony of the moment wasn't lost on him.

His hearing was sharper, though his ears never pointed; his smell was crisper, still able to sense certain emotions, the same way he'd begun experiencing just before his birthday, but it was more complex now.

Sadness smelled like wet dirt after a brutal rain.

He lifted his chin to the wind and took a deep breath as the scent of devastation danced along his nose.

And he let Earth Mother carry him to his own.

He saw her from a distance first, propped against a tree, her knees to her chest, shaking with sorrow.

"Hey, Mom." Kalen approached slowly, his feet crunching through the fallen pine needles. "Can I sit?"

She scooted over, making room for him, and quickly wrapped her arms around him.

"I sure have missed you, my love," she said. She pressed her lips to the top of his head, stroking his hair as she spoke softly. "Two years was a long time without you."

Two years?

"Two years?" He sat up now, turning to face her. Eyes wide in confusion.

There's no way it has been two years.

"I know. I can't believe it either. You've grown so much." She grabbed his chin.

"No, Mom." Kalen's ears were ringing, his chest was rising and falling quickly.

How could I have been gone for two years? What have I missed? What have I–

His mother quickly sensed his panic.

"Hey. Take a deep breath." She grabbed his hands now. "Ground yourself." She rubbed her thumb over the top of his hand. "I'm right here."

"I-I-I just woke up today," Kalen stuttered. "From the Awakening."

His mother's eyes grew wide with concern. "Oh, honey." She pulled him back into her arms. "Do you want to talk about it?"

"Not yet, if that's okay?" he responded truthfully. The idea of going right back into his suffering made him dizzy.

"I'll be ready when you are." She let go, wiping her tears, exhaling a deep breath. "Quite the day for you, huh?"

"That's one way to put it." He leaned back against the tree. "Should we talk about Dad?"

He felt his mother stop breathing briefly, considering her response.

"Not yet, if that's okay?" she echoed back to Kalen, a soft smile on her face, despite the tears that continued to fall.

"I get it." He rested his head on her shoulder.

Two years.

They sat together silently, basking in the nothingness. And despite what he'd just endured—things that had driven him to the point of breaking—he finally felt completely whole again.

Kalen felt heavier on his trek back home. He was so grateful his mother was back, so thankful for the opportunity to spend time with her alone.

But he dreaded the fact that he'd have to tell his father she wasn't interested in seeing him.

Not yet.

Her voice bounced off the walls of his mind. At least she didn't say never.

It gave him hope, and somehow hope felt dangerous.

Kalen knocked on the door of his home, one quick tap to alert the folks inside that he had made it back before walking in. He was looking forward to being with all of them, to sharing more about his new power.

To catch up.

Two years was a long damn time.

He stepped inside his home, fully taking in his surroundings now that his mother wasn't the centerpiece. His father really had decorated while he was away.

A large woven tapestry hung on the wall behind his sitting area. It looked handmade, with a large oak tree in the center. It reminded him of the Sanctwood.

But what caught his eye most was the small wooden crow on the tea table. Another thing that looked handmade, a reminder of the bird who had sacrificed nearly everything to keep him and his mother safe all of these years.

Kalen loved that his father had left these large pieces of himself in his space. That even though he'd been gone for so long, he never stopped thinking about him.

The door to his bedroom opened slowly, his father walking out first, Liam in tow.

Here goes.

He could sense the hope in his father's eyes. The anticipation of the reunion with the love of his life.

"She's...not ready."

It was all he could say.

And he watched as his father's face shattered the illusion of confidence. He was a broken man standing in front of his son.

"Understood," was all he responded, as he walked over to Kalen and kissed his head.

"I'm glad you're back. I'll see you tomorrow."

He couldn't get out a word before his father shifted to his bird form and flew out the door.

The heaviness of the moment could have broken him, but he'd just experienced much worse in the Awakening.

At least he's alive.

Kalen stood in his doorway, watching as his father flew away. Wondering if he'd somehow be drawn to where his mother was. Knowing he'd likely spend the next few hours watching over her if he found her.

Old habits.

"Just us, then." Liam's voice cut like a dull blade through the silence. "You missed Tessan and Eugenia."

Kalen gave a soft smile to the Overseer before sitting down in his common room. Liam joined him shortly after.

"What a day." Kalen laughed. "I thought the most exciting thing would be waking up."

Liam chuckled in return, creating a lightness in the room he didn't realize he'd needed. Kalen swore he could still smell his Dad's sadness lingering behind.

"I'll tell you what, this is the most action Wyrdbrook has had since you fell asleep..." Liam paused before continuing, but Kalen could read the room. He knew the Overseer didn't know how to tell him what came next.

"I know I've been gone for two years," Kalen responded directly.

Liam dipped his head.

"Mom let it slip unknowingly."

He watched as Liam peered around his small cottage, admiring one of the spaces he'd worked so hard to curate, to protect, all of this time.

"I'm sorry, Kalen. I had no record of anyone enduring the Awakening for more than a fortnight. I would have tol–"

"It's not your fault," Kalen cut him off abruptly. "None of us knew what we were getting into."

"Your capacity for kindness hasn't changed, it seems," Liam responded fondly.

"Well, you can learn a lot about what matters to you when you're forced to live through your father's torture and death on a loop for two years straight."

Liam couldn't hide the pain on his face at Kalen's admission.

Kalen looked away as the memories of what he endured tore through him.

He could still hear the heavy thud of his father's head as it fell against the marble floor of The Hollow. Could vividly remember the way it rolled to the edge of the stage, his father's lifeless eyes staring straight into his own. He could still smell the blood that lingered in the air from the torture.

But the steady hum through his body was the reminder of what the cost of the suffering was. Magic he'd never known, magic he wasn't sure *anyone* had ever known.

Nature didn't just bend to his will; it shifted to his desire. He could turn a giant pine into the illusion of a building. Make it disappear completely. Or double it.

"Rootweaving with a hint of shifting," Liam said in awe, "Like a mix of your parents' power..."

Of course, the Overseer could understand his thoughts somehow.

"Would you show me?" Liam responded gently. "If you're ready."

Kalen paused, considering the gravity of the moment. Truthfully, he wasn't even sure he could. He could feel something different stirring inside of him, but this magic didn't have a name.

He guessed that if anyone could help him understand what came next, Liam would be his best bet.

Kalen let out a breath and dug deep into the well of his magic. It was different out here than it was while he was in the loop; this magic had a limit, and he could feel it. He didn't know what would happen if he hit the bottom; he hoped he wouldn't ever have to find out.

He looked around his home before closing his eyes and sending a burst of magic forward. This power made him feel like he was in communion with Earth Mother Herself. His relationship with nature had always been a partnership, and he wasn't willing to give that up—to abuse all he'd been given so freely for so long.

You take, but you give, too.

Eugenia's words kept him grounded. Like an anchor tethering him to himself, refusing to let him drift for the sake of having more than he needed.

Kalen leaned into it, giving way to his power, whispering a quick prayer to the divinity he believed in most.

Let's impress the hell out of him.

In the blink of an eye, the elements had spun together in perfect harmony to create an exact replica of Liam's office. Right in the common room of Kalen's home.

They hadn't moved an inch, but they were in an entirely new place.

He was reeling now. His spirit soared as he saw his power in action for the first time after waking.

He looked at Liam with pride in his eyes.

The Overseer's jaw was wide in wonder.

"My Gods," Liam gawked, walking toward the illusion before him. Reaching forward to touch the replica of the stained glass window he'd poured so much of his own time into.

Kalen quickly waved it away, pulling his magic back in. Reminding Liam they'd been standing in the same place the whole time.

The Overseer spun quickly to face him, his eyes reflecting the pride that shone in Kalen's.

"My Gods," Liam repeated in awe, as he walked over to Kalen.

"Could you show me again?"

Chapter Twenty-One
Ria

*A*live.
    Here.

Seeing Kalen had restored her. The hole that had sat empty inside of her for the last two years was suddenly full again. Her beautiful boy, standing in front of her as a man.

It had been so hard without him.

She laughed to herself, recalling her first thought as she laid eyes on her son.

He looks so much like his father.

Until the man himself was standing directly behind her son.

Their son.

She could have sworn she was seeing double, an illusion, even, until she felt his face. Felt the invisible string that tied them together, pulling tightly again. The thing that had made their love so unexplainable and impossible to resist.

The stubble of his shaven beard poked her hand as it rested gently on his face. And in that moment, she swore she was just a young witch falling in love again.

Alive? All of this Gods damn time.

Alive and not with his family. How could he do that to her? She still felt the sting from smacking him.

She hoped he did, too.

When she decided to follow Eugenia she couldn't have anticipated things unfolding this way. Could never have anticipated ending up in Wyrdwood, seeing Westin. She just knew her friend was off, that something was wrong.

And she was tired of feeling like she was in the dark. The notes from Kalen were becoming more scattered, sharing less and less about his life. They were signed by him, but they had changed over time. His handwriting wasn't quite right–and she *knew* her boy. Eugenia had noticed it too, affirming the feeling deep within her gut.

So, she finally listened to her intuition.

And to be honest, two years was just too long for a mother to be without her son, which made the decision to follow Eugenia through the forest an easy one to make.

Eugenia never turned around once, though Ria suspected she knew she was being followed. She always knew.

That's what she loved so much about her best friend. The way she didn't make things a big deal. The way she always knew what Ria needed, without her having to say it out loud.

Her life had been full of love, even without West. Kalen had healed the part of her that shattered when she lost him...and Eugenia was the glue that held her together. Held *them* together.

They were her family.

His showing up didn't change anything.

His showing up...changed everything.

The familiar flutter of wings flapped overhead, a welcome distraction from her complicated and scattered thoughts.

Wen.

The crow landed on the tree overhead, perched silently as if it were listening to her grief—eavesdropping on her heartache.

"Hi, Wenny," Ria said warmly, standing up. "Let me grab you a worm, and you can get back to the Sanctwood." She began searching for a nearby rock to flip to find a bug for the crow.

Wen cawed twice in response.

No?

"What? You love worms!" Ria responded before finding a large rock.

Silly crow.

Cawing twice more, Wen flew down to where she was standing.

"I don't understand why you're saying no. You've never said no before."

This day really is weird.

Regardless, she stopped searching, and the crow flew up to perch on her shoulder. His presence calmed her. He was here, with her, keeping her safe in some way.

He always was.

She reached up to pat his head, "I'm going to stay here for a few days. Kalen asked me to stay in Tessan's cabin to...avoid some other people here."

She spoke to the crow as she had every day since he showed up in the Sanctwood. He was her faithful friend.

"I'll be home in a few days. Don't wait up for me," she said, before moving the crow off her shoulder, and encouraging him with a steady lift of her hand to fly away.

And off he went, weaving between the trees, headed back home.

But not until he rang out five steady caws.

She wondered what he meant as she sat back down under the tree.

And reluctantly thought about Westin Vale.

Chapter Twenty-Two
West

I will always love you.

Chapter Twenty-Three
Kalen

"**H**ow's *that* for pretty cool?" Kalen joked, waving away the forest he'd just resurrected in his living room.

"It's *incredible*, Kalen," Liam responded truthfully. "It may even be enough to keep our people safe for a very long time."

Our people.

His heart bloomed with gratitude at the small acknowledgement from the Overseer.

But safe from what?

"What do you mean by safe?" Kalen asked, entertaining the statement. But he knew, deep down, what Liam was going to say.

Please don't say it.

"The Order has taken over Evermere."

Gods damn it.

Kalen's ears were ringing again. When he began the Awakening two years ago, The Order was on the rise to power, but he was hopeful that the goodness in people would prevail. That they'd see another way to live together in peace, that they'd see people like him as valuable—not a plague to their way of life.

A boy's wishful thinking.

But he *was* good. He knew he was good. If he could just convince them. Go to Evermere. Show them a different way.

There's that hope again.

Between his parents, Eugenia, and this, he almost wished he were still in the Awakening.

Almost.

"Their leader has become more charismatic than before," Liam scowled before continuing. His face contorted in disgust.

Kalen watched Liam as he cycled through his emotions before landing softly back into himself.

"He's creating chaos out of nothing. Saying hybrids are more than just a sin against Athero, but that the power those like you hold is enough to destroy Evermere entirely."

Only for restoration, for peacemaking. Never for harm.

"But that's not true," Kalen spat out. "I've never wanted to use my magic to destroy anyone."

He wasn't raised to fear others—to fear himself. He was raised to see the good in all things, and in all beings.

The Order was lying. At least about him.

"It doesn't matter if it's true, little crow." Liam stood up anxiously. "Power is the point, not truth."

If The Order really had taken over Evermere, they already had more power than anyone needed.

"Before the Awakening..." Kalen started, recalling the memory. "There was a man. I saw him the night I got here...in the forest."

Liam's eyes went wide with fear.

"He was led here by an Orderly, but they couldn't figure out a way into Wyrdbrook, so they left," he continued. "I'm sorry for not telling you sooner. I meant to before I went under. I didn't think that I'd be gone for so long."

The Overseer began to pace.

"I saw him again. In the Awakening." Kalen closed his eyes, and Hauke's cruel smile slithered into his thoughts. He pushed it away. "He was so powerful. Everything felt...so real."

"And everyone listened to him, no matter what he was saying. No matter how ruthless. They were encouraging him to continue, to keep causing pain."

Kalen's voice was trembling.

"He was in complete control. Like they would believe anything he said. I've... I've never seen anything like it."

Granted, Kalen hadn't seen much. But he'd seen more now, *lived* more now, than he had when he got to Wyrdbrook.

Liam nodded in response, continuing his pacing. Kalen's anxiety began to tick up. He was used to seeing the Overseer calm and centered. This version of him confirmed what Kalen already knew. It was bad.

"His name is Hau–"

Liam cut him off: "Hauke Elowen. The Head Cleanser of Evermere. Immensely charming and convincing, despite his brutality."

"You know him?" Kalen was surprised to hear The Cleanser's name fall so freely from Liam's lips.

The Overseer stopped pacing and turned to face Kalen before shaking his head in disbelief.

"He's my brother."

If Kalen hadn't been sitting down, he would have fallen to the floor.

The man who haunted his thoughts shared blood with the one standing in front of him. The one he trusted with his life. The one who had been watching over him the last two years, while his *brother* was torturing his mind.

The juxtaposition of the two thoughts made Kalen feel physically ill. *How could this be possible?*

"Hauke and I have the same mother," Liam continued, sensing the confusion in Kalen.

"She was an amazing and kind witch. The greatest woman I've ever known." Liam walked toward Kalen now, dragging a small stool from the kitchen, and sat across from him.

Was.

"I'm very sorry for your loss," Kalen responded genuinely.

"Me, too," Liam exhaled, wringing his hands.

"Hauke never knew who his father was. Neither did my mother. She had a rough start to her life." Liam lifted his eyes to Kalen's. "She did what she needed to do to get by."

Kalen understood.

"When she became pregnant with Hauke, she made a commitment to give him the best life she could." His lips lifted into a grin, recalling the memory of his mother. "To change everything for herself, for him. And she did."

"She became our village's counselor. Helping people to understand their thoughts, to make sense of their minds." He tapped on his temple. "I think people were disarmed by her kindness. By her history. They knew she wouldn't judge them for what they'd been through."

Liam's gift was making more sense to Kalen now. His mother understood people inherently. And in so many ways, so did he.

"A few years after Hauke was born, she married and had me. We were a family. We were happy." Liam's voice started to shake.

"But the older he got, the more curious he became about who his father was."

Kalen hated that he could relate at all to The Cleanser of Evermere. He wished he could scrub his skin clean of Hauke Elowen.

"So he left home when he was around sixteen to find him. My mother begged him not to go...but he said it was something he had to do."

Liam's voice grew quiet as he continued.

"Years later, we saw him at the Evermere Market, dressed in all white. He had become an Orderly."

"But it was more than that; he was obsessed with their teachings. He was prophesying to the people in the market. Telling them of the purity of The Order and what they stood to gain if they joined him. Of Athero and the covenant." Liam shook his head in disbelief.

"We tried to get him to come back to us, to come home...but he'd changed. Mother was convinced he was still himself, but I could sense something...different lurking within him." Liam dipped his head again. "Something...evil. He wasn't the same person who left home. My brother was gone. I knew it, but my mother couldn't accept it."

Kalen felt his throat tighten, listening to the sadness in Liam's own story.

"I think that's what killed her, in the end. Losing him. When he didn't come to her burial, I knew he was really gone forever."

Kalen was quiet. Liam had laid his soul bare, and he couldn't think of a single thing to say to the Overseer of Wyrdbrook.

What was there to say?

That he didn't deserve to lose his brother? He didn't deserve to lose his mother?

That he just simply deserved more?

He reached out to touch Liam's arm, hoping he could sense his thoughts.

Thank you for telling me everything. I'll keep it safe.

But even in the midst of the Overseer's deep sorrow, Kalen couldn't stop his brain from flickering through the horror he'd endured at the hands of Hauke Elowen.

Knowing that The Order's popularity had risen, that they were more powerful, sent a chill down his spine.

He shook the feeling away.

If that's what he'd endured in some version of a dream, what would they do out here? In the real world?

He didn't know what gifts Hauke possessed. But being the son of a witch, he was sure to have some.

Power.

His body began to buzz in defense of the fight raging within his mind. As if it was reminding him of the reward of what he went through.

Power of his own.

He was Kalen Halrowe, the son of Ria and West. A powerful witch and fae. A friend to the forest and the shadows. A memorywalker, a rootweaver. A hybrid.

He was everything. He was nothing.

And he had to do something.

"Those thoughts are dangerous, little crow," Liam whispered. "You have no idea the power Hauke possesses...what he can do."

Kalen felt himself deflate at the Overseers' words.

Maybe this is a child's dream.

But it was a dream they shared, wasn't it?

Kalen thought about Liams' office, and the stained-glass window that framed his desk. It wasn't just a wish of what the world could be–it was his wish to be with his brother again. To be a family.

And family, Kalen had learned, was worth risking everything for.

Kind. Gentle.

Brave.

"No," Kalen said, standing up. "He should be scared of me." His power flared in response. As if he'd finally walked into full acceptance of who he could become.

Of who he *will* become.

The room grew silent in his defiance. Kalen wondered what Liam thought of the man standing in front of him. Of all the ways he'd changed in the last two years. Would it be enough?

Could it be enough?

Would someone like the Overseer of Wyrdbrook believe in him?

Liam stood up, walking closer to Kalen, his face unreadable.

Shit.

It wasn't until he extended his hand and grinned that Kalen let out an exhale. Kalen grabbed Liam's hand with force.

An agreement. A promise.

Hope personified.

"Let's go change the fate of Evermere, Kalen Halrowe."

Chapter Twenty-Four

West

West was flying to Gods only knew where.

Away.

Just for now, not forever.

Never forever, never again.

Just far enough to clear his head.

He knew now there would never be peace in his mind again. He could never erase the way Ria's face looked when she saw him.

She was so beautiful. So fully there. So close to him in a way he hadn't experienced in so long.

She was also terrified and unsure. Shocked and betrayed.

Disgusted.

If he wasn't already broken by the thought of what could have been, he would have shattered.

And then she touched him.

Him.

Not Wen.

Him.

As a human. For the first time in over twenty years. He was a fool to lean into it. To assume that it meant she had missed him as much as he'd missed her.

He wasn't sure that was even possible. That anyone had ever missed someone else the way he missed her.

He was grateful the sting of her slap was still burning—it served as a small reminder it was real.

She was here.

My Ria.

The thought stopped him mid-flight. His wings beat steadily in the air, keeping his body still as his mind raced.

What was he doing? If she needed space, that was fine. But he didn't. He'd *had* space.

He'd longed for her, for as long as he could remember.

He loved her. More than he'd ever loved anything.

He died a million different deaths to make sure she survived. To make sure Kalen survived.

She didn't owe him anything.

But he owed her everything. And he'd start with the truth.

Without another thought, West took off back toward Wyrdbrook, back toward Ria.

To make things right.

Or to promise to spend the rest of his life trying.

Chapter Twenty-Five

Ria

She should probably get up.

Wen hadn't been gone long, but loneliness was weighing heavily on her heart all the same.

She needed to be with Kalen, with Eugenia.

She just needed a hug.

She heard the familiar flapping of wings growing close to her before they disappeared again.

Weird.

And then she heard footsteps.

She wasn't alone.

"Ria," Westin's voice echoed from within the forest behind her. She didn't turn to face him.

He was the last person she wanted to see. She wasn't *that* lonely.

His voice cut through the aching in her brain, and everything stilled.

She fucking hated that. The way he could calm her down with nothing more than her name.

She wished she could let him go now. Now that she knew he'd been alive all of this time, *choosing* not to find her.

How could he have chosen not to find me?

She couldn't even begin to think about what he'd missed with Kalen. How sweet their life could have been together as a family.

It made her sick. It made her angry.

She wasn't ready to do this. Would she ever be?

She didn't look up at the sound of her name.

"I know you don't want to see me." She heard the shuffle of his feet as he moved closer to her. "I wouldn't want to see me, either."

Gods damn his charm.

The unfortunate truth was that Westin Vale's voice was like her favorite song; soothing and familiar. She knew the way every word would sound, and she could listen to it forever.

"I'll make it quick. Could you please just turn around and look at me?"

She refused, almost feeling his breath linger on the back of her neck. A small chill snuck its way through her body. What would it mean to turn around? That she forgave him?

She didn't forgive him.

"Please, Ri." The ache in his voice was tender.

Gods damn him.

Reluctantly, she turned and looked into the eyes of Westin Vale.

Sweet, steady Westin.

"My friends call me West."

What would she call him now?

What do you call a stranger with the face of your soulmate?

She took him in. His beautiful face was laced with the sadness of a life that hadn't been kind to him.

And his ears. Butchered and mutilated, a brutal reminder of the suffering he'd endured at the hands of The Order.

Because of her.

He began talking softly, "I have loved you from the very second I laid eyes on you in the Evermere Market."

Her breath caught in her throat.

Why is he doing this?

"I think I ate cloudberries every single Gods damn day after because they made me think of the witch who dropped her basket." He laughed deeply. "And they aren't even good."

Her stomach flipped.

His laugh.

But she wouldn't break.

She couldn't break.

"I need you to know that I have never regretted our love. Not once. You healed me, Ri. You changed me. You made me see the good in myself without The Order. You made me a better man."

His voice was shaking.

Why was his voice shaking?

"I have spent the last twenty years of my meaningless life missing you. And I know I'll likely spend the rest of it doing the same." His bottom lip began to tremble. "And that's okay. It really, truly is."

She felt her own lip wobble, too.

"But you deserve to know the truth. All of it." His voice came through with clarity now. "So, I'll start with this. I will love you until the last leaf falls off our Gods damn oak tree in Autumn. Until every bird has flown to warmer weather in the winter. Until every star placed in the universe by Earth Mother has burned out."

Our oak tree.

"I will love you in every lifetime. In every version of us. Forever. And you don't have to forgive me now." He laughed, exasperated. "Honestly, you don't have to forgive me, ever. But even if you don't, it doesn't change a thing for me."

She felt her cheeks redden. She wasn't sure if it was because of anger or something she wasn't ready to talk about yet.

She didn't know how to feel.

He grew serious in front of her. "Because you are it for me, Ria Halrowe. And you always will be."

And then he went quiet. He was waiting for her to respond. But he wasn't *really* done, and she could tell.

"What else is there, Westin?" The words fell from her mouth like a threat.

"I just told you I'll love you until the day I'm gone, and you're asking me what else?" he said smoothly, trying to charm his way out of the question.

It wasn't going to work. Not this time.

"You think I can't tell? You're hiding something. You've always been a terrible liar," she spat back at him.

This was venom.

He was lucky she was talking to him at all.

"Ria."

His voice was quiet, timid.

"Westin."

Hers was not.

"I will tell you everything, but it is not the right time," he pleaded.

"You don't get to tell me what's right or not when I haven't seen you for twenty Gods damn years!" She hated that she was yelling now, but she didn't owe him her kindness.

"Tell me now, or I will leave this place and take Kalen with me. And you will never find us again."

She flinched at the pain that flashed across his face.

She was baiting him. Would he take it?

"I have been with *our* son every single Gods damn day as soon as I knew where he was." His voice was calm–a bit *too* calm.

Our?

She raised Kalen. *She* kept him safe.

Not West.

Her.

"Oh, so you sat by his side while he was asleep for two years? What does that change, Westin?" she snapped back. "You don't know him! You don't know me. And actually," she raised her voice, "you definitely can't know if you still love me."

How could he still love me?

"Open your Gods damn eyes, Ria!" He wasn't yelling, he was begging. "I've been with you and Kalen since the moment I found out you were in the Sanctwood Forest."

What?

She froze. No one was supposed to know of her home in the Sanctwood. It was private. It kept them safe. Their privacy, Eugenia, and Wen.

Wait.

"No." She began shaking her head in protest.

No.

"It was the only way." He clasped his hands together, pleading for her to understand.

She'd never understand.

"No."

This can't be happening.

Because she wished every day that he was still alive.

And now she knew that every day he was.

Right in front of her face.

Because Westin Vale shouldn't know where they lived. He shouldn't have known anything about their life in the Sanctwood.

But he could shift.

And that meant...

This was a betrayal beyond what she could have ever expected from him.

Wen is West.

He took a step toward her now, panic on his face. She knew he wanted to fix it, to fix them.

But this was beyond repair.

She put her hand up to stop him from coming closer. She didn't want him to be near her any longer.

He didn't deserve to be.

"I will tolerate being in your presence until Kalen and I can go back home. Until then, do not speak to me."

"Ria, please. Ple–" he started, reaching toward her.

She didn't care.

"That was not a request. And it starts right now."

She watched as Westin Vale, the great love of her life, shrank into himself in shame and nodded once.

A confirmation.

And then he shifted into a beautiful black crow, the one who had spent so long keeping her company, and flew back toward Wyrdbrook.

Toward their son.

Away from Ria.

And her heart shattered all over again.

Chapter Twenty-Six
Kalen

K alen jolted awake.

Where am I?

His senses were on high alert, his chest tightening. He couldn't go back into his dreams.

Taking a deep breath, he recalled the way his mother used to calm him down when he was young.

Cradled in her arms, she'd ask him very simply, *"What can you see, smell, and touch, little crow?"*

He glanced around the room for anything to latch onto.

My desk is right there.

He inhaled deeply.

I can smell something. Maybe Dad is cooking?

He rubbed his hands along the soft linen sheets.

I can feel my bed.

He felt himself steady.

I'm safe. I'm home.

He exhaled slowly, wondering how long it would take him to reintegrate into this version of the world each morning.

Wondering when Hauke Elowen would stop terrorizing his thoughts.

His talk with Liam had changed something within him. Something that had been waiting for him to acknowledge its existence.

Now that he had, he couldn't go back.

Power.

His gifts whispered to him like they were sharing a stolen secret. If he didn't know any better, he'd think they were taunting him. Reminding him of what he'd lived so long without.

He slowly threw his legs over the bed, slipped on a shirt, and headed into his common room. He was right, his Dad was cooking something on his stove top, and it smelled delicious.

"Nice hair, bud," he chirped at Kalen playfully.

Kalen laughed, running his hands through it to try to tame his wild locks. There was no use; it was going to do what it wanted to anyway.

"Where'd you fly off to last night?" Kalen questioned his father as he picked up a biscuit, savoring every bite of the warm bread melting in his mouth.

"I talked to your mother."

Kalen coughed as he took another bite of the biscuit, his eyes wide.

"Yeah, I know. It didn't go well. I didn't think it would," he said, casually taking a bite of the charred meat from the skillet. "But, it's worth a shot."

"What'd she say?" Kalen was curious. Would they ever be a family? He hated how much he wished they were.

But he'd never tell his mother that. He'd never make her feel like she had to do anything for him before she was ready. Especially forgive his father.

But he'd be lying if he said his heart didn't hurt for his father, too. After knowing what he'd done for them.

"Ah, it's not worth talking about." His father turned back to the pan in front of him and began cooking again. The sizzle of the food against the hot pan became a placeholder for the words his father couldn't say.

"Alright," Kalen knew the pain in his own voice was obvious, but he'd learned long ago not to push the people he loved before they were ready. "If you change your mind, you know I'm here, yeah?"

"Yeah," his father said, plating the two of them a full breakfast, and gestured to the kitchen table for a meal.

His first meal with his dad.

"So, what's on the agenda today? First full day back in the real world." His dad moved his food around on his plate, making it seem like he was eating more than he was. The conversation was casual. As if they'd done this very thing thousands of mornings past, but Kalen could tell his father hadn't recovered from the run-in with his mom.

"I was thinking we could all head to the Veilhold for a chat, actually."

His dad stilled briefly before taking a bite of his food, ignoring the thick tension filling the room.

"All of us, huh?" His dad kept his eyes on the plate in front of him.

"I think it's going to take all of us," Kalen said as he put his fork down. "Liam told me about the rise of The Order. About how bad it is in Evermere."

"Gods damn him," he heard his father whisper under his breath.

"I know what they did to you, Dad," Kalen said calmly. He wasn't scared anymore, not like he used to be. "We can't let them hurt anyone else."

He watched carefully as his father slowly exhaled, noticing that the man before him was weighing his options.

Would he show up in this moment as the protective father he'd always strived to be, or would he let his son forge his own path? Try and change things?

The stillness of the room was deafening.

"I'm listening."

Kalen's power hummed at the simple response.

And so the two had breakfast–father and son–scheming to come up with a way to stop The Order from the inside.

To put an end to Hauke Elowen's reign.

In Evermere, but also in Kalen's brain.

Kalen was standing in the middle of Liam's office.

On his left was his mother, Eugenia, and Tessan.

To his right, his father and Liam.

An invisible line drawn right through the center of the room. Kalen knew they couldn't stay that way. If this plan was going to work, he'd need everyone on the same page.

He'd asked them all to meet at the Veilhold after breakfast, careful not to share why, just that he'd needed to talk to them all together.

It was risky. Beyond risky, really. But he knew the cost of his actions, and he'd accepted what could be.

Death.

Because he wasn't *just* a hybrid. He was the son of Westin Vale, the escaped fugitive that The Order had been hunting for years.

The Overseer's office was silent as the people he cared for the most stood on opposite sides of him. He could feel Eugenia's glares piercing through his father. He wasn't sure if this meeting was a good idea.

Here goes.

"Could we just pretend everything is okay for a few minutes?" Kalen started gently, slowly looking toward his mom, hoping she'd hear his unspoken ask.

Please.

She slowly uncrossed her arms.

Progress.

"I don't know how to say this, so I'm going to just go for it." Kalen exhaled. "I've spent my entire life being sheltered."

His mother and father both flinched.

Shit, this is not off to a good start.

"Protected. I've spent my entire life being protected."

That's a little better.

"And I am so grateful for the role you *all* have played in making sure I stay alive in a world that wishes I didn't exist. But things have changed. They're worse."

"But Kal-" his mother interjected.

"Please, Mom. Just let me finish." He had been expecting her to protest. "The Awakening challenged me in ways I'm not sure I even understand yet. But the thing I learned most is that I can't be a bystander to suffering," he continued, shifting his gaze from one side of the room to the other, making sure they all really heard what he was saying.

"People like me are hiding who they are because they are scared. And when they are caught, Gods forbid, The Order shows no mercy. It's not right," Kalen whispered.

His father slowly walked toward him, putting his hand on his shoulder. An acknowledgement that he was standing with him. That he trusted him. A nudge to continue. That he would be by his side for the hardest parts.

"So, I want to go to Evermere."

A sarcastic laugh came from his left. "I've heard enough. This is ridiculous, Kalen. Evermere isn't safe for you," Eugenia started.

Kalen turned to face her and watched as his mother squeezed her best friend's hand.

"Let him finish, Genie." She nodded toward Kalen, tears pooling in her eyes.

"I've thought about this a lot. And I think the only way to make any real difference is to be on the inside. To become...one of them. An Orderly."

"Well, I'll go," Tessan said first, without a second thought. "I have no desire to be an undercover Orderly, but I've learned Wyrdbrook kind of sucks without you."

"No offense, Liam."

"None taken," the Overseer laughed in response.

"So anyway, I'll go."

Kalen's heart warmed.

"I'll be there in black." His father winked.

Wen.

"I'm sure it goes without saying that I can't leave Wyrdbrook. But I will make sure you have all of the provisions you need for your travels," Liam chimed in.

The Overseer believed in him.

"This is a horrible idea, Ria." Eugenia turned to his mother. "You can't let him do this. They'll kill him if they figure out who he is."

His mother turned from Eugenia and looked Kalen in the eyes. A single tear fell down her cheek.

"Are you sure?" The question was pointed. No hidden agenda. It wasn't a trick. It was a knowing that passed between the two of them. He imagined they were back in the Sanctwood, talking about their day. When life was easier.

"I...don't know. I don't know if I can change anything." His voice was strong. Even if he wasn't certain, he knew his magic was pulling him to Evermere somehow. "But I think I have to go anyway."

She stood for a moment, staring at him. Kalen had no idea what she was thinking, if she'd ever really give him her blessing to go after what his father had experienced at the hands of The Order.

"I need you to tell me it's okay." Kalen walked toward her. "I can't do it without knowing you'd be okay."

She peeked around his shoulder, looking at his father. Kalen turned around, eyes pleading with him.

Help.

"He can do this, Ria." His father nodded. "You know he can."

She hesitated before she walked toward him, bridging the gap between what is and what could be, and grabbed his hand.

"Then count me in, my love." His mother never said things she didn't mean. That's why sometimes she never said anything at all.

He knew how hard this would be for her. Accepting that he would actively be in harm's way every day. That the risk she was taking was losing him forever.

She'd said yes anyway.

How did he get so lucky?

Standing here between his mother and father was everything he had ever wanted.

His family.

"Well, Gods damn," Eugenia interrupted his thoughts. "I guess I'm in, too. When do we leave?"

It was enough to make him weep. They were all on board.

I did it.

"Tomorrow," Kalen responded. "We leave tomorrow."

Chapter Twenty-Seven
Kalen

"We couldn't have waited until the sun came up?" Tessan yawned, tossing her bag over her shoulder.

Kalen laughed.

The morning air was nipping at their heels, telling them to pick up the pace. As if the forest was waiting for their return. For *his* return.

They'd spent the rest of the day yesterday planning their accommodations and travel plans. Tessan had protested then, too, at the mention of the early morning start.

She was outnumbered by the rest of the group. They'd leave at first light and not a second later.

The group decided Tessan and Eugenia would stay in Evermere at Eugenia's home, keeping her safe from her father at all costs. Kalen would be able to sleep there if he were ever in the city too late.

On most nights, though, he would stay in the Sanctwood with his mother and father. His father had to spend most of his time as Wen—his mother wouldn't let him stay with them otherwise. At night, he and his father would sneak deep into the forest to train his new magic, just as Liam had suggested before the Awakening began.

It wasn't a foolproof plan. There were so many things that could go wrong. But he couldn't worry about what came next yet—he just needed to move forward.

For now, they'd go back to the Sanctwood and exist as they'd always unknowingly been existing. The forbidden trio.

He couldn't help but wonder how this would all work out with his mother and father. Would they be civil? Or would his dad stay in crow form long enough that they'd avoid each other altogether?

He hoped not.

He found himself daydreaming of his parents forgiving one another. He could almost picture the quiet moment.

Maybe he would be getting home one evening from Evermere, and see them sitting together at the kitchen table, talking quietly, leaning in close, hands intertwined.

Maybe he would find them sitting under the oak tree one morning while he was foraging.

Some days, he felt like he had grown up quite a bit during the Awakening, but then he would have thoughts like this and realize there were moments when he still felt like a child who just needed his parents to be okay.

The group had broken off into steady pairs now, he and Tessan walking just ahead of his mother and Eugenia.

His father flew overhead, keeping watch, diving and swooping from tree to tree, with the promise to alert the group of anything that could deter their trip.

He was grateful for that, considering everyone he cared about, save for Liam, was here together. If anyone was looking for one of them, they'd find them all.

And that was a thought Kalen couldn't stomach.

He just needed them all to get home safely.

Home.

The word tasted different in his mouth now that he had been in Wyrdbrook. A place where he could fully be himself, without having to hide. The idea of retreating to the life he had known before felt like he was moving backward. But he wasn't, not really.

Because this time, he didn't plan to hide. This time, he wouldn't be scared. This time, it was what *he* had chosen.

He hadn't been back to the Peaks since he made the trek up to Wyrdbrook over two years ago. He knew a grueling descent was coming, but for now, they enjoyed the flat walk out of his safe haven.

His mother and Eugenia had fallen into conversation, catching up on the last few days, soft whispers of their own language shared between them. His mother was oblivious to the lies her best friend had been hiding from her for so long. The ones she was still hiding.

He wondered if his mother would forgive her best friend when she found out about how the web of lies they had woven had led them all to this moment. His mother was an angel, but that type of forgiveness might take an act from Earth Mother herself.

Kalen had made the decision to tell her himself if Eugenia wouldn't tell her on her own. But for now, his mother needed her best friend just a tiny bit more than she needed the truth.

"You know, you've been a lot nicer to me since I got back from the Awakening." Kalen turned back toward Tessan. He felt more confident in their friendship now that he knew she had stuck by him for two years.

"I figured you'd need some time to reacclimate without my bullshit for just a few days," Tessan replied. "Don't worry, I'll be back to my typical self before you know it."

"Good. I like your typical self," He responded without thinking.

What the hell was that? Just go with it.

He winked.

Oh my Gods, I have lost my mind.

"Gross, Kalen." She laughed.

Maybe death out here wouldn't be too bad.

He had to change the subject.

"How are you feeling about being back in Evermere?"

"I'm a little nervous, actually. I just..." Her voice broke just a bit. "I just don't want to see him. You know?"

"Yeah. Maybe we should come up with a safe word? When it all feels like too much and you just want to get away," Kalen suggested. "And no matter what, we stop what we're doing and go to the forest. Take a walk. Anything."

If she was making this trip for him, the least he could do was make sure she was comfortable while she was there. He wasn't even sure how long they'd need to stay.

"I like that." Tessan kept steady, though Kalen noticed her thoughts seemed far from her.

"What about *crow*?" She said straight-faced, her voice playful.

"Stop."

"What!" she exclaimed. "I thought that one was solid."

"Fine. We'll go with it, but only because I can't think of anything better," Kalen conceded. He liked the idea of letting her win *sometimes*. Though he knew she wasn't the type of witch to expect a handout.

"Crow it is, then," Tessan sang back.

This group–his family, found and otherwise–headed back to the Sanctwood Forest. The place that had kept their secrets for so long.

He wondered what other secrets they'd all uncover when they arrived—if they'd ever be the same as they are right now.

He didn't have much time to consider it, as they began to crawl down the side of the Peaks, straight toward a future he knew none of them could possibly predict.

Chapter Twenty-Eight

Ria

*G*ods, *it's good to be home.*

Ria's cottage sat exactly as she had left it when she took off through the forest after Eugenia earlier that week.

If she had only known then what she knew now.

Her signature spices were strewn across the counter of her kitchen. The fragrance of her house was the same as it had always been—lavender and vanilla.

It was Kalen's favorite smell, so she made sure the scent remained the same, just in case he ever popped home for a visit.

He never did. She now understood why.

If she had any idea she would be coming back with Eugenia, Kalen, Tessan, and *Westin*, perhaps she would have cleaned up a bit.

But maybe not. It was her home, after all. Mess included.

The group arrived at her cottage as the sun was setting. Their timing was perfect, though they didn't consider how drained they'd all be after such a long day. Their legs were burning, their lungs on fire.

The trip was taxing, and somehow felt longer to Ria, knowing her home was waiting for her on the other end.

They'd decided in the last three miles that everyone would stay at Ria's tonight to eat and rest. They hadn't relayed that message to Westin, as he was too busy keeping watch.

Keeping them safe.

It pissed her off. He was so self-righteous. She didn't ask him to protect her or Kalen.

She ushered the small group into her home, considering what she had to cook for them. She was sure she could throw something together that would fill their bellies for what came tomorrow.

Everyone was getting settled, collapsing onto the floor, on chairs, on whatever could brace their fall. All but Wen–Westin. He sat perched where he had always been, all these years. Just watching her from the outside.

She asked him not to talk to her. She meant it. And he listened.

She hated that he listened. She hated even more that she wished he hadn't.

Her love for him fueled her hate for him. It was blinding. It was honest.

It was going to tear her apart.

She walked over to him, slowly, and watched as the bird tilted his head.

This is not a peace offering.

"We've had a long day. I know you're exhausted." She kept her voice gentle, considering what story he was going to believe in this moment. "I'll be right back."

Ria walked out of his sight, just long enough to quickly flip a few rocks, knowing exactly what she was foraging for.

"Enjoy your dinner," she said, putting a worm in his beak, before walking back inside and slamming the door.

It felt powerful.

It felt horrible.

She briefly looked out the window, watching as the crow threw the worm up in the air and gulped it down, keeping his eyes on her the whole time.

Gods damn it, Westin Vale.

The evening ended quickly after their stomachs were full. She was able to gather enough ingredients for a mushroom casserole, and though it wasn't her best meal, no one had the energy to complain.

Eugenia walked over to her slowly. "Goodnight, honey." She gave her a quick hug. "Thanks for dinner."

Ria settled into the safety of her friend's embrace. No matter which way her heart was pulling her, to or from Westin, she would lean into the warmth of her truest companion, her Genie.

The house was quiet now as Eugenia and Tessan headed off to Kalen's room to rest. He insisted they'd sleep in there while he stayed on the common room couch for the night.

Her boy and his big heart.

She walked over to him, sleeping soundly, though his long legs were dangling off the edge of the furniture that had once swallowed him whole.

The time was moving too fast, but she was grateful for every day she had with him.

She sat down on the side of the couch, running her fingers through his hair. Wondering what she had missed while he was away–what he had endured while in the Awakening.

She could tell he had changed. But it wasn't in a bad way. He was more himself. More sure. He looked people in the eyes when they spoke to him. He laughed without abandon, never feeling shame.

She knew he was special. He'd always been special. But this felt different. Like maybe he knew it too. Guilt swirled in her stomach as she wondered if she had done him a disservice by not getting him to Wyrdbrook sooner.

She had missed him here. Her home felt whole again. Here, on the couch.

Here.

He slowly woke up. A sleepy haze covered his eyes, but he smiled up at her anyway.

He was worth the pain of meeting Westin.

She would do it again if it meant she got Kalen.

She'd probably do it again if she didn't.

She hated the hold he still had on her. It didn't feel like an embrace; it felt like a noose around her neck. One wrong move and it would kill her.

"Thanks for letting everyone stay here, Mom." Kalen yawned, sitting up to make room for her.

"I was happy to." She leaned back into the couch, her legs still tingling from the day's travels. "I like Tessan, for what it's worth."

He chuckled. "Well, I like Dad. For what *that's* worth."

Kalen Halrowe.

"That's not funny." She pulled him into her shoulder, continuing to stroke his hair. It had grown so long since he had been away.

But he sat up abruptly, breaking her touch.

"I'm not trying to be funny," he answered, his voice no longer covered with exhaustion.

What in Earth Mother's name?

"Then you're being cruel. And I don't know you to be cruel." She hoped he would hear the pain in her voice. She was begging him not to do this. Not tonight.

They just needed to sleep. They'd talk about this some other time.

"Mom." He grabbed her hand, begging her to look at him. "I don't know how, but during the Awakening..." He exhaled shakily, "I saw his suffering. All of it."

Her heart stopped.

"I saw the way they mutilated his ears. His torture," Kalen kept on as if he were in a distant place, dissociating from the words he was speaking. "He showed me his memories, too. When we first met," he continued. "The guards...they'd ask where you were. And every day, he would tell them to fuck off. That he'd rather die than endanger you."

Kalen was speaking in a flurry, and she couldn't dodge the words being hurled at her.

He needed to stop. Now.

"Why are you doing this, Kalen?" she interrupted.

"Because I've been mad as hell, too." His voice raised just a bit. "He left *me*, too."

"*Shhh.*" She nodded toward his bedroom, a reminder of the sleeping witches behind the door.

"Sorry," he whispered. "I'm just saying I know how you feel. And forgiveness feels better."

"You're wise beyond your years, Kale. But this isn't something you could understand fully. Not quite yet," she responded tenderly. "You've never loved someone the way I've loved him."

"I know." He shrugged. "But he's been through a lot, Mom." He squeezed her hand tightly. "Just hear him out."

"Kale–"

"For me?"

Ria sighed. He never did this–asked her for things. He spent his whole life not pushing her, not asking a single question about his father, just so she would stay comfortable. It wasn't fair of her to ask that of him now.

If Kalen could forgive him, could she?

For Kalen, maybe she would try.

"Okay," she responded slowly.

"Okay?" He smiled in return.

"Only for you. Always for you."

Kalen leaned back into her now, his warmth a reminder of the gift of knowing Westin Vale.

"It's kind of for you, too." Kalen nudged her. "I see how you look at him."

"Okay, that's enough from you." She laughed. "I'm headed to sleep." She pushed his head off her shoulder playfully.

"I love you, Mom," he called to her as she walked away.

Making a quick stop in the kitchen for an extra serving of casserole, she called back quietly, "I love you more than you'll ever know, Kalen."

She took a few steps toward her room, waiting patiently for Kalen to turn around and lay his head down before she changed course and headed out the back door.

It was embarrassing how quickly that conversation changed her mind. Like it gave her permission to forgive.

She wasn't ready yet. Not completely. But this was a start.

It didn't take her long to find the crow, still perched, watching over her home.

"Sorry for earlier." She looked at the bird squarely in the eyes before placing down the leftovers. "Enjoy your dinner, Westin."

She scratched the bird's head before jogging softly back to her cottage. She slipped in the back door. Kalen was still fast asleep on the couch. At last, her head hit her own pillow.

She closed her eyes tightly, willing sleep to come and restore her after such an exhausting day.

Instead, she thought about West.

Over, and over, and over.

Until the thoughts became dreams.

And he met her there, too.

Chapter Twenty-Nine
Kalen

Kalen smiled to himself as the back door quietly latched shut–his mother's feeble attempt to sneak out and give his father a proper dinner. He would play along for now, acting as if he had no idea.

Maybe fae hearing wasn't so bad, after all.

Kalen walked into the warmth of the morning sun, the blades of grass wedging between his toes as if they were hugging an old friend. He needed to ground himself in who he was before the day ahead. He was going to take his first real trip since childhood to the village that lay just beyond the forest that raised him.

The village he had been curious about for so long.

He wondered how his body would react to seeing the places that haunted his dreams. Would he freeze in fear? Would it affirm that he made the right choice by coming here?

Would he still smell the blood of his father's suffering? Would the white marble floor of The Hollow carry a slight stain of red?

What if there was a Severing while he was there today? It was something he wasn't prepared to face in person.

Not yet.

He carried what happened to him during the Awakening close to his chest. He could sense that the others were curious about what he saw and how he had changed. And he would tell them one day. But it wouldn't be today.

Today, his brave thing would be Evermere. And that would be enough for him.

His father was the only one of the group who knew Kalen was unsure of his own plan. Their conversation in the kitchen was simple; Kalen's magic was calling him back here to finish what had been started in the Awakening. No one deserved to suffer like that again. Not if he could help it.

Sometimes the first step was to just...go. And he trusted his instincts, maybe for the first time in his life.

He would figure it out when he got there.

Maybe.

If he didn't get caught first.

He wondered if that was the point of all of this, of being called back. To stay open to what could come and what he would learn. For the first time in his life, he was the one in charge of his own destiny.

Whatever was going to happen would happen. He would just have to be ready for it when it did.

"Do you remember what we talked about?" His father walked toward him, finishing up his morning foraging. He handed Kalen a handful of berries to snack on for his trip to Evermere. He hadn't seen much of his father since they arrived back. He had kept his distance, perched on a tree in his crow form. Kalen was grateful to see him standing on two legs today.

"Yes." Kalen popped a berry into his mouth, "I am a witch who has been studying the teachings of Athero for the last few months. I'm looking for community and to grow in my faith and understanding of the covenant."

His Dad nodded, confirming what they'd discussed just a few nights prior.

Maybe he had more of a plan than he thought.

"And if they ask about your parents?"

"My mother and father were both witches. My father died when I was a boy from an incurable disease. It plagued my mother's mind, as she was a healer."

"Perfect." He pulled Kalen into a tight hug. "I'm so proud of you, you know? For trying to make a difference. You're braver than I ever dreamt of being."

Kind. Brave. Gentle.

Their conversation was interrupted by the squeak of the front door opening. His three favorite witches were filing out of his mother's small home. He didn't know if it was still his anymore, or if he'd go back to Wyrdbrook when this was all said and done.

Maybe she would come, too.

He enjoyed being back in the Sanctwood last night, even if his aching back was a reminder that he hadn't slept in his own bed.

He didn't mind, though. It was better than his most recent long bout of sleep.

Tessan passed him a grin, her eyes clear. So blue. *At least she had a good night's rest.*

His mother's face, though, was worried and still. She walked toward him quickly, and the scent of her sadness filled the air. He wondered if his dad could smell it, too.

"I'll be back tonight, Mom. Everything will be okay," he said confidently, trying to calm her fears before they overwhelmed her.

"I know. I just worry for you," she whispered.

"That makes me pretty lucky." He squeezed her hand. "I'll tell you everything when I get back later. Deal?"

She nodded.

"Take care of him!" she shouted toward the group.

"I will," they all answered in unison.

It prompted a smile.

Kalen looked at the group of people around him. It was more than he'd ever wanted–his *family*. Chosen, found, and blood. And somehow, someway, they'd found their way here. To each other despite it all.

"Hey, Dad? Why don't you hang back?" Kalen asked his father.

He may not have much of a plan for Evermere, but he definitely had a plan with his parents.

His mother and father whipped their heads toward him in unison. His mother's stare was beady, his father's was playful.

Kalen smirked. They were so different, and both so good. He felt grateful to finally have them together.

"Eugenia knows the way better than any of us." Kalen doubled down.

His father looked at his mother, his eyes full of hope, of desperation.

"What do you think, Ria?" he questioned sincerely.

Would she ask him to stay? Would she say it was okay?

Please tell him to stay.

"*Apparently*, you've always been around," she quipped. "Since when do you need my permission?"

Shit.

His father dipped his head.

"Be safe, Kale," he responded quietly, before shifting and flying deep into the Sanctwood.

His mother lowered her gaze in shame. Kalen didn't blame her for the response. It would take time to figure it all out.

Hopefully, time was a luxury they could afford.

With nothing left to say, Kalen gave his mother a quick hug, and the small group headed off to Evermere.

Toward the mystery of The Order.

Toward whatever the hell lay ahead of him.

He sent a quick breath of gratitude to Earth Mother for the beauty of the morning. Then, one simple plea.

Please keep me safe.

Their trip to Evermere was uneventful at best and loud at worst. Eugenia and Tessan still had a lot to catch up on, so Kalen made himself small and listened to the love shared between aunt and niece. Their laughter blended with the sounds of the birds chirping, the wind pushing them all straight to Evermere.

Eugenia's house was exactly as Kalen remembered it from his father's memories. Tinctures of oil and healing salves were scattered about, a perfect depiction of who Eugenia was at her core–the one who made things better. He did a quick walkthrough of the home before he took off toward The Hollow. He needed to confirm everything was exactly as Eugenia had left it. Especially now that Tessan was here.

He owed that to her.

He found comfort in knowing Eugenia would take care of her if anything happened–if her father showed his face. Not that Tessan needed anyone to take care of her.

Regardless, he had seen the way Eugenia had always watched out for him. At whatever cost. Even if it meant lying.

He still hadn't confronted her about her involvement in his father's lie. He understood why his father did what he did. But in some unfair and cruel way, the betrayal felt bigger coming from her.

She could have told his mother at the very least. He didn't understand why she hadn't and couldn't imagine she had a good enough reason.

He was going to talk to her about everything soon enough, but today wasn't the day. If he didn't take one thing at a time, he would never make it through.

So today, he focused on The Order.

Kalen headed out the door and toward the town square, deciding he would retrace his steps from what he experienced during the Awakening—hoping it would lead him to where he needed to go somehow.

Evermere was bustling, just as it had been every time the loop reset. He felt his pulse start to quicken at the idea that somehow the last few days had been a dream that had ultimately led him back here.

The one thing that tipped him off was that it wasn't Market Day—and it didn't smell like fish.

He could breathe again.

Kalen quickly learned he wasn't dressed for this weather. He had been used to the shade of the towering trees of the Sanctwood, but here, in Evermere, he felt exposed. His dark hair was burning as the sun shone brightly, beating down on his scalp.

If he had money, he'd be bartering for some type of cap. Instead, he would seek solace from the sun by traveling to the High Seminary.

The thought of the stone building made his stomach turn. He wondered if it would seem as big in person as it did while he was in the Awakening.

He followed the beaten path to The Hollow, carved out by the footprints of those before him. Those who would rush to witness the horror awaiting someone innocent for simply existing in a world that didn't want them.

In a way, he felt like he was walking toward his own death sentence.

He understood his mother's worry more now than he did before. He understood her trust in him more, too.

She had experienced the ache of losing someone she loved at the hands of The Order. He wished he had thought about how it would feel for her to lose him, too.

But it was too late to turn back. It was too embarrassing to turn back, if he was being honest with himself.

After the speech he gave at the Veilhold? He couldn't imagine showing back up to Wyrdbrook and saying he couldn't do it.

Looking Liam in the eye and telling him his belief in him was for nothing.

No, he wouldn't do it.

The trip to the High Seminary was a mirror of what he had experienced while he was asleep. It was just him and a few other travelers making their way to and from the building that towered over the city. No scheduled Severings, no smell of blood, the white marble floor of The Hollow shone bright.

All that was left was to go in.

To face the terrors on the other side of the door.

He took a deep breath.

You belong here. You belong everywhere. You can do this.

He pushed open the heavy stone door.

His senses were on high alert, though he needed to keep the fact that he was half-fae under lock and key. He was just a witch from Evermere. Nothing less, and certainly nothing more.

"Hi!" a sweet voice rang out from across the room. "Welcome to the High Seminary. I'm glad you're here."

That makes one of us.

He couldn't see her yet, the owner of the voice. The space was so open and vast. It was a direct contradiction to the feel of the Veilhold. These walls told different stories entirely.

Where the walls of the Veilhold were meticulously carved as a reminder of the horrors that could be, these stood firm in the horror. Blank and slick, as if they were a canvas wiped clean of any stories the walls could tell on their own.

Everything was so grand. The ceilings felt taller than the towering trees of the forest. The floor was spotless, nothing like the dirt paths he had spent his life running down.

It was unnatural—it was forced.

Maybe he *didn't* belong here.

Maybe that was the point.

Just play along.

He faked confusion, acting as if the voice was echoing along the empty halls, though he knew exactly the direction it was coming from.

"Over here!"

It worked.

Kalen saw her now—the owner of the voice—sitting behind a large desk, a bright smile stamped on her face. He didn't expect to meet someone his age here. He thought The Order was reserved for the old men he'd seen during the Awakening.

But she...she was not an old man. She was not an old man *at all*.

He found himself wishing she were.

"Hi. I'm, um, I'm new here," Kalen stuttered out.

Gods, Kalen.

"That's an interesting name." She laughed in response.

"Sorry, I'm Kalen." His palms were slick with sweat.

Why was he so nervous?

"It's nice to meet you, Kalen. I'm Bryn. I'm the greeter here at the High Seminary." She gestured toward the large desk in front of her.

"So now that the greeting part is over, what can I do for you?" Bryn looked at him with a kindness he didn't expect from someone in The Order.

"I was hoping to get some information about how to become an Orderly?" he responded. "I'm new to Athero's teachings and looking for ways to get connected with others who believe like me."

Okay, settling in.

"Oh, wonderful," she responded. "We are always excited to welcome new folks." Bryn's green eyes sparkled while she talked.

He hated that they sparkled while she talked.

"I just need you to fill out this form, and then I'll give you a tour and we can chat more."

She slid a piece of paper in front of him, and Kalen looked down at the big, bold letters.

Registration of The Order

They register everyone who walks through these doors.

The registration was simple, but this wasn't something he and his father had talked about. He wasn't prepared to be filed away in a system, or whatever would happen with this paper.

A declaration that he had been here.

They hadn't thought that far ahead.

How could they have?

"Is something wrong?" Bryn curiously leaned forward. Her blonde hair covered the corner of his registration sheet.

He'd been staring at the form for a beat too long.

"No. Sorry. Just trying to understand what I'm signing up for here." Kalen kept the conversation light.

"We don't even use these. To my knowledge, at least," she followed up. "The Head Cleanser just asks that everyone fill them out regardless."

"The Head Cleanser?"

Of course, Kalen knew of Hauke Elowen. But what did other people think of the evil face of The Order?

"Yes." She grinned. "Hauke Elowen." The name rolled off her tongue in familiarity. "He's wonderful. I'll make sure to introduce you two on our tour if he's around."

Gods, I hope he isn't.

Kalen looked again at the sheet in front of him before putting pen to paper and filling out the registration form.

He was nervous, but his hand held steady as he signed his false sense of safety away.

Who else had done this? What was this for?

He just figured out the first part of his half-baked plan: find out what these forms were for, and how to destroy all of them.

Registration of The Order

First Name: Kalen

   Surname: Halrowe

   Underline one:

- <u>Witch</u>

- Fae

- Human

- Other:

Residence: Evermere

Lineage: Halrowe Witches

Shit.

He really was not prepared for this.

He passed the paper back anyway and sent up another prayer to Earth Mother.

It may take a miracle for him to get through day one.

"Kalen Halrowe," she repeated his name back after reading the registration form, and a small smile bloomed across her face.

Their eyes met, and a small smile bloomed across his, too.

This can't be happening.

"Ready?" Bryn grabbed his form, tucking it under her arm, before walking around the desk. "Fingers crossed we can deliver this to The Cleanser ourselves."

Kalen hated that Bryn was somehow more beautiful walking toward him than she was sitting down.

When she was behind the desk, she was out of reach. But here she was, walking toward him now, and he felt his cheeks grow warm, a new kind of danger coursing through his veins.

If he had any real experience with women, maybe he wouldn't even notice his attraction to the greeter. Maybe, she would just be another pretty person he met in passing.

But would she, really?

With her blonde hair and green eyes. The dimple that sat on top of her cheek when she smiled at him.

Why did she keep smiling at him?

This could be a fleeting thought if he had grown up around other people. Instead, he was stuck wondering about what her favorite color was. About what she dreamt of. Who she loved. *If* she loved.

He was being so immature. It was so dangerous.

And it felt impossible to stop.

His mind bounced between Bryn and Tessan.

His *friend*, Tessan. She made that much clear.

He hated that he was in enemy territory, walking toward the man who haunted his dreams, and couldn't think about anything other than the way Bryn smelled.

Like daisies.

This was going to be more difficult than he thought, in ways he couldn't have possibly anticipated when he arrived.

Chapter Thirty
Kalen

He couldn't get over how massive the High Seminary really was.

He and Bryn had been walking together in a comfortable quiet, nothing but the echoes of their footsteps bouncing off the walls. They hadn't made it to the first stop of her tour, but Kalen didn't mind the silence as he took in his surroundings. Casually looking for exits, for clues on what life was like as an Orderly. Anything he could take back to the Sanctwood and share with his parents.

He couldn't ignore the light buzz of his power the entire time he was with Bryn. It felt like a warning, but of course it was–he was walking through a lion's den.

"So, *Kalen Halrowe*," she said his name playfully, "Why haven't I seen you around Evermere before?" She spoke quietly, trying to avoid her voice carrying down the hall. "I'd remember a face like yours."

Is she blushing?

"Um." He tried to play it cool amidst the obvious flirting. "I stick to myself, really. I spend a lot of time in the Sanctwood." He tried to mirror her volume. The last thing he needed was to draw more attention to himself.

He decided he wanted to stick as closely to the truth as he could while he navigated what was to come with The Order. If he spun up too many lies, he risked getting caught in them. He saw it happen with his father, with Eugenia. The truth would come out, and it would hurt people.

He didn't want anyone else to hurt. That was why he was here in the first place.

"What could possibly be in the Sanctwood Forest that isn't here in Evermere?" She seemed curious, and it felt genuine. He wanted her to stop being nice to him.

"Everything." He shrugged. "Trees, berries, birds. All of the good stuff."

"Hm. I've never thought about what lies beyond the edge of Evermere," she replied simply.

Thank Gods for that.

Because aside from the trees, berries, and birds, she would have found him and his parents. And no one could know that. Especially not someone in The Order.

"Maybe you can take me sometime?" Her voice was vulnerable.

Hell no.

"Yeah, maybe." He kept his cool, but his lips tilted to a smirk.

He would never take Bryn to the Sanctwood.

"So how'd you get the job as the greeter of the High Seminary?" He would try to convince himself later that he wasn't actually curious about Bryn. That he was just figuring out how she fit into this world he was forcing himself into.

"My family has a pretty storied connection to The Order." She slowed her walk, hinting that they'd be stopping soon.

Kalen wondered what that meant, but he was toeing a fine line.

Would too many questions raise a red flag? Right now, Bryn was his in. He wanted to keep her close, but not too close. He wanted to keep her interested, but not too interested.

"Okay, we've reached our first stop." She held out her hand, showcasing a large door with a placard that read *Age of Athero*.

"This is where new Orderlys spend their first few months learning more about Athero's plans for all of us." She spoke as if she were reading from a script.

"Oh, okay, great," Kalen mumbled. He was not looking forward to this.

"We have a new cohort starting up in a few days, actually. I hope you'll join us. Class is only once a week in the early afternoon. I attend each one to keep my history sharp."

"Yeah, sure. I'll be there."

Gods, what was he getting himself into?

"Great. I'll save you a seat." She smiled.

Please stop smiling at me.

"Our next stop will be the Head Cleanser's office." She nodded her head to the right, a signal to change direction. "We'll just do a quick introduction, drop off your form, and then we'll be on our way."

Kalen nodded in response.

"How long have you known The Cleanser?" Kalen asked, an attempt at casual conversation.

"Oh, forever. He's been around for as long as I can remember," Bryn responded plainly. She walked just ahead of him, casually looking over her shoulder to speak.

"His office is just right here." She pointed to a door ahead on their left. It was cracked open slightly.

He was here.

The Head Cleanser of The Order. The man who tortured his father. The man who was responsible for tearing his family apart. For perpetuating the lie that people like Kalen weren't good enough–that they were *unclean*.

His power began pulsing, calling out to him to do something. To end him. To end all of this.

Not yet.

His body hummed with anticipation as Bryn knocked softly on the door before poking her head in. "Excuse me, sir? We have a new Orderly I'd love for you to meet."

"Okay, we can come on in," Bryn said, looking at Kalen with joy on her face at the invitation to enter. Oblivious to the fact that the man behind the door was a monster.

She had to be. No one would smile like this to meet The Cleanser. Not after what Kalen had seen him do.

He followed her anyway.

He lost his breath when he stepped into the office of Hauke Elowen. It was a sharp contrast to the rest of the huge building.

Small, uneventful, spotless. A sign hung on the wall directly behind his desk with The Order's motto, *Purity Above All.*

This motherfuc–

"Welcome to the High Seminary." Hauke's voice sent a chill down his spine.

He looked up to face the man for the first time. He seemed older here, in this version of reality. His long white hair hung down his back. His beard was well-groomed and kept close to his face. The golden cages still trapped the rounded tips of his ears.

He didn't seem capable of so much evil sitting in front of him like this.

Bryn walked over to Hauke and handed him Kalen's registration sheet. He smiled at her. It was genuine. Real. If he didn't know any better, it would have warmed his heart.

But he did know better. Because Hauke Elowen was a monster.

The Cleanser looked down at the paper, his eyebrows furrowed.

"Halrowe," he started thoughtfully. "I'm not familiar with that name."

"We're a pretty small family. Just me and my mother."

"Ah, that may be why." The Cleanser set the paper down on his desk before locking eyes with Kalen for the first time.

His magic spiked in response.

He stayed calm as the Head Cleanser tilted his head to the side. His eyes squinted slightly, a look of recognition.

This was a horrible idea.

"Just you and your mother? I'm sorry for your loss," he said skeptically.

Shit.

"Thank you, sir." Kalen bowed his head just a bit. "I was very young when he left us, but my father was a good man."

"I'm sure he would be very proud of you for showing up here today."

More than you know.

"Thank you, Head Cleanser. I believe so, too."

"Well, thank you for bringing him by, Bryn," he said as he looked at the blonde standing by his desk. "It's always a pleasure to meet our newest members."

"We appreciate you for making the time, Head Cleanser." She curtsied slightly.

It was time for them to leave.

He just needed to see what Hauke was planning with that paper. What had he signed his name to? Where did he keep them?

If he could just stick around for one more minute...

Bryn started toward the door, and recognizing that it would be weird to stay in the same place, Kalen followed.

"Oh, and Kalen?" Hearing his name from Hauke's lips would give him nightmares for the next month.

He turned around to face The Cleanser. He wouldn't be afraid. He could handle what came next. He would go down swinging if he had to.

"I look forward to getting to know you," Hauke smirked at him, his eyes locked again on Kalen's.

Was that a taunt? Did Hauke know who he was? He couldn't, right?

"Thank you, sir." The words tumbled out of his mouth as he stepped quickly into the hallway.

Deep breath.

Kalen could feel Bryn's joy radiating from her. She grabbed his arm in excitement. "He never says that to anyone!" she sang out.

"Lucky me." He grinned back.

He really shouldn't have come here.

The sun was setting as Kalen arrived back to the Sanctwood.

What a day.

He spent another hour walking around the High Seminary with Bryn, learning more about the ancient structure. Learning more about her, too.

She told him that young Orderlys who had left their family to join The Order were offered free meals and housing in the West Wing. He couldn't imagine anyone choosing to leave their family for The Order. Maybe especially now that he had a shot at having a family of his own.

Regardless, Bryn lived there by choice. She moved in when she was young, and that's how she ended up with the job as the greeter.

"Thank Gods." His mother was standing outside her door when he came into view of the home. She ran toward him, wrapping him in a tight hug.

"Mom, I've barely been gone a full day," he said, squeezing her back.

"I know. I know." She released the hug and rubbed her hands up and down his arms.

"Ready for dinner?"

Kalen nodded, lifting his head toward the horizon to look for his father. He didn't see him perched on his typical branch. He wondered how their day together went without him there to mediate.

"He's inside," his mother said reassuringly.

Kalen jerked his head toward her quickly.

Inside?

"Relax. He's joining us for dinner, that's it."

"I'm relaxed, Mom," Kalen barked back. He absolutely wasn't. "You relax." He nudged her shoulder.

They both let out a light chuckle and walked arm in arm toward their small, hidden sanctuary.

Their first real family dinner. A proper kitchen table sit-down. Maybe today wasn't so bad after all.

His father was already seated at the table when they walked in. He pulled up a chair from the common room to make their kitchen table a place for three to sit.

Three. As it should have been from the start.

"Welcome back from Hell, bud." His father kept his voice light, though Kalen could hear the small notes of fear.

"It wasn't too bad." Kalen sat down, relaxing into the back of the chair, arms lifted over his head in a deep stretch. "I even met Hauke Elowen."

Kalen's mother dropped her spoon. He watched as his father jumped up from the table immediately, walking toward her to help.

"Sorry. Sorry," she spoke softly as she leaned down to pick the spoon back up.

"It's no problem, Ri." His father continued to the bowls of ladled soup, picking them up and carrying them to the table.

Another glimpse into the way his world could have been.

The three of them sat quietly for just a moment, the tension in the air thick with a mixture of fragrant fiddlehead ferns and palpable anxiety.

"They make you register when you enter the High Seminary," Kalen started from the beginning. "I signed my name as Kalen Halrowe of the Halrowe witches." He scooped up a bit of soup and blew on it before continuing, "I know that no one knows who you are, Mom, so I thought it would be safer to try not to spin myself into a lie I couldn't keep up with."

"That's probably smart." She twirled her spoon in her bowl nervously. "What else did they ask?"

Kalen told them of the registration form, and how they were filed somewhere in Hauke's office. He told them how his first order of business would be to find out why they made people register in the first place.

He didn't, however, tell them about Bryn.

Why would he? He knew proximity to her was dangerous. But it was also necessary. And there was no reason to worry them more than he had to.

"I did tell them that I lived in Evermere, though," Kalen finished up. "So I'll probably need to visit a few times a week just in case they start to wonder why I'm not coming around."

"Just stay with Tessan and Eugenia when you can, and you'll be fine," his father said as he stood up to get himself another bowl of soup.

"Anyone need anything?"

Kalen and his mother shook their heads no. He watched her intently now. The fear was overwhelming her.

"I'm going to be okay." He reached out and squeezed her hand.

"I know." She looked up sadly, but squeezed back three times regardless.

Kind. Brave. Gentle.

"Ria, this soup is delicious," his father said, sitting back down, oblivious to the shared moment between Kalen and his mother.

"Better than the worms, huh?" Kalen poked fun at his father, and they all fell into an easy laugh.

"So much better." He kept laughing as he watched his father look his mother directly in the eyes. "*This* is so much better."

Get a room.

Kalen took that as his cue to stand up and get cleaned off.

"Ah ah ah," his father tisked, waving a finger in his direction, letting him get just close enough to the bathroom that it felt like a tease. "It's time for us to train."

He had forgotten about that part. The idea of using his power in this way was exciting. He didn't have to hold back or hide. He could just unleash. It might be exactly what he needed after a day like today.

"We'll see if you can keep up, old man."

"Meet me outside in two minutes," his father taunted. "Good luck trying to catch me."

In a flash, his father transformed into his feathered black form and flew out the window.

"I will never get used to that," his mother sighed sadly, before picking up her empty bowl and heading toward the sink.

"Me neither," Kalen replied truthfully.

But he wasn't talking about the way his father shifted before their eyes.

He was talking about the way they sat together peacefully, coexisting as a family, for the first time in twenty years.

"I'll be back. Wish me luck," Kalen said, taking off toward the door.

"Go for his right knee," his mother called to him. "That's always been his weakness."

Kalen grinned at the intel and at the fact that his mother remembered the small detail.

"You're the best," he yelled as he crossed the threshold from his house into the forest.

To the place where his magic hummed in perfect harmony.

He stopped outside the door, focusing on where his father could have gone. He whispered to the wind, "Take me to the crow."

And the wind responded with a light push to the left.

With a nod of gratitude, Kalen followed the whipping breeze through the forest. Running along the pine and the yew. The oak and the maple. They all called to him, too, whispering directions to the boy they'd helped raise.

Straight. Turn here. Keep going. You're close.

Until suddenly they stopped. And he knew his father was around here somewhere—

"Took you long enough." He hopped down from a tree and landed directly in front of him.

"I don't think it was too bad for my first time," Kalen spat back matter-of-factly. "So now what?"

"Now," his father looked at him lovingly, "we train."

Kalen watched, stunned, as his father brought his hands together and, with one quick clap, they were encircled in a ring of fire.

"Hope you like it hot," his father growled, crouching low into a fighting position.

Kalen's lips lifted into a smirk.

"*Actually*, I don't."

And Kalen clapped back, sending a blanket of rain falling from the sky, extinguishing the fire in mere moments.

His father looked at him in awe.

"But I hope you do." Kalen quickly stopped the rain and sent out a quick burst of flame toward his father, trapping him in a circle just big enough for him.

His father's laugh rang out through the forest. It was full of pride, of wonder, of joy. And it was because of Kalen.

What a gift.

He lowered the flames surrounding his father, just enough for him to step through before he extinguished them again.

"You, my son, are remarkable." His father put his hand on his shoulder. "How'd you learn all of this?"

"You wouldn't believe what I've been through in the last two years." He shrugged. "What it took to get out of there."

They stood quietly, his father giving him the space to recharge.

"I want to see what else that magic can do." His father's voice filled the silence before he shifted and took flight, as Wen again, soaring around Kalen. Weaving in and out of the trees, taunting him from above.

Kalen knew he didn't inherit his father's ability to shift into an animal during the Awakening, which was kind of a bummer. He always wondered what it would be like to fly.

He did, however, inherit shifting magic of his own. Magic he had never known before. The ability to manipulate environments into a brand new space. The only person who had seen it up to this point was Liam, but that was about to change.

He dug deep into his well of power, still unsure of where his limit existed, knowing that he was safe enough to test those limits now. His father wouldn't let him get hurt.

Kalen put his palms out and closed his eyes, then slowly lifted them up, casting the illusion that more trees had appeared in the forest.

Dense and never-ending. His father was dodging trees that Kalen knew only existed because he, himself, had put them there. It wore him down slowly, until his defenses had fallen just enough for Kalen to call up one final tree.

His father dodged it at the very last second, shifting back to his human form just in time to land on his feet.

"What the hell?" He was running toward Kalen now. "I've never seen anything like that."

"I don't know what it's called. But I can manipulate elements to look like other things," Kalen gasped, the weight of what he had just done began pulling him down.

His father's mouth was open in awe. "Who knows?"

"Just Liam. I shifted my living room to look like his office back in Wyrdbrook."

His father ran his hands through his hair in disbelief.

"Don't tell anyone else, okay?" he said, his face stern. "You can tell your mother, obviously," he amended. "She doesn't deserve to have anything else kept from her. But no one else."

"Okay," Kalen answered quickly. He felt like he was in trouble somehow. Like he had done something wrong, though he knew he hadn't.

He spent his whole life just listening to what other people asked him. He never pushed back, never asked why. If he needed to grow, maybe he needed to break that cycle now.

"Actually," he looked at his father, "why can't anyone else know? I'm not ashamed of what I can do."

"I'd never want you to be, Kale." His father put his hand over his chest, as if showing Kalen he was being genuine, honest.

"But that magic isn't fae or witch, buddy. It's hybrid," his father continued. "If someone else found out you could do that and it somehow got back to The Order..." his voice trailed off. "It would be a dead giveaway of who you are. Of what you come from. It just wouldn't be safe."

Was safe the point?

He found himself regularly vacillating between the world he wished existed and what it could cost him to get there.

Would there ever be a day he woke up and didn't have to worry about being different from other people? Where he woke up and wouldn't have to pretend he was someone he wasn't?

He guessed that was what he was fighting for in the first place.

"Yeah, I understand," he replied. But his understanding didn't change the fact that it made him feel small. He was living in the shadows for his safety, but at the root of it, it was because people didn't think he should exist as he did.

If he weren't so well loved by his mother for all of his life, that thought may have crushed him.

He couldn't change everything in a day. It wasn't possible. But he could keep training to prepare for what came next. No matter what it was.

"Let's go again." He cleared the trees he had sent sprouting from the forest floor with a wave of his hand.

His father laughed.

"Show me what you got, little crow."

Chapter Thirty-One
Kalen

K alen rolled over in his bed, throwing the cover over his head to protect his eyes from the beaming sun. He had no idea how long he had been asleep.

His body was aching. His mind was far away. He had pushed too hard last night. He could almost taste ash in his mouth, and his blood felt muddy. This was new.

He did not like it.

He had felt himself slipping away from who he was during his training session. Attack after attack, he felt himself caring less about the impact of his magic on his body, caring less about any harm it could cause others, too.

He knew then that it was time to stop, but he couldn't. He was drunk on how powerful he felt. He hated that he understood Hauke better than he ever had in that moment. A little power can change someone's brain if they aren't careful. If they didn't have the right people around them.

He needed to keep himself in check and stay close to the ones who loved him most. He couldn't lose himself to gain something else. It wasn't worth it.

He racked his brain trying to remember how he stopped and how he had made it to bed. He didn't know. But here he was, head tucked under his cover, the world hazy.

Sore as hell.

He groaned as he stood—his muscles screaming at him to stay in bed. If it were another day, he would have listened. But he needed to go back to Evermere and be seen by a few Orderlys around town in an attempt to make his story more believable. He had always been here—but no one had noticed him before. Maybe he and Tessan could go for a walk and catch up a bit. It had only been a day, but he missed her anyway.

The floor creaked as he stepped into the common room, surprised to see his mother and father sitting and talking at the kitchen table.

It was enough to snap him back to reality, despite the fog that existed in his brain.

"Good morning," he called out, his voice gravelly with the deep sleep from the night before.

"It's actually almost time for lunch, sleepy head." His mother got up quickly and walked over to him, putting her hand on the back of his head. "How do you feel? Your father told me you pushed pretty hard last night."

"I kicked his ass." His father chuckled and took a sip of water.

Kalen would remember this moment forever. The picture of waking up to his parents together. His father was at the table, like he had always been there, and it wasn't a big deal.

But it was. To Kalen, it was a really big deal.

"I'm fine. Just sore. It's good for me," he said, hugging his mother before walking over and flicking the back of his father's neck. "I was taking it easy on you, by the way," Kalen chirped back before stealing his mother's chair. His legs were weak, not quite awake. He just needed to sit a bit longer.

"I'm going to head back to Evermere today to hang out with Tessan and Genie," he shared, while his mother set down a plate with toast and cloudberry jam spread on top in front of him. It looked divine.

"I have a class tomorrow for The Order, so I'll probably just stay the night in Evermere if that's okay?" He took a bite of the bread and threw his head back to savor the sweetness of the berries.

Gods, this is good.

"Told you, Ria." His father grinned in his mother's direction.

"Told her what?"

"That I kicked your ass. I knew you wouldn't want to train two nights in a row."

His parents both laughed. His mom's eyes were a bit brighter when she looked in his father's direction than they had been.

Kalen recognized this slow and steady pace toward forgiveness. If this were all it ever was, it would be enough for him. He wondered if it would be enough for them, too.

"Believe whatever makes you feel good, Dad," he continued, eating his toast.

His dad absolutely kicked his ass. But it wouldn't stay that way much longer. Kalen's power came naturally to him. It had been harbored away in his body, waiting for the right time to show itself. He knew it now as the constant buzzing in his veins. He had always considered magic as a companion, but he was learning it was more than that. It was a steady presence; it was a loud and consistent part of who he was, not just a passenger. Though right now the buzz felt more like a tired whisper.

"Hey, Mom? Would you want to come with me today?" he asked casually. She still needed to talk to Eugenia. If he could just get Tessan out of the house, maybe they could have that conversation.

"I think I'll hang back today, my love. Thank you for the invitation." She moved through the kitchen now, focused on everything but Kalen. "Next time, though."

"Next time for sure."

He was going to tell Eugenia today that she had until the end of the week to talk to his mother. To tell her the truth about his father and everything since then.

If she chose not to, he was going to tell his mother everything himself. He had a feeling it would land better coming from Genie, if it were going to land at all.

The only thing he knew for certain was they couldn't move forward until they faced all of this head-on.

Kalen gave his parents a quick wave goodbye before he threw his pack over his back and took off through the forest. He still didn't feel quite right from the previous night's training, but he could feel himself gaining some strength. He stopped before he got too far away from the house and threw a few berries in his pack just in case he needed a boost.

The air was crisp today, flowing through his hair, kissing his scalp.

Gods damn, he belonged among the trees.

He had no idea why he'd always felt so connected to the physical world around him, but the more he learned about the mechanics of his magic, the more it made sense.

These trees raised him, in a way. They gave him a safe place to hide, shade on the days the sun wouldn't let up, and plenty of provisions for their meals day in and day out. How could anyone not see the beauty that lay within the Sanctwood Forest? How could anyone live in Evermere their whole life and never venture out here?

Kalen focused on his trip back to Evermere. He hadn't told Eugenia and Tessan he was coming, though he didn't think they'd mind.

Here's to a safe day.

His feet were aching as he arrived at Eugenia's front door. He was looking forward to sitting down again for just a bit. He sent a few quick knocks against the wooden frame and waited for their answer.

"Coming!" he heard a muffled voice yell beyond the door. "I'm coming!"

A few locks unlatched and Kalen was greeted by Eugenia's smiling face.

"Hey, you." She opened the door wider, giving him some space to step inside. "I didn't know you'd be here today."

"Tess! Kalen is here!" she yelled through her small home.

"He's here now?" Tessan called back with worry in her voice. "Be out soon!"

Eugenia laughed. "She slept in today. You should see her hair before she tames it."

Maybe one day he would.

"Do you think we can talk while she's getting ready?" Kalen requested. He found himself grateful for the bit of privacy, no matter how short-lived.

Eugenia nodded and headed toward her couch–the same couch from his father's memories, where he had convinced Eugenia to keep his secret. Where Eugenia had told his father about him.

And now he was here to tell her it was time to come clean. The irony of it wasn't lost on him.

Kalen let loose a big breath. "Dad showed me his memories. How he asked you to keep his secret from Mom."

Eugenia wouldn't look at him, sitting with her head down and hands in her lap. A painted picture of shame.

"How could you do that to her?" Kalen wanted to be kind and gentle–he did–but his anger was boiling now, threatening to spill over and burn them both.

"This is what I warned you about before you left," she started. "I don't expect you to understand why I made my choices." She stood up confidently, turning to face him.

"But I'd do it again. I'd do it all over again if it meant you and Ria were safe and left alone." She was looking at him now. The shame was gone, replaced with something firmer. She wasn't going to budge.

"We were never safe, Eugenia." Kalen stood, too, looking down at her. "Ever." His voice was rising now. "People were always looking for us. For him."

"You don't think I know that, Kalen?" She matched his tone. "You don't think I've spent the last fifteen years trying to keep track of every move the Gods damn Order has made?" She squinted her eyes and shook her head. "You can't possibly understand what it's like to carry a secret so big that if you share it, people die."

Oh, that's rich.

"*I* don't understand?" He laughed in disbelief. "I *am* the secret, Genie. *Me.* I was the one born unclean. I am part of the reason my father was sentenced to death in the first place. ME!" He yelled, pointing to his chest. "I do understand what it's like," he continued. "I also know what it's like to find out that the people you love have been lying to you. They're both hard. And almost impossible to reckon with."

Eugenia was quiet now. Her flames turned to embers right in front of his eyes.

"You're right. I'm sorry."

Woah.

He didn't know what he was expecting from her, but it wasn't an apology. Not this fast. Maybe not at all.

"You need to tell her. If you don't, I will." He was a bit calmer now that she had apologized.

"I'll tell her."

"Soon," Kalen warned.

"By the end of the week." She looked at him straight in the eyes; her resolve had returned. "You have my word."

"Thank you." He was uncomfortable now, the two of them sizing each other up in the small common room. This may have been the first time he was ever uncomfortable with Eugenia. But the conversation had to happen, despite the awkward silence that followed.

The door to Tessan's room flew open, though Tessan moved slowly and with intention.

"Well, to what do we owe *this* pleasure?" She smirked, walking toward him. "And what was with the yelling?"

"Noth–" Kalen started before Eugenia cut him off.

"Kalen told me my pastries were no good. Can you believe it?" She looked at Kalen. "Maybe The Order is right after all. Down with the hybrids!" She rubbed Kalen's arm before laughing and walking toward the kitchen. Kalen smiled after her.

They were going to be okay.

Maybe.

Hopefully.

"I thought we could go on a walk through the village. What do you think?" He moved closer to Tessan.

"Oh, wow. So all it took for you to show your face around here was a two-year magical sleep, and now you're ready to explore the town?" she joked.

"Yep. That's *all* it took." He rolled his eyes, laughing. "So? Walk?"

She didn't answer, just breezed past him and headed toward the door. He was frozen in place, watching her exist the way she did. So certain of herself and how she moved through the world.

"Well?" she called back. "Are you coming or not?"

Of course he was. He was pretty sure he would follow her anywhere.

The breeze welcomed them both as they stepped outside Eugenia's cottage.

"It's Market Day! I almost forgot," Tessan started. "Want to go check out the vendors?"

Kalen stopped abruptly.

Evermere Market. Fish. The Hollow. Hauke.

His breathing picked up rapidly. He didn't know how he expected his body to react, but it was clear he had a long way to go before he really processed all he experienced in the Awakening.

The noise of Evermere was falling away, replaced by a high-pitched buzzing between his ears. His breath was escaping him quickly now, just small, hurried puffs of oxygen leaving his body. He couldn't anchor to anything except this terror.

"Kalen?" He heard a voice, but it was distant. His sight was growing blurry.

"Hey, Kalen?" A hand rested on his shoulder.

He flinched, but the voice began to come through more clearly.

Tessan.

"Hey. Hey." Her face snapped into frame, his breath slowly filling his lungs again.

"Look at me."

So he did.

"Big deep breath, okay?"

Inhale.

The darkness slowly began to fade away. And when the fog cleared, all he could see was the witch with the icy eyes.

Exhale.

"I'm sorry," he whispered. "I don't know what happened."

"You have nothing to apologize for." The kindness in her voice was a balm. "How about we skip the Market?" she followed up. "I don't have any purits, anyway."

"No." He steadied himself. "I think I need to go."

He couldn't let what happened to him in the Awakening control his life. The only way to get through all of it was to face it head-on. He already faced the worst of it with Hauke. This was just another step toward accepting his power. Toward healing.

"You know when you're ready to talk about it, I'm here." Tessan looped her arm in his, the way she always did.

"I know." He grinned at the witch. "You're the best friend I've ever had."

And he meant it. There was no one in the world like Tessan Duscaire.

"I am quite literally the only friend you've ever had." She nudged him playfully.

"I did an amazing job picking you, didn't I?" He nudged her back. "Lead the way."

They walked toward the sound of the crowd, and though his mind was still protesting just enough—his panic was at bay thanks to Tessan.

He just hoped it stayed that way.

The voices of the Evermere Market washed over him. Deep, vibrant, rough. Not at all like the gentle streams he was used to in the forest, but instead like a roaring ocean.

He and Tessan were jammed shoulder to shoulder, the smell of body odor and sourdough swirled together in a pungent aroma.

Better than fish.

The longer they stayed at the Market, the thinner the crowd got. Unlike most other folks, they didn't have anywhere to be and nothing to buy. They slowly admired the work of the artisans, and Kalen watched as Tessan disarmed even the grumpiest of them when they learned the two of them were just there to browse.

He loved that about her. She was so tough to read, and so tender. She was so clever, always one step ahead, but continually compassionate. He was so grateful to know her.

"Kalen?" He heard someone call his name in the distance. He knew it wasn't Tessan—he was watching her talk to the gruff candle maker in front of him.

He turned around and saw her blonde hair bobbing toward him first. Bryn.

Shit.

"Hi!" she yelled again after they locked eyes.

"Hey, Bryn." He stuck his hand up in an awkward wave. "It's good to see you."

"You, too!" She reached out and touched his arm. "I don't think I've ever seen you in the Market before?"

"I typically come earlier," he replied. "Got a late start today."

Kalen felt a shift in the energy and realized Tessan had made her way back over to him.

"Who are you?" Tessan asked directly, her eyes full of skepticism and concern.

"I'm Bryn. I work at the High Seminary." She reached her hand out to shake Tessan's. "I gave Kalen a tour yesterday."

This ought to be good.

Tessan looked down at Bryn's outstretched hand before looking back up at her. She didn't take it.

Oh no.

"Nice to meet you, *Bryn*." She dragged out her name in condescension. "I'm Tessan, Kalen's–"

"Cousin," he responded quickly. "Tessan is my cousin. She's staying with me at my mother's house tonight, so we came to the Market to grab something to eat."

Cousin? Why did he do that?

"Sorry about that. She's protective of me." He put his arm around Tessan's shoulder. "I don't have much family, as you know." Kalen looked at Tessan, a plea in his eyes to play along.

Bryn stood in front of them awkwardly, her gaze bouncing between Kalen and Tessan as they fumbled through a story they hadn't rehearsed. Kalen wondered how obvious it was that they were lying. He hoped it wasn't evident at all.

"Oh, for sure. Kalen here tends to fall for every pretty girl he sees, so I'm just looking out for him," Tessan droned, her tone flat.

Oh Gods.

"Anyway." Kalen kept his arm around Tessan's shoulder and pulled her away hurriedly. "It was great to run into you, Bryn. I'll see you tomorrow for class."

"You, too, Kalen," she called back, defeated.

He moved them quickly out of earshot.

"What the hell was that about?" he snapped at her.

"What do you mean? I was just playing along, *cousin*," Tessan responded calmly.

"Did it bother you that I called you my cousin? What else would I have introduced you as? My best friend? My girlfriend?"

"Don't be gross." She rolled her eyes. "I just didn't expect cousin."

They walked in silence now, the cheer of the day left behind with Bryn.

Kalen didn't understand what happened—why Tessan got protective that way. He hated that she had met Bryn in the first place. Now he had to explain why he hadn't mentioned her before. He planned to leave out the part about not intending to tell any of them about her at all.

"Do you just want to go back to Eugenia's? It's been a long day, and we're both exhausted–" He tried to change the subject. To get them back to where they had been before. She cut him off before he could finish.

"Nope. I want you to tell me about her," Tessan replied, turning to face him fully.

"There's nothing to tell, Tess."

And it was mostly true. He didn't know Bryn. They'd just met the day before. What was there to tell? Why was she picking this fight?

"Do you like her?"

"I don't know her?"

"Just be careful, Kalen. She *works* for The Order. You have no idea what they are capable of."

Kalen felt his blood rising. He was sick of being told he didn't know things. That he didn't understand.

"I know th–"

"Tessan?" a voice called out to their left. Kalen instinctively stepped in front of the witch. Even in the midst of their fight, he would protect her from anyone. Whatever it took.

"It's okay, Kalen." She spoke softer now. "He's an old friend."

"Hi, James," she responded cheerfully. A violent shift from the conversation they were just having. "It's so good to see you."

"You, too." He looked her up and down, smirking. Kalen hated that. "It's been years. I was worried I was never going to see you again."

"Well, lucky you. I'm just with my cousin here." She slapped Kalen's back before moving past him. "Walking around the market."

"Nice to meet you, man," he said as he punched Kalen in the arm.

Is this how adults greet each other?

"Mind if I steal her away for a bit?" James looked at Kalen. "I don't mean to interrupt family time, but I'd love to catch up." This time, directed at Tessan, his smile was bright, and his eyes lingered.

Kalen wanted to punch him back.

In the face.

"Oh, *he* doesn't speak for me. I'd love to catch up." Tessan walked toward James now, looping her arm through his. The same familiar thing she had always done with Kalen. Did she notice? Did she do that with everyone? Was she trying to make a point?

"Don't wait up." She smirked at Kalen before walking down the alley. Kalen heard her laugh even as they turned out of his view.

Just two old friends. Catching up. It didn't bother him–why would it? Tessan was his friend.

Just his friend.

He would head back to Eugenia's and get some rest. He was still a bit wobbly from the night before, anyway.

The sights and sounds of Evermere were so incompatible with who he was. He was used to the chatter of birds, not people. The running of rivers, not toddlers. He didn't see how anyone chose a life like this when the serenity of the forest was just beyond the village's border.

Maybe he would have been like this, too, if things had been different for him and his mother.

"Hi, again."

How did she find me?

He turned. "Bryn." Kalen smiled. "If I didn't know any better, I'd think you were following me."

"Oh yeah right, I ran the other way after that interaction with your cousin." She laughed. "She's...intense."

"Yeah." Kalen didn't really want to keep talking about Tessan. He knew they'd sort it out at some point over the next couple of days, anyway. "She means well, though."

"I'm sure she does," Bryn responded awkwardly.

Where would this conversation go from here?

"Do you want to hang out for a little while?" Kalen heard the words falling out of his mouth before he realized what he was doing.

She was dangerous. She was a part of The Order. But she was so...*nice.*

"I'd actually really love that." She grinned. "I'd like to know more about you, if I'm being honest."

She'll never know me. Not really.

The sentiment made his stomach stir. She wanted to know more about *him.* Has anyone ever cared to know more about who he was outside of his identity as a hybrid?

The thought was enough to crack open his heart, just enough to feel a small piece of the blonde in front of him begin to nestle in. He didn't like the lies he was starting to spin, and alone time with her just meant he would have to weave more of them.

It would also mean she'd learn to trust him more, though. He supposed that would be worth the risk.

"How about that trip to the forest?" Kalen responded.

He laughed as her eyes widened with fear.

"Now?" she responded hesitantly. "But it'll be dark sooner than later, and what if the animals come out and–"

Kalen cut her off, laughing, "I'll keep you safe, you just have to trust me."

She squinted her eyes at him, her nose crunching playfully as she grinned. "I think I can do that."

You really shouldn't.

Kalen walked with Bryn toward the opposite edge of the Sanctwood Forest. Far enough to stay hidden from his father, and for his mother's cottage to remain safely unseen.

"Okay." Bryn sat up from the meadow she'd been lying in. "I get what you see in the forest. It's peaceful."

"Told you." Kalen chuckled. "There's no place like the Sanctwood." He opted to lean on a tree instead of lying next to her. He was trying his best not to get too close, but every time she leaned up to talk to him, he realized it wouldn't have mattered where he was in relation to her. Proximity to Bryn was intoxicating all on its own.

"Then why do you live in Evermere? You seem like the type that could, I don't know, build a house with your bare hands."

Kalen let out a deep laugh. "What does that mean, Bryn?"

The moon reflected off her eyes as she continued. "It means you look strong and seem capable. It's a compliment, Kalen Halrowe." She waved him over. "Lay with me?"

Shit. Think, Kale.

"Well, actually, we should probably get going. Tessan worries if I'm out too late," he replied, his sentence was full of conviction, but his voice was trembling. He hoped his insistence would be enough to avoid lying with her altogether.

"You're right. I don't want to be on her bad side. Help me up?"

That was easy.

Kalen reached out to help Bryn to her feet. His magic flared as their fingers brushed. Like it was roaring at him, telling him to pay attention to the greeter of the High Seminary. It was a warning he didn't need to heed–he couldn't take his eyes off of her.

Did danger feel like this?

He wondered if she'd felt it too.

He didn't have time to consider it before she gave him a hard tug, pulling him to the ground beside her.

"Bryn!" He yelped as he tumbled over her, falling into the meadow. The smell of clover rushed his nose, like the forest floor was finally welcoming him. "What the hell!"

She cackled. "I can't believe you didn't see that coming." She turned her body toward his, her hands resting under her cheek. "Just a few more minutes?"

He accepted his defeat easily and scooted closer to her, closing the distance from where he fell to where she lay. They'd never be able to do this again–what's the harm in one night? In a few more minutes?

"Okay. But just a few." Kalen flipped onto his back, an attempt to keep from staring at the blonde beside him. "I'd love to live out here, to answer your question." He kept his eyes on the stars shining above him, his hands interlocked behind his head. "Maybe one day I will."

Maybe one day I'll be back and can live freely and openly. Maybe one day I won't have to hide.

"I bet it feels nice to have dreams like that," Bryn spoke softly. "My whole life is already planned out for me."

Kalen knew how that felt in his own way. Your next steps being scheduled, forced to do things you didn't plan on your own.

"What if tonight we forget about the future and focus on right now?" Kalen replied. He was reminding himself that his problems would still be there when he woke up in the morning. "If you could snap your fingers and be anywhere in the world at this very moment, where would you go?"

Bryn was silent. The croaking of a toad in the background filled the void their voices once occupied. "I think...I think I'd stay right here."

Me, too.

"Okay, I have one for you." Bryn inched closer to him. "If you could change one thing about yourself, what would it be?"

That I'm not a hybrid.

The thought slipped through his mind before he registered what he'd considered. Did he really feel that way about himself? Or had the words of The Order sunk its claws into his self-worth that easily? Regardless, it wasn't a thought he could share with Bryn. It wasn't a thought he wanted to share with anyone.

"I think my nose is too big," he answered instead.

She reached out and ran her finger along its ridge. "I think it's perfect."

He was glad he was lying down because he was pretty sure her touch would have sent him to his knees.

An owl hooted in the distance, a reminder of how long they had been together. The sun had set a while ago, but their conversation was too full, too interesting, for them to have ended it before now.

"We should really get back to Evermere," he said, hoping he could get out of here before anything else happened between them.

"Dang it, Tessan." Bryn scoffed playfully. It made Kalen laugh. "This is the most fun I've had in a long time."

Kalen thought about it for a moment and resented the fact that he agreed. Bryn was amazing, kind, and surprisingly funny. There was no hard edge, no mystery. She was just who she was.

And who she was, was an Orderly.

"Me too." Kalen was amused by the Greeter of the High Seminary. "Can I walk you back?"

Stupid.

"Oh wow, handsome *and* a gentleman?" Bryn responded. "Where have you been all my life?" She moved her hand to her forehead and pretended to swoon.

Kalen blushed, huffing out a laugh to keep his cool. He stood up first, brushing off his pants, before reaching his hand out to Bryn. "Don't even think about pulling me down again."

"You can't blame me for wanting to spend more time with you," she said plainly, taking his hand.

Kalen was taken by her openness. Handsome? Gentleman? So freely admitting she enjoyed spending time with him? He wasn't used to anyone being so forward.

"Please." He didn't know what else to say. "I'm not sure the greeter of the High Seminary is supposed to flirt with the newbies."

"I won't tell if you don't." She grinned again, her dimple making an appearance on the top of her cheek.

That won't be a problem.

"I'm kidding. The Order usually encourages relationships between Orderlys." She was reciting again, back in her tour guide voice.

Panic crowded her face. "I'm not saying this is a relationship." She was speaking quickly now. "I'm sorry." She covered her face with her hands.

He reached out to move them, and his heart fluttered at the first touch of her fingertips on his. "Stop." He grinned. "It's okay."

She really was so beautiful.

She really was so off limits.

He wondered if this was how his father felt when he met his mother. Carrying a secret he knew would change everything—too afraid to be honest.

He had to stop thinking about her like this.

"Tell me...Why The Order for you?" Kalen was sure he had built enough rapport with her now to dig more into the history. "Most people our age don't care much about Athero, I've learned."

"My family has just always followed the covenant." She shrugged. "Ever since I was young, I never missed an opportunity to go to the High Seminary. It's just what I did."

Kalen wasn't expecting such a loose answer from her. Those were not the words from someone who was convicted by their beliefs.

"But, I do love it. You know?" She looked into the distance, smiling.

Those words were, though.

"It gives me a purpose. And, at the end of the day, I think Athero had it right with the whole purity thing."

His stomach dropped. The crack that had formed in his heart earlier, now threatening to grow in a different way.

But of course she felt this way. He didn't know why he was surprised. He knew who she was from the beginning and chose to spend this time with her anyway. Maybe the Awakening hadn't matured him as much as he thought it had.

"Yeah?" That was all he could muster up.

"I mean, I guess I can't *really* know," she continued. "But from what my grandfather has told me about hybrids, it seems like it's best. Apparently, they're very powerful and have a hard time controlling their magic."

He could feel his own buzzing now, a warning, fighting against every other feeling he was having. Telling him to get out of there.

He was having a hard time listening to it.

"But what if he was wrong?" Kalen questioned her. "Have you ever met one?" he continued. "I mean, I haven't...I just can't imagine they are all exactly the same." He was wading in dangerous waters now.

"Yeah. There's one who comes to class. They're allowed as long as they have vowed not to use their powers," she continued. "Hauke even allows them to stay in the High Seminary. Maybe you'll meet her tomorrow." She was curious. "If you're still planning on coming to class?"

"Yeah, I'll be there," he mumbled quickly, his mind still stuck on the fact that he could really meet someone like him. "But how will I know when I meet one? A hybrid?"

If there was a tell, he would need to know it now. It may be able to save his life if the time comes.

"Hybrids wear a golden bracelet on their wrist." She unknowingly reached down to touch her own. "Hauke gives them to each hybrid that converts to the covenant as a gift. He's so good to them, really."

"And that's the only way you know?" He was gaining so much information now that he didn't want it to stop. He needed to get back to Eugenia's so he could write it down and remember to tell his parents.

"You're really curious about this." She laughed.

"Sorry." He was embarrassed. He'd pushed too hard, too fast. "I just don't get to talk about this kind of thing with anyone else."

"Please don't apologize. I like talking to you. About anything." She smiled at him.

Fuck.

He grinned in her direction, continually surprised by how forthcoming she was.

Kalen saw the spire of the High Seminary off in the distance. His night with Bryn was ending.

And that was probably for the best.

"I'm going to take this last bit on my own." She stopped, facing him. "Thank you for today."

"Are you sure? We're so close–"

"I'm sure. Prying eyes, ya know?" she said quietly.

Who would be watching her?

He nodded. He had asked enough for tonight.

"Good night, Bryn."

"Good night, Kalen." She leaned in for a hug and, rising to her tiptoes, planted a kiss on his cheek. "I'll see you tomorrow."

Kalen gulped, flustered by her proximity, by the kiss still lingering on his cheek. "Yeah, tomorrow."

She waved before turning to walk toward the High Seminary.

Her home.

Kalen's hell.

An angel.

She would end up destroying him if he weren't more careful.

Chapter Thirty-Two
Tessan

*H*e *should be here by now.*

Tessan's decision to hang out with James wasn't about James at all. She didn't even like him.

Cousin?

She wasn't sure why it had burrowed under her skin the way it did. Maybe it was because she didn't like to see Kalen lying like that. Or at all.

It felt like he was already drifting too far from who he was, somehow. Maybe it was because it made her feel ashamed—like she had been reading into their relationship a bit more than she should have. He made it clear they were just friends. And that was fine with her. She thought so, at least.

For now, it had to be.

Regardless, she'd stay up and wait for the stupid boy. Because she couldn't imagine a world in which he didn't come back here.

Her thoughts were interrupted by the unlatching of the front door.

Finally.

She was lying on the couch, watching Kalen fumble through the pitch dark, tiptoeing around the room, trying not to wake the house. Like she would have possibly gone to bed without knowing he was safe.

"Took you long enough," she said from the darkness.

He jumped with fright before flicking a quick flame toward the lamp in the corner.

"What the hell, Tess?" he hissed. "Why would you do that?"

"Thanks for waiting for me to get home, Tessan," she mocked him in a deep voice, mimicking his own. "It means a lot to me that you care so much."

"Oh, don't wait up for me, Kalen," he mocked back. "Or did you forget you said that?"

"Well, here we are, huh?" she sighed. "Are we going to argue all night, or are you going to tell me what you were up to?"

"It's none of your business," he muttered back.

"Okay?" she responded, offended. "Sorry for caring."

Was he trying to hurt her? She thought they'd talk it out–that they'd go to bed fine. She didn't expect this version of him. He was on edge. He was hiding something. And he didn't want to tell her about it, which honestly made it worse.

"How was your time with *James*?" he scoffed.

"Lovely, actually."

Lie.

"We caught up for hours. We made plans to meet again soon. I'm really looking forward to it."

Lie.

"Great. Seemed like a nice guy," he stated plainly. She could have sworn she saw him roll his eyes.

She could tell him some version of the truth. That she didn't like the way he blurted out that she was his cousin when she wasn't, that she didn't actually want to leave with James, but was just trying to bother him the same way he bothered her. That she sat here all night waiting for him to get back because the alternative, him not coming, was too much for her to fall asleep on.

"Yep. I'm going to bed," fell from her mouth instead.

"Cool. Sleep well, then."

"Sure thing. See you in the morning, *cousin*." She rolled her eyes.

Close enough.

Chapter Thirty-Three
Kalen

"Morning, Kale," Eugenia sang, opening up the blinds to the common room. The light from the day poured over him, but the smell of breakfast was enough encouragement to get up from the couch and join the two witches at the table.

"Did you all have fun yesterday?" Eugenia took the last bite of eggs from her plate, sensing the obvious rift between Tessan and Kalen.

"Oh, it was a blast," Tessan responded stoically. "Best day ever."

"Yep," Kalen replied. "You know Tessan, a real joy."

What the hell is up with her?

"Okay, well, clearly something is going on here, and I don't want to be in the middle of it. So I'm going to head to the Sanctwood to visit your mother." She looked at Kalen, sadness settling in the corners of her eyes. "I'll be back before nightfall, Tess." She squeezed her niece's hand.

"I trust you two will work out—" She waved her hands in their direction. "—whatever this is."

Eugenia was out the door quickly, leaving Tessan and Kalen to their silence.

"Just tell me if you saw her last night," Tessan started.

This is about Bryn?

"Yeah, we went for a walk," he responded truthfully. "Why does that even matter?"

"You just need to be careful, Kalen," she started, but he could tell she wasn't telling the whole truth. "She's dangerous."

"I heard you when you said it the first time, Tessan." His voice was softer now. "I need you to trust that I know what I'm doing."

But the truth is, he didn't know what he was doing. He *did* enjoy his night with Bryn. He could still feel the soft outline of her lips on his cheek. What was worse was that he found himself looking forward to seeing her today. And he knew how stupid that was. He didn't need Tessan to remind him every time they spoke.

"I do trust you," she snapped back. "I don't trust her."

"You don't know her."

"And you do?"

They were quiet again.

He hated this. He and Tessan hadn't had a real argument until now. It wasn't something he'd expected either. And over Bryn? This version of them wasn't the right one.

He'd be patient, but they couldn't stay like this much longer. He needed her back on his team.

"You're right. I don't know her. And she'll never know the real me. But for now, she's my best shot at learning anything about The Order, so I need to lean in." Kalen's voice was calm now. Surely he could get her to see his side. Or a version of his side.

"I just need you to be careful," was all the witch responded. "I really can't articulate how boring my life would be if you weren't around again."

"I'll be careful." He put his pinky out to her. "Pinky promise."

"We don't need a fucking pinky promise, Kalen." She laughed.

"What?" He laughed. "I thought those meant you were serious."

"We're not children." She rolled her eyes, laughing. "Stand up."

So he did, and she pulled him into a tight hug, an agreement that they were okay again, at least for now. He rested his chin on top of her head.

"Hey Tess?"

She pulled away just a bit, arms still wrapped around his middle, and looked up at him.

His breath caught in his throat from being this close to her, staring at her so intently.

"I've been meaning to tell you this for a while now," he started, and her eyebrow raised curiously. "You...you..." he paused, "You have spinach in your teeth."

She pushed him away, laughing.

"Wait! Let me get it." He reached for her playfully, trying to pick at her teeth.

They both started giggling as Kalen chased her around Eugenia's small common room. Maybe he would always be chasing her somewhere. Maybe he was fine with that.

For now, he was just grateful they were okay again.

"Purity Above All," the teacher's voice boomed through the classroom. Kalen had arrived right on time—hoping he could slip into the back row and avoid being seen.

Of course, that's not what happened, because Bryn had saved him a seat right next to her. Just as she had promised.

Great.

He navigated to the chair as the class repeated, "Purity Above All," back to the teacher.

Oh Gods.

"Hi," she whispered, as he sat down.

Daisies.

"Hey," he murmured back. "Thanks for the seat."

"I'm just glad you showed up," She smiled at him. He believed her. Why did he have to believe her?

He scanned the classroom, taking a quick mental note of the exits if somehow this went south. He could almost picture Hauke Elowen storming in, demanding they arrest the hybrid. He sunk into his seat.

Age of Athero was written on a green chalkboard in front of the class, the professor's name was scribbled in the top corner.

"Welcome, all, to *Age of Athero.*" The teacher had a thick accent that Kalen couldn't place. "My name is Acer Jules," he continued. "In this classroom, you may call me Orderly Jules. Outside of here, though, please call me Acer."

Acer? From the woods?

"How many of you are new to The Order?" Orderly Jules posed the question to the class, lifting his head to see who would raise their hand. There were only a few people with their hands up, but one in particular caught Kalen's eye.

A gold bracelet on the right wrist.

The hybrid.

"Thank you so much for joining us. You may put your hands down."

He had to get to that person. Somehow, someway. Even if it meant showing up to this Gods damn class every week.

Bryn had some paper for note-taking in front of her, doodling in the corner as Orderly Jules spoke about the history of Athero. Kalen found it challenging to listen for several reasons.

One, he didn't agree with anything being taught.

Two, everything that was being taught was about how people like him shouldn't exist.

And three, and *almost* more frustrating than the previous two, Bryn.

Bryn and her doodles and her smell and her blonde hair. Bryn and her job as the greeter of the High Seminary. Bryn and her kindness and warmth. Bryn and her honest smile and green eyes. Her dimple on her cheek and freckle above her lip.

She nudged him and tapped her pencil to her paper.

Are you paying attention to this?

He took the pencil from her and scribbled a response.

Will you tell on me if I say no?

She snickered softly.

Depends. What do I get for keeping your secret?

Shit.

What do you want?

Shit, shit, shit.

How about a date?

Holy shit.

Are you hitting on me, Bryn?

What if I am?

His cheeks grew pink.

A date it is.

She scribbled out the words they had written before she elbowed him softly and smirked. It seemed that Bryn had some secrets of her own.

He needed to find those out, too.

That's what he needed to keep telling himself about her in general, really. He would go on this date to find out more about The Order. That's all it was. It was intel. He could weasel his way into her life just enough to know what was happening in the High Seminary. To find out what Hauke Elowen was doing with those registration forms. And then he would burn it all down.

That was it.

But she had kissed his cheek. And he wondered how it might feel to kiss her lips.

His stomach turned with anxiety.

Because in the midst of so much uncertainty, one thing was abundantly clear–he was feeling just a little too much for the greeter of the High Seminary.

"Thank you for your time and attention today. I hope you found this lesson valuable." Orderly Jules was droning on. Kalen was so relieved to hear the end was near. This class may be more torturous than the Awakening.

Kalen had a plan to catch up with the hybrid as soon as they were dismissed. He would introduce himself for now as a new Orderly, maybe see if they wanted to hang out after class one day.

But the idea, the *knowing*, of being this close to someone else who was like him made him feel less alone somehow.

He began to pack up his stuff as the other students filed out of the classroom, each of them passionately talking about parts of the lesson that stuck out to them. The excitement over The Order and its teachings was palpable. It was hard for Kalen to grasp it.

What a miserable life. To believe others don't belong just because someone else is telling you they don't.

"Excuse me?" Orderly Jules called from the front of the classroom. "You, with the brown hair."

Kalen put his finger on his chest–his eyes widened.

Orderly Jules nodded.

Gods damn.

"I'll see you later?" Bryn turned to him. "Enjoy your conversation—he's really nice."

And off she went. Somehow, her presence made him feel a bit more at ease, even knowing that she felt the same way as everyone else here. Kalen wondered if that made him a masochist.

He walked to the front of the room, his heart thudding in his chest.

Orderly Jules extended his hand to shake Kalen's. "Acer."

He took it and gripped it firmly.

"What's your name? You look so familiar to me." Acer squinted at him.

"Um, my name is Kalen Halrowe," he fumbled. "I've been told my face is very unremarkable." He laughed, trying to play it cool. He didn't think it was working.

Acer let out a chuckle of his own.

"And how long have you and Ms. Elowen been a pair?"

"I'm sorry?"

What is he talking about?

"Bryn. How long have you two known each other? I saw you passing notes." He smiled. "I don't miss anything from up here."

Kalen's hands went numb, and his magic jumped up to his throat as a reaction to the name that haunted him.

She's an Elowen? That can't be right. How could that be right? Maybe there's another Elowen family?

"We're just friends," Kalen replied firmly.

"Sure," Acer responded playfully. "Nevertheless, you just reminded me of an old friend, so I wanted to say hello." He said softly, "It's been a while since I've seen his face, and yours reminded me of his."

How could Bryn be an Elowen? She's so...opposite of Hauke. There's no way.

"Well, thank you for saying hi," he started, still flustered by the reveal of Bryn's last name. "And...I'm sorry about your friend. I hope you see him again soon."

"I don't believe I will," he chuckled again. "Seeing ole Westie would be like seeing a ghost."

You're fucking kidding me. I have to get out of here.

The silence stretched a bit longer than Kalen was comfortable with before Orderly Jules thanked him for his time and sent him on his way.

His head was spinning. This was too much. His initial plan of finding the hybrid would have to wait; he needed to get home and talk to his parents. And he guessed he had to plan a date with Bryn.

Bryn Gods damn *Elowen.*

Tessan was right; he needed to be more careful. The solid ground below him was at risk of collapsing with one misstep.

He knew, somehow, this was only the beginning. More secrets would begin to unravel around him. And he had come to learn he really, really, hated secrets.

Chapter Thirty-Four
Ria

"**G**et out." A tear fell down her cheek.

"Ria, please," Eugenia pleaded. "Please, just listen to me."

"Get out of my home, Eugenia," she said firmly, raising her voice. "Or I swear to Gods I will remove you."

Ria had made a promise to herself that she would never use her powers to harm anyone. But Gods damn, what she wouldn't give to summon a vine to wrap around Eugenia's mouth to shut her up.

"Ria."

"OUT." She pointed to the door with force. "I do not want to look at you for one more moment."

"Just talk to me!" Eugenia's words were earnest, unyielding, the way Eugenia always was. "You're my best friend."

"Best friend? Ha!" The witch's words made her feel crazy. "I would *never* do something like this to you. Best friends *don't do* shit like this," she yelled. "You knew how much I loved him. You held me as I cried myself to sleep. How could you?"

"How could I?" Eugenia snapped back. "It was to protect you and Kalen!" She raised her voice, matching Ria's tone. "*Everything* I do is to protect you and Kalen. You were careless with Westin. Do you think we had the same luxury with Kale?"

Eugenia's voice continued to rise. "They would have killed him if they found him. And you, as a matter of fact."

It was just like Eugenia to make a final stand on her own terms. Everything was always on her terms. Even showing up here today, ruining the illusion of stability Ria had begun to believe she would have again.

But it was just that, wasn't it? An illusion?

"So yes, Ria, I know I hurt you. And I will carry that with me for the rest of our lives." She stopped, tears rolling down her cheeks now. "But at least you are *here*. To hug your son. To even see Westin again." She paused. "The only thing worse than this would have been losing you and Kalen completely. So I made my decision."

The audacity of this bitch.

"Send a flower to my doorstep if you want to talk, and I'll come back." She grabbed her bag and headed toward the door. "I do love you, Ria. And I'm sorry."

"Get out," Ria begged. Her tears burned her eyes as she held back the sobs she wanted to scream. She wouldn't let Eugenia have the satisfaction of seeing how bad it hurt. Though Ria had a feeling she already knew, anyway.

Eugenia stepped out of the door, heading back toward Evermere, and Ria felt her already small world shrinking. She couldn't imagine her life without her best friend. How could she? She'd always been here–always around. Her one true constant for as long as she could remember. Now she was gone, and Ria didn't know if she ever wanted to see her again. The betrayal sat on her chest, stealing the air from her lungs. The silence Eugenia had left behind was deafening, while her own sadness was crippling. How would she ever recover from this?

"Wen?" She walked outside, calling for him. They'd agreed not to use his real name while he was in his crow form, just in case anyone was around to hear.

"Where are you?" she whispered under her breath, fuming.

How could he have asked Eugenia to keep this secret for so long? How could he have told *her* best friend? Put all of them in this position?

"Wen!" she called louder. "Meet me at the oak tree."

Fuck it.

She took off walking into the forest. It was time to end this where it all started so many years ago.

She heard his caw and knew he was close. She steadied her breath.

Finding out he had been alive all this time almost broke her. This, though–knowing her very best friend had carried the secret, too–she couldn't do it anymore.

She expected something like this to happen. Their story was fated for tragedy from the start. Why did she think having him back here meant they might, one day, go back to the way it was?

The *way it was* didn't exist anymore.

"Hey, Ri," he said as she walked toward him. Her stomach tightened as she watched him run one of his hands through his hair, catching his breath from his flight. He was always so casual about things. Like nothing affected him. Every single thing just rolled off his back.

Ria had never been that way.

"I just saw Eugenia running toward Evermere. I hate that I couldn't say hi."

She looked him in the eyes; the whites of her own were bloodshot, and there was no point in hiding this sadness any longer. She didn't have it in her to keep it up anymore, not after Eugenia.

He rushed toward her, unaware of what had unfolded while he was away. "Hey," he said gently. "Are you okay?"

She took a deep breath, before her exhale carried her into the admission of grief she didn't know she would ever be able to articulate.

"I have never known pain like losing you." Her voice was quiet. "I have cried every single day for most of Kalen's life."

"I know." His head dipped low. "I heard you."

"Just let me talk," she pleaded in return.

He nodded.

"He just looked so much like you, you know?" She sniffed. "It was torture wrapped up in the shape of this perfect child." She put her hand on her heart, closing her eyes, a physical attempt to try to hold herself together.

"I would spend my nights *begging* for peace. Praying to Earth Mother to give me the strength to be present for him. To be able to set my grief down during the day to be *with* him. To give him the mom he deserved. But the night would come, and so would this..." She clutched her tunic tighter. "This... never-ending pain."

The forest was ringing with silence. She wasn't sure he was breathing. She hardly could.

"You know how you said you knew you loved me when you saw me in the Market?" She let out a weak laugh. "I knew I loved you before then, somehow."

He chuckled softly in return, his eyes remaining glued to hers.

"Like every single fiber of me knew you were out there, and I'd find you."

She watched as a tear fell down his cheek. She reached up to wipe it instinctively, rubbing her thumb over his rough skin.

"And when I did find you, I told myself I would do everything to keep you. The big, great, love of my life," she continued. "But..."

"Please, Ria." He shook his head in protest, begging her to stop before she said the thing they'd never come back from.

She took his hands.

"Eugenia...she was the one thing that was *just* mine." She let out a sob. "My *best friend*. My sister. And you took that from me—*her* from me—the moment you asked her to keep your secret."

"Ria," he interjected.

She put her hand up, her voice still calm.

"I can forgive you for so many things, Westin." She reached out and cupped his cheek. "And I need you to hear this from me, okay?"

Here it comes.

"I will *always* love you," she choked out, finally admitting to him what they'd both been dancing around. There wasn't a version of this lifetime where she wouldn't ache for Westin Vale. But saying the words out loud was her final bow—an acknowledgement that her soul would always long for his. "But this...Eugenia? This part is too big."

He dipped his head in shame.

"I want you to be in Kalen's life." She tilted his head back up so their eyes met. "He loves you so much, Westin, and he needs you. We both do."

She wished she hadn't made eye contact. Seeing his tears was almost enough to make her change her mind. To suck all of the words back up into her throat and say something different to the man she would be missing until her last breath. This man, who had known her, every part of her, down to her bones.

I will never recover from this heartbreak.

"You are a great father," she affirmed. "But we'll never be more than what we are right now. And I hope I can find it within me to forgive you, one day." She wiped her eyes. "I do," she sniffed. "But right now, I can't trust you'll take care of my heart when you're the one who keeps breaking it."

His shoulders shook with his sobs. This was devastation. Years of longing, lost love, missed connections. This was the red thread of fate unraveling. But she didn't regret sharing how she felt. She owed him what he had kept from her for too long–the truth.

"I never meant to hurt you." His voice was barely audible.

Her beautiful, kind, charismatic Westin Vale. The love of her life.

The loss of it, too.

"I know, West," she hushed. "I know."

Chapter Thirty-Five
Kalen

"Again!" his dad yelled from across the forest.

Kalen was drenched in sweat, the salty beads falling into his mouth, the tips of his hair sticking to his face. They had been training for hours, and his father's magic had been lashing him around. His own power had barely recovered from their last session.

"Dad, please," Kalen called. "I'm tired."

"Do you think Hauke Elowen would *care* about how you felt?" he retorted coldly. "I can tell you firsthand, he wouldn't. Now go again."

His dad was almost unrecognizable when Kalen got home from Evermere. There was no greeting, no questions about how things went or what he learned; he just nodded in Kalen's direction and told him to meet him outside in ten minutes.

Where his father was usually calm, caring, and patient, he was lost in an emotion Kalen couldn't place. Was this his own version of sadness? Of grief? He didn't know, but it smelled like fire, and it was enough to make him choke.

His mother was in her room when Kalen arrived back, the door latched and locked. He wasn't sure she had ever done that. She had always said hi to him when he returned from anywhere, even if it had just been a day of foraging. He could hear her sobs through her door. This was heartbreak dipped in betrayal, and it made him ache. He wished he could sit with her and protect her from all of it, the way she'd always protected him.

Was this the fallout from Eugenia's visit? It had to be. He'd never seen either of his parents so wrapped up in their own thoughts. And he'd certainly never been on the receiving end of their pain. Had he miscalculated how much the truth would cost all of them?

Kalen dipped down into the well of his power, growing irritated that he was caught in his dad's volatility. Why did he choose brutal training instead of just talking to Kalen about how he was feeling? Shouldn't *he* have some kind of say in whether or not his family fell apart? In whether or not this was going to be their new normal?

Apparently, he didn't. Because here he stood, his knees trembling, willing his magic to end this stand-off between him and his father so he could rest. So he could check on him.

He called the roots from the forest floor with a whisper. They moved through the air like snakes, slithering against the wind, dodging blasts of fire from his father's counterattacks until finally they latched onto his wrists and snapped him back into a tree. The impact was forceful. Kalen was growing angry.

"Okay, you win," his dad called, wriggling his wrists trying to break free of the vines that held him back. "Let me go."

But Kalen wouldn't, not until he got answers about what was going on.

"Tell me what happened." He walked closer to him. "Tell me what is wrong." He wasn't leaving space for his father to protest. He wouldn't live like this–stuck between his parents and forced to pick a side.

"Eugenia came by."

Kalen stayed quiet.

"She told your mother about the day in Evermere—when she found me." He was staring blankly ahead, a man beyond his breaking point. Kalen hated seeing him like this. "She's devastated."

"Did you expect her not to be?" Kalen questioned curiously.

"I don't know what I expected," he yelled, before softening his voice, a sadness lifted to his eyes. The volume of his father's voice made Kalen jump. "I thought maybe we'd figure out a way to make this whole thing work as a family."

"What do you mean?" Kalen's pulse began to pick up as he called the roots to dissipate back into the soil, releasing his father's wrists. "Did she say you had to leave?"

Please Gods, no.

"No, no," he responded quickly. "I just don't think she'll ever forgive me." His dad slumped down the tree until he was sitting on the dirt, his head resting in his hands.

Kalen took a seat beside him, melting into a moment of rest. Everything felt tender, painful. This is what the end of his magic felt like.

Pain.

"Would it change anything if she didn't?" Kalen asked carefully. "I mean, if she didn't ever forgive you," Kalen spoke softly, preparing to ask the question he feared the most since his father came into his life. "Would you leave us anyway?"

His father's face fell, and he shook his head. It made Kalen instantly regret asking.

"I've done a lot of shit wrong," he responded firmly. "And I know that. I own it. But I would never forgive myself if I missed any more of your life."

Kalen exhaled.

Thank Gods.

"It's going to be okay, Dad." Kalen looked over at the man who'd sacrificed so much for them.

"I know," he whispered. "Because I still have you." He blew out forcefully before he put his arm around Kalen. "Sorry for yelling. And for pushing you tonight. None of this is your fault."

Kalen knew that, inherently, but there was something about hearing it out loud that calmed the voice that told him maybe things would be different if he really hadn't ever existed. Like maybe, The Order was right all along. Hybrids don't belong. He really was unclean.

They sat there in silence as the world turned dark, and under the cover of the night, he listened as his father cried.

He decided he would sit there until his dad was okay again. Until he transformed into Wen and flew deeper into the woods to rest. He would sit there forever if it meant his dad didn't leave.

He said he wouldn't leave.

Who needs to sleep, anyway?

His father took flight about an hour later. Kalen was grateful for the respite from training, for the quiet comfort of sitting with his father and knowing he was safe, even in the dead of night in the middle of the forest.

He hit a jog to get back to his house, though his legs were trembling from exhaustion.

Run, little one. He heard the trees calling out to him, the words sent a chill up his spine. What was happening?

They're coming, Kalen, they warned him again.

He heard them before he saw them. Horses' hooves beating against the ground, the low voices of several men. Kalen focused on the voices, listening intently for any indication as to what they were doing here.

"Straight ahead," one of them called out quietly.

"You heard him," another answered. "We don't have all night." Kalen could pick that voice out from anywhere. The one that haunted his dreams.

Hauke Elowen was in the Sanctwood Forest.

Fuck.

Adrenaline took over Kalen's body. His exhaustion took a back seat to his desperation. He had to get home *now*. Before they got there first.

And he wasn't going to make it.

"Dig deep, little crow." A branch lowered itself to him, an invitation to the top of a tree. He could see his house. He needed to shield it; he needed to change what they could see. He had to save his mother.

So he closed his eyes and prayed to Earth Mother.

Please, protect her. Please. I'll do anything.

He watched in disbelief as the house disappeared, leaving nothing but the appearance of trees and scattered sky. A partnership with Earth Mother. A deal had been made. Kalen wondered what the cost would be. He hoped Earth Mother was as kind to him as her creation had always been.

The tree had barely snapped into place when the men came into view.

"Someone's been here, sir. I can feel their magic. He's close."

He knew that voice, too.

Acer.

"Then where is he, Acer?" Hauke spat at the Orderly.

"I—I don't know."

"I don't know is not good enough for me anymore," he yelled. "We've been looking for fifteen years!" The words flew from his mouth in anger, and the men flinched in response.

Kalen's nightmare had been confirmed—Hauke was looking for his father. He had *always* been looking for his father. And he was never going to stop.

Kalen put his hand over his mouth, doing his best to muffle his own deep breathing. Praying again he wouldn't be caught.

"Kill him," Hauke said to the two other men, nodding toward Acer. "You are no longer welcome at the High Seminary."

"What?" Acer gasped. "Sir, please," he pleaded, dropping to his knees. "Please show me mercy. I beg of you."

"You've run out of chances." Hauke looked down at him in disgust. "This is the third time in the last year alone that you've pulled me from the High Seminary for nothing!" Hauke snapped back. "I simply do not have the time to follow your false leads."

"Hauke. Please." He reached for Hauke's shirt. "I've been a loyal Orderly to you and a faithful follower of Athero." His voice shook with fear.

"Now, men," he snapped at the two others. "Meet me back in my office when you've fulfilled your orders." Hauke walked toward his horse before turning around. "Make it look like an accident."

Kalen's heart was pounding out of his chest. He was about to witness a murder in cold blood. Another person dying at the hands of Hauke Elowen. He watched as Hauke took off toward Evermere. No remorse, no second thought. Brutality in the name of power. Just because he could.

How does Bryn share his blood?

"Carver." Acer looked at the burly one to his left. "Nic." His gaze shifted to the man on his right. "Please, brothers," Acer continued. "Please spare me."

"I'm sorry, Ace," the large one remarked. "You know he'd kill us, too, if we let you go."

Kalen had a choice to make. Would he sit up in this tree, complicit in the death of Acer Jules? Would he have nightmares of this moment, the same way he had nightmares about what happened to his father?

No.

If he let it happen, if he chose to sit back and watch it all unfold, he was just as bad as the rest of them.

He flashed back to the Awakening, to the moments where he had to use his magic to make his next move. His body was trembling at the memory, though what was ahead of him now was different. If he made one wrong choice, he wouldn't get another chance. There was no reset; this wasn't the loop.

Here goes nothing.

With the sliver of power Kalen had left, he once again summoned the vines from the forest floor. They crept, like thieves in the night, along the ground, unnoticed by the two men circling Acer.

Now.

He pushed the thought out as the vines slithered up their legs, around their torsos, and began to constrict their necks.

Do not kill them.

He commanded the vines, but it was a bit of a reminder to himself, too. These were violent men, but they didn't deserve to die at his hands. He couldn't bear that stain on his soul.

Acer jumped away as the two men before him clawed at their necks, an attempt to try and pry the vines from their throats. Kalen was fading, balancing burnout with precision. If he went too fast, they'd die. If he went too slow, Acer would.

The smaller of the two men hit the ground first with a thud, before the powerful one fell with a mighty roar.

Kalen watched from above as Acer stood between the two men in disbelief before looking around him, trying to find the one who'd saved his life.

"Come out, please," he announced to the silence. "I can feel that you're near."

Kalen released the vines from the necks of the unconscious men. The branches lowered him to the forest floor, directly behind Acer.

"Hi, Orderly Jules."

Acer spun around, his hands up in a fighting position, before they dropped as he recognized Kalen.

"It's you." He looked at him, stunned.

"Yeah, Kalen...from class," he responded, assuming he was still in shock from all he had seen.

"No...it's you." He walked closer to Kalen, studying his face. "Athero be damned, Hauke was right."

"What are you talking about?" Kalen backed away, regretting making himself known. He should have just stayed up there in the Gods damn tree.

"A son." Acer continued to walk toward him, backing Kalen into a tree. "Westin had a fucking son." His eyes were wide, crazed.

"I don't know what you're talking about." Kalen's voice shook in response.

"Of course you do." Acer laughed. "How's he doing, anyway?"

Kalen heard a caw in the distance. His dad was coming. He must have heard the disturbance and turned around, heading back toward their home. If he could just hang on a little longer, he'd know what to do. He always knew what to do.

In a flash, his father was standing right in front of Acer, blocking him from Kalen completely.

"Just fine, old pal." Kalen couldn't see his face, but he could hear the smirk in his voice before throwing his fist back and letting it fly. "Thanks for asking."

Acer Jules was out cold.

And Kalen was in big trouble.

"Dad?" The realization of what he had done was slowly sinking in.

"Not now, Kalen," he snapped back. "Help me get these two tied to their horses and back to Evermere."

His dad worked quickly, and Kalen was trying to keep up with him, but he was drained. Fully and completely. The world was growing blurrier each moment he stayed on his feet.

"You'd better pray to whatever God you believe in that these two don't remember anything when they wake up." His father slapped the horses' hindquarters and sent them back the way they came.

Kalen looked down at the face of Acer, terrified of what would come of him when he woke up.

The Order was closer now than it had ever been.

And it was all Kalen's fault.

Chapter Thirty-Six
West

"RIA!" West shouted, throwing the door to her home open, carrying his old friend's limp body over his shoulder. Kalen was right on his heels.

Acer Jules. What the hell was this kid thinking?

Ria's door flew open within seconds. Her bloodshot eyes were a reminder of the pain she experienced today, because of him. And it was about to get worse.

"Someone explain what is going on, please." She gawked at the man thrown over his arm.

"Our son decided to save an Orderly from his death sentence tonight."

Ria paused, working the words over her brain. He had seen that expression on her face a hundred times.

"You did the right thing, little crow." She peered behind him and into the face of Kalen, a small grin on her face.

"If the right thing is putting us all in more danger," West barked back, "then yes, you did the right thing."

"He didn't deserve to die." Kalen stepped forward now. "I couldn't just sit there and watch him suffer," he continued, his voice growing more confident. "I had the power to stop it, so I stopped it."

Ria motioned for Kalen to come closer. She wrapped him up in her arms and whispered softly to him, "You should be proud of yourself." She kissed his head. "I'm sorry I didn't say hi when you got back today."

Thank Gods for fae hearing.

"So what's the plan?" West interrupted the moment. "We just *make friends* with Acer Jules now? Keep him tucked away at the house out of sight?" His tone was mocking.

"What's the alternative, Westin?" Ria snapped. "We send him back to the High Seminary to suffer the same fate that you did?"

Even amidst his own anger, West considered her question. What *was* the alternative? There were so many ways this could go–but there was one thing he wouldn't accept.

There is no Gods damn way Acer is staying here alone with her.

"Ri," he leveled. "You're not thinking clearly."

"You do not get to tell me how to feel." She looked at him plainly.

He wasn't sure they were still talking about Acer, not completely.

"The man stays here," she breathed out and looked at Westin. "And so do you."

What?

"In the house. Both of you," she continued. "You keep him in line. You keep me and Kalen safe."

She turned back to her door. "It's the least you can do."

Kalen turned to him, wide-eyed.

"Mom—" Kalen thought the plan was as crazy as he did.

She simply put her hand up.

"It's final," she declared softly. "You two got us into this. Figure out how to get us through it."

She closed the door, leaving him standing in the common room with Kalen.

"Can you stay at Eugenia's?" His father looked at him, defeated. "I don't know what else to do. You shouldn't be here when he wakes up."

It was *dangerous* for him to be here when Acer woke up. Could he convince his old friend that he had never seen Kalen at all?

"Can I stick around for a few days, just in case something goes wrong?" Kalen responded. "I can take care of myself. I'll sleep on the couch or the floor."

There goes that plan.

"It's your home, Kalen," he answered softly, deflated. "You can do whatever you need to do."

"I guess it's yours now, too, isn't it?" Kalen elbowed him. "'The man stays here, and so do you,'" he repeated back in a shitty version of his mother's voice, chuckling.

"Shut the hell up and help," he countered, dropping Acer to the floor. "Let's get him tied up somewhere."

But inside, his stomach was turning.

If he proved to Ria every day he was worth her love, maybe she would forgive him.

Maybe.

Because sharing a home with Ria Halrowe had always been his dream. And this would be a semblance of the life they could have had together, but likely never would.

Because of him.

What a horrible way to exist.

Chapter Thirty-Seven
Tessan

K alen hadn't been back to Evermere in days.

Eugenia came home from visiting Ria and warned her that it may be a while before she saw him again.

Eugenia told her everything—the truth about the secrets she kept for West, how long she had known. And what finally telling Ria the truth had cost her.

Tessan wondered how Kalen had kept it all to himself, but she was learning that he wouldn't talk about things before he was ready. It needed to be on his terms, and not a moment sooner. She still didn't even know what happened during the Awakening.

She still didn't know shit about Bryn.

Fucking Bryn.

Beautiful, blonde, Bryn.

Bryn, who has done absolutely nothing wrong.

Kalen took up too much of her Gods damn brain space.

Eugenia had basically been in solitary confinement these last few days, leaving Tessan alone with most of her thoughts. It was becoming overwhelming—all of the things she was making assumptions about.

Does Kalen like Bryn?

Does Kalen miss me?

Does Kalen even think about this same shit?

She needed to get out of here.

"I'm headed into town," she called into the quiet house. She knew Eugenia didn't care. She'd barely come out of her room for food over the last few days.

Stepping into the breeze was restorative. A reminder that there was a life to be lived outside of her aunt's home. She wasn't sure if she would have agreed to come back here had she known how little time she would be spending with Kalen. It was a huge risk, wandering around Evermere alone, but it was one she was willing to take today to get away from her thoughts.

She could outrun her father anyway.

She walked the stone streets of Evermere, wondering how Shu and Victoria were doing. If they were still in love like they were when she left to come back here. She would write to them soon. Maybe she would even go home to Wyrdbrook.

If she could stomach the idea of leaving Kalen.

But today wasn't about him; it was about her. And since it was about her, she was going to visit a couple of her favorite places, starting with Hydro's bakery.

Tessan could practically smell the pastries from here. Before her mom passed away, they'd go after Market day each week. Her mother would grab a croissant, and she would grab whatever looked the best to her that day.

They'd touch pastries like they were giving a cheer at the end of a long week, and her mom would always say, "To my darling, Tessan Duscaire."

Tessan could still hear her laugh.

She hadn't visited Hydro's bakery since her mother passed away. She wondered if Hydro was still the baker or if he had passed it on to someone else. She smiled thinking of the man's bushy eyebrows, lying like a caterpillar across his face. He was so kind to her. He sent her a basket of croissants when he heard the news of her mother's passing.

Tessan should have visited before now, but she couldn't find the strength to. And her father wouldn't let her.

The bell on the shop door rang as she pushed it open, and the rich fragrance of bread and dough greeted her like an old friend–another reminder of the way it once was. The bakery was mostly empty, save for a few folks with their noses buried in books.

And there he was, Hydro and his giant eyebrows. Still here, after all of this time.

He hadn't looked up yet before he called out to her, "Welcome to Hydro's Bakery! I'll be with you in just a moment." He turned to knead more dough. Tessan watched him with a knot in her stomach.

She wished she had Kalen's gift of memorywalking. She wished she could rewind to when her mother was alive, just to see her one more time, to exist in that moment, even as a bystander.

We're not thinking about Kalen at all right now, Tess.

She made her way up to the counter when he finally turned around.

"Well, by Gods," he muttered, setting his bowl on the counter. "It's Tessan Duscaire."

"Hi, Hydro." She smiled, tears welling in her eyes.

"Come around here and hug me, child." His voice was warm. "I've missed you."

They hugged for a while, Hydro planting a kiss on top of her head, and for the first time in a long time, Tessan remembered the magic that existed within Evermere.

"Sit, sit." He waved her off. "I'll bring you one of everything." As he shuffled away from her, he said, "On the house, of course."

One of everything was too much, but maybe Hydro's baked goods would be enough to get Eugenia out of her room for more than a couple of minutes. She just missed being around people. She felt vulnerable admitting that to herself.

Tessan walked over to a bookshelf, thumbing through the ancient literature that lined the walls. She settled on a book about common birds in Evermere and grabbed a small table in the far corner of the bakery, opting for full visibility of the room, just in case her father showed up.

She prayed he wouldn't.

She was lost in the book, learning more about, ironically, crows, when Hydro laid two plates of baked goods in front of her. Her mouth watered immediately.

"How have you been, Tessan?" he asked genuinely. "I've missed your face around here."

"Yeah, I moved a few years ago. This is my first time back since."

"Well, it is an honor that you stopped here." He grinned. "I still think about your mother every time I make my croissants."

Tessan thought about her every single day.

"She was the best," she responded genuinely.

"And she raised the best." He beamed at her. "I'll leave you to your book. Please say goodbye before you leave."

"Thank you, Hydro," she managed to squeak out. "For this." She gestured to the plates of pastry in front of her. "And for your kindness."

"You come see me any time, child," he said seriously. "I will always take care of you." He patted her hand before he walked away.

Tessan took a bite of a flaky turnover. The apples in the middle were tender and spiced. She audibly groaned, then grew embarrassed when she heard Hydro laugh behind the counter.

Good thing it was fairly empty in there.

She sank back into her book, grateful for the respite from her aunt's home, the pastries, and the distraction from everything going on in her brain.

The bell on the door rang. Tessan didn't bother looking up; she could tell it wasn't her father from the corner of her eye.

"Hydro!" The cheerful voice caused her to look up. She knew it from somewhere.

Oh no.

"Hi, sweetie," he responded. "The usual?"

"If you don't mind!" She nodded.

Nooo.

"You got it." He wrote down the order on his notepad. "Grab a seat and I'll have it right out to you."

Of course Bryn was here.

Why wouldn't she be here?

It didn't take long for the blonde to lock eyes with Tessan in the corner of the room. She was hesitant, but put her hand up in a wave anyway.

Tessan waved back this time, and immediately regretted it as Bryn headed her way.

"Tessan, right?" she asked, tucking a piece of hair behind her ear.

"Hey." Tessan acted confused. "Yeah. Remind me of your name again?"

Gods, this is petty.

"Bryn," she responded genuinely. "I'm Kalen's friend from the High Seminary."

"Oh, yeah." She looked back down at her book. "It's great seeing you again."

"Yeah, you too."

Bryn stood there for a few more seconds, the air between them uncomfortable. Frustrating. She wasn't going to walk away; Tessan had to accept there was only one way forward.

So much for a day to herself.

"Would you like to sit?" Tessan gestured to the empty seat in front of her. She had been lonely, but had she been *that* lonely?

"You don't mind?" Bryn cocked her head to the side.

"Nope," she responded plainly. "Go for it."

Hydro made his way over shortly with Bryn's order.

A fucking croissant.

A cruel joke.

"Here you are, Bryn." He set the plate in front of her. "I didn't know you two knew each other."

"We don't, really," Tessan answered too quickly. "We just met the other day."

Bryn looked at her and then back to Hydro. "How do you two know each other?"

"Oh, Tess and her mother used to come see me every week." Hydro put a hand on Tessan's shoulder. "This is the first time I've seen her in years. Anyway, you two enjoy your food." Hydro eyed Tessan's plate. "You let me know if there's anything else you need."

An uncomfortable silence fell between them. Maybe Tessan could come up with an excuse to leave.

"Did I...do something to you?" Bryn was staring at her pastry, her hands in her lap.

What was she going to say to that?

No, Bryn, you've not done a single thing. I just think I might have real feelings for my fake cousin?

"Nope. Why do you ask?"

"It's just...the other day with Kalen," she continued, looking up at her. "I just felt like maybe I did something to upset you." She added, "And I definitely didn't mean to."

Why the hell is she so nice?

"I'm just protective of him," Tessan responded. "He's been through a lot." Which was true, despite the context. "I don't want him to get hurt."

"I get that." Bryn settled into her seat a bit more, grabbing her croissant. "But I really don't plan on hurting him."

Okay, I'll bite.

"Then what *is* your plan with my cousin?" She forced the words out of her throat, dreading the response.

"I don't know, really." She could tell Bryn was thinking about what she really wanted. "I just know that he's different."

Different. HA. If she only knew.

"Different?"

"Yeah." She took a bite of her pastry. "He's kind."

At least she got that part right.

"The people I've dated in the past haven't been kind like he is," she said. "I don't know how to explain it, really."

"You don't have to," Tessan replied, her stomach sick. "I know what you mean."

Bryn smiled at Tessan, grateful for the perceived olive branch. For a moment of understanding shared between two young women.

"He's supposed to be planning a date for us." She giggled, leaning closer to Tessan.

A date.

A date.

"He must really like you," Tessan responded, trying to hide the bitterness in her voice. "I can't remember the last time he planned a date for a girl."

Because he never had.

"You really think so?" Bryn was giddy.

"I really do." Tessan pushed her plate of food away from her, her appetite gone.

Tessan recognized that the line between what was real and what was not was growing muddied.

Kalen was an Orderly.

Not real.

Kalen was her cousin.

Not real.

Kalen liked Bryn.

Real. She thinks?

Bryn liked Kalen.

Real. She knows.

Did Tessan also like Kalen?

Undecided.

Tessan believed Bryn was genuine.

Real.

Gods damn it.

The thoughts echoed through her like they had their own heartbeat.

Had she lost him before she ever had him? Did she even *want* to be more than friends? Or was this proximity to who he was clouding her judgment about what it was she actually wanted?

Maybe she really should go back to Wyrdbrook.

Or maybe, she could help Kalen in a different way.

"Hey," Tessan started. "Do you have plans tonight?"

"Um, if going back to my room to read the covenant counts, yes?"

This was worse than she thought.

"It doesn't." Tessan laughed. "Want to come have dinner at my aunt's house with me?"

Bryn's eyes lit up.

"I'd really love that." She grinned at Tessan.

Keep your friends close, and your friends' love interests closer.

Or whatever the fuck that saying was.

Chapter Thirty-Eight
Kalen

I t was late when he made it to Eugenia's house.

Things at his mother's home were interesting, but stable enough for Kalen to feel like he could leave for a few days to give his parents and their new guest some extra space. Acer woke up confused, lost, and seemed to have forgotten most of what had happened to him.

Kalen knew his father was strong, but seeing him hit a man so hard that he forgot where he was put his strength into perspective.

Regardless, Acer ultimately seemed grateful to be alive. He hadn't said anything about it, but Kalen could sense he was glad to see his father, too. Like maybe beneath all of the bullshit The Order had taught him, he was just someone who needed his friend again.

Kalen guessed that time would tell.

The lights were on as Kalen approached the small home in Evermere. He wondered what Tessan had been up to. Was she waiting up for him each night since he'd been away? Wondering when he would be back?

He doubted it.

He heard the soft giggles of two voices as he got closer to the door.

At least Eugenia has recovered. Mom sure hasn't.

He pushed the door open quietly and stopped dead in his tracks at the scene laid out in front of him.

It wasn't Eugenia and Tessan giggling.

It was *Bryn* and Tessan.

What the hell?

Gods, they were so very different, in so many ways. The juxtaposition of the sun and the moon. Both vital for survival. Tessan was solid and steady, unyielding. Bryn was kind and forward, but somehow still a mystery. This was not the pairing he expected to see.

But here they were, sitting on the couch in the common room, mugs in hand, blankets draped over them, laughing, talking.

"Hey, Kalen," Tessan called quietly. "Welcome home." She smiled, nodding toward Bryn. "Look who I found out and about today."

An Elowen, knowing where he "lived." Tessan had no idea what she had just done.

"Didn't try to bite her head off this time?" Kalen remarked, bewildered. "Hey, Bryn."

"Hi, you." She tilted her mug back to take another sip of her drink. Tessan and Bryn continued to giggle.

"What's in the mug?" Kalen eyeballed them curiously. "That's an awful lot of laughing over some tea."

"Because it's not tea, obviously." Tessan stood up, pushing the mug into his chest. "Try some."

"I think you two have had enough for all of us." He handed the mug back to Tessan.

He turned to Bryn. "Do you know what time it is?" He walked closer to her, gently grabbing the drink from her hand. "It's not safe for you to walk home like this."

"Walk her home, then," Tessan challenged, joining him shoulder to shoulder. She lowered her hand to Bryn to help her off the couch. "I'm so glad we spent the day together."

The DAY?

"Me too." Bryn took Tessan's hand and stood up, wobbly. "You really are wonderful when you're not being so mean."

Kalen let out a chuckle as Bryn fell into Tessan's arms for a hug.

What is happening?

"Don't be a stranger?" Tessan nodded before heading toward her room. "Get her home safely, Kale."

"Kale is a cute nickname." Bryn reached up and pinched Kalen's cheek.

He looked down at her and smiled.

She's an Elowen. Her grandfather tried to kill your Dad.

And *that* was enough to kill the moment.

"Let's get you home." Kalen grabbed her hand, softly tugging her through the door.

She interlaced their fingers quickly, her head falling on his arm as if they'd done this very thing a hundred times.

"Where were you today?" she asked, clinging tightly to his hand as they walked down the gravel road toward the High Seminary.

"The Sanctwood," he responded calmly. "It's where I spend most of my days."

"Hmm. I guess I still don't understand what there is to love about a bunch of trees and grass," Bryn returned.

"Maybe one day you'll learn to love it." The words slipped out of Kalen's mouth before he could stop them.

"I hope so," she whispered.

Was this going too far? Was the way Kalen's stomach twisted when they touched a sign that she was bad for him? Of course she was bad for him.

So why did it feel...like *this*?

Like her fingers laced in his was a promise they were both too scared to say out loud. Like the forest after a light rain–sustained.

When in reality, she was the thunderstorm. Threatening to uproot everything steady.

"Kalen?" she hiccuped, interrupting his thoughts. "I think that I really like you."

His body was burning with something that wasn't his magic. Bryn Elowen may just be the one who kills him after all.

"Well, *I* think that you really had too much to drink," he answered. "Tessan can get a little wild from time to time."

"No." She stopped walking, turning to face him, "Nope."

"What?" He cocked his head.

"Don't do that," she snapped back at him.

Kalen furrowed his eyebrows, confused.

"Don't minimize my feelings because they make you uncomfortable," she struck back, quickly sobering up.

"Bryn, that's not what I meant," Kalen responded calmly. "That's not what I was trying to do."

A silence stretched between them.

"They don't," Kalen pulled her closer to him.

Bryn's eyes grew wide, curiosity of her own written on her face.

"Make me uncomfortable." He wrapped an arm around her waist, fingers still interlocked behind her back. His free hand reached up and brushed a strand of hair from her face. She stood, staring up at him, and closed her eyes.

He could kiss her right now. And Gods damn, it would be *magic*. It would be the exclamation point on all of the small moments they'd shared.

But he wouldn't. Not like this. Not while she's drunk.

If he were smart, not at all.

"We should get you back." He moved his hand down her cheek. "Before someone gets worried and comes looking for you."

Her eyes flew open. "You're right," she agreed, but Kalen could read the embarrassment on her face. "Actually, I can make it the rest of the way on my own."

"Prying eyes, huh?" Kalen asked, knowing the secret she was keeping. *An Elowen.*

"Something like that." She leaned into him and lay her head on his chest. "Thank you," she replied. "For being who you are. For making me feel safe."

Fuck.

He rested his head on top of hers for a brief moment before letting her go. "I'll see you soon."

"I can't wait." She squeezed his hand.

And then, Kalen leaned down to kiss her cheek.

"I owed ya one." He winked and ran back toward Eugenia's home.

Gods damn it, he *really* liked Bryn Elowen.

Tessan had gone to her room by the time Kalen made it back to Eugenia's. He assumed she would stay up to chat about her day with Bryn, or at least catch up. They hadn't seen each other in days.

There was always tomorrow.

The blankets Tessan and Bryn had been curled up in still lay spread on the couch. He gathered them up before lying down, throwing the two blankets over his body.

Daisies.

Every single time he was with Bryn, he wondered how he would ever stop being with her. How he'd eventually have to tell her the truth about who he was and what he was doing. About how he was the antithesis of everything she believed.

He couldn't have planned for this part–to have met someone so caring. To be falling for someone so thoughtful. Someone who made him want to be a better version of who he was.

He stared up at the ceiling, his thoughts whirling through his head, whipping him around with uncertainty.

They would always just be two people circling one another, lost in the possibility of what could be.

An Orderly and a hybrid.

He'd seen a version of this play out with his parents. He knew how it ended.

Heartbreak.

If he were wiser, he would let her go now–tell her they couldn't go on the date he'd promised, that he wouldn't be going back to the High Seminary.

But there were hybrids to save. There were minds to change. And he was already in this deep.

He couldn't lose the point of all of this because a pretty blonde showed up and made him feel seen.

He wouldn't.

He would try not to, anyway.

A pillow smacked Kalen in the face and startled him awake. He groaned.

What a way to wake up.

"Morning, loser," Tessan chirped. "How'd ya sleep?"

She sat down in the chair across from him, handing him a mug of tea. He sat up a bit, squinting at the sun beaming in, and took the hot tea into his hands.

"Fine," he croaked, lifting his mug to Tessan. "Thanks for this."

"Not a problem." She tucked her knees up to her chest now, the silence settling between them.

"I missed you," she mumbled. "Eugenia told me everything."

"Yeah." He took a drink of tea, the warmth sliding down his throat. "I missed you, too. It's been a hard few days." He exhaled slowly. "How's she doing?"

"I don't really know," Tessan responded, still keeping her voice low. "She won't come out of her room."

Despite what they'd been through, the idea of Eugenia being so devastated filled Kalen with sorrow of his own. She was supposed to be the unbothered one. The one who knew everything, accepted it for what it was, and moved on.

This broke her the same way it had broken his mother. Maybe not quite as bad–but it was a pain Kalen hadn't expected to see from the witch who'd held the secret for so long.

"Maybe I should talk to her," he replied, matching her volume.

"Not sure if it would help, honestly." Tessan shrugged. "But I'm sure she'd be glad to see you."

Kalen nodded, lifted his arms over his head to stretch, and stood up from the couch.

"Yeah, I don't know what I'll say," he responded, walking toward Tessan. "But I hate that she's not doing well."

"You and your great big heart," Tessan smirked almost mockingly. "No wonder Bryn likes you so much." She grew serious as the words left her mouth.

"She doesn't like me *so* much." He sat back down on the couch quickly, her words knocking him off balance.

What did they talk about last night?

"Not what she told me," Tessan countered frankly. "What *are* you going to do for your date, anyway?"

"Why are you doing this, Tessan?" Kalen responded earnestly. "Do you have something against her?"

"Her?" Tessan spat. "No. She's actually so lovely and she would be perfect for you—" Her voice was trailing off now.

"Okay, so get off my ba–"

"Except for the very important fact that she's a Gods damn Orderly, Kalen." She set her mug on the common room table. "An *Orderly*. Have you *actually* lost your mind?"

Maybe.

"I already told you I know what I'm doing, Tess," he answered passionately.

"No, Kale, you don't," she snapped back. "You may have before, but things have changed. You look at her like she hung the fucking moon."

Kalen sat there quietly. Tessan was right, and there was no sense in arguing with her.

So he wouldn't.

"You need to be more careful." She reached her hand out toward him. "That's all I'm saying."

He grabbed it, his head hung in defeat.

"I know," he mumbled.

What else was there to say?

"I'm sorry." Tessan rubbed her thumb against his hand. "I know what it feels like to want someone you can't have."

"It's okay." Kalen looked up at Tessan and watched a tear roll down her cheek.

He reached out to wipe it for her, but of course, she smacked his hand away.

"Don't even think about it." She chuckled as she wiped it herself.

Kalen grabbed a pillow and threw it at her, the same thing she had done to him just a few minutes prior.

The two erupted in laughter as it knocked Tessan's head back.

"That's for calling me a loser," he responded as he stood up and started toward Eugenia's room. "I have to go to the High Seminary today, but maybe we'll hang out tonight?"

He didn't *have* to go to the High Seminary, but he did want to see Bryn. And right now, there was a fine line between his wants and his needs.

"If you're lucky," Tessan responded, picking up her mug and staring straight ahead.

Kalen would talk to Eugenia first.

Then head toward Bryn.

Would it always end with Bryn? Her bloodline holding him hostage, like a dagger to his throat? Would he be the one delivering his own fatal blow?

What a Gods damn mess.

Kalen knocked on Eugenia's door a few times before opening it.

The room was pitch black save for a tiny sliver of light peeking through the curtains, hitting her bed like a beacon guiding him to his Genie. He looked at the outline of her body, huddled up under the covers, drenched in an unending despair. There was nothing in here beyond Eugenia and her sadness. And her sadness was big enough to fill the room on its own.

"Eugenia?" Kalen spoke softly.

"Go away, Tessan," she called back.

"It's Kalen." He walked closer to her. "Can we talk?"

He noticed her stir, just enough, her grip on the covers loosening as if she was making space for the conversation.

"I don't know why you'd want to talk to me after all I've done."

"Because I love you." He continued to walk closer to her. "And so does Mom."

A cry ripped from Eugenia's throat.

"I messed up everything, Kale." She sat up, her hair matted to the side of her face. "How could she ever get over this?"

Kalen sat down on the edge of her bed. "You're not giving her much credit. Her life has been full of heartbreak, and so far she's managed pretty well."

"I never wanted to hurt her." She sniffled. "She's my family. The other piece of my heart."

"I know." He put his hand on her leg.

He listened to Eugenia's sobs for a few more minutes, the silence making way for what he hoped would be healing soon.

"I never told you thank you," Kalen whispered. "For saving him that day."

"I shouldn't have done it," she responded firmly. "I should have sent his ass back to wherever he came from before he showed up."

Torture chambers.

"You did the right thing, Genie," he replied. "You just did it the wrong way."

She took a deep breath and wiped her eyes.

"Do you think she'll ever forgive me?" she asked nervously. If anyone knew his mother better than Eugenia, it was Kalen.

"I hope so." He moved closer and wrapped her in a hug. "I know it was hard, but I'm glad you told her the truth."

"I'd do anything for you." She squeezed him tight. "I'm sorry it took me so long."

"I know." He pulled away from her. "I do love you, you know?" He wiped a tear from her cheek.

She smiled, still devastated. "It's good to hear."

"I'm staying here for a few days." He stood up from her bedside. "Join me and Tessan for dinner tonight, and I'll catch you up."

"Deal." She settled back into her bed. "Love you, Kale."

He turned and walked out of the room, gently closing the door behind him. Tessan was no longer in the common room, so he quickly changed his clothes and headed out the door.

Toward Bryn and The Order. Toward the unknown.

His heart picked up speed the closer he got to the High Seminary. The crunch of gravel under his feet and that he was traveling here alone kept him tethered to the fact that this was the real world and not the Awakening.

He pushed the great doors of the building open and turned to his left. There she was, behind the comically large desk, looking down and lost in some thought or doodle.

Bryn.

He cleared his throat.

"I'll be right with you!" her voice rang out, bouncing off the soaring walls.

"Can't believe you'd keep me, of all people, waiting," he called back playfully.

She dropped her pencil and looked up with a smile. "Kalen Halrowe, two days in a row?"

"I know, I know." He walked toward her. "Couldn't stay away."

"From me or the High Seminary?" she asked genuinely.

"Both." He smirked, lying.

You.

"Think you can show me more of this place?"

She looked out the giant window, taking inventory of the time of day. "I think I can spare an hour or two." She put a sign on the desk, signaling to those who came in that she would be back soon. "Can we stop by my room first?"

Her room.

This was just stop number one on a continued tour of the High Seminary. Nothing more.

"Lead the way." He put his arm out in front of him. She grabbed it and interlaced their fingers again. The gesture surprised him. How was she so confident in these small displays of public affection? And what happened to the prying eyes she was always so worried about?

They hadn't talked about what they were to each other. Because they were nothing. Maybe she knew it too, deep down, that something was different about him–that he didn't belong here. Maybe she also wanted to live in this imaginary world together a little bit longer before things inevitably imploded.

They walked together, going the opposite way they did the first time here. Kalen was doing his best to take in the newness of his surroundings. If he was being honest, nothing really seemed different.

He wondered where the door to the basement was. *If* there was one at all—to the room where his father had been kept all those years, being tortured right below their feet.

"Thanks for walking me home last night." Bryn looked up at him. "I felt like shit when I got back to my room."

His eyes grew wide. "Are you allowed to cuss here?"

"It's allowed but frowned upon," she continued, laughing. "If Hauke heard me, he'd definitely give me a slap on the wrist."

Hauke. She still hadn't told him they were related. He wondered if he could get it out of her now.

"He seems to think pretty highly of you," he started, treading carefully. "So I doubt it."

She looked at him, amused. "Here's our stop." She turned the knob of the door in front of them.

She didn't keep it locked?

She pushed the door open, gesturing for him to go first. The room was small, just big enough for a bed, a dresser, and a desk. The walls were lined with books, her desk covered in intricate doodles. Everything was in perfect order, in the perfect place.

And he couldn't even get started on the way it smelled. Like her.

Like everything.

"This is nice," he said, walking into the space, running his finger along the books on the wall.

Age of Athero, Athero's Way, The Order's Promise, The Covenant.

She closed the door behind them. "Thanks." She opened her dresser, digging through her clothes.

Is she looking for something?

"It's small, but it works for me."

He nodded, dropping his hands from the books. "How many other people live here?"

"There are about ten of us that live in permanent rooms, and there are a couple of hybrids that rotate in and out," she responded, closing her drawer and tucking something into her pocket.

"Why do you distinguish the two?" he asked curiously.

She looked at him, puzzled.

"You said us and then hybrids..." he followed up. "If they're here, aren't they one of *us*?"

"Not really." She shrugged. "They'll never *really* be one of us."

"Hm," he responded quietly.

She walked closer to him. "Ready to go?"

He had suddenly lost his desire to spend time with her at all.

He reached down into his magic, begging for the fire that lived within to heat him up. He slowly felt his face begin to grow warm.

"I'm actually really not feeling well," he responded, faking a stumble and putting his hand to his head. "I'm sorry." He sat down on her bed dramatically.

She followed him to the bed, leaning low to put her lips on his forehead. "You're burning up." She looked worried. "Are you sure you don't want to just hang out here for a bit and get some rest?"

"I don't want to get you sick," Kalen responded, letting out a cough. "I should just head back home."

"No, please. I'll go back down to the desk," she responded genuinely. "Please just stay here."

Gods damn it.

"Okay." He gave in, kicking off his shoes and settling into Bryn's bed. "I'll stay."

Bryn's bed.

"I'll see you later," she said, lifting the cover and tucking it around him. "Make yourself at home."

He thanked her and closed his eyes, his fae hearing on high alert as he heard her dresser drawer open again, the same rustling of her clothes as before.

She's hiding something.

And as soon as she walked out of this room, he was going to find out what it was.

Kalen lay in her bed for a moment longer, patiently waiting for her footsteps to fade down the hallway, thanking his magic for its quick work.

He popped up and ran his fingers through his hair before taking a deep breath. He had shit he needed to figure out. And he needed to do it now.

Part of him felt guilty for invading her privacy like this, but the other part of him—the one that needed the information—tucked the thought away in the back of his mind. Bryn had secrets of her own. This would be one of his.

Well, this and the fact that he was a hybrid infiltrating The Order, and thought he was falling in love with the granddaughter of the Head Cleanser.

Love.

That thought alone made the Awakening feel like a stroll through the forest.

Focus, Kalen.

He put his ear to her door to double-check the hallway was clear and quickly walked over to her desk. He would start by looking through her notebooks. She was always carrying one of these Gods damn books.

Bryn and her doodles.

The pages were covered with notes, small signature doodles on each corner, her name written several different ways. Never a trace of her last name, but he did spot a trace of his.

B+K scribbled in cursive in the footnotes of one of the pages. Maybe the K didn't stand for Kalen, but what if it did?

BE+KH scribbled on another confirmed that it did.

It made his heart soar.

It made his heart break.

This wasn't supposed to happen.

He flipped through a couple more notebooks, feeling grateful for his gift of memorywalking. He'd be able to put everything back exactly as it was.

Thank Gods. Bryn was the kind of person who would notice.

He knew he should check the drawer, but the likelihood he would ever have the chance to look through anything in her room again was low, and he wanted to see everything he could. He glanced around the small space, a notebook still in hand, looking at the decorations on the walls.

The bits of her spread throughout—the tapestries that hung above her bed, the knick-knacks that lined the edge of her desk.

This was Bryn unfiltered, a look into what life would be like outside the walls of the High Seminary.

A life that would never exist.

He set the first journal down gently, making space to look through the worn leather book that had sat underneath it. He watched in dread as a note fell from it and hit the floor.

Gods damn it.

He had no idea where it had come from, so he had no idea how to put it back where it belonged.

The paper was worn and tattered. Like she had been holding onto it for a while. Like she would reread it on the days she needed some kind of boost. He unfolded it carefully, trying not to tear the thin edges.

My dearest Bryn,

I am so proud of you. I count it all joy to see you grow in your faith, following Athero's teachings. People who know your heart are better for it.

I know I am.

Having you here with me at the High Seminary has made my life abundantly more meaningful.

You will make an impactful Cleanser one day—when I'm called home to Athero. Oh, what a day that will be for us both.

Purity Above All,

Grandpop

Kalen's eyes started to burn.

What?

He reread the letter two more times.

Bryn is the next Head Cleanser?

Sweet Bryn? Was she capable of evil like that?

Did he know her at all?

He tucked the note away in his pocket. Better for her to think that she lost it than for it to be in a different place altogether.

He took a deep breath, trying to steady himself. He didn't know where to put information this massive. The Head Cleanser? Did it matter anyway? He knew they were nothing, but how could she be like Hauke in any capacity?

Maybe he didn't need to fake his sickness after all. He wasn't sure he'd felt this bad in a very long time.

A distant bell rang in the distance, a reminder that his time was limited. He had to keep looking.

He opened up a few more books, flipping through the pages quickly, and the fear of too much passing time sent a chill down his neck. He needed to get out of this room.

He needed to find a way to the basement. He had to.

He set the last notebook down, rearranging them so they were in perfect order–just as they were when she left.

The dresser was burning a hole in the back of his head, calling him to look through it, to figure out what the hell was inside. He could feel his magic stirring at the thought of what lay within.

Would it change everything between them? More than learning she was the next Cleanser already had?

Was there anything at all to change?

He made his way over to the drawer, his heart thudding as he reached toward the handle.

Footsteps. Voices. Shit.

Kalen moved swiftly, hopping back into Bryn's bed, praying whoever was in the hallway hadn't come for him.

A knock confirmed his fear.

Had he been set up?

"Bryn?" a woman's voice called from the other side of the door. Kalen's heartbeat was thrumming through his ears.

Another knock. "Oh, wait, I think she's working today."

The voices carried down the hall, away from her room. Away from Kalen.

It had been too damn close.

He waited another moment before peeling the covers back and going straight to the dresser. Time was not a luxury here, so he opened up the drawer to begin the search.

He moved her shirts carefully, being mindful of the way they were each folded and in what order. The scent of Bryn was wafting through the air each time he moved one, a steady reminder of where he was—a darker reminder of what he had to do.

He kept digging until he got down to the last shirt, but he came up empty. He ran his fingers along the inner edge of the drawer.

Still nothing.

He knew for sure something was here; he had seen her grab it in the first place, and he heard her put it back. At least, he thought he did. Had she kept it with her?

Maybe she didn't trust him the same way he didn't trust her?

He sifted through the drawer for several more minutes before frustration took over and he slammed it shut. Whatever she's hiding, she didn't want Kalen to be the one to find it.

And, somehow, that made this horrible situation feel much worse.

Kalen opened Bryn's door slowly, peeking his head into the hall to see if anyone was near. He took off in the opposite direction, leaving all he had just learned behind.

All except for that note.

The next Cleanser.

If Kalen could pull this off, there would never need to be another Cleanser at all.

He sent up a quick prayer to Earth Mother that no one would find him roaming these halls.

Maybe he would be able to spin some kind of web of lies if he did? He didn't know where he was; he was new to The Order and got lost in the massive building.

They weren't completely lies. But they were definitely a stretch of the truth.

He needed to be doing more of that anyway. Kalen the hybrid was more important to keep safe than Kalen the Orderly.

It seemed like every part of the High Seminary was the same. Long stone hallways, rich alabaster floors. Each ceiling was tall enough that a whisper would turn into an echo. His footsteps created a thundering beat no matter how softly he walked. It was a chilling reminder that Hauke Elowen would do all he could. That he would *learn* all he could. He had eyes and ears everywhere, even the walls.

Kalen had no idea what he was looking for. He ran his fingers along the wall, trying to notice if there was anything that felt off. If his magic called him to something.

Nothing.

How could he not find anything?

Because they didn't want him to. They wanted to keep a secret.

Kalen froze, stunned by his own train of thought. How had he missed it?

Liam had a secret room in his office. Could that kind of clever run in the family?

Kalen pivoted quickly, turning back the way he came, doing his best not to hit a light jog.

He needed to get to Hauke's office.

Something was telling him there was more to the small room than met the eye. He just had to figure out what it was.

There was an unfortunate snag in Kalen's plan to get to Hauke's office. He would have to pass by Bryn.

Bryn, who thought he was sick in her room.

He could see her blonde hair from the other end of the grand room. She had a pencil in her hand, writing something with a small smile on her face.

He approached the desk cautiously. Bryn saw him almost immediately and rose from the desk, walking quickly to where he was before pulling his forehead down to her lips.

"You've cooled down," she said with relief, checking his temperature. "Thank Athero."

"The bit of sleep really did wonders for me," he lied, trying to make his voice sound tired. "Thanks again for letting me steal your bed."

"Any time," she answered joyfully. "Well, not *any* time." Her eyes grew wide. "Like, at the appropriate times."

Kalen chuckled in response. There was something so charming about these moments with her.

"Hey, where's the nearest bathroom?" He pivoted. "Is there one around here?"

Please be near Hauke's office, please be near Hauke's office.

"Oh, of course, sorry I didn't show you where the communal one was in the wing." She shook her head. "There's one right by where we hold Age of Athero." She pointed toward the way to Hauke's office. "I can walk you there?"

"Oh no," Kalen responded simply. "I've taken you from your job already once today. I got it."

Bryn headed back toward her seat behind the desk. "Great." She flipped her book shut quickly. "I'll see you later?"

"Maybe." Kalen winked, taking a page from his Dad's book of charm. *Stupid.*

He made quick work of finding the bathroom Bryn had directed him to. While it was near Hauke's office, it wasn't close enough to look like he was lost. Being in the halls like this could put a target on his back.

It was a risk he was willing to take.

Fortunately, it paid off as he stood outside Hauke's office. The door seemed to cast a shadow that made him feel small.

Kalen's bones were shaking. Not his hands, not his feet—his bones. A full body quiver, standing in front of the door of the one capable of so much evil. He had seen the cruelty of Hauke Elowen over and over and over again. Could he really do all of this alone?

He was a nobody from the Sanctwood that somehow ended up here. Wasn't that how every great story started? Someone seemingly insignificant, believing they could make a great difference?

He wouldn't let his story end the way The Order wanted it to. Hybrids lost to history, a stain on the way they thought things should be.

He was more than that. And he deserved to be free exactly as he was. No matter what it costs. No matter who he lost.

He took a deep breath, quelling the voice inside of him, and listened intently. Having trouble hearing over the sound of his own heartbeat, he pressed his ear to the door.

Silence.

He rapped lightly against the wooden frame.

Silence.

Here goes nothing.

Kalen reached his hand to the knob, his fingers trembling as they made contact with the brass handle, preparing for whatever lay beyond the door.

Would he find something that could change everything?

He turned the handle.

Stuck.

The door was locked.

Shit.

He would have to come back when the devil himself was home.

Chapter Thirty-Nine
Kalen

The next few days passed quickly. He and Tessan had spent time catching up, and Eugenia slowly began showing her face more. Kalen was grateful to be with them both, trying to forget all he'd learned.

Today was his second Age of Athero class. He hadn't seen Bryn since he left the High Seminary a few days ago. It was what was best for both of them, after he'd invaded her privacy and found out the truth about her lineage; about her future.

The next Cleanser.

He pulled the note out from under the couch cushion. He had read it a hundred times since he took it from Bryn's room. He wondered if she was missing it–if she knew it was gone at all.

He was lying on the couch, note open on his chest, when Tessan's bedroom door flew open.

"Morning." She walked toward the kitchen. "How'd you sleep?"

Kalen quickly folded up the note, stuffing it under his pillow, praying Tessan hadn't seen it.

"What was that?" Tessan changed course, her face full of curiosity. "A love note?" Her voice rose in a taunt.

Of course she saw it.

"Something like that," he huffed in response, folding his hands behind his head, weighing what it would be like to tell Tessan all he knew now. It had been tearing him apart the last few days.

He had been quieter, less engaged, stuck in his head. Bryn was the next Head Cleanser—the next person to enforce Athero's beliefs that hybrids weren't meant to exist.

She wouldn't have held his hand so tightly, wouldn't have kissed his cheek, wouldn't have let her gaze linger for so long, if she had known that he was one that they called unclean.

How could he reconcile that?

"What's going on, Kale?" Tessan sat down in the crook of his outstretched body, resting her hand on his arm. "You've been off."

He took a deep breath, slipping his hand under his pillow, feeling the edges of the note.

"You know I like Bryn," she replied. "You don't have to hide how you feel about her."

He silently handed her the note.

Tessan unfolded it cautiously, tilting her head to the side in confusion at the worn paper. Realization settled in that this wasn't a freshly written letter.

She slowly began to scan the page. Kalen's stomach churned as he watched Tessan's eyes slide across the letter, before finally growing wide with understanding.

Tessan lowered the paper and looked at Kalen, exasperated. "This can't be real."

"I know," Kalen said softly. "I found it the other day in her room."

"Her room?!" she exclaimed. "We'll come back to that." Kalen was grateful for her pivot back to the note. "I can't believe this," she gaped. "Hauke's *granddaughter*? The next Head Cleanser?"

"Yep," Kalen responded. He let his head fall back against his pillow with a thud.

"I'm sorry." Tessan motioned for him to scoot over so she could lie down next to him. She draped her arms around him in a hug.

It felt nice to be with her right now. To finally tell someone the truth.

Tessan reached up, resting her hand on his face. "I know how much you like her."

"I don't–" Kalen started, before Tessan laughed, interrupting him.

"I know you do," she said without judgment.

She was right.

And he would have to spend forever without her.

"It changes things." It was all he could manage to say as he looked into the witch's icy eyes.

"Does it, though?" she said softly as she took a deep breath. "You two never really had a chance, huh?"

Kalen winced. "I guess not."

"You're just like your dad." She pinched his cheek jokingly. "Wanting what ya should have never had."

She was doing her best to diffuse his sadness. And while it hurt, she was right. He'd always known there was no possibility of a life with Bryn Elowen in it.

"Does that make you Eugenia?" he clapped back. "Keeping everyone's secrets?"

"There are worse people to be." She shrugged.

He agreed with that.

They settled into an easy silence as Tessan nestled into his chest. Kalen wrapped his arms around her now, grateful for the ways Tessan kept him connected to himself.

"Hey, Kale?" she whispered. "I really am sorry about Bryn."

"Thanks," he responded, rubbing her back. "I am too."

Kalen couldn't believe all that had happened since the last time he attended The Age of Athero. Just last week, he had been talking to Acer Jules in front of the class. And now, Acer was holed up at his mother's house in the Sanctwood Forest after Kalen had saved his life.

A lot could change in a week. He knew that better than anyone.

He wondered how it was all going. Were his parents doing okay living under the same roof? Had his dad's charm lowered Acer's defenses? His mother's?

He needed to visit soon. He *wanted* to visit soon. He missed them.

The classroom door was propped open as he approached. He saw the empty seat by Bryn—saved for him. Just like last week. Though, unlike last week when he arrived exactly on time, he decided to show up a few minutes early today. He didn't have anything better to do.

Or at least that's what he told himself. He knew, despite all he learned, he just wanted to spend more time with her. Before the inevitable happened, and they never saw each other again. Before he would do what had to be done to destroy The Order altogether.

Whatever that meant.

Would he have to take her down, too? Would he be able to live with himself if he did? He paused, admiring her from behind. The way she sat hunched over, nose in her notebook, scribbling away at Gods only knew what.

He wondered how she had spent this much time alone. How no one else at the High Seminary knew how amazing she was. Or maybe they did, and she hadn't been interested?

The thought sent a pang of jealousy through him. He didn't want to think of her with anyone else.

He would have to get over that.

"Hi." She smiled as he slid into his seat. "I missed you."

"Hey," he grinned back. "It's only been a few days."

He really missed her, too.

"Too long for me," she responded, cracking open her notebook. "How's the date planning going?"

It's not going at all.

"Great." He fumbled his words. "Are you free tomorrow night?"

"I am now." She smiled. "Meet at your mom's?"

He nodded, his response interrupted by a spike in his magic. The hair on the back of his neck began to stand. He knew this feeling; he only felt it when–

"Good afternoon, everyone."

Hauke swept into the room, his powerful presence causing half of the class to hold their breath, and the other half to swoon in the presence of the Head Cleanser.

"I regret to share that Acer Jules will no longer be teaching this class," he continued casually, setting a book down on the desk. "So you will have me for the next couple of weeks while we work to find a suitable replacement."

Regret my ass.

The classroom was completely silent in response.

"Please, dear friends," Hauke said with a smile. "Let us take a breath together, hm?" He inhaled deeply, encouraging the class to do the same. "I may be the Head Cleanser out there." He gestured to the door. "But in here, I am nothing more than a loyal follower of the covenant, just like you."

Bryn let out a soft laugh beside Kalen, her eyes showing so much adoration for Hauke. *Her grandfather.*

"Now," Hauke continued. "Let's pick up where Acer left off."

He walked over to the chalkboard. "Today's lesson is one of my favorites." He laughed casually. "Open your notebooks, please."

Hauke began to write on the board, U-N-C-L.

No.

E-A-N.

He underlined the word twice before turning back to the classroom. "Today, we'll be learning about the Unclean."

Kalen's shoulders tensed, his breath caught in his throat.

"You okay?" Bryn whispered, staring at him for a beat longer than usual, her eyebrows curious, as if noticing the sudden shift in his posture.

"Yes," Kalen managed to squeak back. "I must have just slept wrong or something," he continued, moving his head in a slow circle. "Just a spasm." He reached up, grasping the back of his neck—hoping he could convince her he was telling her the truth.

She pouted her lips in response and placed her hand over his. She began to give his neck a gentle squeeze, trying to massage the knots that didn't exist in the first place.

His magic flared at her touch.

The way she cared gutted him. He wished she didn't care at all.

Kalen looked back toward the chalkboard to see Hauke staring at him—an evil grin plastered on his face. He had seen this grin in the Hollow, moments before Hauke sent the blade of the guillotine soaring down through his father's neck.

The memory flashed through him again, Hauke's teeth bared, *"You're going to have to do better than that."*

He knew. Gods damn it. Somehow, Hauke knew who he was.

"Bryn?" Hauke called after her as they walked out of class. "Can I speak with you, please?"

She turned to Kalen. "I don't want to say bye yet. Meet me in my room?"

Say no.

"Yeah," he answered. "I'll see you up there."

He turned and walked out of the classroom, made a sharp turn to look like he was headed to the bathroom, and patiently waited for the last person to leave the class before he crept back over to the door frame.

How often would he be able to hear a conversation between Hauke and Bryn?

"You don't know him, Bryn," Hauke said in a low voice.

"He's good, Grandpop," Bryn responded with conviction. "I've even been to his home. I've met some of his family," she continued. "He's different from the other Orderlys."

"His home?" Hauke inquired. "Here in Evermere?"

"Yes?" she responded, annoyance lacing her voice. "It's close to Hydro's, the one with the terracotta colored roof. It's a safe walk from here."

This can't be happening.

"And he lives with his mother?" Hauke inquired curiously.

"Grandpop, please," she whined. "Yes, he lives with his mother." Kalen heard her feet shuffling. "Can I go now?"

Shit, he needed to get out of here.

"You can't blame me for being protective of you, Bryn," he retorted. "People aren't always as they seem."

"I know." Her voice was muffled, like he had scooped her up in a hug. "But he is."

"Tell him to come by my office tomorrow," he replied. "If you're going to date him, I would like to spend some time with him."

No, no, no.

"Deal," she confirmed. "Don't scare him either."

"No promises." Hauke laughed.

He was going to be sick.

He couldn't go to Bryn's room. He couldn't be here at all. He needed to go home.

He sprinted toward the door of the High Seminary, running straight toward the only safety he's really ever known.

His mother.

Chapter Forty

Ria

Having Westin in her home was a bad idea. His patience with Acer, his care around the house, felt too real. Too close to the life she almost had. She never had to wash a dish, sweep the floor, or make a bed. And she felt so...safe. Even in the midst of having an Orderly in their home.

The three of them had fallen into a routine that went something like:

Ria foraged, came home, and made breakfast.

Westin and Acer woke up, and they talked for a while.

They joined her for breakfast, and the table was silent.

Acer stared at Westin in disbelief.

Westin stared at Ria when he thought she wasn't paying attention.

She was always paying attention.

Westin would take Acer out of the house. They'd talk more.

Ria wished she could hear them.

Ria wished she could send post to Eugenia. She missed her friend.

But she wouldn't send a letter.

Westin and Acer came inside.

Ria would leave to sit under the giant oak tree and wish for a life that had turned out differently. Full of the truth, not the lies they'd all spun to keep each other safe.

This was the cost of that safety.

Loneliness.

Repeat. Repeat. Repeat.

Wish. Wish. Wish.

"Westin?" She walked back into the house from her evening under the oak tree. There was no response to her call.

"Westin?" she called again, peering into Kalen's room. She was surprised to see Acer sitting there instead.

"I won't bite," he joked. "West told me if I left this room, he'd kill me," he huffed. "I believe him, so here I sit."

Against her better judgment, Ria leaned against the doorframe, settling into the conversation. "At least *you* believe him," she muttered under her breath.

"I heard you, you know?" Acer responded. "Do you want to talk about it?"

"Not with a stranger who has been on the hunt for my family, no," she answered frankly.

"That was before your son saved my life," Acer responded. "I believe I owe you one."

"I think you owe us all more than one," she replied sharply.

"I think you're right," he chuckled. "You know, West was one of my very best friends." He trailed off. "We couldn't believe it...when everything happened."

"This isn't helping," she responded, turning to leave the room.

"Wait!" he exclaimed. "We couldn't believe it because we thought we had everything we needed in The Order, you know?" He spoke softly. "Hauke makes you believe the world starts and stops inside those walls. West was always looking for more, somehow." He stared into the distance. "Like he always knew more than the rest of us about life."

"He's always been like that," she remarked.

"I think he wishes he really did die that day." Acer looked into her eyes. "So you and Kalen could have just been free."

"I'm glad he didn't," she responded easily, returning his stare.

Now that he was alive, Ria couldn't imagine the alternative. Not being able to see him again or talk to him. Missing the moments between him and Kalen.

"Does he know?" Acer asked. "That you're glad he's alive?"

"I don't know," Ria said simply.

"You should tell him, then." Acer leaned back on his hands. "Trust me, life changes fast...one day you're hunting for your ex-friend in the woods and the next you're saved by his hybrid son and living with the love of his life." He huffed out another laugh and shook his head.

Love of his life.

"Anyway," he continued. "They don't make them like Westin Vale," Acer said casually. "And I get it, you really are beautiful. Anyone would be lucky to have you."

Is he...flirting?

"Thanks, Acer," Ria responded with trepidation. "I appreciate the talk."

"Of course," he responded. "If you want to talk any more, you know where to find me."

She nodded, shutting the door behind her.

What the hell just happened?

"Dinner's ready," she called through the house, keeping to their routine.

Westin arrived home minutes after Ria had left the conversation with Acer. He dropped off some vegetables on the counter before dipping his head and going into Kalen's room to check on Acer.

Did they talk about her? Is that why Acer shared what he had earlier? *Love of his life.*

The words echoed through her mind.

Would she always love Westin this way?

"Mom?" The door opened swiftly as Kalen hurried inside, breathing heavily.

"Kalen?" She rushed to him. "What's wrong?"

"I just need you." He fell into her arms, and his tears began flowing before she understood what was happening. She held him tight and walked them toward the couch. Having Kalen in her arms like this felt like he was a toddler again. Like this was a scraped knee after a long day of foraging.

She heard the door to Kalen's room open and noticed Westin sticking his head through the crack with curiosity.

She shook her head no in his direction, a gentle ask. *Please, let me have this moment with him.*

He nodded in return and closed the door softly.

Yes, she decided at that moment, she would always love Westin this way.

She turned her attention back to Kalen. "Start from the beginning, my love." She ran her hand through his hair. "And tell me everything."

Chapter Forty-One
Kalen

Kalen told her about Bryn, about Hauke, the hybrid he saw in class, the letter in Bryn's room, and about the mess he was walking himself into.

She sat there, nodded along, squeezed his hands when he needed comfort, and scoffed in disbelief when he needed that, too.

There was no one in the world like his mother.

"It's a small world, isn't it?" she said, running her fingers through his hair absentmindedly. "The man who tried to kill the man I love is the same man who helped raise the woman you love," she whispered.

"I didn't say I loved her," Kalen responded. "I don't know what I feel."

Did he love her?

"How did you decide you wanted to be with Dad, despite everything?" Kalen asked curiously.

"He made me feel the most *me*," Ria sighed. "There's no other way to explain it. He looked at me, and I felt like he understood my soul. Like he wouldn't change a single thing about who I was."

"He still does." Kalen nudged her. "Look at you like that."

"Yeah, I know." She turned her gaze toward the door of Kalen's room. "But things get more complicated as you get older."

Things feel complicated now.

"Do you think you'll be able to forgive Eugenia for all of it?" Kalen questioned her, changing the subject. "She's hardly left her room."

"I don't know," Ria responded truthfully, still staring into the distance. "Like I said, things get more complicated as you get older."

"I don't think they always have to be," he said. "Maybe life is too short to spend time mad at the people you love?"

She chuckled. "Who made you so damn smart?"

"Well, it definitely wasn't the bird." He laughed before leaning up. "There's one more thing I need to do, but you can't tell anyone." She looked at him curiously. "Just trust me."

Kalen turned toward his mother, grabbed her hands, and lifted one to his temple.

He transported her back to the Evermere Market fifteen years ago, when her best friend tried to save a wounded crow. Their Wen. Her West.

He had no idea what his future was like with Bryn. What his future looked like at all, really.

But he did know his mother deserved to be happy. *Truly* happy.

He knew he couldn't fix everything. But maybe, just maybe, he could fix this.

It felt good to get all of it off his chest. To get away from the High Seminary, from his fake life, and exist in the world that raised him.

A reminder of who he really was—away from the lying that was burning a hole through his soul.

He shared real parts of himself with Bryn. Almost everything.

Except for his real mom. And his dad. And his home. And the truth about who he was.

Maybe he hadn't actually shared much at all.

Shit.

He decided to stay for dinner, curious about how things had been going here since Acer arrived. He was surprised to see the routine they'd all fallen into. Though the food had gone cold thanks to Kalen's abrupt arrival.

"Kalen." Acer nodded to him. "Thank you for your kindness in saving my life."

Oh, we're jumping right into this.

"It was the right thing to do." Kalen shrugged. "I'd do it again."

Kalen watched his mother light up out of the corner of his eye. "Actually, Acer," she mentioned. "We could use your help, and I think you may owe us one."

"We could?" his father chimed in, casually taking a bite of greens. "With what?"

"What do you know about Bryn Elowen?" she continued.

Kalen dropped his fork.

"I was wondering when this would come up," he chuckled. "You two were awfully close that first day in class."

Kalen sank into his seat, his cheeks turning a bright red.

This is so damn embarrassing.

Kalen glanced at his father, the confusion covering his face. His mother cleared her throat, bringing the attention back to her question. "So?"

"Bryn is wonderful," Acer started. "She's been around the High Seminary most of her life because of Hau–"

"Who the hell is Bryn?" his dad asked, still eating his food.

"I'll tell you more later," his mother chimed in.

"Well, how am I supposed to follow this conversation if I don't know Bry–"

"Westin," his mother said softly. "I'll talk to you later, please."

He nodded.

"Anyway." Acer cleared his throat. "She's just a sweet girl. A loyal follower of the covenant and Athero."

"Is she dangerous?" his mother responded curiously.

"If she's spent any time with Hauke, she's dangerous," his father chirped back.

"Westin, I swear." His mother's eyes were beady.

"Sorry, sorry." He put his hands up in submission. "Sorry."

"She's not dangerous in the way Hauke is," Acer placed his fork down. "She wouldn't try to murder us, for instance." He gestured between himself and Kalen's father. "But she is in the way that she only knows tradition, and carries the teachings of Athero very close to her heart." Acer's voice grew steady. "I'm assuming she doesn't know more about...you?"

Kalen shook his head no.

"Yeah." Acer shrugged, shaking his head. "That's a hard place to be."

"Tell us about the registration cards," his mother followed up, grilling Acer. She wasn't leaving a single moment for Kalen to process what he was hearing.

"Ria, I'm a bit uncomfortable with this line of questioning." Acer shifted in his seat.

"I'm sorry to hear that," his mother responded. "If you'd like to continue to stay in my home, I do need you to respond."

"Ruthless," Kalen heard his father whisper with a chuckle.

"Protective," his mother corrected. "They have our son's information," she continued. "Whether all of it is true or not, they know who he is."

Acer took a deep breath. "He tracks every person who sets foot into the High Seminary."

"We know that much," his mother snapped. "Why?"

"In case one of them is...you," he responded. "Any of you."

The table grew silent.

"He has not stopped looking for you," Acer said, turning to Kalen's father. "Since you broke free. And he knew you would try to find her." He pointed toward Kalen's mother. "And figured there was a child involved, based on how unbreakable West was in the basement."

The unclean trinity. Would they always be chased like this?

"But why can't he leave us alone now?" his mother shouted. "Why is he still trying to find us after all these years?"

"Because *no one* has ever bested Hauke. Especially the way that West did," Acer said plainly. "An Orderly fae, in love with a witch, right under his nose for years? That doesn't happen to Hauke Elowen. *And* throw in the fact that you escaped the basement?" Acer shook his head. "He's obsessed with finding all of you. He won't stop until he does."

Kalen pushed his plate away. He had always known coming back here, being visible the way he was, was dangerous. But hearing the words from Acer's mouth made it more real.

And he won't stop until he does.

The silence between them clung to Kalen. The words stuck to him like sweat on a hot day in the Sanctwood. Peace would never find them.

"Tell me about the hybrid from class," Kalen said, breaking the tension. "Why are they there?"

"Hauke hunts them," Acer said simply. "If there's a hybrid in Evermere, he knows somehow." He shrugged. "I'd be very surprised if he didn't know the truth about you already."

His father slammed his fist on the table. "We shouldn't have come back here. We should have just stayed in Wyrdbrook, and none of this would have ever happened."

"*Wyrdbrook*?" Acer asked curiously.

Shit.

"He meant the Sanctwood," Kalen cut in quickly. "Slip of the tongue."

"Sure," Acer smirked. "Hauke gives the hybrids a choice–submit to the order and surrender your power, or be exiled."

"So, the hybrid from your class—" Kalen started before Acer cut him off.

"Her name is Olive."

"Okay, Olive," Kalen continued. "She's there because she wants to be?"

"She's choosing to be there for her own survival," Acer responded flippantly. "Wants are thrown out the window when the other option is death."

"But you said he was just exiling them?" Kalen questioned.

"Exile from Evermere almost always means death," Acer said. "You're cut off from everything and everyone. Those who don't die of starvation die of loneliness."

Maybe living in the forest all this time wasn't so bad.

"But we've heard of a secret place, run by an Overseer who shows them kindness–gives them another shot," Acer continued. "Sound familiar?"

Kalen gulped. "No, but it sounds like it would be nice."

"Very," Acer squinted at Kalen. It was a challenge, but Kalen wouldn't break.

"That's enough for tonight," his father cut in. "Ace, thank you for sharing all of this with us." He stood up from his chair. "Ria, can I see you in your room, please?"

She nodded and stood up, then leaned over to kiss Kalen's head. "Are you heading back to Eugenia's?"

"Yep." He leaned back in his chair. "I'll see you all soon?"

"You better," his dad called back. "You've skipped out on training too many times to be worth a shit when this inevitably goes south."

His mother elbowed his father in the ribs. It made Kalen laugh. "I'll be back to beat your ass in a few days, don't worry."

He watched as his parents walked into his mother's room and heard his father's voice faintly through the walls. "Okay, who the hell is Bryn?"

Kalen smiled before standing up, tipping his head to Acer. "Thanks for everything tonight," he said genuinely. "It really helps."

"Like your mother said–I owed you one," Acer responded. "Be safe heading back to town."

"I will," Kalen said, sticking his hand out for a handshake. Acer obliged.

"You're a good one, Kalen," Acer said with a sadness Kalen couldn't place.

"I learned from the best." He looked toward his mother's room. "See you around?"

"See you around." Acer stayed seated as Kalen headed out the door and back to Eugenia's.

He had a date to plan.

The night air was cool on his face, a welcome relief from the thoughts burning through his brain. Acer had told them so much over the course of dinner that Kalen wasn't sure he was making the right move by heading back to Evermere right now.

Especially if Hauke knew who he was.

Leaves crunched under him as he followed a new path to town, doing his best to stay hidden among the shadows–making sure no one could track which direction he was coming or going. He did that every time he came back home, just in case someone was watching him.

"*Run,*" the trees began to whisper in a hurried tone, doing their best to protect the boy they helped raise. "*Quickly, Kalen.*"

Kalen took off in a dead sprint, but it was too late as a body came crashing onto him, pinning him face down in the dirt.

"What the hell!" he cried out, terrified, as the stranger grabbed his hands, holding them behind his back. "I'm just trying to go home," Kalen responded, thrashing against the restraint. "My mother will be worried if I don't make it for dinner." He dug deep into his well of power, calling for the fire deep within him to fight back.

"I think we both know that's a lie, Kalen." A familiar voice taunted him.

"Acer?" Kalen's breath caught in his throat. "Please, let me go," he pleaded. "You don't have to do this."

"Sorry, kid," he exhaled. Kalen's scalp screamed as Acer ripped his hair back, pulling his face off the ground. "This is the only way I can go back home." He slammed Kalen's head to the ground. His illusion of safety had officially shattered. This game was over. And Kalen's life likely was, too.

I tried my best.

It wasn't enough. He would never be enough.

The world went dark, and the flame that had been building in Kalen's stomach had extinguished, too.

Chapter Forty-Two

West

"How could he get involved with her?" West paced the room. "He knows better than that."

"I don't know, Westin," Ria answered sarcastically. "That story doesn't sound at all familiar to you?"

He paused, looking at her. "It's not going to end well for him."

"It may not." She walked over to him slowly. "But what if it does?"

"How could it?" he responded plainly, sitting down on her bed. "They've built their relationship on a lie."

"To protect themselves from each other," Ria followed up, sitting down beside him. "He has to learn all of this on his own, the same way we did."

"I don't want him to get hurt," West sighed. "Or killed. They're dangerous, Ri."

"I know," Ria spoke softly, reaching up to put a hand on his face. He foolishly leaned into it again, testing the waters. "But he's brilliant and brave. He's going to be okay."

"Okay," he replied, lifting his hand to lay on top of hers. "I trust you."

He stood up, stretching his arms over his head. "I'm going to get back out there and talk with Acer." He headed toward the door. "Sleep well, Ria."

"You, too, West," she answered simply, a sly smirk slid across her lips. *West.*

She called him West, and she knew how much it would mean to him. After weeks and weeks of *Westin*, of the formalities, she finally called him West again.

He would never give up on her. On them. He'd never push, but he'd never move on.

He walked into the kitchen, the smile still plastered to his face. "Ace?" he called.

Silence.

He didn't know why he felt it, or what he felt. But his magic perked up in the absence of something.

Of someone.

Acer.

"No," he whispered, moving swiftly toward Kalen's room. The room he and Acer had been staying in for the last several days. Reconnecting, talking about life, about Ria. What things could be like for Acer now that he wasn't in The Order.

Empty.

"No," he said again, louder, the panic began to build in his body.

He turned toward the desk and saw a slip of paper sitting on top of a notebook. He walked slowly toward it, his magic buzzing in panic.

Please, Gods, No.

I'm sorry, West.

- Ace

"NO!" He slammed his hand on the desk. "RIA!"

"What?!" She came sprinting into Kalen's empty room. "What?"

Westin held up the piece of paper. "Acer is gone."

Ria snatched the note from his hand. "How?" Her eyes met his in a panic. "What if he has Kalen?"

West froze; the thought hadn't crossed his mind somehow. How could it not have crossed his mind? "We have to go. Now. They will come back for us."

"They have our boy, West." She was frozen in fear.

"I know," he replied. "I promise you that nothing will happen to him."

"How can you promise that?" Ria turned to him. "You cannot promise that."

"Because I'm the one they really want," West responded. "So I'm the one they're going to get."

"West, please." She grabbed him. "Please don't leave me again."

Please don't leave me again.

"If there's another way, I'll find it," he said. "I need you to go to Wyrdbrook. Okay?" He paced. "Liam will keep you safe."

"No," Ria said firmly. "No, I'm coming with you."

"Ria," he responded, grabbing her hands. "I can't let anything happen to you."

"Then don't. But we will go together."

"Ri-" he choked out.

"I am not sitting in the shadows while they have my son. *Our* son." She stood up. "And I will not lose you again."

"Okay," he conceded. How could he say no to her now? To a mother who would go to the end of the earth for her son?

"Okay?" Ria looked at him, surprised.

"Okay. Let's go save our boy."

He squeezed her hand, and together they sprinted out of their small safe haven, leaving every version of what could have been behind.

Chapter Forty-Three
Kalen

It was dark and damp.

Kalen heard a steady drip in the corner of the room–it matched the slow rhythm of his heart.

He didn't have to be told where he was. He already knew. He remembered it from his father's memories–from his own Awakening.

He was locked in the basement of the High Seminary–like a monster–while the world continued on above him. He wondered if Bryn was sitting at her desk. If she knew he was down here.

"Hello?" he spoke softly into the darkness.

There was no reply.

He was alone.

What was the point of coming here? What was the point of any of it? Why did he save Acer just to have him turn his back on him and end up here? Did being good matter at all?

Where was Earth Mother? He had nothing left to believe in.

This was the end.

He was stupid to think he would ever live a life outside of the one he'd always had. What he had been building was fake. He didn't belong here in Evermere. Maybe he didn't belong anywhere at all.

If he had never existed, maybe his mother would have been able to enjoy her own life. Maybe his father would have given up on the idea of finding her. She could have been truly happy.

Instead, his mother hid away in a forest for Kalen, missing out on her own life *for him*.

He only caused people pain. He was nothing more than an unclean bastard. He understood now why Hauke wanted him to disappear. Why everyone hated hybrids. Didn't they understand that he would always hate himself more?

More. More. More.

He started clawing at his skin. If he could just rip this feeling off of him, this grime from his own life. This idea that he would have ever been more.

More. More. More.

That he could have ever made a difference.

Stupid. Stupid. Stupid.

People like Kalen didn't belong.

Kalen didn't belong.

He was going to die here.

Maybe that was best for everyone.

And for the first time, Kalen wondered what it would be like if he just...gave up.

Chapter Forty-Four
Tessan

It was late, and Kalen wasn't back. This had become a routine Tessan didn't appreciate.

A knock at the door startled her out of her chair.

About time.

She walked to the door, turning the knob. "You really have to stop getting back so late–" She looked up. "Ria?"

"Can we come in?"

We?

She noticed the crow perched on her shoulder.

"Of course, please." She moved to the side, letting Ria and West in. "Is everything okay?"

Why are they here? Where is Kalen? What is happening?

"No, actually," Ria answered in a hushed tone as West shifted swiftly. Tessan watched as he ran to each window, drawing the curtains closed.

"We think they have Kalen," West responded breathlessly. His attempt to steady himself was frail–Tessan could see right through him. She could see through both of them.

And because they were this worried, she felt herself begin to crumble, too.

"Who?" The words fell from her mouth quickly. "How?"

A door behind her creaked open slowly, a sound Tessan had almost forgotten with how much time her aunt had spent in her room these last few days. She turned to look at Eugenia, to prepare her for what she would soon learn.

They have Kalen.

But her aunt wasn't looking at her. She was locked in on Ria. Confusion settled into her brow, and Eugenia tilted her head and began to speak.

"Ri?" Tessan noticed her aunt's voice was tender. "What are you all doing here?"

"We need your help." Ria's vulnerability was exposed like a wound. "Both of you." She reached out to Tessan, grabbing her hand.

Tessan turned back to her aunt and watched in adoration as the light flickered back to her eyes for the first time in a very long time. "Anything for you, Ria. *Always.*"

The group made their way to the common room quickly. Ria and West swapped lines and shared the story of the last several days. They explained what Acer had told them over dinner, and why they believed he was the one who had Kalen.

Kalen not showing up here tonight confirmed they were right.

"How can we help?" Tessan started the conversation. "None of us have ever been to the High Seminary. I wouldn't even know where to start."

"Well, I have," West responded, cutting in. "They have to have him in the basement...where they kept me." He shook his head while Eugenia lowered hers. "I just don't know how to get *in* there."

"What about Bryn?" Ria was throwing ideas against the wall to see if they would stick. "Would she know?"

"I can find out," Tessan replied. "I think she trusts me *just* enough."

"Tess, this is dangerous," Eugenia cut in. "Are you sure?"

"I'm positive," Tessan responded firmly. "And I imagine we don't have much time."

"We have more than you think," West said. "Kalen is probably suffering, yes." He flinched at his own admission. "But Hauke isn't going to kill him. Not yet."

"How can you be sure of that?" Ria asked in desperation. "He's vile."

"I know," West responded. "But the goal *has* to be to lure us there first."

The words were hardly out of West's mouth when another knock rang out against the door. It was aggressive, powerful.

And they weren't expecting any visitors.

Eugenia's eyes grew wide. "Everyone hide," she mouthed to the group. "One moment!" She called toward the door, gesturing for Tessan, West, and Ria to hide in the house.

The knocks continued, growing louder and more forceful. "You have thirty seconds to open the door by Order of Hauke Elowen," an unfamiliar voice called from the other side. "Or we will break it down."

Shit.

West pointed toward Tessan's room before shifting into his bird form, a nudge to get somewhere they wouldn't be seen before it was too late.

Ria grabbed Tessan's hand, pulling her into the room, quietly shutting the door behind them.

"We need to stay calm," Ria said softly to Tessan, looking around the small room to determine where they should hide. "We're going to be okay. I've got you."

They settled on Tessan's closet, and held each other tight in the back corner, their rapid breaths seemed to sync somehow. They were covered in clothes, and Tessan found herself praying it would be enough to keep them both hidden.

Tessan's heart was pounding as she heard the front door open. Her aunt's voice rang out calmly in the distance.

"I apologize for my delay, gentleman," Eugenia started. "What can I help you with?"

"We've been told by the Head Cleanser to retrieve you. Grab your things," a gruff voice demanded.

"The Head Cleanser himself sent for me?" Eugenia kept her voice light. "Well, how lucky am I?"

"He doesn't take kindly to those who harbor hybrids," the man spat. "I'd say goodbye to your pretty home."

"I'm not sure what you're talking about," Eugenia said, her voice faltering just enough to reveal her terror. Tessan's stomach churned at her response. Genie was never scared.

"I'll make this simple," the man replied. "Come with us or the boy dies."

She felt Ria flinch beside her. Tessan pulled her in tighter.

"Where are you taking me?" Eugenia's voice was high-pitched now. "Let me go!" The sound of a fight rang through her and Ria's ears. Tessan felt a tear fall on her shoulder. They were both losing Eugenia, and there wasn't a single thing they could do about it.

The door slammed shut, and the house was quiet—a stark reminder that she was gone. Genie was gone. Tessan and Ria remained still in the closet. Tessan wasn't sure the men had left. Would they come back looking for *her*?

Footsteps clomped across the living room floor, and the two witches froze again.

"Ria? Tessan?"

West.

"In here," Ria called out as they climbed out of the closet.

Tessan watched Ria and West embrace. Ria collapsed in his arms, sobbing. West looked Tessan in her eyes, despair flooding his own. "We have to do something."

Tessan nodded in agreement.

But what the hell could they possibly do?

The three of them stayed up all night plotting against The Order, trying to determine how they'd get to Kalen and Eugenia. They begged sleep to come, but there was too much on the line. Peace never found its way to the common room.

Ria retired to Eugenia's room to be alone, leaving Tessan and West together in the quiet. She was grateful for the time with him. They'd not been able to catch up since they left Wyrdbrook, and they'd formed quite a bond as they waited for Kalen to wake up.

He walked over to where she was sitting and handed her a cup of tea. "You hanging in there?"

"I think I've had better days," she responded softly. "You?"

"Same, kid," he huffed. "Same."

They sat together quietly, each taking small sips of their tea. She sent up a prayer that it would give them the energy they needed to get through what was to come.

"Can I ask you something?" Tessan turned toward West curiously.

She watched as he set his cup down on the table, nodding at her to continue.

"How did you..." she fumbled over her words. "How did you keep hope down there? In the basement?"

She needed to know Kalen would be okay. If he were still alive, would there be any way he would get through it? After all he'd been through in the last couple of years with the Awakening? His Dad? Bryn? Was there too much stacked against him to assume he could come out of this the same? That he would come out of it at all?

"I don't know," West whispered. "I don't know how I did it."

"Hm," Tessan responded, taking another drink.

"Maybe knowing there were people on the other side of it I wanted to see again helped," he continued. "But thinking about how the world kept moving on without me almost made me give up completely."

"Yeah," Tessan answered simply, unsure of what else to say. She wanted to ask him how he refused to give up on Ria, too. If he ever imagined getting over her, or if he just resigned himself to loving her from afar forever. How it felt to be stuck, wondering if they'd ever be anything. Did the wondering pain him the same way it pained her?

"You can ask," West said. "I see your wheels turning over there."

"It just seems so small compared to everything else happening." Tessan looked down at her cup, scared to make eye contact, but she knew he could see right through her. She needed the advice of someone who had been through a version of what she was going through. Can you love something you may never have?

"Look, I don't know what's going on between you two," Westin started, and Tessan's body clenched. "And I don't need to."

"There's nothing going on," Tessan responded, shrinking into herself. "I don't know what we are. *If* we're anything."

"I've been there," he chuckled, looking toward Eugenia's room at Ria. "I think I am there now. But all you can do is keep showing up. Keep showing up every day exactly as you are. And it'll either happen or it won't."

"But what if it never happens?" A tear fell from her cheek.

This is so embarrassing.

"Then he isn't the one." Westin stood up and moved toward her. "And he's an idiot–just like his ole dad." He winked. "For now, let's make sure we save him tomorrow so you have the ability to figure out the rest. Deal?"

"Deal," Tessan sniffed. "Thanks, West."

"You got it." He reached his hand toward her, gesturing her to come in for a hug. She obliged, grateful for the way he showed up for her in the midst of everything. "Try and get some sleep."

Tessan sat back down on the couch as West hurried to Eugenia's room, toward Ria. Always toward Ria. She was still sitting on the bed, still sobbing in her hands. He wrapped her up, brought her to his chest, and closed his eyes as he held her shaking body. Tessan really hoped he ended up with everything he wanted. Gods damn, he deserved it.

Tessan got up, deciding to give them the privacy they deserved. She stumbled to her room and fell flat on the bed, unaware of the time of day–just that sleep wasn't on the table for her tonight. Instead, she replayed the conversation with West on a loop in her mind until the sun began to peek through the blinds, and she knew it was time to get moving.

She hoped Bryn was up for a visit.

Tessan and Ria headed toward the High Seminary—her heart pounding as Ria led the way.

The plan started and ended with Bryn Elowen. Which, of course, was just Tessan's luck. She wasn't going to tell Bryn everything, just that Kalen was *missing* and she needed help finding him. It wasn't a complete lie, not really. She'd conveniently leave out that her grandfather was the one responsible.

A foolproof plan.

They were all banking on Bryn jumping at the opportunity to help. And despite her own feelings, Tessan was grateful the white lie would ultimately keep Bryn busy while West and Ria did what they needed to do. At least it would mean she was safe, and Tessan knew that would mean something to Kalen–if they could save him at all.

The High Seminary towered over Tessan and Ria. In all her years living in Evermere, she never bothered visiting. She always saw the grand spires in the distance—but to her they were the city's symbol of hate; even before getting to know Kalen. She didn't feel like visiting was ever a good use of her time.

She looked over to Ria. "Ready?"

"Yes," she said calmly. "Please be safe in there."

Ria slipped around the corner of the building, and Tessan took a deep breath as she pushed open the giant door. She looked both ways before entering the High Seminary for the very first time.

It was kind of boring. Grand, but boring.

"Welcome in!" she heard Bryn call from her left. "I'll be with you in just a second."

Well, she definitely doesn't know anything is going on.

"Hey." She walked frantically toward Bryn's desk, building a sense of panic. "I was hoping I'd find you."

"Tessan?" Bryn stood up. "It's good to see you." She walked around the edge of the desk to give her a quick hug. "Is something wrong?"

She hated lying. She hated *this*. But there was too much to lose for her to concern herself with a guilty conscience.

"It's Kalen," Tessan breathed out. "He didn't come home last night."

Bryn stilled, her eyes wide. "What do you mean he didn't come home?"

"He didn't come home, Bryn," Tessan repeated quickly. "We can't find him."

"Well, what can I do?" Bryn quickly shuffled back behind her desk. She closed her notebook and threw her things into a bag. "What can I do?"

She really cares about him.

"That's why I came," Tessan responded. "I'm heading to the forest to look for him. It's the last place he said he was going to be." She wrung her hands, an attempt to twist away the guilt. "Can you please help? We need more eyes."

"Yes." Bryn didn't hesitate. "Absolutely. Yes."

Bryn threw her bag over her shoulder, and they quickly ran out of the High Seminary. Straight to the Sanctwood Forest—toward their own safety, and away from Kalen.

Phase One was complete.

Chapter Forty-Five

Ria

Tessan and Bryn ran past her, the two so very different. And they both meant so much to her son.

She understood why Kalen fell for Bryn–it hadn't been more than three minutes before she was out the door with Tessan to help "find" him. She would have done the same thing for West. She still would.

Maybe they'd all make it in the end.

Unless this *was* the end.

Her part of the plan was risky. She needed to find an unknowing Orderly and tell them she had a meeting with Hauke Elowen and wasn't sure where his office was.

There was no one at the front desk, thanks to Tessan, so she was clinging to the viability of a believable story. And to the fact that no one knew what she looked like. No one, except Acer Jules.

She wasn't worried about running into him, though. He, on the other hand, would rue the day he saw her again.

She walked down the long, silent hall, stunned by the gravity of the situation she'd found herself in. Stunned by the size of this building.

No one needs this much.

She scoffed, getting lost in her thoughts.

"Can I help you?" She heard a young voice behind her. "You look lost."

"Oh!" Ria gasped. "Sorry, I didn't hear you," she added with a laugh. "Maybe. Do you know your way around this place?"

"A little." The young woman looked to be around Kalen's age. Her eyes were careful not to meet Ria's. "I'm newer to The Order." She reached up to tuck a piece of hair behind her ear. A gold bracelet hung from her wrist.

A gold bracelet.

The hybrid.

Holy shit. Thank you, Earth Mother.

"This is going to sound crazy," Ria said, treading lightly. "But is your name Olive, by any chance?"

The woman looked at her, puzzled. "Um, yes." She tilted her head. "How...do you know my name? No one knows my name."

"I know Acer Jules," Ria replied. "He recently shared your story with me."

"Oh," Olive responded. "Well, it was nice to meet you. I should get going." Olive turned abruptly.

Ria reached out to grab her arm, a calculated risk she was willing to take. "I need your help," she begged, whispering. "Please."

"I can't help you." Olive pulled her arm away. "I'm sorry."

"Please," she urged. "My son is a hybrid." Ria dropped her arm and clasped her hands together. "They have him."

Olive stilled. "He's...like me?"

"Yes," Ria confirmed. "And he's going to die if I don't find him."

"I think I know where he is," Olive responded. "I can take you. But you need a gold bracelet to get in." She lifted her arm, showing the jewelry enclosing her wrist.

"How do I get one?" Ria asked quickly. "I'll do whatever it takes."

"How can I trust you?" Olive squinted at Ria. "How do I know you're not lying to me?" She shook her head. "What if you're just like everyone else in this building?"

"I wouldn't blame you if you didn't trust me," Ria said honestly. "But you know why I'm here. You could go straight to Hauke and turn me in and be hailed a hero. Honestly, you'd probably want for nothing else for as long as you live."

Olive was quiet. Ria wondered if she had said too much.

"Please, Olive," she begged. "He's my world. Help me save my son."

"Okay," Olive reached out and grabbed Ria's hand, "I'll help you."

"Thank you–"

"On one condition." Olive cut her off.

Gods damn it.

"Take me with you," she pleaded. "Please. I have to get out of this place." She spoke faster, "I can't live like this anymore."

"Oh, sweetheart." Ria looked her straight in the eyes. "I wouldn't dare leave you behind."

And she meant it. She *was* going to get them all out of here. If it was the last thing she ever did.

The two moved swiftly, Ria whispering the next steps in their plan as they walked down the hall toward Hauke's office.

It was only a matter of time before West–

"HAUKE!" Ria heard his voice screaming from the lobby. "THE PRODIGAL SON HAS RETURNED!" West taunted, still yelling. "DID YOU MISS ME, YOU BASTARD?" She heard the echo of his hands clapping together. He was creating a scene, the way only West could. Just as they'd discussed.

Ria grabbed Olive and pulled her into the bathroom as the door to Hauke's office flew open. Three men sprinted past the door–headed toward West. One of them was Acer. That motherfucker. If she didn't have more important things to do right now, she would have put him on his ass. Instead, she sent up a quick prayer to Earth Mother.

Please keep him safe. Please let him come back home to me.

And then she saw *him*. The Head Cleanser, Sir Hauke Elowen. If she thought her blood boiled while looking at Acer, she was worried she might burst into flames looking into the face of Hauke. He was the last person out of what she assumed was his office, his long white robes flowing behind him as he walked down the hallway. His eyes were beady, and a small grin was plastered on his face. She was a ball of nerves.

They were playing into his hands.

She just hoped their plan was better than his.

Chapter Forty-Six

West

"What's taking you all so long?" West mocked a yawn. "I thought you'd send the whole battalion after me. Especially after all this time."

He kept shouting through the High Seminary, taunting the men he used to call friends. Brothers.

That was before he knew the real meaning of family.

He heard their footsteps before he saw them, knowing Hauke would send his soldiers after him first. But he was prepared. And he planned to stay right here until he looked Hauke Elowen in the eyes.

He would have to restrain himself from killing Hauke on the spot. He wondered for a moment why that hadn't been their plan all along.

West saw the men down the hall. Acer was leading the group.

"Well, look who it is," he called down to Acer. "Your betrayal certainly didn't take long." He laughed. "You've always been Hauke's bitch, though. I don't know why I was surprised that you left."

Acer clenched his fists and sprinted toward him, but West held his ground. He would stay planted, still, until the very last possible moment. To give Ria all the time he could to try and find their boy.

"ACER." He heard a booming voice coming from behind them. "Do. Not. Touch. Him." It wasn't a suggestion, it was a demand.

Hauke.

"You've grown *much* slower in your old age," Westin called to him. "The long white hair looks good on you, though."

Hauke's robes flowed behind him as he made his way closer to West.

"It has been far too long, Westin Vale." Hauke walked ahead of the men now, close enough that Westin could see the green of his irises. "Have you come to join us again?"

"Aw, Haukie, I knew you missed me, but surely even *you* can play hard to get?" Westin blew him a kiss.

Hauke scoffed.

Westin called a flame into both of his palms. "You have my son. I'm here to get him back."

"I'm afraid that's not possible," Hauke replied, grinning. "I don't know why you'd care about a worthless hybrid anyway," he continued, walking closer to West. "Blood or not, I thought I taught you better than to care for unclean filth."

"Shut your Gods damn mouth," West spat in his direction, the fire in his palms roaring to life.

Keep your cool, West.

"Ah, does it *upset* you, Westin?" Hauke pouted his lip. "You knew he had no life here in Evermere. No life at all, really." He stepped closer. "And you? You really thought you could run from *me*? Forever?" He let out a laugh that echoed through the building. "You really thought *I* wouldn't find *you*?" Hauke was yelling now.

"Technically, you didn't find me." Westin shrugged. "You almost did, several times. But you lot," he gestured to the group of Orderlys in front of him, "are just too *damn* dumb to really execute. Or I'd be dead already, huh?"

"Get him," Hauke snarled, and the men charged West.

"Oh, and it was just getting fun," Westin growled, throwing a flame toward the group. "Catch me if you can." Westin waved and took off in a dead sprint toward the door.

"GET HIM!" he heard Hauke yell from behind him.

West planned to stay on his feet just a little while longer. Long enough for Hauke to grab his horse and get them into Evermere, where he could shift into his crow form and get lost among the crowd.

He pushed through the large doors with ease and took off down the gravel path. He heard muffled yells from the stable and glanced over to see a group of Orderlys readying the horses for Hauke and his men.

I can't believe that used to be me.

It wasn't long until he heard the gallop of hooves growing closer to him.

"Stop that man!" Acer yelled to anyone on the path. Lucky for West, no one listened.

But they were gaining on him. It was time.

So he took flight as Wen, and the wind gusted beneath his wings as he flew into the village.

He wondered how many times a crow had bested a Hauke.

Chapter Forty-Seven

Ria

Ria and Olive stood in the bathroom, waiting for the High Seminary to grow quiet again.

Olive moved first, checking to see if the hallway was clear. It didn't take long for her to peek her head back in. "Come on."

The two made their way down the hallway, walking as quickly as they could without drawing attention to themselves. Though Ria wasn't sure anyone would be back here for a while after what had just transpired.

Gods, she hoped West would make it out of this alive.

"We're here." Olive stopped abruptly. "This is it."

Ria took a deep breath before putting her hand on the knob, praying it would be open. That the surprise of West showing up here was enough for Hauke to forget to lock his office.

She closed her eyes and turned her wrist, and she heard a simple click.

Click.

Click.

The sound would echo in her brain forever. She made it into his office. *They'd* made it into his office.

She looked at Olive. Tears began welling in Ria's eyes. She didn't know when she left this morning that they'd get this far. She just knew she was willing to die trying to save her son. Trying to save her Genie, too.

"Everything with Hauke has a reason," Olive said, shuffling into the office. "These bracelets suppress our powers, but they also get us into our living quarters." She moved swiftly, opening his desk. "He knows if we take them off, we won't have anywhere else to go, so it's like a two-for-one kind of thing." She began shuffling through his desk drawers carelessly. "It makes us completely reliant on what he provides for us here. Which isn't much, obviously."

Evil.

Ria jumped in beside her, digging through the desk. Olive stopped her. "Check the bookshelf." She pointed to the wall. "I got this."

Ria ran to the bookshelf, pulling the contents down in a frenzy. She wasn't putting any thought into the mess she was making. She didn't care, anyway.

"I can't find anything," Ria cried in frustration. She felt the burden of time creeping up on her. "How's it going for you?"

"Nothing yet," Olive responded quietly. "Keep looking." She encouraged Ria. "Look everywhere."

"Wait, didn't he give you yours?" Ria stopped her search. "Where were you all when that happened?"

"I...I don't remember," Olive answered, confused. "I've never thought about it."

"You don't *remember*, or you've never thought about it?" Ria responded, her skepticism apparent.

"Both." Olive stopped searching and looked down at her wrist. "I don't remember anything about the day I got here."

Ria walked over to her. "May I?" She reached her hands up to Olive's temple.

Olive hesitated and then shook her head yes.

"Just think of the day you arrived," Ria whispered. "I'll do the rest."

Olive closed her eyes, granting Ria permission to memorywalk.

But Ria saw nothing.

Darkness.

Like she was hitting a wall. Over and over and over. No matter how hard she tried to dig. There was no memory here.

Ria dropped her hand, puzzled. "I...I don't see anything."

Olive shook her head and shrugged. "I told you," she replied. "I don't remember."

What the hell?

"Keep looking," Ria responded. "Something is bound to show up here." She turned, heading back to the bookcase.

"Got it!" Olive yelled, holding up a gold bracelet identical to hers. "Let's get out of here. Quickly."

Ria's heart soared. She was going to do this. She was going to save her family.

Chapter Forty-Eight
Kalen

He had been drifting in and out of consciousness. His power was useless thanks to this Gods damn gold bracelet.

And he was still alone.

That's all he'd ever be.

Alone. Alone. Alone. Alone. Alone. Alone.

Someone cleared their throat.

"Hello?" he called to the darkness.

His mind was playing tricks on him.

Alone. Alone. Alone. Alone. Alone. Alone.

"Kalen?" the voice called back.

He knew that voice. That voice reminded him of fragrant kitchens and healing salves. Of foraging for berries and sneaking through the woods.

"Genie?"

"We've really done it now, haven't we?" She laughed. "How are you holding up?"

Alone. Alone. Alone. Alone. Alone. Alone.

"Are you really here?" he responded.

Why would she be here?

"I'm really here, honey." Her voice was gentle, like she understood what kind of shape he was in. "You're not alone."

"I'm sorry," he cried. "I'm sorry you're in here."

"Hey, hey," Eugenia hushed him. "I'm okay. *We're* okay."

"We're not okay!" Kalen yelled. "We're going to die here."

A sob broke from his throat. He couldn't believe this was the way it would all end for him. For Eugenia.

That this whole damn thing was for nothing. Hybrids would still be unclean. The Order would still hold all of this power. Hauke Elowen had won.

Evil had won.

And he and Eugenia would rot in this Gods damn cell.

What was the point of being good if this was what it amounted to? Locked in a cage with no way out. Sitting and decaying. He could almost see his story etched on the walls of the Veilhold–the hybrid who *almost* changed everything.

Almost didn't mean shit.

"Kalen." Eugenia's voice broke through his thoughts.

He didn't answer her.

"Kale," she said, trying again. "Listen to me."

He didn't answer her.

It was better when he was alone down here. Suffering in silence. No one else should have to die this way. They could have all just moved on without him.

Alone. Alone. Alone. Alone. Alone. Alone.

"I don't know what the hell is going on in that brain of yours. But cut it out."

Alone. Alone. Alone. Alone. Alone. Alone.

"Kalen Halrowe!" Eugenia yelled firmly.

He broke from his trance.

"I'm here," he called back weakly.

"You *will not* die down here," she called to him. "There is not a world that exists in which your mother and father do not risk everything they can to save you."

"I don't want them to save me!" he yelled back. "Don't you get it?" he cried. "Everyone who has ever loved me is in danger *because* of me."

Eugenia was quiet.

"Everyone would be better off if I were dead," he whispered, still crying. "Then maybe you'd all have your freedom."

"Sweet boy." She sniffled. "Don't *you* get it?"

Kalen sat in silence, his head in his hands.

"We wouldn't change one single Gods damn thing," Eugenia said, punching every single word like a declaration. "*You* have been worth every moment. Don't you see that?" she continued. "You've given us all purpose. A reason to dream about a better world. To believe there is good worth fighting for."

Is it worth fighting for?

"You gave us hope. Just by being who you are." She paused. "That's the cost of loving you. Nothing else."

Kalen felt a spark flicker in his chest. The words of the woman who'd loved him all his life, slowly bringing him back to himself.

"Thank you," Kalen responded as he wiped his tears.

"KALEN?" Another familiar voice cut through the darkness. He could see a tiny light held up in the distance.

"GENIE?" the voice continued, the light growing brighter.

Mom?

"Mom?" Kalen choked out.

"I'm here," she yelled. "I'm coming!"

Kalen heard two sets of footsteps running toward him, a jingle accompanying every step.

"Mom!" he yelled again, hoping to guide her through the darkness to where he was. "We're over here!"

"I told you," Eugenia called to Kalen. "I told you she'd come."

His mother stopped in front of his cell.

"My boy." She reached between the bars, cupping his face. "My sweet boy."

He was getting out of here.

Hope.

Chapter Forty-Nine
Ria

Ria held up a set of keys to the lamp Olive was carrying. They'd have to move quickly before the guard woke up.

Olive had guided Ria beyond the West Wing to a tiny corner. To the untrained eye, it was just the end of the hallway. To Olive, it was the door to her home. This disgusting, wet basement was her *home*.

Ria watched in disbelief as Olive held her wrist up to the wall, a tiny click signaled an unlatching, and she pushed the hidden door in, just enough to slip through.

Ria waited for a moment before she heard it—a loud crash and then a slight knock on the inside of the wall. Olive was ready for her. Ria held her own wrist up and quickly glided into the space.

The guard on duty was slumped against his desk. Olive had punched him in the face. Sweet Olive. He was knocked out cold. Ria couldn't have done any of this without her. And one of these cells was her room.

It made Ria sick.

Olive was being hidden away in the depths of this hell. And The Order offered it up to her like it was an oasis. She was able to come and go as she pleased during the day because of her pledge to their teachings and her suppressed power. But when the night fell, this was where she stayed.

If only Hauke Elowen could see her now.

If they didn't hurry the hell up, he would.

Ria flipped through the keys, trying every single one on the lock to Kalen's cell. She was doing her best to remain calm, to keep her hands steady and still, so she could get him out of this place.

She slid in the sixth key, and with no resistance, Kalen's cell door unlocked.

He flew out in a hurry, almost tackling her to the ground in a hug.

She held on tight, worried that if she let him go, she'd wake up from some horrible nightmare where none of this was real. Where he was still stuck down here, unreachable, and she couldn't save him. She hadn't thought she would ever have this moment again. Ever smell his hair or touch his face again. She squeezed him tighter.

She let go of him and nodded to the woman beside her. "Kalen, this is Olive."

"The other hybrid." Kalen gaped.

"Nice to meet you," Olive said simply. "Your mom is a badass."

"I need you both to go." Ria turned to Kalen. "Eugenia and I will be right behind you." She shuffled through the keys again. "Go to the forest, Tessan is waiting, and your father will be there soon."

Ria reached over to Kalen's wrist, carefully using the small pick on the key ring to release the golden bracelet.

He was free. Thank Earth Mother, her boy was free.

She waved Olive over to remove her bracelet too, squeezing her hands tightly when it crashed to the floor. "Thank you, Olive," she said genuinely. "If we do not show up..." Her voice grew louder so Kalen could hear her. "Do not wait for us."

"But Mom–"

"No buts." She put her hand up. "Get to Wyrdbrook. Tell Liam everything."

"Okay."

"I love you, Kale," she said. "Now go."

"I love you, too." He ran down the hallway with Olive.

"I love you, Genie!" Kalen called out, right before he disappeared beyond the door.

Ria walked swiftly to Eugenia's cell, shuffling through the keys again, starting from the beginning.

"That boy of yours," Eugenia said to her. "He needs you."

"He needs both of us," Ria responded, putting a key in the lock.

Doesn't fit. Next.

She put the next key in.

And the next.

The silence between them was building, the tension of time spent pressing in on them, making it hard for Ria to breathe.

"Both of them," Eugenia continued calmly. "They both need you."

"Stop talking so I can get you out of here," Ria responded, trying the seventh key.

The eighth.

The ninth.

The tenth.

The eleventh.

The twelfth.

"Gods damn IT!" Ria screamed. "They're not working!"

"Ria," Eugenia said, reaching her hand through the bars, resting them on hers. "Look at me."

"No, Eugenia," she said. "No, I just need to try them all again."

"Ria," Eugenia insisted. "Please."

"I can't leave you here," Ria cried. "You can't make me leave you here."

"It's okay," Eugenia said. "You need to go."

"No!" Ria yelled again. "No. I can't do any of this without you. I won't."

"Of course you can, Ri," Eugenia rubbed her thumb against Ria's hand. "You can do *anything*."

"I'm sorry," Ria choked out. "I'm sorry I said those horrible things to you, I just didn't know how to–"

"I know," Eugenia was crying softly now. "I know. Promise me something, okay?"

"Genie, please don't do this." Ria kept trying the keys.

One of them had to work.

"Take care of Tess?" she sniffed. "She's a good girl, and when I'm gone, she won't have anyone else."

"Stop," Ria whispered.

"Promise me?" Eugenia said firmly. "Please."

Ria dropped the keys and looked Eugenia in the eyes. Her best friend had given up. Accepted her fate. Ria began to shake her head in protest. She couldn't do the same–she'd never accept this.

But it was the end, wasn't it?

Ria and Genie. Genie and Ria.

Just Ria.

"I am so sorry." Eugenia reached for her other hand. "I never meant to hurt you. I just wanted to keep you safe."

They were both crying now.

Her best friend. Her sister.

"I know," Ria said. "It's okay, I forgive you."

"Thank Gods," Eugenia said, laughing softly. "It would have sucked to die down here without making things right with you."

"Don't say that," Ria snapped. "You're not going to die."

A sad smile settled on Eugenia's face. "You need to go. You need to go now and live your great big life, Ria."

"I can't."

"You have to." A tear slipped from Eugenia's cheek. "For me, please."

"Anything for you. Always." Ria looked at Eugenia, hoping she understood the weight of the words Eugenia always said, reflected back to her.

"Everything you've ever wanted is right in front of you, Ri," Eugenia whispered. "Take it."

"But what does it mean if you're not there?" Devastation covered Ria's voice.

"Everything," Eugenia replied with conviction. "Every. Single. Thing." She grabbed her hands tightly. "Plus, Earth Mother promised I'd reincarnate as a crow, just to haunt West." Eugenia laughed.

"It's not funny," Ria cried in return. "I don't want you to leave me."

"And I don't want to go," Eugenia's voice wobbled. "But I'll see you again. I promise."

"I love you, Genie," Ria wept. "I love you so much."

"I love you, too," Eugenia said, squeezing her hand three times.

Kind. Brave. Gentle.

"Now go." Eugenia waved her off. "Go before you're stuck down here with me."

Ria stood frozen. How could she leave her behind? How could she *almost* have it all? Why was the world so cruel to her?

"I promise you, I'm okay." Eugenia nudged her. "Go get your boys."

Ria reached into the cell, pulling Eugenia into a hug. They sobbed in each other's arms.

"I'm sorry I couldn't save you," Ria cried, holding her best friend close.

"Oh, Ria, you did," Eugenia hushed her. "You did."

Chapter Fifty
Kalen

Kalen and Olive sprinted through the High Seminary and didn't look back. They'd get to the forest. They'd get to Wyrdbrook.

They all would.

They had to.

"There!" Olive called to their right, pointing to a door at the back of the building. It would lead them straight to the forest.

Kalen slid to a stop before changing directions, willing himself forward. If he stopped moving, even for a moment, he would end up changing his mind about leaving his mother and Genie in the basement.

Eugenia and I will be right behind you.

Her words bumped against his brain as a reminder. Kalen had trusted his mom's plan his entire life. Why would he stop trusting her now? He had to keep going.

He dug deep into his magic, sending a burst of air forward, flipping the unsuspecting door off the hinges. He and Olive barrelled through, the silhouette of the forest swaying in front of them. The limbs of the trees waved in excitement upon his arrival. Their boy had almost made it.

Sirens began wailing shortly after they exited the door. Kalen reached up to grab his ears to keep them from bleeding–he'd never heard anything this loud before. He wondered if Liam could hear them all the way in Wyrdbrook.

"Attention Citizens of Evermere!" a voice boomed over the village speaker. "Dangerous hybrids are on the loose within the city."

Shit.

"Move into your homes and lock your doors," the voice continued. "Do not approach anyone."

The recording looped, and the sirens flooded his brain, making it hard to focus on what came next.

One step at a time.

He looked over at Olive, gasping for breath.

"Are you okay?" he yelled over the siren song.

"Barely," she puffed, yelling back. "I just need to focus on running."

Fair. They could talk when they got to safety.

"I hope they got out of the basement." He couldn't help but say it out loud. Just in case Earth Mother was feeling generous.

"They did," Olive responded, still breathing heavily. "Nothing will keep them from you."

Kalen's heart warmed.

The only thing keeping them from reuniting would be death. And death was no longer in their plan.

They'd made it this far.

"Think you can run a bit faster?" Kalen questioned hesitantly.

Olive nodded as they kicked up their speed, in a dead sprint toward the safety of the Sanctwood Forest.

Chapter Fifty-One
Tessan

Tessan heard the siren from deep within the Sanctwood. She just hoped Bryn couldn't.

"Is that..." Bryn turned her ear up. "Is that the siren?"

Well, shit.

"I don't hear anything?" Tessan responded innocently as she kept walking deeper into the woods.

"Wait, Tessan." Bryn grabbed her arm. "That *is* the siren." She squinted at her. "Something's wrong."

"Yeah, something *is* wrong. Kalen is missing—and he is my priority." Tessan shook Bryn's hand off her arm. "Are you coming or not?"

Bryn stopped moving, hesitation crept across her face.

Shit.

"Why did you bring me here?" Bryn's eyes pierced through Tessan's. "Is he even missing?"

"Of course he's missing." Tessan rolled her eyes. "Come on."

"Tessan," Bryn warned. "*Why* did you bring me here?"

Could Tessan tell her the truth? What would it change? At this point, probably nothing. They were all leaving Evermere, anyway. There was nothing left for them here. Not safety, not home.

"Okay, fine." She threw her hands up in frustration. "Kalen was taken by The Order."

"What? No–" Bryn stumbled back. "Why would they do that?"

"Do you really want to know, Bryn?" Tessan walked toward her. "Do you want a glimpse into how evil your *grandfather* really is?"

"What are you talking about?" Bryn shook her head and continued to walk backward. "How did you–" She fumbled over her words. "He's not evil...he's just...he's following the covenant."

"He's *torturing* people. Wiping them from existence because of who they are," Tessan countered. "That's evil."

"No." Bryn stood up straighter. "You don't get to say that. You don't know him. You don't understand."

"Actually, I do," Tessan challenged. "I do understand." She continued to close the space between them. "I understand The Order exists to oppress people for things they can't control. For who they are. For love that never hurt anyone."

"Tessan, stop," Bryn demanded, putting her hand up. "Stop."

"Why? You wanted the truth!" she yelled. "Well, here it is, ya ready?"

Tessan probably should have toned down the dramatics, but damn, it felt good to get it out.

"Kalen is a hybrid, Bryn." Tessan's face was stone cold and serious. "A hybrid."

Bryn froze. "No, he isn't."

"What the hell do you mean he *isn't*?" Tessan looked at her, puzzled. "Open your eyes."

"No, he's too..."

"Too what? Good? Kind?" Tessan barked back. "Yeah, he is. And he's a hybrid."

"Yes, Tessan. He's too much of all of that!" Bryn yelled back. "What do you want me to say?"

"I want you to say it doesn't matter to you." Tessan walked closer to her again. "I want you to say Athero is wrong. That Kalen is *proof* that The Order is wrong."

"I—" Bryn was cut off.

"TESS!" She heard Kalen's voice in the distance.

Her head snapped to the side, following the sound of her best friend's voice.

Ria did it.

She really did it.

Chapter Fifty-Two
Kalen

"Tessan!" he kept calling. "Where are you?"

He and Olive dipped under tree branches and wove between stumps, doing their best to keep moving, despite the siren's continued wail and the aching in their legs.

"Over here!" he heard her shout from his left.

Thank Gods for fae hearing.

"This way." He nodded to Olive.

"Yeah, I heard her, too," she chuckled.

"Oh, right." It was going to take him some time to get used to being around another hybrid.

He smelled her before he saw her.

Daisies.

"Bryn?" he yelled curiously.

"She's here," Tessan answered, but Kalen heard it in her voice. Something was wrong.

It didn't take him long to find them both. These weren't the two friends who sat together drinking just a few nights ago. Something had exploded. Their arms were crossed. Bryn's eyes were on him, Tessan's eyes were on Bryn.

Kalen ran to Tessan, scooping her up in a hug. "Thank you!" he exclaimed. "I don't know what you did, but I know I wouldn't have gotten out without you."

Tessan didn't respond, still glaring at Bryn.

He turned to her next. "Hey," he grinned, relieved to see her safe and away from the High Seminary. "I'm so sorry I missed our date." He chuckled. "I got held up."

"Tell me," Bryn responded, tears in her eyes. "Tell me the truth."

Kalen snapped his head toward Tessan, a questioning look on his face. She shrugged at him, rolling her eyes.

"She was going to find out eventually," Tessan replied.

Shit.

"Are you really a hybrid?" Bryn's voice was soft.

"Bryn," he started. "I can explain."

"Tell me the truth." Her voice grew firmer. "Are you a hybrid?"

"Yes," Kalen stated simply. "I was going to tell you when the time was–"

Bryn released a breath, cutting him off while shaking her head, "I trusted you." She glared at him with disgust.

Kalen heard Tessan whisper to Olive behind him.

"We'll be over here, Kale," Tessan interjected. "Come when you're ready."

He nodded as the two walked deeper in the forest, leaving him and Bryn alone.

He would never be ready for this.

Kalen walked toward her again. "I'm sorry."

"So what?" Bryn yelled at him. "What was this for?" She gestured between the two of them. "A means to an end?"

"No," he responded honestly. "No, I promise."

But that *was* the plan, though, wasn't it? To use her? Before he really got to know her. Before he felt her lips on his cheek or her hand wrapped in his. Before their conversation in the forest, or walking her home drunk.

Maybe he deserved this fallout. He knew the first time he ever heard Bryn's voice that he never stood a chance. If he could just make her see—

"Your promises don't mean anything to me," she responded, tears welling in her eyes.

"But nothing has changed." He reached out to grab her hand, but she pulled back. "I'm still me." He clutched a fistful of his shirt in his hand. "I'm still me."

"No." She shook her head. "You're not." A tear fell down her cheek. "You're a hybrid, Kalen! You're one of the unclean."

Unclean.

The words sliced through his heart, red hot and painful. She didn't mean it. She couldn't mean it.

Could she?

He stared at her, speechless.

"I really thought this might have been it for me." She laughed softly, wiping a tear before it fell. "I saw it all, somehow. A house in the forest, visiting the High Seminary a few times a week to study the covenant." She shook her head. "But it wasn't real. None of it was real."

"Bryn." Kalen moved closer to her again. "It was real. Just let me—"

She held her hand up, cutting him off again. "I can't do this," she responded. "I can't love you and be an Orderly. I can't love a hybrid."

I can't love you.

The words knocked him off balance. He began to speak—to plead. They could figure this out. Wasn't he worth it? Weren't *they* worth it?

Three sharp caws rang out above him, stealing the words from his lips. *Run.* His father was here.

"Kalen!" Tessan sprinted back toward him. "We have to go."

"Come with me, please." He grabbed Bryn's hand. "We can have the house in the forest. We can have anything you want." He pulled her closer. "No more secrets."

He knew the answer before she said a word. Her face dropped, her green eyes bloodshot from the tears pooling in them.

This would be how he remembered her. Crying in the middle of the forest. This was how it was always going to end.

"I can't." She lowered her head. "You know I can't."

Kalen stood frozen, though the world around him was still tilting. This was the confirmation he had been dreading. He would never be enough for her. He was stupid to think that *Bryn Elowen* would ever really choose him–an Unclean hybrid–over what she had always known. Over the beliefs she'd always carried.

I can't love a hybrid.

He had hoped.

He was tired of hoping.

He would ask one more time. One more time. "I don't want to let you go, Bryn. Please."

"In another life," Bryn whispered, as she reached up and ran her finger along the ridge of his nose. "I'm sorry."

She leaned in to kiss his cheek, and everything began to move in slow motion. He closed his eyes, feeling the weight of her lips against the stubble of his face. This was really the end.

How could this be the end?

The end of a story that never had a beginning.

"Kalen!" Tessan ran behind him and tugged his shirt. "Now."

"Bye, Bryn," Kalen breathed, as he let go of her hand, their fingers unlacing for the last time. Her hands flew to her mouth to muffle her sobs.

He would never see her again.

He would never be the same.

Nothing ever would.

"Where's Ria?" His father called out from in front of him.

"I'm here!" she yelled, running to catch up with the rest of the group.

Thank Gods.

Kalen ran to her quickly, sweeping her up in a tight hug before setting her down to keep running.

"Bryn?" his mother asked curiously. Her question was full of the things she didn't have to say.

Where is she?

Why isn't she here?

Are you okay?

Do you want to talk about it?

Kalen couldn't say it out loud and instead just shook his head no.

"I'm sorry, little crow."

"Me, too." He bit the side of his cheek to keep himself from crying. Blood pooled in his mouth in protest.

"I lost Hauke and his dipshits back in Evermere," his father yelled from the front. "But we have to keep moving."

"Wait!" Tessan yelled. "Where's Eugenia?" She looked back at Kalen's mother.

She didn't respond.

"Mom?" Kalen followed up. "Where's Genie?"

She closed her eyes. "I couldn't save her. I tried...and I couldn't save her."

Tessan stopped abruptly in her tracks, turning back to face Evermere.

"We have to go, Tess," his father called to her.

"I can't leave her. I won't leave her!" Tessan cried, sprinting back toward the village. Kalen took off after her, stopped by his father's touch, watching as he ran forward instead.

"You'll die if you go back, Tessan." Kalen heard his father's plea as he grabbed her.

"I'd rather die trying to save her than live knowing I left her behind." Tessan squirmed in his father's arms. "Let me go, West!" she screamed, sobs breaking through her throat.

"She would never leave me," Tessan cried. "She has never left me behind!" She continued trying to break free from his father's arms.

Kalen's tears came quickly. There was too much heartbreak. Too much grief. They'd come here with hope, and they were leaving with heartache.

All of them.

Would evil always win? Would it always be this way?

Kalen watched as his father brought Tessan into a strong hug, whispering something in her ear that was too quiet for him to pick up on.

His father stood with Tessan for a little while longer, and he felt the presence of his mother draw closer to him.

"I tried to save her," she repeated through her muffled cry.

Kalen didn't respond; his eyes were locked on Tessan as they made their way back to the group.

Kalen hugged Tessan tightly. He couldn't fix this for her. He could only be there for her—together in their devastation.

His father's warning to keep moving in the back of his mind prompted him to let her go. "I'm so sorry, Tess."

"I know." Tessan turned to look at the group. "Let's just keep moving," she breathed, her voice cracking. "It's what she would want, anyway."

His father nodded and hit a jog. "Keep up, please," he called out, and the group fell into an easy rhythm behind him. Running toward their new life.

Or a version of it they weren't quite ready to accept.

They got to Wyrdbrook early the next morning, barely stopping for more than a drink of water. Exhausted wasn't the word.

Kalen's heart was shattered. His brain was groggy. His legs were jelly.

But he'd made it back. They all had.

Well, almost all of them.

His parents went ahead to his cottage, and Olive followed Tessan to hers.

Despite his body's plea, he couldn't rest. Not yet.

His heavy feet carried him to the Veilhold. The warmth of the building enveloped him immediately. The rich woods and earthy greens were a stark difference from what he experienced at the High Seminary.

It was good to be back here.

Mostly.

He traveled the hall slowly, wondering if Liam would be disappointed in him. He had left here with so many grand ideas. To infiltrate The

Order, to change the minds of people, to expose Hauke Elowen for the monster he was.

Instead, he lost Eugenia.

He lost Bryn.

And somewhere in there, he lost part of himself, too.

He wasn't sure that was anything Liam would be too proud of.

"Let me decide that for myself," the Overseer said, walking up behind him. "I've missed you."

"Liam." He hugged the Overseer tightly. "I'm sorry."

"Nothing to be sorry for." He released the hug and held onto Kalen's shoulders. "Come to my office." He walked down the hall. "I have some tea waiting for us."

"How did you know we'd be ba–you know what?" Kalen walked in stride beside him. "Never mind."

Liam chuckled softly. "So tell me, how's my brother doing?"

Kalen huffed. "He really is the worst." He stopped abruptly and turned toward Liam. "You could have warned me about Bryn, by the way." He lobbed the sentence at Liam like a joke–but he wasn't kidding. Not really.

Liam looked at him, puzzled. "I'm afraid I don't know Bryn."

"Your great-niece?" Kalen answered, confused.

Liam pursed his lips and shook his head. "I didn't know Hauke had a granddaughter." His voice held a certain sadness Kalen hadn't experienced from Liam. "Would you tell me about her?"

I can't love a hybrid.

Liam lifted his chin and nodded, understanding Kalen's thoughts. "I see." The Overseer put his arm around Kalen's shoulders. "I'm sorry. Do you want to talk about that, instead?"

"I haven't had enough sleep to have *that* conversation yet," he groaned in response.

"You know, I have a bed in my office if you need one." Liam nudged him. A playful moment passed between them in the midst of their sadness. Kalen needed that more than he knew.

"Don't remind me," Kalen grumbled as they walked into Liam's office. Kalen sat for the first time in what felt like forever. He slowly sank into the soft chair, settling in as Liam made his way around his desk.

Kalen stared up at the stained glass window that towered over them both. A devastating, visual reminder of what he failed to do.

He was safe. But was this still home? He was safe. But at what cost?

He'd heard it said that home is where the heart is. If that was true, hadn't he left his behind in the Sanctwood Forest? In Evermere? With Bryn?

Broken.

Hidden within the fractured edges were the whispers of what could have been, and what would never be.

The next couple of days were filled with quiet sorrow. Grieving the lives they left behind. Grieving the people they left, too.

Kalen thought about his last conversation with Eugenia often. Wondering if she was still alive or if they'd killed her for what the rest of them had done.

His hands felt sticky, slick with the blood of Eugenia Duscaire. Most nights, it felt like too much to bear.

Every dream was exactly the same. They were stuck in the basement. He would look across his cell bars and see Eugenia's rotting body across from him. Slumped against the wall. Lifeless. He would yell her name, scream for her to wake up. She never did.

And then he'd wake up screaming her name, taking just a moment to catch his breath before realizing that his nightmare continued the moment he opened his eyes, too. She was gone.

Would he ever know peace again?

Because when he wasn't thinking about Eugenia, he was thinking about Bryn.

Bryn Gods damn Elowen.

Sometimes, when his heart couldn't settle after one of his nightmares, he would memorywalk back to their night in the woods after the Evermere Market. Her phantom kiss would land on his face, and he'd reach up and trace his fingers along the outline of her lips. He wondered if she ever thought about him. But then reminded himself it was a waste of time.

Through it all, he was grateful for the support of his parents. He watched as his mother and father comforted each other in quiet corners of his cottage, both lost in versions of their own unending sadness–but holding each other through it. That was the one single part of all of this that may have a happy ending.

His parents.

If anything, or anyone could be truly happy again.

He hadn't seen much of Tessan since they returned. She hadn't said it out loud, but Kalen could see she needed time and space to be alone. Alone, except for Olive.

Today, he would be a little selfish with her. Today, he needed his best friend.

He knocked on the door of her home. Olive answered, hesitantly peeking through the crack as if she were waiting for someone to come snatch her up and take her back to the High Seminary.

"It's me, Olive," he said reassuringly, and smiled softly when she opened the door wider. "Is Tessan here?"

"No, she left before sunrise," Olive replied. "She's been gone since."

He knew where to find her.

Kalen waved goodbye and headed toward the woods, toward Tessan, retracing the steps to the spot that had become their own.

He walked up behind Tessan slowly. Her long black hair sat messy on her head. The steady stream of water cleansed him somehow, just enough to forget why they had to come back here in the first place.

"I can hear you, idiot," she called, not bothering to turn around.

"Has anyone ever told you how sweet you are?" Kalen responded as he sat down on the rock beside her.

They sat there for a second in silence. Tessan's knees were pulled up to her chest, her chin resting on top of them.

"I don't think I'll ever be okay again." A tear fell from her cheek.

He reached up to wipe it away, and instead of smacking his hand away like she typically would, she let him. He pulled her close.

"Me neither," he said.

"What was it all for?" Tessan sniffed. "Going back? What did it even change?"

"Us," Kalen responded honestly. "All of us."

"That's a horrible answer." She let out a soft laugh.

He laughed too.

"I'm sorry about Bryn," she whispered. "I really thought she was going to come with you."

"It's okay." He rubbed her arm as she leaned her head against his shoulder. "I guess it wasn't meant to be."

"What do we do now, Kale?" Tessan asked.

"I don't know." He sighed. "I don't think we give up, though."

"Do you think she's still alive?" Tessan responded cautiously.

"I don't know," he answered again, staring ahead. "I hope so."

"Hope is dangerous." Tessan looked up to the sky. "It gives us too much to believe in."

"What's the alternative?"

"A life without pain, I think." Tessan's tears continued to fall.

"I think pain might be the point, sometimes," he responded carefully. "It means all of it mattered."

"Maybe you're right." She leaned back into him. "For once."

The two chuckled.

They would spend the rest of their life missing Eugenia.

"I love you, Tess," Kalen kissed the top of her head. "Thank you for being who you are."

"Gross." Tessan nudged him. "I love you, too."

Chapter Fifty-Three

Bryn

Bryn had lost track of how many days it had been since their goodbye.

She hadn't eaten, and she had barely slept.

How could everything change so fast?

A soft knock rapped on her door; she wasn't going to answer. She'd ignored everyone up to now—she would keep ignoring everyone until she felt like herself again.

If she ever felt like herself again.

"Bryn?" She heard her grandfather's voice from the other side of the door. "Could you let me in, please?"

About time.

She was surprised it took him this long to show up.

He was the one person she wanted to talk to.

She walked over to her door and swung it open. "Come in," she said coldly; his face was stoic in response.

He closed the door behind them, took a deep breath, and prepared to talk. But it wasn't his turn.

It was hers.

Everything she had done in her life had been for him. Being here in this stupid building. Sitting at that stupid desk. Going to that stupid class.

"Why?" The words ripped off her tongue, poison spewing in his direction. "Why couldn't you just leave them alone?"

She watched him move slowly across the room, carefully deciding his next words.

"I have my reasons, Bryn," he started. "When the covenant is broken, I enforce punishment. It's the way of The Order."

"It doesn't have to be," she cried. "You *knew* how I felt about him." She raised her voice. "You could have chosen another way. For *me*. Once."

"There is no other way, child." His voice was rising too. "There is *one* right way, one *pure* way," he continued. "You are being foolish."

"No," Bryn fought back. "You're being archaic." She pointed her finger at him. "You used me to get to him. To get to his mother."

"And I'd do it again." He smiled at her. It made the hair on the back of her neck stand up. She had seen this version of him in the Hollow. But never here, and never to her. "I'd do it again, and again, because that is *my* job," he said calmly. "To keep you and everyone in Evermere safe from people like him."

"He's not dangerous." Bryn puffed her chest in defiance. "He's just–"

"Of course he is!" he yelled, interrupting her. "And he's *infected* you with his thoughts already." He looked disgusted. "He's a threat to our way of life."

"Then maybe *we* should change, Grandpop," Bryn replied boldly. "Maybe we're the ones who are wrong."

He laughed. "Ah. I was really hoping we could resolve this on our own." He walked toward her, cornering her in her small room. "But, it's clear to me that you're too far gone."

"What are you talking about?" Bryn backed up slowly before her hip ran into her desk. She had nowhere else to go.

"Acer?" he called to the door. It didn't take long before it swung open, an evil smirk plastered on Acer Jules' face.

"Grandpop?" she questioned. "Stop. You're scaring me."

But he ignored her and continued to talk to Acer. "I fear my beloved granddaughter has lost her way." He shook his head in disappointment.

"Grab her, please," he spoke softly.

Acer sprang at Bryn. She grabbed a book from her desk and swung it fast at Acer's face. He dodged it, smacking it from her hand. The fight was over before it started. She had no chance.

She never did.

"Acer," she pleaded. "What are you doing?" She struggled against Acer's grip. "Please."

"Hold still, Bryn." Her grandfather lowered his voice, gently removing the golden cuffs that caged his ears. That had always caged his ears. The same golden hue as the bracelet the hybrid from class wore.

Wait.

Jagged.

Scarred.

Severed.

"Your ears?" Bryn muttered, the truth snapping into place in front of her. "But you can't be..."

"Grandpop has a few secrets of his own," he sneered. "It's a shame you won't remember any of this," he said, kissing her forehead.

She continued to thrash against Acer's body. "Stop!" she yelled. "Help!"

"No one is coming to save you," he spoke softly, and raised his hand to her temple.

Her body seized as every memory of Kalen came rushing back to her in slow motion, the feeling of his hands slipping from hers, his lips on her cheek, every little smirk, every single *hey*.

All of the moments that made her fall in love with the one she would never be able to have.

Playing in reverse in her mind, until she was back at her desk in the High Seminary, doodling away in a notebook to pass the time. It was just another day as the greeter. And Kalen Halrowe never existed to her at all.

Bryn gave in to the darkness that enveloped her brain. She was tired, she was hungry.

And she forgot what she was upset about in the first place.

She woke up the next day feeling lighter than she had in weeks. She grabbed her notebook and headed out the door of her room.

It was a beautiful day to be an Orderly.

"Hi!" She waved at some of her friends in the West Wing. They looked at her with concern.

It's good to see you too?

She shook her head in confusion as she headed to her Grandpop's office. The way she always did, to drop off the tea she had made him in their communal kitchen. He never had time to do things like this for himself, and it had always been their morning ritual. A nod to how they took care of each other.

He always took care of her.

The hallway was busier than usual. It made her happy to see everyone out of their rooms. Was it market day? Were they headed into town? Maybe she would go, too? She noticed this morning she was running low on tea, anyway. Bryn continued to wave at the people she passed, noticing their smaller gestures, their smiles never quite reaching their eyes.

What is going on?

She knocked on her Grandpop's door before pushing it open. Her mouth fell open in disbelief at the mess in front of her.

His office was destroyed, the contents of his desk spread across the floor, his books thrown from their shelves. He sat at his desk with his hands on his temple.

"Grandpop?" she whispered, entering the office slowly. "What happened?"

He looked up at her. "Bryn." His eyes were bloodshot.

Has he been crying?

"Shh." She put his tea down, moving quickly to his side to comfort him. "Shhhh."

"Hybrids," he responded. "We were attacked."

What?

"What hybrids?" She fumbled for her words, her heart racing. "There is only one hybrid here?" She began searching her mind for more information–for anything that would help her connect the dots.

But nothing came. Like she was hitting a wall she couldn't get past.

Her grandfather pulled a piece of paper from the floor, putting it on his desk. "The hybrid left with them," he responded. "We were attacked in broad daylight."

But how did she miss that? Wouldn't she have been at the front desk? She opened her mouth to ask her grandfather when it happened–but a simple question stopped her train of thought.

"Do you remember meeting this young man?"

Bryn looked down at the paper, *Kalen Halrowe of the Halrowe Witches.*

Her palms grew sweaty, her heart pounded in her chest at the name. Like her body remembered something her brain couldn't access.

Who the hell is Kalen Halrowe?

"I..." She closed her eyes, trying to remember giving someone this registration form. "I don't know."

"Exactly as I thought." Her grandfather stood up from his chair in a fury. "We've heard hybrids can steal memories."

What?

"I'm so sorry you were violated in that way." He spoke slowly, moving in to hug her.

Someone stole my memories?

"What do we do? What should I do?" Bryn spoke strongly, her anger making way for courage.

"Hybrids are a threat to our way of life, Bryn." He let go of her. "They're coming to steal what is ours. To ruin the covenant Athero has called us to protect and maintain." He paused. "To harm *me*."

Bryn shook her head, trying to take in the information. Her eyes scanned the destruction in the office around her. Her blood boiled at the thought of being manipulated. Of this hybrid, *Kalen*, stealing her memories. She'd never been greeted by anger like this.

The worried looks in the hallway this morning made sense now. Their sacred space had been destroyed. In the name of everything they didn't believe in.

The Unclean.

She wouldn't stand for it. Not as the future Cleanser of The Order.

"Tell me what we need to do."

Her grandfather leaned down to look directly into her eyes.

"We must find the one they call Kalen Halrowe." He held her shoulders steady, preparing her for his next words.

"And kill him."

And kill him.

"Whatever it takes."

Whatever it takes.

Acknowledgements

I can't believe you made it to the end! When I set out to write this book, I really wasn't sure if anyone would read it–but you did. And I'm so grateful.

Unclean fell from my heart and onto the page with a lot of ease. It has been a story I've wanted to tell some version of for a long time, but I never would have imagined it would finally be out in the world and in your hands.

There are a lot of people who helped me get from page one to acknowledgements, but no one more than my wife, Cami. Thank you for listening to my wild ideas as I was having them and redirecting me when I got too far from the story. I am so lucky to like you and love you–and I am grateful for the way you love me right back.

To my littlest love (have Mommy read this to you), everything I do that means anything is because of you. Thank you for being my reason why. I love you through and through.

To my sisters, Blaine and Bailey, who hyped me up after every new chapter and called me to talk about these characters as I was writing them in real time. Thank you for arguing about being #TeamTessan or #TeamBryn, for creating my cover, and for giving your opinions even if I didn't agree with them. I love you both.

To the folks who read my book early–Mom, Jess, Carly, Ron, my real-life Liam, and Atlee, thank you for showing up for me and going in without any idea of what I was asking you to do. I'm still cracking up that several of you were thinking of ways to lie to me so you didn't hurt my feelings if it was bad–and I'm thankful that you actually thought it was good. I feel so loved, known, and valued by each of you.

To Brianna, thank you for editing this whole damn thing just because you wanted to, and for inspiring me to finally make one of my dreams become a reality just by being vocal about your own. I don't know how I would have done this without you. (**YOU CAN BUY BRIANNA'S BOOK**: *The Willows: a novel* by Brianna Curtis Sargent on Amazon!)

And finally, to anyone who has ever been told they're different simply for being who you are–you are full of goodness. I'll say it for as long as I live, you belong everywhere and you make the world a better place by existing. I'm so glad that you do.

About the author

Keller Hayden was born and raised in the South. By day, he works a corporate job, and by night he's writing his next novel. When he's not working or writing, Keller is enjoying time with his family— whether exploring his parents' twenty-acre property or savoring quiet moments at home. You can learn more about what Keller is up to at kellerhayden.com or find him on TikTok and Instagram @authorkellerhayden.

www.ingramcontent.com/pod-product-compliance
Lightning Source LLC
Chambersburg PA
CBHW020010120726
47903CB00004B/1223